Un-Solicited Confession

Gene Gerber

BookLocker
Saint Petersburg, Florida

Print ISBN: 978-1-64719-170-2
Epub ISBN: 978-1-64719-171-9
Mobi ISBN: 978-1-64719-172-6

Published by BookLocker.com, Inc., St. Petersburg, Florida.

Printed on acid-free paper.

Un-Solicited Confession is a work of fiction, names, characters, businesses, places, events, locales, and incidents are either the product of the author's imagination or used in a fictious manner. Any resemblances to actual persons, living or deceased or actual events is purely coincidental.

BookLocker.com, Inc.
2020

First Edition

PROLOGUE

Angus McKay thought it was appropriate that graduation was on May 25, 1967 during the week of Memorial Day. To him it was his way of honoring, his father, Connor McKay, and his Uncle Rory McKay. Flags were flying up and down the streets of Texas A & M campus on this warm, sunny day. The Corps of Cadets proudly marched into the G. Rollie White Coliseum, better known by the students as the "Jollie Holler" or the Holler House of the Brazos". The speaker was General Frank Pile. His words were short and to the point. In 1870 Decoration Day, now Memorial Day, was declared a national holiday. The country is proud that the men and women of the Corps are stepping up to protect their families, their friends, and their country from becoming a communist country. He predicted that Russia was about to test another nuclear bomb. He reviewed the Soldier's Creed, stressing the twelfth point - "I am a guardian of freedom and the American way of life."

The general presided over the commissioning ceremony as the seniors paraded across the stage. When Angus McKay walked up to receive his brass bars, the general commented, "I understand you were the only one at this university to be accepted into the Military Advisors of Vietnam Command. Congratulations."

"Thank you, sir." replied Angus.

The Corps of Cadets graduates were instructed to stand and recite the Oath of Office of Military Officers. Some of the graduating class had already received their assignments and had orders to report to various posts around the USA and others to foreign countries. Angus, however, had not received his orders.

Three days prior to graduation the Commander had called Angus into his office to explain why he had not received any information about his military assignment. "McKay, congratulations as you are one of the three percent accepted to that program." The Commander told him, "After graduation, go home, relax and be ready to report to wherever they tell you. You should be receiving your orders as soon as the government completes the background check."

After the graduation ceremonies, later in the day Angus and his family, along with his best friend Rob Palmer, drove back to their Bar MK Ranch in Houston County. The modest ranch was off highway 1733. The 600 acres were surrounded on three sides by the Davy Crockett National Forest. The edge of the forest was Angus's favorite spot. He liked being close to nature and the quietness where he could ponder the next chapter of his life. He often asked for guidance from Above to help him during the upcoming days. An additional 300 acres were south of Grapeton, off highway 2544. The Trinity River flowed along the west side of the property providing water for the Black Angus herd. The native salt grass made it ideal grazing for the six to eight bulls and over one hundred cows.

During the days following graduation Angus and Rob worked the cattle, separating the calves from their mothers and putting them into groups based on their size. Angus loved the ranch's demanding life and the manual labor involved.

Rob lived on the outskirts of Crockett. Rob and Angus were a team. They had been best friends since the fifth grade. The two had met at a Crockett Future Farmers Assoc. chapter meeting. He enjoyed helping the McKays with the ranching chores, cutting and baling hay, branding the calves and ear marking the cows so the McKays could follow the blood line of their herd. They had been following the blood lines since Grandpa McKay brought the first two black bulls to Houston County.

Rob had not joined the Corps. He was more interested in learning about the future of oil and gas in Texas. The fact that the McKays had capped a small oil field find in 1941, right before the beginning of World War II, made him want to know what was under Mother Earth. Rob planned to pursue his Master's Degree in Gas and Oil Engineering when Angus left for Vietnam. He knew he had to get into graduate school quickly because during those times every man not in school was eligible to be drafted.

On June 10th Lieutenant Antony Daniel McKay was elated to find his orders in the mail. "You are to report to Commanding General Steel at Fort Polk, Louisiana no later than June 19th at 0800. You will not be allowed to have your personal vehicle during the 10-day training camp."

Angus called to share his good news with his best buddy. Rob was happy for Angus and agreed to drive him to Fort Polk. "That leaves us a few days to celebrate and say 'good bye' to our friends," suggested Rob.

On Sunday, June 18th Angus went to the church services dressed in his military uniform. Church members prayed for his safety and all the military personnel serving in Vietnam and around the world. The choir sang "God Bless America" for their departing hymn. Well-wishers gathered around Angus to let him know he will be in their prayers.

After the family brunch, the two young men were ready to drive to Fort Polk. His family gave him lots of concerned hugs and teary-eyed kisses before the two drove down the gravel driveway to Highway 1733. They headed northeast toward Lufkin, Texas. They crossed the Toledo Bend bridge and entered the state of Louisiana where Rob turned south on Highway 171. At Leesville a Dairy Queen gave them free drinks with their order of hamburgers and French fries. The restaurant owner had served in Korea and he supported those in uniform. The next stop was Fort Polk.

CHAPTER 1

Angus McKay was happy that his girlfriend, Mary Beth Mason, said she'd wait for him until he got back from Vietnam. He was driving from her home in Matagorda back to his home in Crockett. He had felt that he needed to tell Mary Beth personally that he had gotten his assignment and was heading for Vietnam for the next two years. He felt more like a big brother to her than a boyfriend.

Angus had left Crockett in time to visit Mary Beth when she got off work at her father's boat and guide store on O'Connor Bay. They had dinner at the Spoonbill restaurant. Mary Beth would be a sophomore at Tulane University. They generally met at the Future Farmers of America meetings. She was impressed with Angus for being a state officer and having won the Grand Champion award. He let her hold his Aggie ring until he returned from Vietnam. They had watched a late movie that ended at midnight. The TV station played the Stars Spangled Banner and went off the air until the next morning.

Angus started his 225-mile drive home as a thunder storm blew in from the Gulf of Mexico. The young couple had missed the weather report that had forecasted gusty winds up to 50 miles per hour and heavy rains to hit the coastal area around midnight. Angus had to turn on his windshield wipers at Wallis near highway 60 intersection and state highway 1093. He was driving toward Caldwell where he would take highway 21 all the way to Crockett. The winds and pouring rains began to increase. He noticed there were no cars on the road as the sky darkened and the torrential rains intensified. The visibility and wind made it difficult for him to keep the car in a straight line. Whipping winds were pounding road debris against his car. He was leaning forward and straining to see the yellow stripe dividing the road on the two-lane road. News on the car radio claimed that a tornado had touched down between Conroe and Montgomery. The rapid swish, swish of the windshield wipers didn't do his headache any good. The storm was producing winds and rains that came down in sheets – heavy then light; heavy then light.

Lightning bolts and thunder continually filled the night sky. His headlights were dulled by the darkness due to the low dark cloud level and heavy down pour. He could barely see the trees doing their rain dance swirling and bending with the rhythm of the rain. As the storm got closer, the crackling noise of the lightning bolts and the sound of the rumbling thunder became louder ending in a crescendo

Angus knew he would be stopping for some coffee and aspirin at his usual stopping place on the outside of Bryan, the all-night Corner Store. Over the years Angus had stopped there nearly every time he drove from Texas A&M University to the Bar MK in Crockett.

The bored clerk looked up from reading the Houston Morning News. His big smile showed his happiness that a customer, whom he recognized, was running from the car that still had the head lights on and the windshield wipers rapidly swishing back and forth.

"Up late or is it up early, Mr. Angus?" he warmly greeted. "Havn't seen you since your graduation. What's you need?"

"Just a cup of joe and some aspirins, Ira! Must be my sinus either that or allergies. It's that time of the year when the pollen count seems to be at its worst," Angus replied as he blew his nose.

"Bad storm to be out in this morn, huh, Mr. Angus. Aspirins are on the next aisle," he pointed to an aisle, "They're over there. Maybe you should try one of them new allergy pills. They claim the pills will dry up your nose. You'll find 'em next to your aspirins."

"Think I will. Thanks for the medical advice. I'll give both a try, maybe one or the other will help me get some relief," Angus yawned as he approached the counter.

Ira punched some keys on the cash registrar and said, "Sir, that'll be $5.75. Good lookin' black sweatshirt you wearing there, Mr. Angus. I like that scarf. Here's your twenty-five cents change,"

"Thanks, it's a Tulane sweatshirt and scarf that my girl friend gave me for Christmas. It's supposed to make me look more collegiate. I like it, it's warm ,"he replied looking at his reflection in the big round mirror above the cash register. Angus had typical Irish features of strawberry blonde hair, blue eyes, and fair skin. He was wearing black slacks, a white shirt with its collar sticking out from under the black sweatshirt and a scarf draped over his shoulder.

As he was leaving, a white car sped past by. "Boy, he's in a hurry!" Angus yelled back to Ira with the wind and rain slapping him in the face. Suddenly, a black Lincoln raced by. "It had to be going 80-85 miles per hour, maybe more," he thought to himself as he backed up, turned, and headed toward Crockett. That is when he thought he heard multiple gun shots cracking ahead. He rolled down the car window to listen to the shots more clearly. Several more rounds were rattled off. "Man, that sounds like an AK-47 that I fired last year at the Corps six-week training camp," he whistled as he hurriedly rolled up the car window.

As he came to the crest of a knoll, he saw sparks flying off the white car. Bullet holes were scattered across the back of the car. It began swerving from one side of the road to the other. Then it ran off the highway just past a road side picnic area plowing head-on into a tree.

The black Lincoln slowed down; more rounds peppered the car as white smoke from the smashed radiator began rising skyward. The Lincoln's brake lights lit up as it slowed down until it nearly came to a complete stop, Sparks bounced off the white automobile, shattering the rear window so that half of it fell inside on the driver's side.

The driver of the Lincoln stomped down on the accelerator for more speed, causing the tires to slip and slide sideways. The car squatted as the tires gripped the wet pavement and quickly straightened out. A lightning bolt ripped across the black sky. The lightning up the road allowed Angus to see black fumes as the Lincoln disappeared in the pouring rain.

Angus slowed down and turned into the picnic parking area. He pushed the button to turn on his emergency flashers. Then he decided to park his car so it was facing the wreckage wrapped around the tree and hit his bright lights. He jumped out of his car and ran toward the smoldering car. The motionless driver was slumped over the steering wheel. The back window and front windshield looked as though they were covered with spider webs with bullet holes in the center and lines zigzagging across them. Bullet holes were scattered across the trunk.

Flames began flaring up around the open trunk providing extra light to the headlights in the darkness. Pulling up on the door handle Angus had to yank several times with all his strength. It took several more attempts he finally got it opened wide enough for him to reach in and grab the victim. The heavy odor of cigarette smoke mingled with the black smoke from the smoldering plastic seat covers and began to fill the inside of the car. The smoke burned Angus' eyes and throat; he turned around to breathe fresh air. He felt the heat as flames began to engulf the back of the car. Grabbing an arm and shoulder, he tried pulling the victim out of the car, but the driver's left leg was squeezed between his right leg and the steering wheel.

Angus took the scarf that Mary Beth had given him for Christmas, and wrapped it under the man's arm pits. He was able to free the man from the burning wreckage. The man's weight and soaked clothes made it difficult for Angus to tug and pull him toward a tall pine tree about 20 yards away. The area under the evergreen tree sheltered them from the wind and rain. The temperature dipped farther making the air colder so that Angus felt like he was in a meat locker.

Angus was surprised to find a faint pulse. The victim was bleeding where a bullet or piece of metal from the automobile had torn a big chunk of muscle and bone from his neck including the shoulder area. Blood spurted with each heartbeat. Angus' black Tulane sweatshirt and the driver's jacket were splatted with blood. Angus unwrapped the scarf under the man's arms and wrapped it around his hand and began applying direct pressure as he had been taught in the Corps summer training program.

Suddenly the man's eyes opened wide showing enlarged pupils. He gagged on the blood and saliva that filled his throat and mouth. Using the victim's jacket sleeve Angus wiped the fluids from the man's mouth. The two stared at each other for a long period of time. The man blinked and with a weak whisper murmured, *"Forgive me Father for I have sinned."* Angus was stunned, he could only mutter, "It's OK." The man, never stopped, *"It's been many years, too long, since my last confession. I'm truly sorry for all the sinful crimes I've committed. But I just couldn't shoot those kids.* (cough, gag*) mafia...trying to kill me. I shot the commissioner and his wife,"* he admitted as he coughed and gagged on more bloody phlegm, *"... had...contract to kill his whole family...couldn't pull the trigger, even after...kids saw me. They screamed."* The man gagged and struggled for a breath of air. *"I ran."* He stopped to let Angus clean the bloody mucus from his chin and throat. *"That's wh-* (cough, cough)*...mafia put a hit on me."* His words grew weaker as he choked on more mucus, *"commissioner...figured out (his coughs were coming* harder and deeper*) "the school bus scheme."*

Angus remained silent and continued applying pressure to the wound. The scarf was now completely soaked and blood dripped to the ground. The wreckage was smoldering from the hood to the trunk.

The man lying in his arms, took a couple of deep, hard breaths and with blank eyes ended with, "Tell Maria, I love her." His whole body suddenly began to shake violently and, then went limp. Lifeless eyes stared into eyes of Angus, who realized at that moment the man had taken his last breath.

Angus shut his eyes and with a trembling voice prayed, *"Lord you gave forgiveness to the thief who died with you on the cross. If it be your will, forgive this man who turned to you in his darkest hour."* Angus kept the pressure on the wound.

The sound of a car door slamming frightened Angus. "Was it the black Lincoln?" he thought to himself. Angus twisted his body around and saw a police car with its red flashing light next to his car. "Sir, you alright?" A voice called from the darkness. The flames from the wreckage had died down and the headlights on Angus' car had begun to dim.

"Yes, I am OK, just soaked and cold to the bones," Angus responded his teeth chattering.

"Give me a minute and I'll be right there. I'm fix'n' to get you a blanket from the trunk," the police officer stated as he opened the back of his station wagon and grabbed a blanket and a towel. He approached the scene.

"How's he doing?" he nodded toward the man lying beside Angus as he handed Angus a blanket.

"Took his last breath several minutes ago," replied Angus still applying pressure.

"Let's take a look," the officer bent down to check for a pulse. "Yep, no pulse. Cold skin." He gently pushed the victim's eyes lids downward. He walked over and slowly removed Angus' hand from the victim's body.

"It's OK, son. You did the best you could," the police officer assured Angus. He began to wipe blood off Angus' hands with a towel that he had brought from his squad car.

"So, what in tarnation happened here?" the police officer asked as he took the blanket from Angus' hand and wrapped it over his shoulders. "By the way, I am officer, Jack White, from the Bryan Police Department and, "You are...?"

"My name is Angus McKay. As I was leaving The Corner Store, I saw two cars zooming up the road.

When I pulled onto the highway, I heard shots. I thought it sounded a lot like the sound of an AK-47," Angus replied.

"An AK-47! How is it you come to recognize it was an AK-47?"

"I got to fire one at a Corps six-week training camp last summer. I graduated this year and have my orders to report to Fort Polk in a few days for Vietnam training. I was saying good bye to my girlfriend," McKay explained.

"OK, Mr. McKay. So, how is it that this fellow ended up bulldozing that tree?" asked Officer White.

"Well sir, a black Lincoln was firing at this guy's car. Bullets hit his car. He swerved off the road. The Lincoln fired more rounds and it sped away. I didn't think I could get close enough to get a license number, so, I pulled into the picnic parking area. I dragged him from his burning care over here. The rain must have brought him around from being unconscious. I've been applying pressure to his wound since then," Angus took a couple of quick breaths and continued," He's lost a lot of blood. You'll probably find more wounds."

The officer asked, "Did he ever say anything?"

"Yes, but it was hard to understand him with the thunder, the wind, and the rain. All I could understand was he asked me to tell Maria he loved her and that he was sorry. At least, that's what I could make out. He had a very difficult time with his words. Mostly gasping for air in between clearing his throat," replied Angus.

"McKay, I am going back to my squad car and call for an ambulance for this guy, and a tow truck for this fellow's car. Your headlights look like they could use a charge. We can do that while we wait for them. I will need to see your driver's license when I get back," the officer stated as pulled the blanket over Angus's head. "You got something to drink in your car?" he asked heading back to his car.

"Coffee, probably not so hot by now," replied Angus.

Finally, a couple of cars stopped to render aid, but Officer White waved them on. When he returned, he had a plastic cover for the victim. "Dang it! I helped my grandson with his model airplane last night and got glue on my fingers that didn't scrub off. Sure makes it difficult to unfold this plastic sheet," he complained handing Angus a cup of hot coffee.

"Here, have some coffee. How long have you been sitting under this tree?" he asked as he covered victim's body with the plastic.

"Can't really say. I left The Corner Store a little before 3 a.m. What time is it now?"

"It's quarter after 4. Did anyone else stop to help?"

"No sir. Just those two that stopped a few minutes ago. Maybe no one wanted to drive through the storm. Cannot say I blame them. It was tough driving up Highway 36, especially around Sealy. It was a real Texas gully washer!" explained Angus.

Officer White pulled out a pad and pencil as he checked Angus' driver's license. "Says here, your name is Andrew Daniel McKay? Is that correct?" he asked.

"Yes, sir. My friends call me Angus."

"You live on Rural Route #4, Crockett TX. Is this your correct address?" Officer White continued."

"Yes, sir. But, I'm to report at Fort Polk June 19th."

"The ambulance and tow truck should be here within 30 minutes. Before they arrive, is there anything more you can tell me about what you witnessed?" Officer White asked.

"Can't add too much to it. When I heard the shots, I did slow down because I did not want to get involved with any shooting. I am not certain it was an AK-47, all I saw were sparks when the bullets hit this guy's car. Then, it turned sharply left, ran off the road and crashed into that tree," he explained pointing in the direction of the tree and the charred car. Angus continued, "The Lincoln slowed down and fired off more rounds before disappearing from my sight. At first, I was scared they might backtrack and take shots at me. But then I felt this fellow could use some help. Been applying pressure all the time until you came."

"Are you warm enough in that blanket?" asked Officer White. Then he added, "Reckon I need to find out who this fella is."

Removing the plastic sheet and rolling the body over, the police officer fished the wallet from the man's hip pocket. He shined his flashlight on the victim's license and then on his face, "Holy shit! This is Joey King! He's a 'member of the Houston Mafia. He has been in and out of jail lots of times. The Houston Police and probably the FBI will be interested in talking to you, Mr. McKay."

White's tone of voice changed into man giving fatherly advice, "Son, you need to be very careful what you say, how you say it and who you say it to, ya hear me? This is gonna make front page news. I know you didn't have nuthin' to do with his death, but be aware of the Houston Mafia. They got contacts all over, in local newspapers, even some police men are on their payroll. I gotta get this information to them as soon as I can. You can expect a call from them. I need your telephone number for my report. How many telephones do you have?"

"Let's see, kitchen and the living room. Oh, ye'ah dad's got one in the barn. There's three." he replied. Then Angus added, "Officer White, I'm to report to Fort Polk in a few days. Is all this going to hinder my getting to Fort Polk?" Angus was desperate to know.

Officer White thought a bit and slowly responded, "Tell you what I'll try to do. In my report I'll suggest they wait 'til after 11 A.M. to allow you to get some sleep yet today. That's the best I can do," he looked at Angus and laid the sheet back over the corpse.

"Son," he began, "this can be a real dangerous situation. "This guy is a bad hombre. He is, er, was part of the Houston Mafia. I don't know if you fully understand it or not, but you can bet your britches they will be interested in knowing what you heard. Surely, they know someone stopped right after Joey crashed his car. You can expect 'em to eaves-drop on your phones... home, barn, your friends, neighbors, anyone they can think of who you may confide in. Remember, be aware who you talk to and what you say. Do you have a security system at your home?"

"Only yard lights near the barn," he replied. White's warning words made sense. He had to protect his mom, his dad, and uncle Rory!

They could see flashing lights from the ambulance and the tow truck that was following right behind. "Looks like they're here. McKay go home, get yourself some sleep. I'll have to call this into the Houston Police. First, let's make sure your car starts," White said.

After the two batteries were hooked up, Angus's car started up after a couple of minutes of charging. Officer White called the Houston Police from his car to report the news. A few minutes later he got a call. He said, "Yes sir!" to the person on the other side of the line.

"Whoa, hold your horses," he yelled to the tow truck driver, "STOP! The Houston police called the FBI, who want us to leave everything as is. Their instructions are to tape this area off. Walking over to the ambulance crew, just as they were loading Mr. King's body in to their vehicle, he forewarned them, "You ain't gonna like this, but the FBI wants you to deliver the body to the Harris county morgue right away. Sorry we disturbed your sleep," he apologized to both crews.

"Are we authorized to do that?" the frustrated driver asked.

"According to the FBI you are not only authorized but required to do so." White replied, "This guy is on their list. I'll explain everything to your office. You are to leave here now and not stop any place on the way."

The two vehicles drove away; one headed back to Bryan, the other to Houston. Officer White got back in his car and poured the last of his warm coffee. "It'll be a while before they get up here from Houston," he thought to himself.

The sun was peeking over the horizon when Angus pulled into driveway of the ranch. Based on Officer White's warning about the mafia, he looked around to see if anyone was following him. He could not see any cars from the north, nor from the south. Besides he was too tired and his body ached. He questioned if his mind would allow him to sleep.

Mom and dad were up having breakfast, they were startled to see Angus come in with blood-soaked clothes. He had to explain everything to them about witnessing a mafia hit and stopping to offer first aid to the victim. They were concerned about him being an innocent bystander. Grace, his mother, told him to get out of those bloody clothes and take a long hot shower and she'd have breakfast for him. He stripped off his bloody, wet clothes and headed for the shower where he spent extra time letting the hot water soothe his body. During breakfast he informed his parents that the FBI may stop to talk to him about the mafia hit. Then he went to his bedroom. It was not a sound sleep. The events of the day caused him to have a weird dream. In the dream he was the one involved in the accident and the mafia were after him because they thought he had information. But he did not know anything.

"Angus, wake up. There are two men from the FBI here to talk to you," his mother called down the hallway. He hurriedly got up, put on a robe, and walked into the living room There were two men having coffee and talking to his father and mother.

"Mr. McKay, FBI! Good morning," the agents stood up and introduced themselves. "Is it OK to call you Angus?" one of the agents asked. "We need to discuss what you witnessed and heard last night or should I say earlier today? We're with the FBI in Houston. My name is Al Ramos and this is my partner Bill Williams. We've been talking to your parents and your mother has already given us the clothes you had on at the time of the accident. We know you had nothing to do with the accident, in fact, you were a good citizen for stopping to render aid."

"Well, gentlemen, I told Officer White all that I heard from Mr. King. He wanted me to tell his wife that he loved her." Angus began and then continued, "The thunderstorm prevented me from really hearing him and I guess I was too focused on his wound to pay attention to everything he was saying."

"As we told your parents our department has been looking for Joey King for several months," Officer Ramos explained. 'Did he mention anything to you in his dying moments," Agent Ramos said, " We'd like to hear about it." The agent pressed on for any information the two agents could take back to their office.

Angus stated, "By the time I pulled him out of his car and dragged him 20 feet, Mr. King had only made groaning noises. We looked at each other for several moments. That was tense moment for me. I think he knew he was dying."

"We're sure it was a terrible moment for you. Did he mention anyone's name of previous killings? Did he say who was after him?" questioned Agent Ramos.

"No sir. He was gagging and coughing too much to hear anything. The storm had pretty much passed when he asked that I tell Maria that he loved her," concluded Angus.

"Angus, we have reason to believe he had something to do with the murder of a County Commissioner and his wife several days ago.

Angus looked at each agent and said, "I wish I could be of more help for you, but that's the only thing I heard. As I told Officer White, I made a choice to try to help save the victim, rather than follow the Lincoln. Regrettably I was not successful at saving Joey's life. He had lost too much blood from a shoulder-neck wound. The only thing I was able to understand from his garbling and gasping for air was that he loved his wife and asked me to tell her that he loved her. He had a lot of fluids flowing out of his throat. But between the rain and thunder I just was not able to make out any specific words other than about his wife. Mostly he was grasping for air and clearing his throat of blood and other liquids. That's all I was able to understand. I did not know he was a member of the Houston Mafia. Do you have any further questions for me?" he asked, looking each agent in the eye.

"Just a couple. We want to know if you had any difficulty getting him out of the car. Was he conscious or not?"

"Yes, he'd been wedged under the steering wheel and it took several minutes to free him from the car. There was blood on the windshield so I figured his head had hit it. I dragged him maybe 20 feet to a tree to get out of the freezing rain. Both of us were soaked by the time I got him under the tree. That's when I saw his shoulder-neck wound and saw blood squirting out. I knew direct pressure was needed to stop the blood flow. I think the rain caused him to become conscious. That's when he began mumbling and gagging about Maria. Then he died. Later Officer White arrived and wrapped a blanket on my shoulders and covered Joey after checking his identification. Sorry I just don't have any more details. I will say it was an intense experience for me," Angus concluded.

"I am sure it was," Agent Ramos agreed, "If there is anything else that comes to you later, here is my card and Agent Williams will give you his contact information. Please call us before you talk to anyone else about this case. Your mother has given us the clothes you were wearing at the time. Should something come to mind that you think would help us in our investigation, call us. I noticed your sweatshirt had Tulane U. on it. Did you go to Tulane University?"

"No sir, that was a gift from my friend. She's a sophomore there," Angus replied then added, "I told her yesterday that I would be in Vietnam for at least two years."

"Yes, your parents discussed that with us. Thank you for your service and good luck over there," Agent Williams offered his hand to shake Angus' hand.

After the FBI left Connor and Grace discussed the situation with Angus. They told him that since he was not involved with the shooting and he did the right thing by stopping to render first aid he should go on with his plans to go to Fort Polk. Connor, who had fought in World War II, had empathy for Angus. "Son, I know what you're going through right now. The experience of being with a dying man is tough. Just remember you must live your life. The less baggage you carry with you during your lifetime will help you eventually," his dad said trying to comfort him.

Three days later a reporter from the Houston Morning News called to make an appointment for an interview with Angus about the accident just north of Bryan. Angus suggested they meet at the White Bear restaurant in Crockett the next day. He chose that restaurant because it is a longtime supporter the Future Farmers of America. In fact, among the many FFA photo's on the walls, there was one with him and EZ Boy with the Grand Champion Ribbon.

"By the way, my name is Johnnie Porter. I will meet you for lunch tomorrow at 11:30 at the White Bear restaurant," Johnnie said as he confirmed the interview with Angus.

The next day, Angus parked his pickup in front of the White Bear restaurant at 11:20. Mr. Porter walked through the door at 11:45. He had a camera that belonged to the Houston Morning News hanging around his neck.

"You must be Johnnie Porter," Angus said walking over to meet him.

"Yes, and you must be Angus McKay," Johnnie replied holding out his hand for a handshake. They took a table toward the back where there would be less noise from the others in the restaurant and near the photo of Angus and EZ Boy.

A young waiter quickly approached them with water. Both ordered the luncheon special of the day and sweet tea.

"Mr. McKay you must have be a brave man to have stopped to render first aid to a mafia man," Johnnie began.

"It had nothing to do with bravery. I did not know Mr. King was a member of the Houston Mafia. All I knew was that there was a man trapped inside a wrecked burning car. I got him out and noticed he had been shot in the neck area. I applied pressure to the wound, but he had lost too much blood. He asked me to tell his wife he loved her," responded Angus.

"How long did he bleed? Were there other wounds on his body?" the reporter fired off multi questions.

"It was probably an hour or more. It took some time to get him out of his car. Later, I learned from the police officer that he had three or four bullet wounds," noted Angus as Johnnie pressed on with more questions.

The waiter brought their orders and more sweet tea. In between bites Johnnie continued with his questioning. "Who, err from whom, did you hear that?" Johnnie asked correcting his English.

"The police officer Jack White. He was the only other person on the road at that time. That was when the severe thunder storm came through the area. Smart people were not on highway 21 at that time. Officer White was the one who told me the victim was Joey King." Angus stated as he took a sip of the sweet tea.

"So, you were applying pressure for nearly two hours and the only thing you heard Mr. King say was to tell his wife he loved her? Is that correct?" Mr. Porter continued inquisitively.

"Yes! That is correct. He had been shot before the car smashed into a tree. Remember, Mr. Porter, the thunder and pouring down rain made it difficult to hear anything. Besides he was going in and out of consciousness and struggling to breathe. I never did fully understand his wife's name. Mr. Porter, don't try to make a story about me saving nor failing to save Mr. King's life. I did the best I could under the circumstances," countered Angus.

"I understand Mr. McKay, or should I say Lieutenant McKay? Just a few more questions. Did you get the license plate number of the automobile that shooting at Joey?" Porter kept on questioning while taking bites of his lunch and looking at his notes.

"No, I was too far behind that car, besides the storm was limiting eye sight to just a few yards ahead. All I saw was a black automobile firing at Mr. King's car. His car was peppered with bullet holes that, I believe came from a semi-automatic rifle. I would think, Mr. Porter, you need to find the answer to 'why' the commissioner was murdered. And, with that I cannot help you." Angus asserted, letting the reporter know he was getting a little more than unhappy with the line of questioning.

"Maybe I should. Maybe I should." Johnnie smiled, nodding his head as if a thought had just popped in his head. He quickly stood up from the table, finished his tea, grabbed the tab, and abruptly left. "I'll call you on my follow up story," he commented to Angus, who was surprised at Porter's sudden departure.

Angus drove back to the ranch and told his parents that the reporter had basic questions about the accident and then without explaining got up and left. "It was a crazy interview," he said to his parents.

CHAPTER 2

MAFIA

It was an old 1930's bar between an unknown bayou and the bay south of New Orleans. The loud ringing of the telephone could barely be heard above the song "Yesterday" by the Beatles coming from the juke box. A couple was doing a slow dance on the small dusty space surrounded by 6 tables with 3 chairs each. There were only four stools at the short bar. Two dock workers finished off a couple of bottles of beer, with their Po' Boys sandwiches and crushed their smoldering cigarettes before going back into the hot warehouse down near the bay. Smoke from their snuffed-out cigarettes blended with the smoke caught in the stale air by the squeaky slow turning fans.

Locals were the only customers and, that's the way Tony Bocavinii, alias Trigger, wanted it. Trigger was a flashy dressed 37-year-old. His black hair was slicked down with a greasy gel because he was trying to look like a 19-year-old. His Duck Tail hairstyle was 15 years out of date since he'd missed his latter teenage years sitting in a cell at the state prison for robbing a senior citizen at gunpoint. He had told the judge he needed the money to take his girl to the prom.

The lighting was a dull yellowish since the old light bulbs had not been dusted in years including the ones that had burned out. Christmas lighting still framed most of the beer ads on the wall. The telephone on the wall rang five times. Finally, the bartender yanked the receiver off the hook and in a loud voice yelled, "Ye'ah."

"Oh, hi, Mr. C," Twyla's tone softened after she recognized the voice,

"When you gonna come down and see me?" she teasing asked him.

"Twyla, honey you know I want to, I'm just so busy keeping up with our growth here in Houston. Maybe if you're a good girl I'll fly you to Houston. You do any good tricks lately?" he cajoled back with her.

She responded, "Not much opportunity down in this dungeon. We did get some photos of a mayor over on the Texas border. They may come in handy in crossing the border."

"Look sweetheart, you're the only person I can trust to manage The Last Resort and handle my money," Then he quickly added, "You ain't stealing from me, are you? You get to keep what you make. Be happy." Mr. C sweet talked her, "We'll talk later. Put Trigger on the line."

Twyla set the phone on the bar, turned, and yelled to the back room, "Hey Trigger, it's for you!"

After the usual hellos, "Trigger, what the Sam hell happened in Houston with Joey?" Mr. C asked in a frustrated tone.

"Mr. C, I've been meaning to call you about that. Man, Joey failed us. He left those kids untouched. The newspapers didn't even mention the kids. Our police source told me the kids are in protective custody. He couldn't confirm whether the kids saw Joey. I am taking that as they did not. But at the time we couldn't afford that, could we?" Trigger asked waiting for a confirmation.

"Nah, guess not. It's a shame but, I guess, you did what you had to do. Anyway, it's over. Anyone else witness it? Did Maria get any more money?" asked Mr. C.

"There was one car behind 'em about a half-mile or so. The storm limited Corky's visibility to less than 20 yards ahead. He was the guy the Kansas City office sent down to take care of Joey. There's no way the driver could have gotten the license number. The guy musta seen Joey crash into the tree and that's about all. Ye'ah, Maria got $5,000 cash," Trigger answered each of Mr. C's questions.

"Are you sure that no one got the license number? What measures did your brother Frankie take? You were sure about Joey! Send Maria another 5 G's. She's a nice girl," he rambled on.

"OK, you're the boss. Rooster, Frankie's man, hasn't been able to find out the address of the guy who stopped to help Joey. The kid just graduated from Texas A&M. We will keep checking our police sources on what their investigation has turned up. I ain't worried. Don't yah worry about it, I'll take care of everything," Trigger said attempting to reassure Mr. C.

"Probably the FBI will be getting involved in this. Think they will be able to trace the plane?" Mr. C was worrying and wanted to know.

"Doubt it. They landed in a small town north of Houston. Think it was Navasoda or something like an Indian name. Frankie drove up from Houston to meet Corky. It took 'em a while to find Joey. He was not at his usual hangouts. We figured he knew we were after him. I just wish Joey had finished the job. Oh ye'ah, Corky took that AK-47 with him, says he really liked it. They had to sit in the plane for nearly an hour or so in Navasoda to let a thunder storm pass over. Then Corky flew back to Kansas City," reported Trigger.

"OK. Here's what I want you to do. Have Frankie put his Houston newspaper guy, what's his name? Oh ye'ah, Johnnie something, on this to see if he can uncover anything that may be a major problem for us. Anything further about the kids? How's our assistant county commissioner? Is he all up in arms?" questioned Mr. C.

"Ye'ah, he's threatened to cut the whole thing off. He won't! He's enjoying the money too much. It makes his monthly alimony payments," replied Trigger.

"OK, let me know if we need to have the Kansas City boys send Razorman down to Houston to take care of the assistant commissioner if it becomes necessary. He's their best hit man. Be sure to keep me informed. By the way, Trigger, what about the 25 G's that I paid Joey to do this?" Mr. C inquired with concern.

For several seconds Trigger did not respond, "Mr. C, nobody has reported finding any money. It must've burned up with the car," he speculated. "I'll get Frankie to double-check with Officer Deggs, our Houston Police contact to find out if they know any more about the money. I'll let you know, all right?"

"Ye'ah. You do that!" Mr. C said abruptly, slamming down the phone.

"Damn, Mr. C's not happy about the situation. I've got to call Frankie to see what he's done so far," Trigger muttered at the telephone as he hung up and dialed Frankie's private line in Piney Hills, a bedroom suburb north of Houston.

"Frankie," was the answer on the private line.

"Frankie, it's Trigger. Mr. C just called about Joey and the $25,000. He wants to know what the police know about the shooting. What about the assistant commissioner, how's he taking all of this?"

"Everything is mum at the police station. Newspapers reported only one guy who stopped to render first aid, but his only comment is that Joey's last words were 'Tell Maria I love her.' I'm not worried about it. Mr. C need not be worried about it. And I'm damn sure I don't know nothing about any $25,000!" stressed Frankie. He hung up disgustedly. Staring at the phone and shaking his head, "I said everything is OK!"

Then he yelled out to the showroom, "Hey Rooster, come in here a minute."

"What ya need boss?" Rooster asked entering the corporate office of the World-Wide Rugs Company in Piney Hills. His wrinkled striped shirt had a heavily worn ring around the collar that showed him to be a man in his mid-50's. His trousers did not hide the bulging belly and they had been out of style for ten years. His unshaven face showed signs of aging as grey whiskers dotted his beard. Rooster had little concern about his overall appearance. His yellow-tipped fingers showed years of heavy smoking and he was beginning to get a smoker's cough.

"We need to get current information from our Houston Police contact. See what information Deggs has on the commissioner's shooting. Maybe he can find out what the FBI knows. Go!" Frankie commanded Rooster pointing to the door.

Trigger and Frankie were twin brothers who had replaced the mafia men who cheated the mafia out of too much money. Their bones were resting at the bottom of the bayou near Gretna, LA. Trigger managed the unions, casinos, drug traffic and pimps in New Orleans, Baton Rouge, and west to the Texas border for the mafia.

Frankie had the Houston to Fort Worth area. His responsibility to the mafia was the same as Trigger's. He had no contact with Mr. C, who owned The Last Resort in Gretna, Louisiana, and a gas station less than three blocks from the Houston ISD Bus Maintenance Depot.

Rooster headed for the Caboose Bar right after leaving a phone message for Officer Deggs to meet him at the usual location. The Caboose Bar was near the Houston train station. He checked the massive bulletin board which was covered with various 'For A Good Time' messages and attorney business cards. He found a small opening and tacked up his message, blocking out several other notices - CALL ROOSTER. It was on a yellow index card in BOLD black ink and in 20-point type size. He would hang out at the bar until Officer Deggs contacted him either by phone or in person.

Frankie had decided to personally handle the newspaper contact. He left through the back door of the World-Wide Rug's office, backed up his black Lincoln and headed for Houston. He knew where to find Johnnie Porter.

Johnnie was where he usually hung out. South Ellen was an old warehouse district of Houston where hippies and artists now congregated. Amazingly Johnnie was still with the Houston Morning Daily. The editors had caught him expanding on a real estate deal scam taking place in South Houston.

The newspaper checked out some of his sources and found out that he had paid several real estate firms to make certain claims. Had Johnnie not had some photos of the chief editor exposing his extra marital activities, he would have been released from the newspaper by the chief editor. Johnnie was now a freelance newspaper reporter.

He was at his usual spot at the Pinky's Sunshine bar. He was snuggled up to a cute blond about half his age with messed up hair. Two half-empty beer mugs and two empty shot glasses were on the tiny table in front of them. Her pale skin and dilated pupils were her life story. She was showing Johnnie a lot of leg and cleavage while hitting him up for some 'good times' money. He was leading her on.

When Frankie walked in and adjusted his eyes to the dense smokey air, he got a whiff of the sweet smell of marijuana. Frankie finally recognized Johnnie sitting near the back. Johnnie always wanted to know who was coming in and out of Pinky's.

"Here, baby, here's a twenty. I'll meet you tonight at your place," Johnnie prompted the young lady as he ran his fingers through his hair and patted her butt when she stood up to straightened her skirt and blouse. She quickly grabbed the money. She gave Frankie a nasty provocative smirk as they passed each other. Both men watched her swish back and forth while making sure all the males in the bar noticed her.

"Up to your old tricks, huh?" Frankie asked with grin as he plopped down across from Johnnie. He took a swig of Johnnie's beer.

"Ye'ah, she was about to tell me how a gang is obtaining drugs with fake medical prescriptions. I'll get a lot more out of her tonight. Maybe you need to weasel in on some of that action," he grinned at Frankie. "What brings you to my jungle?" he asked. Then he quickly followed up with, "Bet you're looking for some detailed information about the commissioner's murder, right?"

Frankie fired back, "Maybe, what can you tell me about it?"

"Nothing, notta. I do know that neither the police nor the FED's have yet come up with anything. Their only witness saw nothing, knows nothing other than that Joey loved Maria. Basically, they are scrambling to come up with something. City Hall's screaming for answers. Right now, they'll take anyone. Wanna volunteer?" smirked Johnnie.

"You need to interview the witness to see what YOU can dig up. So, go dig up something. Find out about the kids! Anything! Let me know when you get some worthwhile information. Sooner the better. You'll get your usual fee. Here's a fifty. Should help you keep your young lady friend on the ropes for a while," remarked Frankie as he stood up to leave, leaving a fifty-dollar bill under an empty beer mug.

"Frankie, I've already met with the witness. He knew nothing, only what the newspapers have reported. I didn't even do an article on our meeting. The kid's on his way to Vietnam," Johnnie casually replied. "Thanks for the money. If I do find any information, I'll call you."

Chapter 3

Fort Polk

"Welcome Soldiers to the United States Army. Stand Proudly" was a big sign at Gate 1. A security guard stopped them at the gate, "This is a restricted military area," he stated.

"I have orders to report to General Steel," replied Angus handing over his orders.

The guard studied the orders and compared them to his file. "Yes sir, I see you are to report to the Bachelors Officers Quarters. They are located straight down this road to the circle." he said pointing to the circle, "Take the second turn off from the circle. Look for Bravo Street. You will see the BOQ sign about 4 or 5 blocks on your right." He handed the orders back along with a vehicle pass, "This pass is good until 1900 hours tonight," the guard explained to Rob. He raised the gate bar and waved them through with a sharp salute.

The Officer of the Day at the BOQ reviewed the orders, "You're in room 105 down the hallway. If you plan to have dinner, the Mess Hall closes at 1900 hours. It's to your right down Bravo Street. Your guest can eat with you, but he needs to turn his pass in before 1900 hours."

"Thanks, but we stopped a while back for a bite to eat. He will help me unload and then he'll be on his way back to Texas," responded Angus.

"Here's a map of this area. Colonel Debarba's office is to the left near the circle. Uniform of the day is fatigues. Just a warning, the colonel goes by Lombardi Time. I suggest you be there ten to fifteen minutes before 0800 hours, else he'll embarrass the hell out of you!" the Officer of the Day said as he returned to his desk. "Oh, for $5 a week your area will be cleaned and your clothes washed and ironed. Would you like for me to put your name on the list?"

"Why not? Yes. Who do I pay?" Angus asked.

"There will be an envelope on your bed along with your ironed clothes," the officer of the day said without looking up from his book.

Rob helped Angus unload the car. Both walked back out to the car to say goodbye. As they hugged, Rob said, "I'll try to help your mom and dad whenever I can. Don't you go over there and try to be a hero. You hear me?"

Rob got into his car and headed back to Texas. He knew it would be a long drive since he had to face the setting sun on his way back to Crockett.

Angus watched as Rob drove down Bravo Street. The new lieutenant turned and walked to room 105. This was going to be his home for the next ten days. He began to put his clothes in the foot locker. He could hear other soldiers coming in as he dozed off into a light sleep.

At 0527 hours the platoon sergeant entered the barracks and yelled down the hallway, "Get your butts up." Angus got up showered and shaved, put on his fatigues, and headed for the mess hall. He could smell the bacon and sausage. The mess hall had breakfast ready by 0600 hours. He could see soldiers already eating when he walked in. Some were in fatigues, while others were in full dress uniforms. Angus ate a light breakfast because he was a little nervous about his first day at Fort Polk.

At 0745 hours he walked into the office building to meet Colonel DeBarba. Master Sergeant Jenkins was at the front desk. Angus handed his orders to him. The sergeant studied the orders then said, "They're meeting in Room B, down to your right. Be sure to sign the Sign-In Sheet." Sergeant Jenkins added as he handed the orders back to Angus. There were twelve officers in fatigues already in the room. Angus was the thirteenth to sign in. At 0750 hours someone in the back yelled, "Attention!" when Colonel DeBarba entered the room. He, too, was in fatigues. As he walked up to the podium, more men could be heard rushing in and making noise with their chairs. The newly appointed officers stood at attention. Two were just coming through the door after the colonel had entered the room.

"At ease!" commanded the colonel. "Good morning, gentlemen. Welcome to Fort Polk. Here, we are on a very tight schedule. This is not a college class. As officers it is not good for you to be late for the men who you command. So, as leaders you need to be there to greet your men. It shows respect and leadership. You expect respect, so show it! Do I make myself clear?" he asked.

"Yes Sir!" echoed off the walls. The last two officers found a seat and sat down.

He continued, "Gentlemen you are to get a four-week training course in the next ten days. We will start by covering Uniform Code of Military Justice's and 'Character Guidance.' You will have reading assignments at night. You will watch a film introducing you to Vietnam, "Jungle Jim in Vietnam", for the initial purpose of training Vietnam forces. There will be one full day on 'Field First Aid-Treating Wounds.' On Saturday, you will have two hours on the rifle range and learn how to properly board a helicopter. Today, Captain Tom Thurston will take you to the Quartermaster to get the necessary clothing and field gear that you do not already have. I now turn it over to Captain Tom Thurston. "Captain!"

As Colonel DeBarba, walked down the aisle, he stopped by the two late arrivals who were sitting in the back row. "Never, never be late to any of my meetings the next ten days! You do not want to ruin your clean record this early in the game. Do you read me, gentlemen?" he glared at them.

"Yes sir!" was their reply, their faces red with embarrassment.

Captain Thurston stated, "Here is the list of clothing and gear you'll need for this program. Some of you may already have a few these items. If you do, do not take any item that you have already been issued. Check only the items you need," They then marched in columns of two to the Quartermaster. "Once you get what you need, take the items to your bunk. We will assemble at 1100 hours in Room "B," the captain explained.

The rest of the day was crammed with information on handling grievances, misconduct, and character guidance.

There was a fifteen-minute break and then back to the classroom. At 1530 hours 'Character Guidance' was the topic. When the two-hour session ended Captain Thurston informed them, "Tomorrow you may be called on to recite the Creed or explain one of the tenets," as he handed each man a pamphlet. "Tomorrow at 0750 hours we will take head count. Enjoy your evening, gentlemen."

On Tuesday there was a paramedic in class to demonstrate Field First Aid. He covered bullet wounds, insect bites, snake bites, burns, major wounds of eyes, deep severe wounds, etc. There were actual photos of various wounds. Some were gruesome photos. The major question was " how would you handle this one?" The answer was "It has to be done, so do it!"

On Sunday, Angus attended church services in the chapel. The chaplain spoke about the fact that Jesus forgave the men who lowered their friend from the roof down to Jesus. Service to others is an important trait to have. Sunday night the trainees found a bag with black pajamas bottoms and shower thongs. There was a message attached. *No underwear. Do not eat breakfast! Trainees are to gather at the rear of the BOQ at 0500 hours.*

For the rest of the evening there was much discussion among them about the note and what would be happening next.

At 0445 hours Colonel DeBarba was standing at the doorway. Every man was accounted for. He stated, "Gentlemen, today and tonight you will get a feel for what prisoners of war endure every day." The young officers were marched out to the training area known as Tiger Land. This was the area where jungle survival was taught.

A tough looking sergeant was standing on a makeshift podium. He wore an olive drab military undershirt, fatigue pants and combat boots. "My name is Sergeant Jack Olson. I escaped a Vietcong POW camp 13 months ago. My job today is to give you a taste of what it feels like to be a prisoner of war. The next several hours of this course are going to be rough," he bellowed at them with a bullhorn in his hand. "First, there will be no talking, no communicating. You will be penalized if caught. Your meal will be reduced by half with each penalty. You did not have breakfast because you were captured. That is a disgrace in the eyes of the Vietnamese soldier. They believe there is no dignity, nor pity for a prisoner of war." The men began to look at each other with some concern. They were already getting hungry.

"Break up into two groups. Group number one, you will be digging a ditch twenty-five feet long, two feet deep and two feet wide. This will be done with available tools," barked Sergeant Olson. "Your tools include three shovels, six hoes and three pitch forks. Group two, you will haul the rocks ten yards from the ditch using hands only."

The diggers picked up the tools and began digging between two strings stretched out to twenty-five feet. They found it was difficult digging in the dry rocky soil. There were rocks ranging in size from twelve inches wide down to pebble size. Guards poured water on the rocks. Haulers began carrying the wet, dirty top rocks ten yards away while the guards constantly yelled at them, calling them names for not putting the rocks into piles by size.

The hot Louisiana sun and high humidity was taking its toll on the "prisoners". The diggers started taking turns as muscles began to ache. The haulers hands were beginning to get raw from carrying the rough rocks. There was no break because the guards determined the men were not working hard enough to earn one.

It was after midday according to the sun and a break was allowed for lunch. A five-gallon water pail with raw fish and weeds was brought out. Each prisoner got an old rusty metal cup. There was enough for each man to have one cup of the mixture but some only sipped the water. Angus sipped and kept the wet weeds in his mouth to suck on as long as he could taste the moisture.

Then the groups exchanged their assignment. The diggers became the haulers and the haulers began filling up the ditch. The guards continued calling the prisoners names and yelling at them to work faster. By 1700 hours the twenty-five foot, two-foot-deep, project was completed.

At "Wash Time" each man was given a gallon of water and three minutes. Some splashed the water while others sipped it. A drying towel was distributed to every third person. The men looked at each other. This was carrying the experience too far.

Entering the barracks, they saw three dimly lit light bulbs strung down the full length of the bare room. At the end of the room were four "night jars" because the sinks and commodes had been removed throughout the barracks. Inside and outside guards were posted. The large room was hot and stuffy. A few of the men were able to fall sleep. Some were so exhausted they slept periodically. Most were too mentally exhausted and too tired physically to immediately fall asleep. Crickets and the outside noises disturbed everyone's sleep. Some of the men were sniffling as they could not believe the US Army would allow them to be treated in this manner.

"Good morning, gentlemen," Colonel DeBarba greeted them the next morning. "Today is the best day of your life. You've escaped from the POW camp! Enjoy the freedom. This is why you are soldiers fighting for the many freedoms we enjoy. We just wanted you to get a feel for what your fellow soldiers who are trapped in POW camps north of the DMZ line are experiencing every day. Go back to your rooms, shower, and shave. We will meet at the Mess Hall at 0630 hours for a decent breakfast. We have another full day ahead of us."

"Dismissed!" the captain commanded.

There was relief among the men. It had been a tough lesson. Attitudes improved. Angus' hands were raw and sore, but he had survived.

At breakfast the Colonel stood up and pointed out, "Gentlemen, you see there are three of your colleagues who decided they did not wish to continue with the program. The rest of us will return to Room B and continue."

At 0755 hours Sergeant Olson yelled "Attention." as Colonel DeBarba entered the room. He looked around the room and said, "At ease men. Sergeant Olson spent over sixty days under conditions harsher than what you experienced yesterday. He knows what it feels like to lose your identity, your dignity, and your self-esteem. We had him design this program to give you a slight taste of what it's like in a POW camp day after day. Any questions?"

Questions and comments began immediately, "What about the peace agreements?

Sergeant Olson stood up, smiled and remarked, "The Vietcong and the ANV play completely by their own set of rules. The ditch was an actual thing for me. We had to dig a ditch 500 yards down a hill. This allowed the Vietcong to tap into a spring and have fresh water for themselves. We learned to wet our lips by wetting our fingers and any clothing we could dampen. I sucked every last drop of water from the pieces of weeds floating during our water breaks. I did not eat the potato peelings nor the pig's feet. I kept them in my closed mouth for as long as I could. This helped me make it through the night. The noise was a nuisance but over time it became part of our environment. Now you can get coffee, cokes, and water in the back of the room. You do not need permission to go back and help yourself. The donuts are on me."

The rest of day was spent on what to expect if they should become a POW. They even learned some Vietnamese words, including a couple of vulgar ones.

The dinner that evening was Vietnamese. The men got a taste of various types of meats, fish, and chicken meals Vietnamese style. "The Lotus flower is the country flower. It is edible. It has nutrient value," the former POW stated. "I point that out if you get separated from your unit, it is good to know this flower is good to eat." Each table had a Lotus flow decoration. " In Vietnam there are various combinations of grains but rice is by far the basic food," he explained to the men.

Another topic discussed during the evening was that the People's Army of North Vietnam (PANV) military chain of command is very strict. They were told, "Vietnamese soldiers are expected to obey orders or pay the consequences. Life is cheap there. For advisors, how things are said is as important as what is said. Advisors are to pass on their findings and not disagree with the commanding Vietnamese officers. Their decisions are final. It is their war, their country. Some of the commanders do not want nor appreciate our presence."

The former POW continued, "Advisors are to learn to transmit and receive a minimum of four words per minute in Morse Code. If you earned the Boy Scout First Class badge, you should already be able to do four words per minute. Most downed pilots know Morse Code and communicate with one another by that code. That's the reason it is introduced in this training program."

"Also, one of your free nights will be used to learn the military alphabet. Most of our messages are transmitted using the military alphabet. You should not have any trouble learning Alpha to Zulu."

"One other point," he added, "You need to be aware that the Vietcong are mostly southern rebels fighting for a change in their government. The problem is they blend in with south Vietnamese. The PANV is the Communists who want to control all South Vietnam."

Rifle range was on the schedule the next day. The men were taught how and when to disassemble and assemble the various rifles. They experienced firing the M-14's, M-16's, M-60's, and the Car-15. They were able to choose the weapon they preferred to use on their day in Tiger Land's surviving in the jungle. Angus had never fired a pistol. His qualifying score was higher with Glock 19 than the .38 Colt caliber. He chose the Car-15 rifle because the sergeant had recommended it over the M-16 because the shorter barrel handled better in the jungle and field tests showed it held up against the moisture and the humidity in Vietnam. Angus decided on the Glock 19 pistol and holster because it fit his grip better.

More hours were spent watching training films on various land mines like the claymores and other explosives. The Vietcong had devised a lot of different types of booby traps to maim and kill the enemy. The films had examples of both grenade and punji traps made from bamboo sticks with sharp points. A punji pit could be five to fifty bamboo sticks. Some traps were designed to just injure the foot like the "can bullet". This was a bullet resting on a nail inside a can covered by grass and leaves. When someone stepped on that area the bullet was pushed down onto the nail and it fired. The films included actual photos of the results of the punji traps. They also pointed out where to look for the traps. The message was to be aware of where you step or place your hand.

"OK gentlemen, tomorrow is Tiger Land day! We need to arrive there around midnight because there are some night practical skills you need to experience as well as day light skills. Be ready to ship out to Tiger Land at 2300 hours. Be in fatigues. If you have mosquito spray, bring some with you. You will be given night goggles when we get to the jungle. Remember what you learned from the films. See you tonight. Dismissed!" ordered Colonel DeBarba

At 2300 hours Sergeant Olson handed out night googles and said, "Follow me. Stay on the path."

Suddenly, a soldier rose from a mound. He had a flashlight and was pointing to a punji foot trap. The men gathered around the soldier. The trap had been exposed so the men could see the foot-deep trap. The light went out. Flares were fired and an opening to the jungle appeared before them. The dampness of the night heightened the smell of the jungle plants. The course even had sprinkler systems to provide a realistic rain fall. The path in the jungle was narrow and low. Bigger, taller soldiers had difficultly maneuvering along the path. Limbs and large leaves would often hit them, knocking them off the path. Every once in while a flash light would light up showing a different kind of trap.

After 0100 hours they were allowed to take a break and rest. "Be careful were you sit, lean on or grab hold of because there are traps all along this trail," was the warning announced as the men sought rest.

The buzzing bugs were bigger and louder than back on the post. It was close to 0600 hours when they came to a clearing. A mess tent was set up and there was a hot breakfast for the soldiers. The sun was just beginning to rise. Their heavy clothing was wet from sweat on the inside and from the wet jungle conditions on the outside. The breakfast tasted the best they had tasted since being at Fort Polk. "Don't expect this type of service in Nam," pointed out the colonel with a chuckle.

Following breakfast, the men kept walking through the jungle until they came to another large clearing. Here they practiced throwing hand grenades at precise targets. They got to test the M-79 grenade launcher. They learned the sharp "crack crack" sound of the AK 47 of the Vietcong compared to the American made automatic rifle sounds. The men were able to fire their chosen pistols at still and moving targets. A few decided to change the type of pistol they had originally chosen. Learning and practicing basic hand to hand combat was on agenda.

At the tank training area, the soldiers were astonished at the fire power and sound of the tanks. They were amazed that the tank's flame thrower could shoot out over 100 yards.

The last training exercise was how to enter and exit a helicopter six feet off the ground since the pilots had learned that some landing areas were mined. As they finally entered a helicopter for the last time that day, they felt confident in the practical experience they had gained. The C-47 Chinook crew explained the various advantages of their helicopter as all twenty-five of the soldiers who took part in the exercise were loaded aboard the helicopter. It lifted off and headed back to Fort Polk. It had been a long fifteen-hour day.

The next day was Sunday and a day of rest for the young second lieutenants. Angus was at the morning services. He had offered to help the chaplain set up the altar for the Protestant services.

On Monday, those with overseas assignments were scheduled to have medical exams and shots. Two of the officers were to report to Washington D.C. to be assistants to various staff members coordinating the war efforts. Ten were to report to Hickam AFB, Hawaii to coordinate air transportation for supply shipments, as well as including Air Medical Evac to and from Vietnam.

Angus and the others were to report to Saigon for further orders. Those heading for Hawaii and Saigon were bussed to Lackland AFB, San Antonio where they met other Advisory officers heading to Vietnam. He called his parents to say he was on his way. "Don't worry about me," were his last words before leaving for Vietnam.

CHAPTER 4

FLIGHT TO VIETNAM

Boarding older model of a Pan American jet at 1000 , they were told the next stop was San Francisco. His hands were still red and sore from his POW experience at Fort Polk. The training program was too rushed to have time to absorb everything. His closed his eyes and tried to recall the past ten days. The POW experience had taught him the seriousness of the war. He reviewed the Marines' pamphlets, "The Armed Forces Officer" and "Warfighting".

During the last hour of the flight, Angus drifted off into a light sleep with the constant noise of the jet's turbines. The pilot's announcement that flight 1288 was being diverted to Los Angeles instead of going to San Francisco and they would be landing in twenty minutes interrupted Angus' dream. The pilot informed the passengers to expect a two to three-hour layover as the plane needed to have some light maintenance work. It was suggested that everyone take their overhead luggage with them. The captain concluded, "No one is to leave the terminal. This is flight 1288 to Hickham AFB, Hawaii so keep an eye on the flight monitors."

Angus bought some post cards and wrote to Rob. A lot of the passengers headed for the bar. He joined them and ordered a glass of ginger ale. He scribbled a few words on a Los Angeles post card: *Made it to LA. Should be in Hawaii around 9:30 am. In Crockett, it would be 2:30 pm.*

It was 1530 hours when the wheels of flight 1288 lifted off the runway at Los Angeles, "This is the Captain, sorry about the delay.

There were some nuts and bolts that needed tightening. The crew decided it best we stop in Los Angeles rather than San Francisco. Our next stop is Hickham AFB, Hawaii. Our flight time is estimated to be a little over six hours. Local time there will be 1630. The weather report is to expect choppy headwinds. We'll see if we can find some smoother air."

Angus' thoughts wandered back to the ranch and what his mom and dad will do without him helping with the chores. And, Rob, his longtime friend, what will his life be like back at Texas A&M as he works on his Master's Degree in Gas and Oil Engineering for the next two years. Leaving Mary Beth was more difficult than he imagined. The image of Joey King's last moments on the earth kept reappearing in his head and he wondered if the FBI would solve the commissioner's murder.

He recalled Uncle Rory reminding him that the Lord is always there. He carried the pocket size, WWII military bible that his uncle gave him before he left the ranch for Vietnam. He turned to 1 John, chapter 3, verse 16. It had been underlined and Angus closed his eyes and meditated on what it meant to him. The reading helped reduce some anxieties he had about going into battle to harm a human being.

The day he asked Uncle Rory about being a chaplain in WWII, he asked if he ever heard a catholic soldier's dying confession. His uncle explained to him that was not of his concern. If he had heard any confessions it was between the soldier and his Maker. "Don't you ever ask me that again, you hear?" his uncle said in a tone of voice that Angus knew not to ever ask it again.

It was 1900-hour Hawaiian time when the Air Force plane rolled into the designated parking space. Most of the passengers got off to stretch their legs and to breathe some fresh air. The warm ocean breeze felt good. The crew and passengers rushed through the terminal and got in lines to purchase a Hawaiian hamburger and drink before being called back to the plane for the final segment of the flight to Saigon. His watch showed the local time at half past nine when the plane left Hawaii. At the ranch it was 2:30 am and he hadn't had a solid sleep since leaving Crockett.

Snacks and drinks were served. A meal was available to those who did not get any food while in Hawaii. Angus fell into a slumber right after the cabin lights went off. A couple of hours later he woke up. Looking out the window, he saw the blue skies had turned to a dark black with bright stars sparkling above. He could see the scattered clouds below drifting by. He felt he was being suspended by the stars, gliding through a black bliss. He could hear the steady hum of the engines gulping up the night air.

As Vietnam got closer, the early morning light began peeking through the windows of the plane and the passengers began stirring, stretching their muscles to work out the soreness of time travel. The clouds below the plane were increasing and getting darker. Breakfast was served at 0700. Later that morning the men got restlessness, patience ran out, and more were walking up and down the aisle conversing with anyone who would talk to them. Some played cards and others read.

It was noon when a light lunch was served. They were still 1,000 miles from the coast line of Vietnam. Bodies were getting stiff from the cramped conditions. The clouds and winds had increased. In another hour the pilot would start his long descent to Saigon.

Runway 25-L at Tan Son Nhut Air Base was wet from the monsoon rains. The pilot liked being vectored to that runway because it was the longest at 12,468 feet. He knew from years of experience that he would need the extra length with the rain-soaked runway.

Angus was amazed at the number of USAF aircraft that were parked around the airport. He recognized old C-47's, C-123's(known as the Mule), C-54's, and C-130's prop driven cargo airplanes. He saw F-100's, F-101's and F 102's Jets from the United States and some from other countries. Scout and Photography planes included the USAF Cessna (called the Bird Dog) and the Skymaster.

CHAPTER 5

JULY 1967

Angus stepped off the commercial Pan American at Tan Son Nhut Airbase outside of Saigon July 1st. From the terminal he was bused to the Command Headquarters. The steady gentle rain was marking the midpoint through Saigon's monsoon season. The weather in College Station had well prepared Angus for the heat in Vietnam. The rains freshened the Vietnam flora scents that filled the air. Soldiers, with rain ponchos, were scurrying from building to building. Lieutenant McKay found himself last behind a long line of recent arrivals. Finally, he was admitted to meet Major Shepard. The major picked up the last file folder on his desk and went through the orders of 2nd Lieutenant A.D. McKay.

"Texas A&M, huh?" The major asked.

"Yes sir. I am an Aggie."

"Says here your name is Daniel Andrew McKay. Is that the name you go by?"

"That's my name. I go by Angus."

"Angus? Ain't that some kind of a bull?"

"Angus is a breed of cattle we raise on the ranch, sir."

"OK Angus. See ya' got your shots stateside."

"Yes sir."

"You're being assigned to the Citadel unit in Hue. You will only be in an advisory capacity to General Tran's staff. He speaks Vietnamese and some English. You OK with that?"

"Yes sir. I know a few words. Had six hours of basic Vietnamese.

"Well, you're about to learn a helluva lot more! You are to report to Major Lathon at the Military Assistance Command, Vietnam. That's the MACV on your orders. Lathon is an eccentric officer. You're lucky, Hue is known to be a party assignment. There's an Air Force Communications Center in the compound. Just do what Major Lathon says, any questions?"

"Only one. Did I see a South Korean flag flying at the airbase?" Angus asked.

"You did. They are supporting the South Vietnamese police force. You may see some in Hue. Show'em respect. They don't take crap from anyone, enlisted or officer," he responded. Then he returned to what he was saying, "You're replacing Lieutenant Odell Danielson up in Hue at MACV. The MACV is on the south side of the Perfume River. General Tran oversees the 1st Division of the Army of Vietnam (ARVN) at the Citadel on the north side. The Citadel has been the home of emperors for hundreds of years. Danielson will fill you in on your duties as an advisor over the next several weeks. He's a short timer and anxious to go home. You'll need your MACV/Vietnam orders. Don't lose them, else you could be in Vietnam for the rest of your life."

"I will not lose my MACV orders, sir," Angus answered with conviction.

"Good. Here're your Vietnam gear issue papers. Go to Building C and they will give you your Vietnam Advisor's clothing and fatigues. They'll tell you where to go from there. It's all in your orders," the major said handing Angus his Vietnam files. "Welcome to Vietnam, McKay."

After getting his Vietnam Advisor's clothing allowance and a duffel bag to carry everything, the time passed quickly. It was 1600 hours. The sergeant in charge of clothing had suggested he go to the Transit Officers' Barracks, grab dinner at the Officers Mess Hall and wait until morning to catch a plane to Hue.

"Gig 'Em," the sergeant grinned as he saluted. He continued, "Get to the airport early in the morning. I'd suggest before 0600 hours. Show 'em your orders. Wait for the next plane. Base Ops can tell you when that will be. The Citadel is easy duty. Life is slower there. Good luck."

The long flight had tired Angus. He found the BOQ and settled in. Before going for a bite to eat at the Mess Hall, he left a message at the desk to be called at 0445 hours. His plans were to be at the airport by 0530.

There was a C-130 taking supplies and mail to Hue leaving at 0730. It had room for one more passenger for the 300-mile flight. Seated behind the pilot, in the radio operator's seat, Angus was amazed at the wooded hills, the jungle areas and rice paddies he saw dotting land below. What they did not tell Angus was that the flight had two stops before landing in Hue. The C-130 was not designed to be a passenger plane. Loud turbine engines roared and the constant vibration made it difficult to talk to anyone sitting nearby. Angus was lucky he did not have to sit in the seats along the side of the plane. Those seats were made of canvas straps sewn together in a sling fashion.

When the C-130 landed a burly chested Master Sargent came aboard as the crew unloaded supplies. He called off several names and led the men off the plane. The engines roared and the body of the airplane rattled as the plane lifted off the ground to a second destination where a similar event of unloading men and supplies took place. At Hue, the C-130 made a sharp descent at 1200 feet above the China Sea shore line toward the runway that looked too short to land the big plane. Angus saw that the compound took up a whole city block. There was a three-story building facing a river. At the touchdown there was a thump and a bounce, engines reversed and the cockpit crew applied heavy braking as the plane came to a jerky stop before slowly turning a quarter way around.

"Sorry about the bumpy landing, Lieutenant, but the runway is too short to make a normal landing," remarked the pilot in a loud voice. .

Angus smiled and grabbed the combat gear that he'd picked up in Saigon. He followed a forklift loaded with three pallets out the back end of the transport as the propellers kept turning. He heard the engines of the C-130 revving up and the plane whipped around churning up dust and debris and headed back down to the runway. The pilot pushed for full throttle. The heavy plane rumbled down the runway and lifted skyward. The nose of the aircraft was at a steep 70 degrees angle heading southeast toward the China Sea coastline. At 1000 hours, July 2nd, Angus walked over to a small hanger with a pad of four or five tanks and one helicopter; each one parked inside an individual concrete barrier. No one was around. Then he heard a jeep coming around the hanger where the helicopter was parked. The brakes squealed as the jeep came to an abrupt stop.

"You Lieutenant McKay?" yelled the young private as he looked nervously up and down the make shift runway.

"Yes, that's me," replied Angus looking around.

"Hurry, get in and let's get out of here, pronto," the soldier said helping load the gear into the jeep. He continued with his concerns, "Two days ago, we had reports of a VietCong, a "Charlie," sniper with an automatic was hiding in the weeds somewhere at the end of the runway. Our K-9 search team combed that area but there was no sign of the sniper nor the gun. We did find some cartridges and two holes in our helicopter, but no serious damage." The private stopped at the three-story building which was the Bachelor Officers' Quarters and helped Angus with his duffle bag. "This is the BOQ. Those buildings are for the enlisted personnel," he explained pointing to three of the two story annexes. Across that enclosed breezeway is the Hooch: bar, snacks, games, books, and gym. Your building is an old, but nice hotel. About every two or three months the Donut Dollies come up here from DaNang. They're USO members. They visit the wounded, write letters for them, take hot meals to the outlying bases and firebases especially on holidays. You'll see them at the hooch performing skits. The flyboys are located back there," he added pointing to the southeast of the compound. He saluted and left.

The sergeant at the BOQ checked over Angus' Vietnam orders and led him to a room that already had the name Lt. Angus McKay above the door along with Lt. Odell Danielson. The room had two beds, pillows, and brown army blankets. Each bed also had mosquito netting. There was a closet next to a chest of drawers, a small fridge, and a bathroom. Two screened windows with curtains had a couch under them which made the room a little cramped. The sergeant informed Angus he was to report to Major Daniel Lathon at 1300 hours down the hallway to the left. Officer's Dining Hall is across the hall," he informed Angus.

Angus unpacked his duffle bag. He began hanging his uniforms in the closet, putting his folded clothes in the empty drawers, and arranging his toilet items in the bathroom. He was settled in by noon when suddenly the door opened.

"Hi, I'm Odell Danielson. Your roommate. He introduced himself, "We will be working together the next 6 weeks. You'll be getting get on the job training and I'll be counting down the days!"

Odell was a tall, broad shouldered guy with blond hair from Wisconsin. His light-colored mustache was barely visible. It divided his square facial features.

Angus held out his hand to shake Daniel's. "Glad to meet you, Odell. Call me Angus. Come on in," he replied,

"No, it's time for lunch. Let's go over to the dining hall and discuss your OJT program," recommended Odell. "Major Lathon will be asking you some questions and making some comments tomorrow at our 1300 meeting. He's about to retire. He does not care much about regulations but he's a thorough officer who knows more than he lets on. He makes it a lot easier being here," Odell concluded.

There were several other officers having lunch. The two grabbed trays and joined the chow line. Angus was hungry and took the corn beef with mashed potatoes. Odell took some Vietnamese fruits with fried chicken. "You can never go wrong with chicken," he said as they sat at a vacant table.

"McKay, it's not always this way. Some mornings you're up at 0200 and heading north to scout for signs of northern Vietnamese and VietCong hauling supplies to various locations. The unit we're working with now is pretty well trained. Major Lin is the lead officer with about fifteen men under his command. His English is very good. He reports directly to General Tran. I get the feeling the major doesn't care for the involvement of the United States. Major Lin is always pushing for updated field equipment and modern weapons. Some of his men use the old M-1 from WWII. Others even have French rifles and whatever other weapons the French had left behind after they retreated from Vietnam. They don't have much compared to the NVA, that's the North Vietnam Army. Our main function is to keep track of the North Vietnam Army crossing the DMZ and to report the number of enemy killed or captured. "About three months ago we estimated the number of VietCong and North Vietnamese Army using Ho Chi Minh Trail was down, but now there seems to be more activity. This month there has been a significant jump in numbers. The NVA accepts that a lot of their soldiers take off in the spring to plant and then in the fall to harvest the rice crops in the fall. After the planting and harvest seasons they return to duty and the numbers go up. So General Tran does not seem overly concerned about numbers but where the enemy is heading and, more importantly, their locations. . The North has two major bases just a few miles on the other side of the of the DMZ. We need to determine if there's ever a major buildup. Mostly they raid the smaller villages for food and medical supplies that the USA gave to them. We can get into it in more detail after meeting with Major Lathon. Just remember to cross your 'T's' and dot your 'I's' when you turn in your report to him. By the way, where did you go to college?" Danielson asked.

Texas A&M. My grandpa and my dad were in the Corps. So, I kept it in the family. What about you? "Angus asked Odell.

"I am a Badger from University of Wisconsin. Majored in civil engineering. President Johnson sent me a letter congratulating me on my commission and said he needed my service. I came from a dairy operation close to the Wisconsin Dells. We were milking over fifty Holsteins. The biggest dairy herd in the county. I've seen as many as one hundred head in the next county," the lieutenant said. Then he asked, "How did you get the name Angus?"

"EZ Boy, my Black Angus won the Texas Grand Champion my junior year in high school. Classmates started calling me Mr. Angus and Angus stuck."

"Well good thing they don't call me Holstein," chuckled Odell, then added, "You know these people could benefit a lot from our agricultural knowledge and experience. They are behind in their farming methods. It's mostly hand labor here in Vietnam."

Returning to a more meaningful discussion, Odell said, "Angus, duty here is not too bad. Don't try to push Major Lin to adopt our military methods. It's OK to point out the differences but I've learned not to try to advise him that our way is better if you know what I mean. It will take some time for him to warm up to you."

Angus asked, "Do we go out on patrol with his men?"

"Yes, the good part is that we do not lead them, we follow them and try to make adjustments to be sure they don't walk into traps. We decipher scouting reports for Major Lathon to determine in what area the enemy is concentrating their troops and supplies. We try to make sure General Tran's units have adequate weapons and other supplies. Major Lathon will decide how many of our marines or soldiers will participate in any given mission. You'll get the hang of it. Remember it may not be the USA way, but we're not in Kansas, are we?" Odell reminded Angus

The two finished their lunch and picked up dessert. Odell had an herbal Vietnamese tea. Angus had water and vanilla pudding. By 1230 hours the dining hall was nearly full of Vietnamese fatigues and red berets.

After finishing their meals, the two men walked to Major Lathon's office. "At ease, welcome to the Imperial City once the capitol of the Nguyen Dynasty emperor. McKay, welcome to Nam," greeted Major Lathon. "As you have been briefed, we are here only in an advisory capacity. We assist the South Vietnamese by helping them to avoid giving up more land and protecting the smaller hamlets from being robbed, raped and anything else the North does to destroy the poor locals causing them to turn against the southern army. We provide support mostly or fire power and the logistics. We also assist in body count. I see you've met Lt. Danielson, who will be heading home in a few weeks. You two will be like twin brothers. Danielson has put in his two-year tour. He has been with one of Major Lin's best units for nearly two years. He is to teach you, and you are to learn how to do the planning meetings with Major Lin. You'll learn we are here only to assist them. We monitor the North's trails to learn where they are building up their forces and supplies. We keep a low profile. We have engagement rules to follow. Danielson will go over some of them with you. Get to know them, there's no guessing during conflict. Understood?" the major asked.

"Yes sir," Angus acknowledged.

The major stated, "We are here to help them neutralize their enemy. That's the North Vietnamese Army, or the NVA. Your major threats are the hidden mines and booby traps they use to maim and kill. Control your fears. Remember what you were taught during your

MACV training at Fort Polk. You'll get a sense of how they mask a fake trail to look like to a real one. Pay attention to what Danielson points out to you."

Having made his point, Major Lathon looked at each man and commented," I see you both are from the farm. I want to send you both back in one piece to your farm or in your case, Angus, to your ranch. You will be meeting with Major Lin after each patrol. Any Questions?"

"Yes sir. When do I meet the unit that I will be working with?" Angus wanted to know.

The major answered, "You and Danielson are scheduled to be with the patrol tomorrow at 0500 hours. Stay close to him the next few weeks. That'll be all for now," The two lieutenants stood, saluted and left the office.

"Well, Angus, you just met Major Lathon. Let's see if Major Lin is available to us. It's a good time for you to meet him," Odell offered as they walked across the bridge over the Perfume River to Major Lin's Office in the Citadel.

"Tell them to come back at 1500 hours and I will meet with them for fifteen minutes," Major Lin commanded his orderly to relay his reply.

While the two were waiting for time to past, Danielson talked about the Malheur I and Malheur II Search and Destroy operations being conducted by the 101st Airborne Division. It was a tactical allied victory, but strategically ineffective as the enemy continued moving freely throughout that area. The small scale-skirmishes did disrupt the enemy about 100 miles southwest of Hue. At 1500 hours the two lieutenants met with Major Lin. The introduction was going well, until the major asked, *"ban tieng VietCong?"* the question was "How good is your Vietnamese?"

"I know very little Vietnamese," admitted Angus.

The major fired back at Angus, "Why does your government send me soldiers who speak little Vietnamese?"

The silence in the office was disrupted by the humming of a small fan on the floor. Angus just stared at the major without saying a word.

"Never mind, McKay. We have people who speak good English. He called in his orderly and commanded, "Find Khoy Le Phoo. I need him to help this American to communicate properly with my soldiers." The orderly saluted, turned and dashed off.

"You two wait outside my office until Khoy shows up," he motioned with a smoking cigarette squeezed between his fingers for the two to leave. Sitting on a bench outside of Major Lin's office, Danielson reviewed the Air Force's rules of engagement: (1) Don't go after SAM sites until they are operational. (2) Bomb a collection of 55-gallon fuel drums not major fuel storage tanks at sea ports, etc. (3) Do not destroy air fields, wait to engage their fighters in the air.

Angus looked confused and asked, "How does this affect our mission?"

"It can," responded his roommate, "The major just wanted you to realize how our Air Force pilots are limited to fighting this war! And, why we do not always get the air support when we need it."

Angus replied, "Alright, thanks. Do you know anything about this Khoy guy that the major wants to teach me Vietnamese?"

"Khoy had been one of the best scouting pilots in Major Lin's unit. A few weeks ago, he got caught in a diversionary trap and his helicopter was hit by ground fire. He was lucky to safely stay on this side of the DMZ. However General Tran was furious that Khoy lost a valuable helicopter. He was disgraced by being demoted to an orderly." Danielson shared the story with Angus. It was 1530 before the orderly and Khoy arrived at Major Lin's office.

Tell the two Americans to come in," he told his orderly.

As the two lieutenants came into the major's office, Khoy stood up from the chair he was sitting in. "Khoy, I am assigning you to teach Lieutenant McKay here, Vietnamese. I want you to be by his side, especially on our scouting assignments. Think you can handle this?" the major belittled Khoy.

"Yes sir. Thank you, sir," replied Khoy.

Again, Major Lin waved the men out of his office. Out doors away from the office Khoy introduced himself to Angus and Odell.

"You have to forgive my major. He's under a lot of pressure. I caused him a lot of pain when I was shot down by ground fire. He is always responsible for any losses," Khoy apologized for his officer.

"Khoy, I look forward to working with you and learning more about your country," Angus said shaking Khoy's hand. "See you in the morning at 0500 hours."

Khoy smiled and said, "That's a Roger," to let Angus know he understood English and military talk pretty well.

CHAPTER 6

August 1967

As the monsoon season continued Angus walked into the mess hall at 0415 and was welcomed by Odell and Khoy. They were already half way through their breakfast. Angus was anxious about going on his first scouting assignment. After gulping down an orange juice, coffee and two egg sandwiches, he was ready to follow the others to meet with Major Lin's unit. The 10 men entered the Sikorsky H19 Chickasaw helicopter just as it was warming up. The mission was to fly northwest to Con Thien. Local villagers had reported VietCong forcefully enlisting some of their young teenage boys to their cause. The VC count and movement had been increasing ever since the attacks on fire bases surrounding Con Thien on May 8th. On May 10th a Skyhawk A-4E was downed by three surface-to-air missiles. They were fired from across the Ben Hai River on the North Vietnam side of the DMZ, downing the Skyhawk. This was the first action reported with the Communists using Sam Missiles against the South Vietnamese. Con Thien was located just six kilometers south of the DMZ on the northwestern side of South Vietnam. Local missionaries called it the 'Hill of Angels'. The marines called it 'Leatherneck Square.' Today the chopper pilot chose to land at Khe Sanh, it was nine klicks south of the DMZ and four klicks from the Laotian border. Daniels explained to Angus, "A klick was a GI term for kilometer and was 62 miles. It's easier to calculate a klick as half mile. You'll get used to the term." The North Vietnamese Army had mined Con Tien's landing zones. The area was known as 'Death Valley' because so many choppers exploded upon landing in the fields and men were killed or wounded jumping out of the helicopters onto mines. Danielson explained to Angus that there had been an increase in troop and supply movement, especially along the 12,000-mile Ho Chi Minh Trail. The North Vietnamese Army was hauling weapons, soldiers, and other supplies across the DMZ border. There were two NVA divisions just north of the DMZ. The NVA 325C Division and the NVA 3249 Division were both major concerns of General Tran.

As the helicopter hovered six feet above ground., Angus and Odell were the last two to jump out. Immediately the helicopter lifted upward and headed east. It was scheduled to return at approximately 1600 hours. The unit met with a few marines stationed at the fire base. Ten were assigned to support Major Lin's unit. After minutes had passed a trail to the west had been discovered in the thick rain forest terrain.

"Angus, beware nothing is ever quite certain, and nowhere is ever safe," Odell warned as the bright sunlight gave way to the shades and dark shadows of tropical plants. The aroma of the wild plants added to the freshness of the morning tropical dew. No one was talking, just slowly walking along looking for signs of humans and booby traps. The men had previously discussed various types of booby traps (Punji) that mostly the VietCong used which were bamboo spikes smeared with animal and human feces hidden under leaves waiting for someone to step on them or grenades attached to hanging vines that would explode at chest height when the vine was pulled on. And then there were the false trails. When scouts found a trail leading off the major trail, the leader would assign two or three to head down that trail. A thousand feet later there might be an ambush or a 'Foot Punji' which were shells sitting on top of a nail enclosed in a can and buried. When someone stepped on the site, their weight pushed the shell down to hit the nail. The shell would then fire up through the boot and into the foot. Several scouts had been killed or injured by these booby traps. The enemy would then disappear into underground tunnels that were covered with foliage and leaves.

Angus was trying to remember the many different types of booby traps. The marines were eager to talk to the Americans during their lunch break. They felt isolated being stationed at the firebases for a month, or as they put it 'Time in the Barrel." Angus' report, same as Odell's, included that often the only signs of VietCong was a red bandanna that had been dropped on the trail. Fortunately, Khoy yelled, *"Dung Lai! (Stop!)* " in Vietnamese just as a young South Vietnamese soldier was about to pick it up. There was a grenade tied to it. Leaves and dirt covered the end of the bandanna that had the grenade's pin tied to it. Picking up the bandanna, would have pulled the pin. That area was marked off for the bomb squad to handle later when they got the map submitted by the men on the mission showing locations of the booby traps. It was 1800 and the helicopter had not returned as scheduled. Thirty minutes later it arrived.

"Welcome to Vietnam time," Khoy said to Angus first in English, then in Vietnamese, *'chao mung den Viet Nam thoi gian.'* It was dark by the time they got back to Hue. It had been a long day and Angus ate a quick dinner, showered, and went to bed. He and Odell would report to Major Lathon in the morning that there had been no signs of an increase in traffic on the trail. Khoy disagreed, but did not say anything.

Later Khoy told Angus of his personal findings about the report. Angus asked why he did not agree with the report that he and Odell had submitted.

"Because there were tracks on top of tracks. The imprints were deeper than normal. There was an increase in number of feet pushing down on the ground. Some must have been carrying heavy supplies like machine guns, maybe light cannons," explained Khoy.

"Why didn't you tell Major Lin?" Angus asked.

"Major Lin does not trust my judgment. He never will," Khoy replied hanging his head in disgrace.

The rest of the month included more scouting assignments including a search and destroy mission. During the mission Khoy explained the history of Vietnam and why there was a difference between the VietCong and the North Vietnam Army tactics. He made drawings of how the punji traps were designed to detonate causing bodily damage and in what areas to look for them. While on the trail he would point out how to recognize which trails were fake designed to lure some soldiers down the path leading them into an ambush or big booby trap. He proudly pointed out the various kinds of plant life and what was edible and what was not. Angus was rapidly becoming knowledgeable about Vietnam. He was learning more Vietnamese words and although Major Lin never praised Khoy for Angus' improved language skills he would let Angus know that he recognized the improvement.

Danielson's time in Vietnam was down to a couple of weeks and he became less concerned about his scouting skills. Once he missed a vine that had a grenade tied to it. Angus stopped him just in time from grabbing the vine. Angus had learned to beware of cut vines. Danielson broke out in a cold sweat. The incident brought him back to the present - Vietnam is now and home is later. On the next scouting assignment Danielson stepped on a spiked shell that exploded through the very tip of his boot and blew off two of his toes. He immediately crumbled to the ground in pain. The marine medic who had joined them at the fire base, took charge. He gave Odell morphine shot and wrapped his boot with duct tape with his foot still inside.

The medic explained to Angus that Danielson would be all right and missing a couple of toes was a ticket back to stateside. Two marines placed Danielson on a makeshift stretcher and headed back to the fire base where a rescue helicopter was already prepared to ferry another wounded soldier to the nearest army hospital. Danielson grimaced in pain as Angus wished him the best. McKay recognized that it would now be only him and Khoy going out with Major Lin's units. Khoy's training had been more thorough than the field films at Fort Polk. Angus knew he was now responsible for the lives and deaths of the men in the units he joined on each mission.

The next couple of weeks Angus listened to Khoy about being keenly aware of fresh cuts in the vines and trees. They could be a sign of possible booby traps or false trails. Angus' heart beat went up on every mission. Each one was intense and stressful, but in Angus' mind it was like stalking an animal in the woods even when he wasn't hunting. He would constantly be looking for freshly bent twigs and leaves. Maybe some leaves were drier where something or someone had rubbed up against it and the jungle dew drops were disturbed. No more glancing around, he had to stay focused, noticing where there were minute changes. In Vietnam the saying was "trees move and talk." Angus learned that every jungle was different. Different vines and thorns under the double canopies hid poisonous snakes, slimy blood sucking leeches and unfriendly mosquitoes constantly buzzing and attacking with each step.

On a Search and Destroy mission named Hickory II in late July, the Vietnamese elders in a small village about twenty klicks northeast of Hue had informed Khoy there had been VietCong soldiers camped west of them up near the river. The villagers normally were afraid to take sides, but the VietCong had taken all the medical supplies and rice that American GI's had given to them. Plus, two young fifteen-year-old boys were forced to join the VietCong or else their parents would be punished.

Angus and Khoy followed the 10 Marines and 10 South Vietnamese soldiers through marsh land and up hillsides laced with small trees. From the top of a hill, the lead marine gave the stop hand sign. He immediately dropped to his knees and wheeled around. Bending over he crawled slowly back to the unit. He reported to his officer and Major Lin that he had spotted movement down near the river in the bamboo trees. It was difficult to describe since the foliage and bamboo trees along the banks limited visibility. The major broke the men into groups of Americans and Vietnamese. They formed lines ten feet on both sides of the path. They silently began to continue the next thousand yards. Shadows from the trees favored the teams as they approached the river bank. They slowly advanced down the hill; the movement of large bushy leaves gave away their position. The quiet atmosphere suddenly erupted as bullets peppered up and down the trail where the marines and South Vietnamese soldiers had been.

Green tracers enabled the marines to return fire on the enemy's location in the thick grass at the edge of the river. Screams of pain and VietCong leaders hollering orders echoed up and down the river. Bullets ripped the leafy plants further exposing the enemy. More rounds were fired. Then it was silent except for the monkey's squealing and the squawking of the birds as they flew over the heads of Angus and Khoy. The battle had lasted nearly twenty minutes. The smell of gunpowder and gun smoke lingered in the nostrils of the men and the quietness of the jungle signaled the end of the battle.

"All Clear!" was the call from the lead sergeant. There were five dead VietCong soldiers scattered throughout the riverside weeds. One soldier had tried to run back to a wooden flat bottom boat. He didn't make it. He died within six feet of the boat.

No one from Major Lin's unit or any American was wounded. Each man had sweat running from his brow from the emotional pressure of the skirmish. The soaring temperatures and high humidity made breathing more difficult. Some of the soldiers just sat down and prayed prayers of thanks that they were spared a negative outcome. Major Lin, Angus and Khoy walked down toward the boat that had been pulled up in the weeds. It had been camouflaged to prevent an American scout pilot from seeing it.

Angus asked the major, "What do you think we need to do with the boat?"

"We leave it here. Set up an ambush, so that when NVA and VietCong use it to cross the river, it will be our turn to surprise them. We will have our people hiding up the hill." the major said. Two marines and two Vietnamese soldiers were selected to comb the area for the best places for reinforcements to position themselves for the ambush. Major Lin pointed out, "I will need five M-60s, four howitzers and two M-179's that we will set up on top of the hill where they will be out of sight. After four or five boatloads cross the river, we will spring our trap."

"Major, that sounds like a good plan. I'll discuss it with Major Lathon when we get back to the base. He will discuss your battle plan and request for weapons with General Tran," Angus replied.

As the unit prepared to leave the area the dead bodies were checked for booby traps. Weapons were collected and photos were taken per the "Body Count" program required by the Secretary of Defense and General Westmoreland. Then ten south Vietnam soldiers were assigned to carry the dead back to the base. Two Vietnam soldiers carried one dead body tied to a bamboo pole.

This was Angus's first encounter with the truth of battle and the smell of death. His stomach felt queasy and his whole body was running on full adrenaline. He silently thanked the Lord that those on his side had come through this battle safely.

Back in Hue, Major Lathon reviewed the report that Angus had submitted. He called General Tran to say that Major Lin's request of M-60s and Howitzers had been approved by Saigon Headquarter. Fifteen marines will be assigned to accompany Major Lin's unit of fifteen. Two Huey helicopters would transport the men and equipment to a landing area south of the site where the battle had taken place. Saigon Headquarters wanted the plan implemented as soon as the heavy weapons were delivered to Hue. Angus and Khoy enjoyed a two-day rest before heading back to take part in the ambush.

As Angus was leaving Major Lathon's office, he asked Cindi Le, the major's Vietnamese secretary if she knew where the nearest rubber tree plantation was. "Why do you ask?" she replied.

"Well, my best buddy, Rob back home is doing some research on rubber tree plants in Texas. I thought he'd like to see some photos of a Vietnamese rubber tree plantation," he innocently replied.

Cindi Le's father was French, her mother Vietnamese. She was taller in statue than other Vietnamese women and had all the qualities of a beauty pageant winner. Her parents had stressed to her that American GI's are not good for her. Yet, there was something about Angus that interested her. He was a genuine cowboy from Texas. She knew he was his own kind of man, especially when he came into the office wearing his cowboy boots and western style jeans and shirts. He was different from the others. Unlike the others stationed in Hue, he had yet to make a pass at her. He was always pleasant around her and she like the fact that he smiled a lot.

"We used to live on a rubber tree plantation. Sometime when you have time, I can show it to you. But now they are cutting down the trees. Wait until the dry season," she replied with a smile. Then without thinking she asked, "Would you like to attend our mid-August celebration with me?"

Angus looked shocked and he grinned, "Glad to hear there's a dry season." Then he asked, "This may sound like a dumb question, but what's the mid-August celebration?"

She explained, "We celebrate the beginning of the harvest. Tet Trung Thu is our Thanksgiving. There will be lots of mooncakes to eat and many lanterns, some will be floating in the air and some will be released into the Perfume river. The children make face masks and there'll be traditional lion and unicorn dances in the streets."

"Really? That sounds like fun. I like cakes. Khoy and I don't go out on our next mission until two days from now. Maybe we can schedule something after we come back," Angus stammered.

For the first time he noticed her pretty eyes. He'd never considered himself a "lady's man." However, there had been a young girl he met at one of the state's Future Farmers of America meetings that he dated several times. Her dad didn't want his daughter to miss the social life at the university. Angus had received a small package a few days ago from his mother. His girlfriend wrote that two years was too long to wait and, besides, she would miss the social events at the university. She noted she was not ready to make a commitment with anyone at this time. Angus was disappointed that Mary Beth had changed her mind and returned his Aggie ring. After a few days he had reconciled to the situation and accepted it because he could do nothing about it. She had made her decision. His goal in life was to be a career officer.

The next day Angus walked over to the medical center and found Odell with a boot cast.

Pointing to Odell's cast he asked, "You holding up alright?"

"Ye'ah, pain pills keep me quiet. Sure, didn't plan to go home this way." Odell said as he grabbed his cane and stood up. "Heard the ambush went well. Tell me about it."

"The odds were in our favor. We outnumbered 'em four to one. They couldn't find us. The mosquitoes sure did though. Man, they're bigger than the ones we have in Texas! We're going back in to set up a bigger ambush, maybe three or four times as many North Vietnam soldiers, or as the guys in the field call 'em, Charlies, may try to cross the river. We will be waiting for them with more weapons and more men. Headquarters approved everything the major requested. He asked for two M-60's, two 179's (better known as bloopers) and four howitzers. We hope to catch them unprotected on the river bank. I'm not comfortable with all the blood and death," he admitted.

Odell put a hand on Angus' shoulder, "You never will be. It's a life time disease with no cure."

Angus said, "I'm heading to the PX to pick up some things. Some of the guys were taking photos. I think I'll buy a camera and send some photo's home." Then he added, "Anything I can get for you?"

"Pick out a good western book for me. I'm shipping out tomorrow on AirEvac for an Army hospital in Minneapolis. Here's my home address, so send me a photo or two," Odell said as he handed his address to Angus.

Angus replied, "Sorry for your wound. You had only a few more weeks. I'll drop a book off on the way back from the PX," Angus confirmed the request as he looked up and down the row of beds. He got a lump in his throat seeing guys with arms and legs missing. Angus said a prayer for them as he walked to the PX. At the PX he chose an Argus 350 and three rolls of film. He picked out a western paperback and dropped it off on his way back past the medical center to say good bye to Odell.

That night he wrote home and to Rob. He mentioned Odell's wound, and that Cindi Le had invited him to a Mooncake Festival to celebrate the harvest where there will be mooncakes and lanterns. He explained it was a Vietnamese tradition. He wrote he would send photos of Cindi Le and the lanterns later. He went on to say that everything had been OK during the first month in Nam.

Mosquitoes are as big as dragon flies. They are everywhere. He asked his parents to send mosquito spray. Guys who've been here for some time tell me they sometimes use two cans of mosquito spray a day. The pungent smell of the spray builds up after a couple days on a mission causing helicopters to reek with an offensive odor when flying back from the mission. The stink inside the copter is unbearable! Some of the marines had started smoking to kill the stench.

That night he read a few verses from Psalms and fell asleep.

CHAPTER 7

September 1967

Angus and Khoy met with Major Lin and his units to set up the ambush. Major Lin was becoming more friendly with Angus because Angus was able to get more of the weapons and heavy artillery that the major had requested. The marines were picked up at the firebase and two helicopters flew toward the location where the boat had been discovered and the skirmish had killed five VietCong soldiers.

The boat had not been moved. The men began setting up the ambush. The howitzers were in place at the top of the hill overlooking the river. The men were well hidden up and down the river bank. Major Lin, Angus and Khoy were up near the howitzers.

On the second morning, just as the sun was half way over the horizon, more than a dozen North Vietnamese soldiers were observed across the river. They had carried three flat bottom boats to the water. Each boat could hold four men. The still morning air allowed Major Lin and Khoy to understand what was being said. The NVA leaders wondered why the one boat had been left on the other side of the river. The enemy had plans to use this location for more future crossings.

Four NVA soldiers got into each boat and poled across the river to the other side. Nine men got out, sat on the sandy beach, and lit up cigarettes. One uncovered the hidden boat and joined the other three as they crossed back to the other side. Eight more soldiers could be seen coming out of the woods on the other side and got into the boats. When the four boats reached the mid-point of the river, Major

Lin gave the signal. The howitzers opened and some of Major Lin's men began firing on the eight who were exposed on the beach while other men zeroed in on the boats stranded in the water. Two of the boats began sinking because of direct mortar hits. The surviving men began swimming back to the shore. The river current was causing them to slowly float down river, where more of Major Lin's men were waiting to pick them off one by one. The eight VietCong who had been waiting on the beach, scrambled for their weapons but the men with the M-60's prevented any of them from reaching their weapons. They never figured out where their enemy was!

Blood stained the clear water of the river. Bodies, some faceup and others face down, were floating with the slow-moving current. Pieces of the wooden boats were mixed with the bodies. Looking through his binoculars Major Lin was pleased with the success of the ambush. The dead were checked for maps and military papers. The American marines from the firebase knew that there would now be another attack on them in retaliation.

The next day after breakfast, Angus stopped to ask Cindi Le if they could go out that evening after she got off work. Cindi Le agreed responding, "Meet me at the Jeanne d' Arc High School steps at 1730. We will just have time to go to Dong Ba Market. Hue is known for its beef noodle soup with lemongrass, fermented shrimp paste and chili oil added. If you don't like spicy food, we can drop the chili oil. There's also a coffee café with the best egg coffee you'll ever taste. Then our dessert will be mooncake and jasmine tea. I bet you'll like it." she smiled at him as she hoped he would agree. She loved his big Texas smile.

The walk along Dong Ba Market was longer than Angus expected. It was like a big food flea market. Vendors had trays and baskets of crickets, ants, silk worm larva, even scorpions, as well as all sorts of edible flowers and tree leaves. Meats included lamb, chicken, fish, pork, and beef. Everything was presented differently than Angus was used to seeing at the Brookside grocery store back in Texas. The street was crowded with various dance teams doing their traditional lion and unicorn dances. Bystanders wearing their No'n La, the traditional, conical hats cheered them on. Colorful decorated lanterns were strung across the wet street. The breeze made the lanterns dance above their heads creating shadows which bounced around the crowd and the vendors. The ceremony of releasing the lanterns into the river would be later that evening.

As they walked and talked Angus learned more about her mother and father. Andre Bonnay, her father, had been assigned to the French ambassador's staff in London after France pulled out of Vietnam. Cindi Le had finished her high school years in France and one year at the Institute Catholique deParis. When Andre was sent to London for two years, she enrolled at the University of Westminster. Later, Andre was promoted to overseer of a rubber plantation in Indochina, but Kim Ly, her mother, did not care for the living conditions there. She moved to Hue because it was her home; where she had grown up, went to school and met Andre. Cindi Le now lived with her mother in a nice, comfortable home along the Perfume River. After she began working at the MACV, Cindi Le started night courses at the University of Hue.

Cindi Le learned that Angus was mostly Irish. He too was an only child and he loved ranching. His family had the largest Black Angus herd in southeast Texas. He had graduated from Texas A&M University last May. He talked about Rob, his best buddy, being a graduate student in the Gas and Oil Department at Texas A&M. He reminded her that Rob was the friend who had the bright idea that the Texas soil and climate could support a rubber tree plantation. He said he liked hunting and fishing with Rob when not working on the ranch. He asked Cindi Le if she had any serious boyfriends.

"Not really," she answered, "Actually, the Vietnamese men do not feel comfortable with a half French woman and the French feel the same way about me being half Vietnamese. I did like London because they're less biased, but my mother needs my help in Hue. I like the city of Hue's old history and way of life," she admitted to Angus.

"Well you seem to be very well educated and you're a very pretty young lady. I like you a lot as you are. I did not know there were racial biases in countries other than America." Then he changed the topic of their conversation, "This noodle soup has a unique taste. Normally I do not care for noodle soup, but this is tasty. It must be the lemongrass and whatever else they've thrown in makes it so unique. Where is the mooncake and egg coffee?" Angus asked as he glanced at his watch. He needed to be back on the base by 2200 hours

"Come on I'll show you," Cindi Le replied as she grabbed his hand. He noticed her long light brown hair flowing over her shoulders as she quickly stood up from the small table. She wore a long, white, fitted silk tunic called an Ao Dai, over her traditional flowing pants. A design of horses racing went from the bottom of her Ao Dai on one side across the front to her other shoulder.

Angus pointed to her tunic and said, "I like your shirt with horses. Do you like horses?"

She told him that she had ridden in competition in France. The best she had done was second place in the Arabian Breed Championship. They talked about horses until Angus said that he really needed to get back to the compound. They walked back to the high school steps and departed with a "Good night, see you in the morning." Cindi Le quickly caught herself and offered, "Angus, if you would like, sometime I'll show some more what Hue has to offer. The next time you need to try Com Tam. It's a favorite of a lot of the street vendors. It consists of rice and bar b que pork or beef, you'll probably prefer the beef, and a fried egg."

"That would be great. I would like to know more about Hue and the surrounding area and have you for a guide. Thanks for the tour tonight. I did enjoy getting out of the compound," he grinned back at her.

It was 0400 when the duty NCO knocked on the door. "Lt. McKay. Wake up! I have an urgent message from the major." Angus staggered over to the door and slowly opened it. "Major Lathon needs to see you in his office immediately. He just received a hot secret message."

Angus was surprised to see the major in his pajamas and house robe sipping a cup of coffee. "Angus, close the door. Sit down. We just received a special message from the green berets. They read your report about the locals telling you that the VietCong have a nun and six or seven young girls ranging in age from eight to fifteen years, in a makeshift POW camp somewhere in Cambodia. They want you to get a tracking position on the location. McKay, this is a dangerous military mission. This is a top-secret assignment. You will not be in uniform. If captured you will be treated as a spy. You are not being ordered to accept."

"Why do they need me?" Angus questioned.

"You have a relationship with this local because you gave him twenty dollars to help cover the cost of the water buffalo the VietCong took from him." The Major continued, "The plan is for you to go back to the village with more rice, meat and other supplies for the locals. He does not need to know this but there will be a device to track him so we can learn the coordinates of the POW compound. He'll have enough pork and chickens to be able to trade for his water buffalo."

Angus considered thoughtfully, "What if this fails?"

"If this fails, it becomes a search and rescue mission, which means lost time. They may move the girls before we can find the compound. It puts our men at more of a risk being in Cambodia," the major responded. Then he added, "Your man needs to make the trade and be able to draw a map of the compound. Once he does that, the green berets will draw up an extraction plan. They need to know how many guards are there and have a general idea of where the nun and girls are being held. Angus, these green berets are specially trained. Once they can visualize the camp layout and know the numbers, they can go into action.''

Angus paused in deep consideration and slowly inquired, "What about the safety of the girls during the extraction? When do we start? Will I be part of the extraction?"

"The team is also concerned about the girls," the major responded. "When they know about where they are located, they will make every effort to protect that area. Yes, you will have a small assignment in this mission. The team will discuss your objective and participation in more detail later. They want to begin today! Angus, you do not have to accept. This is not an order. Do you understand this is not an order? Yes or no, do you accept?"

Angus asked, "What about Khoy? Can he come with me?"

"No! I am the only one who is to know about this. Not even General Tran knows!" clarified the major.

"Yes sir. I understand! How do I get the money for the supplies?" he questioned.

"McKay you'll be required to sign a release before you go, which will free the US government of any wrongdoing, and make clear that this is not a US government order. The green berets are standing by in DaNang. They flew in earlier this morning. There's a driver outside to drive you to DaNang. Wear your uniform there, but take civilian clothes. You'll change in to your civvies after the local gets back to you from meeting the VietCong. Have nothing on to reveal your name or that you are military.

"Good decision," Major Lathon reassured Angus as he signed the paperwork. The major emptied his coffee cup, looked up and said, "Good luck. I'll want to hear all about it when you get back."

There were fifteen green berets waiting for him at an obscure hut at the far end of the Da Nang air base runway. They were sitting around reading and playing cards. The room was musty with cigarette smoke. The success of the plan hinged on Angus getting the local to go back to the POW camp and being able to make a basic drawing of it. They needed to know what kind of fencing was being used, how many VietCong could be seen and where the girls were being held. Every one began changing into their civvies. They grabbed their backpacks and weapons. Angus picked out a Car 15. It looked to be a brand-new Colt Automatic Rifle. It had an ultrashort ll.5-inch barrel compared to the 20-inch barrel on the M-16. It was lighter, too. It could fire over 700 rounds per minute. With 30 rounds it weighed a few ounces over six pounds.

"Good choice, McKay. The CAR-15 is just now being released for field work. We've found it superior to the M-16," said the colonel in charge of the mission.

Twelve men jumped in the helicopter. "Where are the other three?" Angus asked with a concerned tone.

"They are our rescue in case we need them. There is another helicopter for them and for the girls. There's a doctor in case we need one. McKay, keep your fatigues on 'til we know the local is willing to participate. We will be waiting for you a few miles from the village. You get his agreement. Come back to us and change to civvies. Then we execute our plan, do you understand?" the colonel reviewed Angus's mission.

The helicopter ride took two hours. It landed two miles east of the small village that was along a river. At noon Angus walked into the village. He had carried seventy pounds of rice, pork and chicken, plus $100 equivalent in Vietnamese currency, all available for trading for the water buffalo. There also were a couple of bottles of a strong knockout whiskey. The POW compound was west, across the shallow river at nearly an hour of cross-country walking. It would take six hours for the farmer to walk to the POW camp and return with his water buffalo. The tracking device was dropped as the farmer entered the front gate. The impact of hitting the ground that was partially covered by tall grass activated the device.

Back at the helicopter a monitor flashed. "We have coordinates!" a green beret reported to his officer. The colonel checked his watch. It had taken four hours for the farmer to get to the POW site. The colonel then calculated that Angus should return from the village at about 0130.

A misty, foggy night delayed the farmer's return. It was 0200 hours when the happy, tired farmer entered his darkened village with his water buffalo. Angus greeted him and thanked him. The farmer returned the change. He had proved to be a good trader for the water buffalo, or as the local call them, tractors. Angus took the man's hands and returned money that he had brought back. "You keep. Buy a new cart," he told the farmer.

"*Ca'mo n*" said the farmer. Then he bowed to show respect as Angus began the two-mile trip back toward the parked helicopter. At first, he could not see the helicopter because it had been covered with netting to camouflage its location.

"Man, we were getting worried about you. Everything OK?" asked the colonel.

"Yes, the farmer got his water buffalo back," reported Angus. "The tracking device was dropped near the front gate. He counted six or seven guards. The girls are in the far back of the camp in a makeshift shelter. He could see the girls were frightened to death," Angus commented. "The farmer was upset that they would not let him have his cart back." He handed the colonel a sheet of paper with a rough drawing of the POW camp. The men gathered around their colonel as his flashlight focused on the sketch the farmer had provided. Angus changed into his civvies as the colonel began giving each team their assignment.

"OK, McKay and I will approach the front gate. Team one, you circle around to the north side, team two you cover the south side, team three, work around to the back to protect the girls in case a guard or two heads toward the girls. Back team shoot up the flares when you're in position. Each of you take out your target. I do not want any guard near those girls," ordered the colonel.

The men armed with grenades, cluster bombs and their rifles left the helicopter in quiet formation. Angus and the colonel led the squad to the POW camp. The chicken wire fence was the only barrier around the quarter acre where the girls were being held prisoner. The moon light was broken by clouds floating across the sky. The camp was in a meadow clearing surrounded by hills lined with trees. The colonel stopped and each man dropped to one knee. He motioned for the men to take their positions. Turning to Angus the colonel warned, "Be ready if anyone approaches you, but does not stop when you say, 'Halt!' shoot to kill! I've lost too many men who've gotten blown up because the enemy blew himself up within six feet of them."

There was no sound from any of the guards. No one was walking around. With his night goggles Angus could see the cart in front of a makeshift tent. The time was 0300 and two flares lit the area like spot lights beaming down on the camp. VietCong guards woke from their hard sleep induced by the knock out whiskey. They stood up, staggered around, and looked confused about what was happening. Gun fire erupted in the silent night air and three VietCong soldiers grabbed their chests screaming in pain, their knees buckled and they fell dead. Two other guards ran toward the makeshift shelter where muffled cries of the girls could be heard. Two rounds of bullets hit their targets as both guards fell backward from the force of the impact.

The colonel and Angus rushed through the only gate of the compound. There were three dead guards sprawled out near the table with an empty bottle of whiskey toppled on its side. A big pot of rice and chicken sat on the cart. That and the half-eaten mooncake, along with mangos had been the guards' final meal. Two men were cut down on their run toward the girls. The colonel looked at Angus and asked, "Only five?"

Angus shrugged, "Maybe the local was wrong?" He did not have an answer. The dimming flares were slowly drifting toward the earth. The night was darkened by clouds and the air was silent.

"OK teams, click on your flashlights. Be on guard as you walk slowly to the shelter. There may be a Charlie lurking in the weeds," commanded the colonel. "Stay alert!"

Angus slowly walked over to the table. There were four guards lying on the ground around the makeshift shelter. One was a young VietCong soldier lying in the tall grass. He had drunk too much of the 'knock out' whisky and had passed out. He never woke up. Angus pointed his rifle at each man. The colonel gently pushed Angus' weapon aside. He stepped past Angus, pulled out his revolver and shot each one in the head. Angus flinched and turned his head. Two more single head shots came from near the shelter.

"This one must have had too much of our knock out whiskey," the colonel said putting his pistol back in his holster. "OK, check for names, maps, papers, whatever we can use. Pull 'em into the shelter. Burn the shelter and the cart. We have two helicopters landing here in three minutes. Try to calm the girls down. Give 'em the chocolate bars we brought for them," the colonel ordered the men.

The nun followed by the girls, stopped in front of the Colonel. *"Je Vous Remercie, Dieute Benisse,"* she said in French. Translated in English, it meant: "Thank you and God bless you."

Angus was shocked when the colonel began conversing with her in French. Angus understood the word Da Nang. The girls were given water and chocolate bars as they were helped onto the helicopters. Each girl had signs of rope burns on her wrists. The flames from the burning shelter and cart lit the area as the helicopters lifted off the Cambodian soil.

69

It was 0600 when the helicopters landed in Da Nang. There were medical people waiting to care for the nun and girls. A jeep was waiting to drive Angus back to Hue.

"McKay, a job well done. Here's a green beret bar. You can't wear it but you can tell your kids how you earned it. Congratulations! Thanks for your help in making this a successful rescue mission. Regrettably it won't go on your record, but Major Lathon knows about it. I bet he'll take care of you," the colonel complimented Angus and shook his hand. Then the colonel turned toward the hut at the end of the runway.

CHAPTER 8

October 1967

Angus was back in Hue after a full 24 hours. As Angus walked in the hallway, the guard on duty quickly took his feet off the desk. "Lieutenant McKay, must've been some party."

"Ye'ah, it was a blast," Angus yawned, walking toward his room, his mind and body screamed for sleep as his head hit the pillow, he murmured, "Thank you Lord. Bless those guys and girls."

It was noon before Angus stretched his aching muscles. He still had his civvies on. As he undressed to take a shower, he noticed three tree leeches on his legs. He burned them off and climbed under the hot running water. His shave felt good. His stomach told him the trail crackers, he had on the helicopter, were completely digested. He relieved his hunger pangs with a special order of pancakes and eggs, coffee, and mango juice. Feeling a tap on his shoulder, he wheeled around to see Khoy.

"Hey man, missed you yesterday," Khoy said, sitting down across the table from Angus. "Did you find one of our fine ladies of the night," he grinned with a wink.

"No! I missed you too. Had some catch-up work to do for Major Lathon," Angus countered.

"I ain't buying that, but will let it go for now. How would you like to join me on a bicycle ride up to Tiger Arena?" Khoy offered the invitation with a big smile.

"Khoy, we've got a mission tomorrow, remember? How far is this arena?" Angus wanted to know.

"Ho Quyn is only three klicks outside of Hue in the Tuong Da village. We will be back by 1800. If you're up to it," Khoy challenged him.

"Sure, let's do it. You can teach me more Vietnamese," Angus agreed to Khoy's offer.

As the two peddled along the streets of Hue, Khoy began telling Angus about the history of Tiger Arena, "It was built in 1830 for the royal family's favorite pastime of watching elephants and tigers or leopards face off in life or death combat. Since the elephant was a symbol of the emperor's power, the claws and teeth of the cats were removed allowing the elephants to win every time. The last combat was in 1904."

The arena and the ancient gray walls surrounding it had deteriorated over the decades. Climbing wall vines covered much of the chipped walls and exposed supporting rocks. Angus could see small lizards scampering up and down the walls. The barred red gates that allowed the big hungry cats into the arena were at the far end of the field, which was now covered in weeds. Elephants had once entered through the high red barred gates at the other end.

One could only imagine the sounds of the animals as they faced off against each other. Angus visualized an angry elephant hoisting a tiger up over its head and tossing it aside like a teddy bear. The historical arena gave Angus a greater understanding of the Vietnamese culture. The bicycle trip helped Angus to put the previous mission aside. He didn't care to dwell on the experience of the pains and death of a battle. In his first sixty days of Vietnam he had begun to better understand the fears and attitudes of the civilians. His dad and uncle had taught him to respect other cultures and races. He did not have to agree with their beliefs or practices, he just had to be strong in his own beliefs. The Vietnamese just wanted to be left alone to work in their fields and shops.

On the way back to Hue, the two stopped for a quick dessert and cup of coffee. Angus had a question that he had been wanting to ask Khoy for some time.

"Khoy, it seems that Hue is not in the war zone. People walk around and go to work like there is no war going on. Why is that?" he asked.

"Hue has a lot of temples and has been the center for Vietnamese emperors for centuries. You might say it is the most holy part of Vietnam. So, the battles are 30 or more miles outside of Hue. The Americans have established firebases near smaller towns and villages to disrupt the shipment of North Vietnamese soldiers and supplies toward South Vietnam. There are some non-Vietnamese civil workers who have families living in Hue such as teachers at the schools and the college," responded Khoy.

Back at the MACV command post Angus assisted the chaplain every Sunday. He was friendly with the three hundred fifty soldiers stationed at Hue. Most of them had their twenty-four-month calendar checked off day by day. A lot of the GIs felt that if it was not the American way it was the wrong way. Some never left the compound or never tasted the various foods. Many spent their free time in the Hooch, where they played cards, games, watched canned television and drank.

One day, Angus felt he was coming down with something, he had a sudden onset of fever, an itchy rash, and severe joint aches, so he headed to see the doctor.

"You definitely have a fever. Have you been taking the quinine and salt pills? What about being outside the compound recently'? the doctor asked.

"I may have missed some pills during a few missions, otherwise when I remembered. And yes, I have a Vietnamese friend that has taken me around Hue. He was assigned to be my aid and language tutor," replied Angus.

"Well, McKay, I do not think you have malaria or dysentery because the compound is sprayed periodically for mosquitos. I do not see signs of ringworm or lice. You probably have Dengue Fever. It is more associated urban and jungle activity. You need to stay in bed the next four or five days. I can prescribe some medication to ease the pain. Bed rest should get you through this. If you start feeling worse get your butt back here pronto. Go write letters to your family and girlfriends. Let 'em know you're doing fine?" the doctor concluded by handing him a bottle of pills.

Lieutenant McKay spent the next few days in his room. He wrote letters, asking for more mosquito spray. He wrote Rob about his fever and added he'd met a cute Vietnamese/French girl.

He missed the next mission. He could hear the heavy rains pounding on his window and officers cursing the rains as they entered the barracks. Monsoon season was still the main topic of discussion. Cindi Le learned about Angus' fever from Major Lathon. After work she stopped at her Catholic church to pray for Angus' recovery. She began to recognize that her concern for him revealed that she had deeper feelings for Angus. She remembered that Angus had told her how much he liked biscuits. The following two days she brought him chicken and rice soup, and a biscuit. On the fourth day Angus walked up to her desk with two empty pots.

He set the pots on her desk and with a wide grin said, "Thank you for the soups and biscuits. They were very tasty. They helped speed up my recovery." He winked and added, "I owe you a dinner sometime."

CHAPTER 9

November 1967, Part I

Later in the week Angus was doing office work in the upstairs office. "Hey McKay, the major needs you down in the MACV communications center. The center was eight feet below ground level. It had radios and transmitters around the 15 by 20-foot bunker. There were a dozen Air Force staff manning the center, 24 hours 7 days a week. There was a huge map of the northern portion of central Vietnam on the wall. A short door to the outside opened to a narrow bunker enclosed with sand bags on the sides and on the top. As Angus walked in, the major pointed at the map and said, "Angus, we have a major battle at our Firebase, Hill 48! The entire 812 Regiment of the NVA has attacked our 3rd Battalion at Con Thien at 1730 hours. We're experiencing heavy casualties. I'm in contact with the Midway. They are scrambling two flights of their jet fighters. A scout plane is dropping smoke bombs for the pilots to pick up effective targets."

"The communications officer says many of the wounds are due to rocket and mortar fire. We are sending re-enforcements from Hue and DaNang. Get the estimated time of arrival from DaNang. We have about two hundred men, plus a tank battalion and anti-tank battalion holding off two NVA battalions. They need help!" Major Lathon explained. The tiny fans and high humidity did not help with the temperature in the room. The clothing on everyone in the communications center was showing signs of sweat. No one complained but the heated enclosure captured all the body odors. Angus sat down at one radio set and called DaNang for an estimated arrival time of the re-enforcements.

"Blue Bird One calling Big Dog One. Do you read, over?" the pilot of the scout plane called the leader of the jet planes.

"Blue Bird One this is Big Dog One, over." The pilot of the jet replied.

"Roger, I am at 3,000 feet you should see the mortar fire. I am dropping yellow smoke over the target area, do you read? Over."

"Roger that. You need to clear the area. Climb to 5,000 feet minimum. Show us the yellow and get out of the area, we're turning south, you head north. Got the yellow. We're coming in."

Blue Bird One headed north and climbed to 5,000 feet. He was low on fuel and followed the Ben Hai river back to Hue. Red flames mixed with the black smoke blocked out the sunset as the jets dropped their napalm bombs. There were more explosions as bombs hit stacks of rocket shells. The Americans could see debris and bodies flying through the heavy gray smoke outlining the huge orange flames capped with blackish clouds. Then the two jets dropped their cluster bombs. The bombs bounced along the surface and sparks lit the landscape with immediate fires. At 2130 hours the rocket and mortar fire suddenly ceased. The night was quite except for the crackling of the trees as the flames burned out.

Farther west of Con Thien, at 1615 a barrage of 140 mm rocket rounds caught the marines by surprise. This was followed by a ground assault. A whole division 's of the black uniformed People's Army of Vietnam (PAVN) popped up from pits dug all around the rice paddies screaming and firing their weapons randomly.

Tank machine guns began firing in the direction of the noise and mowed the enemy down by the row. Some of the huts collapsed from the steady gun fire. Trees hit by all the firing were splintered and broke in two. Then, flames engulfed the jagged stumps as well as some huts.

"M" company was in a battle with North Vietnam's Army soldiers wearing USMC flak jackets and helmets. The "thing" which is the nickname for a downsized small tank, armed with six mounted 105mm recoil-less rifles on each, was too much fire power for the enemy. As in other battles the North Vietnamese Army stopped their attack and quickly disappeared. The NVA left a lot of their dead lying on the battle field. Many American soldiers were killed during the battle. They were shipped home in coffins with honors. Angus remembered the first time he had joined the marines from Hill 48. There had been a sign at the front gate, '*You are 2 miles from the DMZ. The Place of Angels. Helmets and flak jackets must be worn at all times*'. The Con Thien area was a dangerous location. All night and all morning air medics flew into the area to air lift the wounded back to the hospital in DaNang. Some of the wounded were transported on to the USS Midway.

It was noon before the communications center was handed back to a skeleton crew. Both Major Lathon and Lieutenant McKay headed for the showers and their beds. It had been a long and stressful twenty hours.

Khoy and Cindi Le heard about the battles the next day because local news traveled fast throughout the compound. The helicopter pilots were still flying back and forth from the battlefields to the medical centers. Concerns for future battles were on the minds of many soldiers in north central Vietnam. The monsoon season was slowly ending, but periodic heavy rains continued to flood the low lands. The locals accepted the rains, the soldiers cursed the weather.

In his report Angus stated that the VietCong may be testing various locations for a major assault in the future based on signs of heavy equipment movement up and down the Trail. There were more visual reports from the villagers. They were being targeted for more food and medical supplies.

Angus talked to Major Lathon about doctors, nurses, and dentists visiting some of the outlying villages and hamlets, to render medical aid and advice as well as obtaining more accurate information on the VietCong movements.

Major Lathon agreed and a plan was passed to Saigon headquarters. The plan was approved and Angus was appointed to coordinate the medical and dental staff for a three-day exercise.

Five locations were selected along the Ben Hoi River. Doctors, nurses, and dentists signed up to participate. Medical supplies were ordered and a handpicked guard unit was assigned to the mission. Rains did not prevent people seeking medical help from traveling across miles of soggy fields, muddy paths, up and down the slippery slopes, and by boats to see a doctor, especially young mothers with babies. The rainy weather made for muddy conditions, but the gratitude of the people overwhelmed the medical staff. Some people brought chickens, some bags of rice, or others brought various kinds of fruits and vegetables to express their appreciation. Angus was able to obtain information and locations about the enemy that Saigon had not known. New sites of VietCong and NVA were marked for future missions.

The following week as Angus walked into the office, Cindi Le had a big smile on her face. Her sky-blue Vietnamese outfit complimented her bright blue eyes.

"Good morning, Lieutenant McKay," she said with an emphasis on "Lieutenant" flashing her white teeth. "The major wants to see you immediately."

"Well, good mor'n to you too, Miss Cindi Le. You're looking bright eyed and bushy tailed this mor'n," Angus smiled back.

"Good morning sir, Cindi Le says you want to see me," Angus said walking into Major Lathon's office. Then he noticed a fresh new title on the desk – Colonel Lathon.

"Congratulations Colonel Lathon. You earned it. When's the party?"

"Thank you, Lieutenant. First, I have something for you. Here are your First Lieutenant Silver bars. Congratulations to you! Maybe we can plan a Friday night party together upstairs in the meeting hall."

Angus stared at the silver bars, "How did all of this happen? I thought it would be next summer before I'd be eligible for the silver bars," stated Angus with a surprised expression.

"When Danielson got wounded, I petitioned for a field promotion for you. The manual calls for a first lieutenant to hold that position," he said quoting the manual.

"Cindi Le, come in here," Colonel Lathon called her.

She walked through the door, beaming!

"Cindi Le, would you like to pin these silver bars on First Lieutenant McKay?"

Angus, looked shocked. With pride Cindi Le replaced the brass bars with the silver ones. When she had completed the honor, she kissed him on each cheek in the French tradition. Angus gave her a friendly hug. His face flushed with pride, and turned beet red when he and everyone in the room noticed they were holding hands. He slowly loosened his hands. They grinned at each other. No one spoke, the room was silent.

"Huh, that'll be all for now, Cindi Le," the colonel softly broke the mood. Photographs were taken to be sent home so his family could celebrate also.

Two days later a message came over the teletype. "Report of downed Jolly Green Giant northeast of Khe Sanh. Send help as soon as possible."

The colonel poked his head out the door, " Cindi Le tell the orderly to get Angus over here."

A few minutes later Angus walked into Colonel Lathon's office. He noticed the map on the wall, he said, "Sorry Colonel, I was helping Chaplin Henderson in the chapel. What's this I hear about a Jolly Green Giant going down?"

"Ye'ah, I've been in touch with the captain at Khe Sanh and he's got six of his men, including a medic standing by, plus half-a-dozen of the South Vietnamese soldiers. There's a hamlet somewhere near that location. I want you to go there, talk to the locals and see what they may know. Another Jolly Green Giant who was in the area, was also fired on. The pilot was unable to give us the location because he was running low on fuel and unable to make it back to their base at Nakhon Phanom, Thailand. The crew ended up staying in DaNang and planned to cover the area on their way back to their base in Thailand tomorrow. We had a scout plane fly in that area, but he was unsuccessful at seeing any signs of a downed chopper or the downed pilot of the jet.

"The Air Force guys out in the communications center are paying special attention to that frequency for any call on the emergency radio frequency. So far that frequency has been silent. Angus, this may be a two- or three-day trip. US aircraft are restricted from flying over Laos from 1730 to 0700. You'll need to travel light. I have one chopper warming up. Grab your search and rescue gear and keep in contact with me," directed the colonel.

"Can Khoy be included in this mission?" asked Angus.

"I'll let Major Lin know that Khoy is to be included on this search and rescue mission," the colonel replied.

As Angus passed Cindi Le's desk, their eyes met and she softly whispered, "Be careful."

He gave her a wink and said, "Thanks, maybe we can go out for some egg coffee when I get back."

Twenty minutes later Angus and Khoy boarded the helicopter. Soon it was out of the Hue air space and headed for Khel Sanh to pick up a team of twelve soldiers, including Captain Bell, for the flight to Lang Vo.

The CIA had given Angus a bag full of packs of cigarette and candy bars. Some cigarette packs had ten cigarettes that had been treated with cyanide. Other packs included a slim lighter that would explode in the face of the enemy when he tried to light a cigarette. Also, candy bars that were laced with small amount of a chemical that caused nausea were in the bag. Angus' orders were to drop the cigarette packs and candy bars along the trails for the VietCong and the soldiers of the North Vietnam Army to find.

It was 1400 when the men unloaded at Lang Vo. The nearest border crossing was six klicks south. The small rice paddy hamlet consisted of ten huts with thatched roofs. Flat bottom boats had been pulled up on the banks of a small bay along the Tibetan Plateau River which separated Laos and Vietnam. Rice paddies dotted the leveled terraces around the village.

*"Vang. (Yes) O*ur hunters saw black smoke and a plane twirling around and around up there," the local villager said pointing toward a valley with a ragged looking karst area that had tall limestone rocks pointing skyward. After much discussion two of the locals agreed to lead the rescue unit up through the karst area for a fee of a three-days' pay. The two locals followed by the soldiers headed out crossing rice paddies that reeked with the stench of animal and human waste that was used as fertilizer, and the meadows of tall itchy foxtail grass along the base of rolling hills. They stopped for the night at the edge of the meadow before entering the karst area of slabs of limestone spiraling toward the heavens. They had cold C-rations for dinner since a fire could attract the enemy if any were still in the area.

The night's dew had left a sweet refreshing aroma on the dry leaves and the two locals discussed the options with Captain Bell and

Angus of either climbing up among the jagged karst rocks or wading in the stream that was trickling down the hillside. The locals urged 'de theo dona' (take the stream), but the consensus of the unit was to 'Stay dry'! Climbing over and around the limestone boulders quickly took its toll on everyone's hands and clothes. It took them three hours to reach the top. They saw the Sikorsky HH-3E copter crunched between two spiraling, cathedral shaped rocks. The unit found the chopper stripped of instruments, radios, and guns. The four dead bodies inside were stripped of their flight suits, shoes, and weapons. "The crew must have been killed in the crash because there were no bullet holes in any of the bodies," the captain observed.

Angus asked, "Where is the pilot of the jet that went down?"

"Good question, since the scout plane report did not mention the downed jet pilot maybe the Vietnamese took him as a prisoner. Let's spread out and comb the area and see if there are any signs of another body," suggested the captain. Some of the men began freeing the bodies from the wrecked helicopter. Others began combing the area.

"Captain! Look at this," Khoy called out pointing to small rocks put together like an arrow pointing down a narrow path between two large slabs of rocks that Mother Nature had tilted sideways. The men had to squeeze between the two rocks. On the other side, they saw another arrow scratched in the sandy limestone path. Another ten yards down the path a stream dribbled from the opening of a small cave entrance. The entrance was the size of a large dog house doorway. Angus walked toward the narrow opening. He bent down, "Anyone in there?" he yelled through cupped hands. He, then, thought of what he had just done. "Damn, that was dumb! A VietCong could have been hiding back there with a weapon or grenade."

Khoy just shook his head, "Angus! That was just plain stupid!"

"Help!" a voice echoed from farther back in the small cave. "I can't walk, I badly twisted my ankle in the fall from the Jolly chopper. I may have a broken leg. It hurts like hell."

"I'm going to get a medic and we will get you out of there," Angus assured the pilot.

Thirty minutes later, the medic had made a two-legged gurney and was slowly pulling the pilot out over the rocky bottom of the cave. Both men were soaked from the stream of water that had splashed on them. "I got this idea from watching old Indian movies," the medic proudly declared.

"His blood pressure is elevated, but that's to be expected. He has a seriously twisted ankle and a simple break in his right femur. Otherwise he's doing well for what he's been through," reported the medic.

"Should we torch the chopper?" a sergeant asked the captain.

"No, the smoke may draw attention. Looks like they got everything they wanted," the captain remarked, adding, "let's get back down this karst."

"Faster to take the creek," one of the locals pointed down at the stream halfway down the jagged rocky area. Angus called Colonel Lathon for a helicopter. The colonel acknowledged the request and said "Expect two birds in two hours. How's the pilot?" Angus went over the medic's report and added, "He could stand steak and potatoes and a mug of beer. He smells like he could use a shower! His ankle will keep him grounded for a few weeks."

Back down in the meadow, the unit kept looking for the two helicopters. The men discovered a field of marijuana and began stuffing their pockets and the insides of their shirts with the weeds.

An hour later, a black blip could be seen in the sky. Then the men heard the rhythmic whop whop sound of the twirling blades as the big birds settled down in the tall grass. The two locals turned down an offer to fly back to their village. They said they would rather walk back.

One local grabbed Angus by the arm as he was about to jump into the copter, "Many tunnels in hills," he whispered pointing north where narrow jagged rocks towered above the ground.

"Thanks, will you show them to me someday? We need to get the pilot to a doctor," Angus responded to what the local had said.

The helicopter headed out of Laos by 1530 on a direct flight to Khe Sanh to let the captain and his unit off. The search and rescue mission had been successful. Angus thanked the captain and his unit as they got out of the chopper, "Ya'll did a great job! Thank you."

On the flight to Hue, the pilot discussed his ordeal during the rescue attempt. He had been able to hook himself up on the lifeline, but as he was being hauled up a ground-to-air missile whizzed past him and exploded when it hit the tail of the chopper. The impact broke the cable and he fell about twenty feet bouncing off big boulders. He watched as the helicopter began flying in circles in a downward spiral before flipping sideways between the two towering rock formations. He could hear the squeaking of metal bending and ripping. He could not see the chopper but did see black smoke swirling skyward.

"I figured it would be a matter of time before the enemy would be searching the area. I saw the small opening to the cave about fifteen yards from me. I laid some trail signs and crawled to the back of the cave." He, then added, "The good Lord answered my prayers. I heard the Vietnamese getting the various parts of the rescue chopper and laughing. There was no sound from the crew so I assumed they had been killed in the crash," he sighed. "I owe my life to those guys. I was afraid the enemy would pick up my emergency frequency and then I realized it wouldn't transmit out of the cave anyway."

A medical team was waiting for the helicopter when it landed at Hue. The transfer from the helicopter to an ambulance went like clockwork. Everyone knew exactly how and when to lift the pilot up and into the ambulance. The morphine was wearing off and the grimace on the pilot's face reflected his pain.

Angus spoke to the crew members who went on this mission, "Good job, thank you for making this a successful search and rescue mission." He shook each man's hand.

A couple of days later Angus met Cindi Le at the high school steps which was two blocks from the compound. Angus could not believe his eyes. Cindi Le was driving an old red Dauphine with the canvas top rolled back. He walked over to her and began a slow walk around the two-door vehicle. He glanced down through the open roof at the narrow back seat. Then he noticed that Cindi Le had put her hair in a pony tail. It was intertwined with a golden cord the full length of the pony tail. He studied the dash board, the small steering wheel and a pair of legs belonging to Cindi Le. Her bright red toe nails stood out from her white sandals. Her summer straw hat rested on the passenger seat.

He continued to walk around to check out the back. The engine was in the rear. There was a hole in the middle of the rear bumper.

"What in the world is the hole in the rear bumper for?" he asked bending down to inspect it.

She giggled, "That's where the crank goes in case the engine needs to be cranked to get it started. I've never had to use it," she chuckled then added, "Yet!"

Angus noticed that there was a single bolt in the middle of each hub cap. The front of the car had two small headlights to provide some light for night driving.

"Is this really your car?" he asked again peering over the boot. "Small trunk space," he teased.

"Yes, Angus. Now will you get in so we can go to Thuan Beach. I told you we were going to the beach today. Do you have swimming trunks and a towel with you?" she asked.

"Yes, I bought a swim suit at the Post Exchange. I am wearing it. I procured a Navy blanket from the quartermaster," he replied as he struggled to get his knees and feet inside the car. He finally was able to close the door. He could smell her strong aroma of an alluring perfume.

"Let's go to the beach to catch some sun and sand," she said with a broad smile. "Ready?"

"Yep," was all he could say.

The rolled back canvas allowed the midmorning sun to warm them as they drove east toward the shore of the South China Sea. At the beach there were only two bicycles and a scooter in the parking area.

"Looks like we have the beach pretty much to ourselves," Cindi Le said as she got out. She opened the boot and took out the picnic basket that she had prepared. It included a bottle of white wine and three bottles of ginger ale. She had remembered that Angus limited himself to one glass of wine and preferred ginger ale to other bottled drinks. She giggled as she watched Angus twist and turn to get out of the cramped car. She had a white, full length, knitted camisole coverup. The camisole covered her vibrant aqua bikini which matched the waters of the South China Seas.

Cindi Le's bikini was a strapless top that tied in the back. The high waisted bottom of her bikini had cut outs on both of her hips that exposed bare skin. There were white cords that fully laced from the waist to the bottom. The cords were tied at the bottom in a bow with the short ends dangling against her thighs waiting to be pulled. The bottom of her bikini accentuated her hips. The bikini colors contrasted nicely against the tone of her smooth skin.

Angus looked up to see Cindi Le standing in front of him. The clear blue sky and the aqua colors of the ocean in the background caught his breath.

"Holy cow! He uttered in amazement, "You're the Neptune goddess!" He got out his camera and took a picture to send home. They waded through the shallow water to the narrow peninsula. She smiled as he spread the white Navy blanket on the sandy beach. They tested the waters of the South China Sea, chased, and splashed each other. Angus tried his skill at body surfing while she set out their lunch of cheeses, various fruits, and mooncakes that she baked especially for the day. Later they walked up and down the beach holding hands and throwing sea shells into the clear blue water. The two laid on the blanket and shared stories of their teenage years. Angus told her more about his best buddy Rob and some of the crazy things they did. He liked recalling their fishing and hunting experiences.

She told Angus about the all-girl boarding school she had attended in France. That was after the family moved back to France after three years in London. She had liked London and that's when she attended the University of Westminster, They both liked horses and spent more time discussing riding horses. Then they lay quietly on the beach listening to the waves washing ashore and enjoying being with one another.

Dark clouds began building up from the east and brought a chill wind. It was time to stop for the day before the rains came. Before leaving the parking area, Cindi Le showed Angus how to close the canvas top. Rain drops started falling half way back to the compound.

"It was a fun day. The lunch was really great," Angus admitted to Cindi Le as he struggled to get out of her car. His fingers nervously touched her bare shoulder, as he said, "You are really beautiful. Thank you for a great day."

"No, thank you for making it such a special day. I enjoyed being with you. You're a great guy," she replied blinking her eyes. However, she was disappointed that he had not attempted to steal a kiss.

CHAPTER 10

November 1967, Part II

"One of the locals from Lang Vo, the small village right along the Laos border, who had pointed to the hills as we were loading the chopper indicated there were many tunnels in the hills. Do you think we need to check it out?" Angus asked the colonel after reviewing his search and rescue mission.

"Yes, it might be worth it," replied the commander. "Let me think about it. Maybe the unit at Khe Sanh can check it out for us when they're in that area."

The next day brought news that the elite Black Lions battalion had fallen into a major ambush in October. Casualty count was extremely high, including some high-ranking officers. The NVA had put a bounty on the heads of the men in the Black Lions because of their reputation as fierce fighters but the successful ambush had the Black Lions trapped in the jungle. They were surrounded by three divisions of the Northern Vietnam Army. It was a difficult defeat for the Americans. It was a lesson for all Americans fighting in Vietnam.

Two days later, Khoy was meeting Angus on the steps of the Hue University close the compound for a quick lunch. Khoy liked meeting there because he would engage in conversations with some of the cute coeds. Looking up, he saw someone he knew, "Cindi Le, what are you doing here?" Khoy questioned with a surprised voice.

"I stopped to check out my score on the last test. What are you doing here?" she asked.

"Waiting for Angus. We're going to lunch," Khoy replied.

"I bet you two are looking for a couple of cute college girls?" she teased.

"Not Angus, I think he has eyes for only you. I need help with my book studies," Khoy chuckled.

"Khoy, you really don't mean that, do you?" Cindi Le asked with a grin.

"No, I don't need help with any studies. I don't even have any text books. Oh, you mean about Angus. Ye'ah, he often talks about you when we're together. He likes you a lot, I know that for a fact. But you can introduce me to one of your cute friends and all four of us can get to know one another better," Khoy pleaded.

"Let me see what I can do for you," Cindi Le said, "I've got to get to the office now."

Angus and Cindi Le met as she was descending from the top of the school's steps. "Good morn'. Fancy meeting you. I stopped at the office to ask if you would like go to the Donut Dollies show with me Saturday night," he grabbed her hand, "Say Yes. I mean say Da!"

"I don't think I'm allowed to be with you at the compound. Sorry. I'd love to be with you. Angus, I always love being with you but my presence with you at the Donut Dollies show may not be good for your career," she said pulling her hand from his.

With a hurt look he replied, "Cindi Le, I can only imagine what your friends are saying about you being seen with an American soldier. Khoy has pointed that out to me."

Cindi Le admitted she had not been with a boyfriend since moving to Hue to be with her mother. "You are the only boy I've been with since I moved to Hue. Yes, they're talking, but they do not know my heart."

"Cindi Le I don't want to do anything to disgrace your reputation," Angus replied grabbing her hand again.

"Angus, I've got to get to the office." she said as she started to walk away, then turned around and said, "Meet me tonight on the high school steps."

As Khoy walked up, Angus gave him a disgusted look with both hands pointed at him, "What did you say to Cindi Le?" he demanded.

"I asked her to find a date for me. We could double date," Khoy smiled as he replied. "Oh ye'ah I mentioned you have eyes for her."

"You told her WHAT?" Angus asked shaking his head back and forth in disbelief.

"I think she can help me get a date. If your heart hasn't told you, your face is telling everyone else how you feel about her. Wake up, my friend," Khoy retorted. "Come on, it's my turn to buy lunch."

"I can't right now," Angus turned and headed back to the compound.

"Hi" he said to Cindi Le as he bolted up two steps at a time to the third floor. He needed to talk to Chaplain Henderson. The chaplain had a small office next to the chapel, which had an altar with a cross on the wall and 35 empty wooden chairs. Chaplain Henderson handled all the services for the compound: Protestant, Jewish and Catholic.

"Angus, come in. I was just preparing for our Wednesday night prayer group. What brings you here?"

"I need some advice. You're a married man." he beseeched, "When did you realize that you were in love and wanted to marry your wife? I mean how did you really know?"

"Boy! That's a loaded question. First, tell me where do you think you are in this relationship. Is it about a girl back in Texas or is it Cindi Le?" he questioned Angus.

Angus looked shocked, "I don't have a girl back home. Yes, it's Cindi Le. How did you know?"

"They say the male is the last to know," Chaplain Henderson chuckled. "Tell me about your feelings for her."

"Well, she makes me feel good. We enjoy being together. I can talk to her without worrying if I've said the wrong thing. I feel comfortable when we're together," admitted Angus.

"Angus, do you think about you two getting married!" the chaplain asked, "or, has that not crossed your mind?"

"Well, somewhat. She likes to ride horses and we discussed riding together on my family's ranch in Texas," Angus replied, avoiding the question.

Chaplin Henderson said, "Angus, I know what you are going through, I was confused once like you are now. My wife is Korean. We've been married fifteen years and have two beautiful daughters. She was a nurse when I was stationed at a naval hospital in Yokosuka, Japan. It was a 250-bed hospital handling the critically wounded from the Korean War in 1950's."

"Chaplain, I am concerned about her reputation. Does being with me, an American, cause her to be talked about? I mean I'm just thinking of her. I wouldn't want to do anything to hurt her," Angus responded.

"How many months have you two been seeing one another? 3? 4? Don't you think if she did worry about it, she would have stopped the relationship by now?" the chaplain pointed out.

"Ye'ah, well, I guess so," Angus slowly agreed.

"Angus, I can relate to your situation. In my case, it was me, who wasn't sure of what was happening between the two of us. Do you hear what I'm saying?" Chaplin Hendeson asked, then quickly added, "You came in for my advice. So, here's my advice. Tell her you are very fond of her and there are things you two need to discuss about your futures, because you are becoming very serious about her. Bring the Lord into your discussions. There's a prayer room next to us, you can start there. I believe you to be a man of God because you are helping me with my services."

"Good advice," Angus said absorbing what the chaplain said as he stood up. Chaplain Henderson smiled and just nodded. Angus darted toward the prayer room to ask his Lord for guidance.

Later Angus walked into the office, "Is the colonel in?"

"es, he is." Cindi Le said coldly without looking up from her typewriter.

"Colonel, I need to talk to you," Angus said as he barged into his office.

Looking up from his paperwork Colonel Lathon asked in an aggravated tone, "What is it, lieutenant?"

"Sir, I invited Cindi Le to the Donut Dolly Show and she says she's not allowed to attend it. Is that so?" he asked.

"Well, there's no policy on that. Guess we would like to know a little something about the people our troops are inviting to the shows. I see no reason why Cindi Le can't join you if she wants to go. There may be some sneering from some of your buddies. You know a lot of guys have been hitting on her without any success ever since I've been in this office. Consider yourself lucky. I am sure, she understands what her presence will mean to some of the guys. You two will have to discuss that," Colonel Lathon explained, looking back down at the message about a convoy of American troops having been attacked on Highway 9.

"Then, if she agrees, she can attend. Is that right?" Angus asked for clarification."

"Yes! She can," he said with a grin that Angus missed. The colonel turned back reading the report.

Angus understood the colonel's nonverbal dismissed signal! and left the office. He had his answer.

"We still meeting at the steps?" he asked walking past her desk.

Later that day as Angus waited at the high school steps, he saw the red Dauphine drive up to the curb. He slowly stood up and took his time to get to the car. Then, he took his time squeezing into the small seat.

"Get in and I'll take you to dinner," Cindi Le smiled back at him.

He finally got settled into the seat, turned to her, put both hands on her face, he leaned over and tenderly kissed her on the lips. "I've been wanting to kiss you for a long time," he sheepishly admitted.

"I've been waiting for you to kiss me longer than that," she smiled back at him as she drove off.

"So, that's settled. Where are we going for dinner?" Angus asked.

"I know a small French restaurant near here. How's that sound?"

"With you, anything sounds fine to me," admitted Angus.

Cindi Le pulled into valet's lane at LeParfum, the jewel of Hue. She'd been there with her father and mother when she and her mother first moved to Hue.

"Do you think I am dressed well enough for this place?" questioned Angus, looking down at his blue jeans and boots. He tossed his cowboy hat to the back seat.

"You look fine. Just be yourself," she replied, softly running her fingers through his hair.

The valet waited because he understood the moment, then opened the door for Cindi Le, "welcome to LeParfum."

Cindi Le gave him the keys to her Dauphine and walked over to Angus who was waiting on the other side of the car. He held out his arm and she took it as they walked arm in arm up to the entrance of the restaurant.

A smiling waiter opened the door, displaying an elegant yellow and white room with white table cloths and sparkling glasses surrounding a bottle of water. There were a few couples sitting at tables scattered throughout the room. The people hardly noticed when the tall cowboy walked in holding the hand of a pretty, well dressed Vietnamese lady.

Angus held the chair for Cindi Le. He could smell a hint of an orchid perfume. The water was poured. They grinned at each other as their knees touched beneath the small round table. Menus were handed out and the waiter asked if they would like to order a glass of wine.

Cindi Le spoke first, in French, "a glass of your white house wine, please."

Angus ordered a glass of red house wine in English.

"This is a pretty plush place," said Angus looking around. Then he asked, "Do you come here often?"

"My mother, father and I had dinner here eight months ago when my mother decided to move from DaNang to Hue. They had felt there were too many American GI's in DaNang. Dad flew in from Thailand to help with the move. Last May dad was here for my birthday. We ate here again. Dad likes the French food here," explained Cindi Le.

"So, what day in May is your birthday?" Angus asked, then commented, "I don't even know how old you are."

"I was born on May 2nd, 1948. You were born January 10th, 1945." She grinned looking up from the rim of the glass of wine as she took her first sip. For the first course each chose the Pomelo Salad, with mixed sun-dried squid marinated with nuoc mam crispy prawn crackers. Everything was fresh and tasty.

Angus waved for the waiter to come over. "What is this?" he asked pointing at the nuoc mam.

The waiter explained, "sir, that is a combination of layered anchovies and other small fish and salt. We ferment it for one year. Then the liquid is poured off and used, sort of like virgin olive oil. Sir, you are enjoying the first batch. It's called nhi. It's the finest quality of nuoc mam. Vietnamese grow up with the flavory taste, Americans need to experience the taste to fully appreciate nuoc mam. It can be a little spicy for some Americans."

For the main course, Cindi Le ordered the Vietnamese beef noodle soup containing chicken and beef with egg, onion, and mushrooms.

Angus selected the smoked salmon salad, with scotch quail egg and lump fish egg, sour cream, and citrus dressing.

"Cindi Le, if you elect to go down this road that we seem to be on, we've got a heap of topics to discuss. Don't you agree?" he asked as he finished off his palatable wine.

"I understand that. You go first," she countered.

"First of all, I plan to have a career in the military. That will probably mean living at many different locations," he stated.

"Angus, wherever you live, I will be at your side," Cindi Le flatly clarified.

The two held hands while enjoying their dessert of mango and a small mixture of other Vietnamese fruits.

Driving back to the MACV compound, Angus confessed, "Cindi Le I've never felt this serious about a woman before. You and I come from different cultures. I see a lot of hurdles before us."

"Yes, I agree. I grew up with two different cultures. It can get bumpy. My mother and father have managed for twenty-five years. So, it can be done. Guess it depends on the two of us. Would you like to meet my mother? She would like to meet you," Cindi Le suggested in an urging tone.

"Yes. when?" Angus said between the hugs and kisses before he got out of the car. "It will have to be when I'm not on a mission."

"I'll arrange a meeting agreeable to your schedule. Angus, does your heart hear my heart?"

"Cindi Le, my heart is beating so fast it's hard for me to know anything except to be with you," Angus replied getting his hat and maneuvering his body around in the small compact car to get out.

He walked around to the driver's side. As she lowered the window Angus leaned down. Cindi Le's face was about to meet his face when her foot slipped off the clutch and the car lunged forward. She immediately applied the brakes, but the moment had passed.

Angus walked forward and grinned, "Guess I'd better go! See you Monday, OK?"

She agreed, shrugged her shoulders, and quipped, "Later, " and slowly drove off.

On Monday Cindi Le agreed she would go the Donut Dolly Follies with Angus. Colonel Lathon and Angus were reviewing the report on the downed jet pilot. "I called the hospital Sunday and was told that they got the swelling down on the pilot's ankle. He's doing fine. He's to be transported back to his ship today.

CHAPTER 11

NOVEMBER 1967, Part III

Tell me about the tunnels the local mentioned," the colonel said sipping his coffee. "Sometimes the NVA use tunnels to hide men and supplies. Maybe we can get permission from Saigon to do a search and destroy," he added.

Forty-eight hours later a classified envelope with "Attention Colonel Lathon" arrived from Saigon with the approval for the search and destroy. The plan was to drop leaflets on Ca Lu and Khe Sanh announcing there would be extensive bombing in the hills south of Ca Lu and east of Khe Sanh. "Our experience has been that the locals would take cover in nearby tunnels. The VC would move in and rob them of the food and medical supplies that we had given them. Then it would be easier to locate fresh tracks and trails to the tunnels," stated Colonel Lathon. "Two platoons from the Rockpile Firebase and units from Ca Lu will join Major Lin's unit in finding the locations of the various tunnel entrances"

The colonel continued, "The Rockpile platoons will be backup in case Major Lin's units and the Ca Lu units run into heavier than expected fire power or they run into an ambush. You and Khoy will be with Major Lin. The combat base will be on alert for VietCong traffic on highway 9. The mission will begin twenty-four hours following the B-52 bomb drop."

Major Lin and his troops had planned to set up a fire base on the south side of the Quang River and wait for the bombers. However, cloudy skies and fog prevented the bombers from dropping the leaflets as well as making their bomb drops. It was decided to do the search and destroy mission without the bombers because the forecast was for continuous rain for at least four more days.

Early the next morning, Major Lin and his unit left the fire base and marched past the rice paddies. The heavy, damp fog made it difficult for the lead soldiers to find any paths heading for the hills.

The two lead men that Major Lin had chosen were a few hundred yards in front of the main group, that was slowly searching for signs of traps, booby trap wires and punji?

Suddenly the two men stopped at the sound of cracking limbs. One soldier yelled, "Dung Lai (Stop!) "Birds and animals began squawking and squealing. Both men froze.

A massive twenty square foot punji with bamboo spikes, came crashing down from twenty-five to thirty feet above the ground. The large punji was like a swing set tied to two tall trees on each side of the trail. It looked like an eighteen-wheeler bearing directly toward them at over thirty miles per hour. There were eight sharp bamboo points sticking out from the punji. A heavy stone was tied to the back of it to generate more force as it picked up speed in its free fall.

The soldier who had yelled jumped into the thick leaves along the side of the trail. The other soldier hesitated and turned to run. The huge punji smacked him with enough force to pierce his body with six of the eight bamboo spiked spears. Red blood from each wound began squirting in the air. His blood curdling screams echoed through the jungle. The open wounds were dripping blood down his uniform and shoes before forming a pool of blood as his body dangled a foot above the ground while the punji slowly swung back and forth.

Major Lin and his men ran forward to see what all the commotion was about. Angus and Khoy brought up the rear. When they got to that point in the trail their hearts stopped. Their breathing stopped. There a soldier was pleading for help and every move he made caused more pain. Many of the soldiers fell to their knees. Some men began loudly praying for the man. Major Lin saw who the soldier was. He drew his Colt .45. Aimed at the man's heart and pulled the trigger. The bullet went straight on course. The man was staring at Major Lin when his body went limp. There were sounds from his body as air escaped from the cavities.

Major Lin fell to his knees. His body visibly shaking. He threw his .45 into the jungle. He hung his head. His lips closed tightly. No one noticed the tears running down his cheeks.

Angus was stunned. His stomach began gurgling and turning. He closed his eyes, but his mind couldn't make the moment disappear. The nausea became stronger. He got up from his knees and walked deeper into the jungle. Acids in his stomach reached his throat. Again, he fell to his knees. He could not believe what he had just witnessed. He heard other men emptying their stomachs and the sounds and odor were too much for his system.

It took several minutes for Major Lin and Angus to collect themselves. Four of Major Lin's men had already started prying the limp body from the deadly punji. Other soldiers were cutting down the fifty-pound punji made from dirt and the heavy flat rock tied to the backside which created the momentum for the punji to be effective.

Other soldiers began to put together a makeshift stretcher with bamboo poles. Angus saw one of Major Lin's men take off his shirt to be used for the stretcher. Angus removed his flak jacket and took off his shirt to complete the makeshift stretcher. Major Lin put his arm around Angus's shoulders and said, "Ca'mo'n" (Thank you)"

Khoy grabbed Angus by his shoulders. "It was a mercy shooting. It is accepted in our culture," he quietly spoke, "The soldier was Major Lin's nephew." The dead soldier's body was laid on the makeshift stretcher. An American soldier came over and covered the body with his poncho. Four of Major Lin's men started back down the trail carrying his nephew back to the fire base. It was decided to continue the search for the network of tunnels in the rolling hills ahead of them. The entire search team was somber. The fog began lifting as sunlight made the jungle shadows more vivid. The leaves continued to drop water on the men as they forged ahead.

After two hours of slowly making their way out of the valley which skirted the dense jungle, a trail was discovered. Khoy was first to uncover the trail. He determined it was an old trail. There were sandal prints, some boot prints and even bicycle tire prints. Angus asked why some prints were from sandals and some from boots. Khoy explained that the sandal prints were made by the VietCong. They made sandals from tire treads. The VietCong soldiers preferred the sandals. They were easier to wear in the muddy rice fields and in the jungles. The leaf leaches were easier to detect and could be removed. Soldiers may not take off their boots for several days and the leaches' infections could be severe by then. The boot prints were from the North Vietnamese Army. They were the soldiers in the black pajamas. Bicycles and carts were used to carry heavier loads such as cannons.

Another two hours went by before an entrance was discovered. Each entrance led to a maze of rooms. The darkness of the tunnels lit up when a few of Major Lin's men lit the kerosene lanterns that were hung all along the sides of the tunnels. There was a larger room that must have been used as a hospital. Beds, wrappings and the smell of alcohol and spices could be detected throughout the room. There was another large room for dining. Long tables were arranged in rows. Next to the dining area were stoves and pots and pans. The complex was like a large ant hill.

The men found over 1,600 fifty-pound bags of rice. Hundreds of rifles, cannons, miscellaneous weapons and over a thousand rounds of ammunition were discovered. Statues of Buddha were scattered throughout the tunnels. Major Lin and Angus were busy recording everything. Weapons included AK-47s, M-1's, machine guns, M67 grenades and homemade claymores. Mixed among the rifles were the

French model MAS 36 from 1936, a few 1940 Russian SVT-40s and a dozen or so FN49 sniper rifles from Indonesia. Angus selected a couple of hand grenades to have analyzed because he recalled reading that 20% of the grenades were malfunctioning. These tunnels appeared to be storage areas for future assaults. That was one thing he and Major Lin agreed on. The question was, was the enemy storing supplies for a spring attack? Major Lin had his men blow up some of the entrances and left some open so they could remove the food and the weapons along with the cases of ammunition.

Major Lin assigned three men to each remaining entrance to remain until more men could come to take the rice and weapons back to Hue. Then he turned to Angus, "We can hire locals to help carry everything back to the firebase and have helicopters pick it up there. They can keep some of the rice for the villagers. The two-year drought has hurt the rice crops." Angus was puzzled about why the tunnels had been abandoned, leaving so many valuable goods behind. On the way back to the fire base Khoy and Angus discussed what had been bothering each of them.

"Do you know what I think?" asked Khoy

"What's that?" replied Angus

"I think the enemy had learned about the B-52's orders to drop bombs throughout these hills. That's why they left in a hurry. Remember the leaflets were not dropped because of the rains."

'So, where's the leak?" Angus questioned with concern.

In his report to MACV, Angus suggested that there were three key indications of men and supplies for a buildup: (1) the trail reflected lower level of boot tracks. This indicated fewer enemy soldiers from North VietCong were moving than in past reports, (2) the number of weapons and rice discovered in the tunnels indicated a possible warehouse for future major assaults, and. (3) the enemy had retreated to Laotian and Cambodian safe sites to recover from their losses.

The MACV report read the NVA was replacing some of the VietCong who had returned to their villages. The supplies were stored to be transferred farther south. There was no mention of a possible leak in the MACV system.

The final report was sent to Saigon: NO INCREASE IN ENEMY MOVEMENTS AT THIS TIME!

Angus did not discuss the report with Cindi Le. She had read the final report and she had her own theories but did not mention anything to Angus. In her mind she reviewed everyone who she knew had handled the report. There was one person no one had considered to be a leak. At the end of every day Quan the office cleaner came in dusted and emptied the waste baskets. He always had a smile on his face, asking the office personnel about their families since most of them had family photos on their desks. He had been working there since Cindi Le first started working. The janitor always asked about her mother. Her desk was close to the copy machine and there was a waste basket at the foot of the copy machine. The janitor was there before Colonel Lathon arrived in the morning and his basket was always full at the end of the day.

That evening while the two sat on a couch at her home. Cindi Le asked Angus, "It seems you have had something on your mind that is bothering you. What is it?"

"Well I am waiting for a reply from my folks. You know I've been sending photos of you and me and telling them more about you and about us," replied Angus.

"And, what kind of reply are you expecting?" she asked.

Then he went into more detail about the letter. He had thought it would be nice if Cindi Le and her mother could visit the ranch maybe in mid-May or June. It would allow her and her mother to get acquainted with his folks.

"Angus, you thought of this all by yourself? I am flattered. I love the idea. What do you think they will say?" questioned Cindi Le.

"I'm sure they will agree to it. I was thinking you and your mother could stay at the ranch for a week or so. Honey, I've got to get back to the compound to review a report." he abruptly stated. His mind would not stop thinking about horrors of his last search and destroy mission.

"Sure, no need to be walking in the rain. I'll drive you," Cindi Le suggested with concern in the tone of her voice.

They hugged and kissed at the gate of the compound, "Tomorrow night's the Donut Dollies Follies. We'll get a light dinner and go. All right?" asked Angus.

"OK, if you insist. I'll meet you after work," she said slowly removing her hand from his.

Angus checked in at the night clerk's desk and asked, "Is Chaplain Henderson in?

"Yes, he's working late in his office upstairs."

"Thanks," as he hurried up the stairs.

The chaplain heard someone knock on his door. "Come in".

"Chaplain, I need to talk to you about what happened in the field. I can't get it out of my mind." He went on explain the 'mercy killing' and how it was haunting him. "How can one shoot someone in his own family?" he asked.

"I don't know how to reply to your situation, Angus. Family killing goes back to Adam and Eve in the bible with Cain and Abel. Sometimes the good Lord doesn't provide answers. War does terrible things to people." He picked up a bible from his desk. Turned to John 1, Chapter 3. "Here read verses 15 and 16."

Angus remembered uncle Rory had underlined that passage in his bible. He read it again, "Everyone who hates his brother is a murderer, and you know that no murderer has eternal life remaining in him. The world came to know it was love that he laid down his life for us, so, we ought to lay our life for our brothers."

"Is his 'mercy killing' a choice of love or hate? Only God knows. We mustn't judge the major. I think, in this case, the he considered it a choice of love," noted Chaplain Henderson.

"I do too. It was one of the most horrible experiences I've ever had. Thanks for helping me grasp this as a choice and not as a murder. I just hope and pray I never have to make that choice," Angus softly commented.

Chaplain Henderson then turned to Mark 8:34-37 in his bible, "read this in your room tonight," he said. The verse read, '...whoever loses his life for my sake... will save it.' "I keep this in mind when I deal with those killed in action."

The next night Angus and Cindi Le walked across the bridge for a light meal and then back to the compound to be entertained by the Donut Dollies Follies. They enjoyed the songs, the jokes, and silly skits. They liked being with each other. Angus had to explain some of the jokes pertaining to the US government officials to her.

Later at mid-week Khoy and Angus were walking across the bridge to have a mooncake with coffee. "Khoy why do you think traffic on the Ho Chi Minh Trail is down?" Angus asked as they sat down at an empty table.

"The VietCong soldiers head back to their farms to prepare for planting the rice crop. Traffic will pick up when they regroup and prepare for the New Year and spring assaults." replied Khoy with conviction, "Just wait."

About that time the dim lights in the restaurant began flickering then went out. Mamasan began yelling, "Everyone out! It's a number ten!"

"What does she mean, number 10?" asked Angus.

"She means this is a major problem. Number one is no problem, number ten is a bad one," Khoy replied.

The generator that provided power for the restaurant chugged a few more times and grinded to a stop.

Angus asked, "May I look at your generator, mamasan?"

She nodded that it would be OK for Angus to check out the generator, as she continued chasing everyone out and cleaning off the tables.

Khoy and Angus began checking to see what caused the generator to stop. After a few minutes, Angus noticed that there was no gasoline in the tank. Khoy spotted a five gallon can of gasoline next to the back door. Once the generator tank had some fuel, Khoy was able to start the generator up and lights came on in the restaurant. The two enjoyed free cakes and egg coffee the rest of the evening compliments of one happy mamasan.

The following week Angus stopped at Cindi Le's desk. "Would you like to go to the Coco Club tonight? I've got something I want to share with you," Angus gushed.

"Well big spender, if you're buying the pizza! Yes!" she teased.

At the Coco that evening Angus shared the news with Cindi Le that he received a reply from his mom and dad. They would love to have Cindi Le and her mother visit them in Texas. They suggested scheduling a trip in late May or June. Later the two walked through Dong Ba Market talking excitedly about all they can do in Texas. Cindi Le was thrilled at the news. She loved the opportunity to get some horseback riding. She agreed to speak with her mother and get her permission to go to Texas. Angus was invited to have dinner at the Bonnay home the following week. Cindi Le was to pick him up at the compound and drive to her home.

Her home was on the same side of the Perfume River. They drove along the river for a few miles. Cindi Le pulled up in front of a small white painted home surrounded by a low rock fence. Several different kinds of colorful flowers bordered the sidewalk leading to the blue front door. There was hibiscus, Chinese honey suckle, spider lilies and roses. A small peach tree highlighted the front corner of the home. A chrysanthemum in a big decorative flower pot welcomed the two at the door with a sweet aroma. Cindi Le opened the door to find her mother finishing setting the table for dinner.

"Mother this is Angus," Cindi Le introduced Angus to her mother. "Angus this is my mother."

Kim Ly greeted him with a warm smile, "It's good to finally meet you. I've been hearing a lot about you these last few months."

"Glad to meet you Mrs. Bonnay. Thank you for the dinner invitation," replied Angus as he held out his hand to shake hers and give her a box of chocolates he had brought as a gift.

"Angus, I've prepared a French beef stew with rice that's one of my husband's favorites. I hope you'll like it. Come and sit down. Would you like red or white wine?" she asked leading him to an adjoining room.

"Red will be fine," Angus replied. Looking around the room he saw a large glass enclosed China cabinet with a full-length mirror. It had a French design. "That's a beautiful China cabinet," Angus remarked as he studied the hand carved designs.

"Thank you, Angus. Andre, my husband inherited it from his grandmother. "He had the dining table made to match the cabinet," she pointed out with pride. He noticed a French style sofa with a large yellow chair that was built for two in the living room. Both were facing a small television with rabbit ears.

Angus held the dining chair for Kim Ly, then for Cindi Le. As he was sitting down, Kim Ly bowed her head and said, "let's pray," They held hands and prayed.

A big pot of stew sat in the center of the table. Each place had a salad bowl with fresh coconut, papaya, mango, banana, and jackfruit, which was one of the most popular fruits in Vietnam, providing a sweet aroma along with the sweet taste of a Lotus leaf.

Kim Ly explained to Angus, "Feel free to either put the French Beef Stew on top of the rice or beside it. Your choice. Vietnamese mix the two, the French, according to Andre, do not," she continued, "Angus I've tried to put American vegetables in the stew. There are carrots, onions, and potatoes. Of course, I've added some lemon grass and a couple of other Vietnamese spices that Andre likes. It's a French Beef Bourguignon with a hint of Vietnamese."

"It's delicious! Very tasty. Mrs. Bonnay. I appreciate you going to all this trouble for me," Angus said as he took a sip of wine.

As they finished dinner Kim Ly said, "I understand you like mooncake, so Cindi Le has prepared a mooncake for dessert. Would you like some Jasmine tea or would you care for more wine?"

"Tea will be fine." replied Angus.

Cindi Le got up and began taking the dishes and glasses to the kitchen. She returned with three plates of warm mooncake. Kim Ly wanted more wine and Cindi Le set the wine bottle next to her mother.

"I understand you have something to tell me," Kim Ly stated looking at Angus.

"Yes, mam. I do," Angus answered. "My parents would like an opportunity to meet you and Cindi Le. They suggest you fly to Texas and stay with them at the ranch for a week or so. They think either the middle of May or sometime in June would be the best time to visit Texas." He stopped and waited for a response.

Kim Ly picked up her glass of wine, twirled it a couple of times, then flashing a smile, she nodded her head in agreement and looked directly at him, "Angus, that is a great idea! I will have to look at my schedule and plan accordingly. Why don't you give me the address of your parents so I can write them directly? Don't you think that would be best?"

"Yes mam.," he agreed.

After everyone had finished the dessert, Cindi Le excused herself and began clearing the table.

"Angus, perhaps you and I could go into the living room. I have some things we need to discuss," suggested Kim Ly. She sat down on the couch, tucked her legs under her and motioned for Angus to sit on the yellow chair. Kim Ly pointed to the TV and said, "We don't get good reception here in Hue. We do not have a local station yet. We are told that we should have one in the first half of next year."

"Andre and I have been protective of Cindi Le in the past. Andre had always been concerned about her being around military men. He worries that Cindi Le may react too quickly to some of the promises made by young men. We both recognize she is a beautiful young lady. Years ago, she made a commitment to Andre and me that she would be careful around military men. I think you know what I mean," she picked up her glass of wine and twirled it. "She made that commitment in our church in the presence of our family priest," Kim Ly continued. "We've always been concerned about her reputation and how she would feel about herself as she matured. When she turned thirteen, we had a special Mass to guide her in recognizing her strengths to reach maturity with God's blessings to live her life in union with her beliefs. It is a sign of leaving childhood and entering the age of womanhood. Angus, I don't know if she has told you are not, but I am a psychologist. I have worked with young girls with guilt complexes because of bad choices they made early in their lives. I have my own practice here in Hue and lecture a couple of courses at Hue University. Am I making myself clear to you?"

"Yes ma'am, I understand and agree with you. I do not want to harm her reputation. I would not do anything to cause her to feel ashamed. We both agree on that. I care far too much for her. We have discussed some of the issues we will face. You and your husband have overcome several issues that Cindi Le and I face. She respects your marriage and has lived through some of those issues that you and Colonel Bonnay have experienced. She probably understands them better than I do. I will always honor her commitment," Angus replied in all honesty.

"Good, I'm glad we had this discussion. You know, Angus I like you!" Kim Ly said as Cindi Le entered the living room.

"Me, too!" declared Cindi Le with her sweet smile.

The three discussed the upcoming Thanksgiving holiday.

Kim Ly asked Angus if he would like to join them for a Vietnamese French Thanksgiving.

He replied, "I would like that, but it depends on what happens back at the compound. I may be called on a field mission."

"Well, let's plan on having you join us and if something calls you away, we'll understand," Kim Ly said. "I'm an officer's wife, I know the demands of the military!"

"Thank you, Mrs. Bonnay for the dinner and our discussion. You have my word." Kim Ly watched as the two walked hand in hand to the car. She thought to herself, "It seems like only yesterday!"

CHAPTER 12

November 1967, Part IV

Back at the compound, the night orderly gave Angus the sad news. Colonel Lathon had an aneurysm in his brain and died on the flight to DaNang. Angus wrote his parents a letter telling them that Cindi Le and her mother Kim Ly Bonnay liked the idea of visiting them in Texas. He wrote about Colonel Dennis Lathon dying unexpectedly. He included some photos of Cindy Le and himself at some of the restaurants and one with Kim Ly and Cindy Le in front of their home.

The next in command following Colonel Lathon was a major at the air station. Major James Steel was informed of the death of Colonel Lathon and that he was temporarily in charge until a replacement was assigned.

That afternoon Major Steel called for all officers to meet in the conference room. Major Steel let the officers know that Colonel Lathon had a history of high blood pressure and probably the stress of the work and the demands of Saigon were factors of the aneurism. "Full Colonel Colt Cunningham will be our next commander. He is on his way up from Saigon and has a meeting with General Tran tomorrow. He wants to meet with each officer about the officer's duties and his areas of responsibility. "Are there any questions about what to expect?" he opened the meeting for discussion.

"Do we have a bio on Colonel Cunningham?" asked one officer.

"The only thing I know is he's a West Pointer class of 1942, He served a short time in Korea. Then he was a tank battalion commander at Fort Knox. Westmoreland wanted him on his staff when he took over MACV. Colonel Cunningham will be in command of the First Corps. I get the impression there will be some changes here at Hue. You can expect a full military review with the changing of the guard. Get all your paperwork current. Get your men to spruce up the area. One more thing according to the staff in Saigon, do not try to bullshit this guy."

Four days later, the officers were again called to the conference room, this time to meet Colonel Colt Cunningham.

"Good morning men." Major Steel said. When Colonel Colt Cunningham walked in, Major Steel called, "Attention." The officers came to their feet.

Colonel Cunningham returned Major Steel's salute and slowly looked over the officers. "As you were," he commanded in a deep voice. He was dressed in his starched fatigues. His military hair cut showed some graying around his temples. His deep piercing eyes reflected a man of strong convictions. He appeared to be in good shape for a man in his late-forties.

He began, "I'm sorry about Colonel Lathon. He was a good officer. I know transitions are difficult. Let's all try to make the best of it. I plan to inspect each unit and each department. I will meet with each of you individually. It's important that you and I are on the same page. Believe me, I've seen some reports come into Saigon that caused conflict among Westmoreland's staff. When we send reports to Saigon there should be no doubt as to what you meant to say. Do not water down your report or fluff them up to make you look good. I have reviewed each of your records. You need to know that I am not an office hermit, I will be going to all our combat and firebases from time to time. You will be required to travel with me on some of those trips. I believe we can unite into a strong Corps I unit. That's all!" he concluded.

With that the colonel wheeled around and walked out the door toward his office, which was being rearranged into a different floor plan.

When Angus returned to his desk, there was a note *"See me in fifteen minutes, Col. Cunningham."*

"When Lieutenant McKay comes in, send him in immediately," the colonel told Cindi Le.

Angus walked up to Cindi Le's desk. She looked up, raised her eye brows, and calmly stated, "The colonel will see you now."

He walked through the door with some trepidation, stood at attention and saluted, "Lieutenant McKay reporting as ordered, sir!"

"At ease, McKay, sit down," stated Colonel Cunningham returning the salute without looking up from one of the reports submitted by Angus.

"Am I reading between the lines on your reports? I have a feeling that someone above you is watering down your reports. What are you seeing out in the field? Is there more traffic or not?" the colonel bluntly asked.

"Sir, I do believe there had been an increase in NVA movement on the Ho Chi Minh Trail up until this month. I understand General Tran thinks the decrease is due to the VietCong heading back to their farms. That may be part of it. We've seen less NVA boots, bicycles, and cart tracks than we did earlier this fall. Major Lin thought the tunnels we discovered earlier were definite signs of excessive storage," replied Angus.

"Are you leaning to more of a major offensive this TET or spring season?" the colonel questioned.

"Sir, I am in the trees, I cannot see the forest," Angus replied to the colonel's question.

"Point well taken. OK, I can buy that! McKay, keep me apprised on what you see in those trees. I have reason to agree with what you're seeing out in the field. Do you hear anything from the locals?" the colonel added.

"Sir, that's hard to say. Locals are caught between two forces. If they're caught helping us, NVA punishes them or even kills them for that. It was the locals that led us to the tunnels. They need to be careful. I try not to push them too far," the young lieutenant stated.

"I understand you speak Vietnamese pretty well. Are you fluent in the language?" Cunningham pushed for more answers.

"No sir. Major Lin pulled a man from his unit to help me with learning the language. I understand more than I can communicate. In fact, that's to my advantage, if locals think I understand them, they tend to have less discussion among themselves then when I am around. I try to pick up the gist of what they're saying. Then Khoy, that's my sidekick who Major Lin appointed to help me with the language, helps me to better translate what I heard. Sometimes, it is best that Khoy not be with me. That way I can ask him later what certain words mean. Khoy has also helped me with how to detect fake trails, punji traps, as well as the Vietnamese language. He's been helpful. I hope we can continue working together," Angus said as he showed support for Khoy.

"OK, McKay or is it all right to call you Angus?" the colonel grinned.

"I respond to either one, sir," Angus grinned back.

"What does Cindi Le call you?"

At that Angus's face turned beet red? He was slow in responding, "She calls me McKay at the office and Angus when we're not at the office," he responded slowly.

"Angus, it's OK with me. Just don't let your relationship get in the way of your work. I know you've been successful at your field missions. I see from the report you recently helped locate a downed pilot. Your medical assistance program to get the medical aid to local villages idea was a great success. Saigon was impressed with the additional locations you discovered. We need to discuss this in more detail soon. Do you have questions?" Colonel Cunningham stated in wrapping up the discussion, "By the way, you can call me Colonel Colt around here. Pass it on to the troops. I'm used to it," he admitted.

"No questions sir, I look forward to being under your command," McKay stood up, saluted, and left the new commander's office.

"How'd it go?" Cindi Le asked as Angus passed her desk.

"OK, I guess. He knew more about me than I expected, "See you tonight at the steps?" he asked her.

"I'll be waiting for you," she replied with a big smile. He winked and left.

Khoy was waiting for Angus at the steps of the office.

"We still partners?" was his first question.

"Yep! We're still perdners," Angus replied with his Texas slang, slapping him on the back.

"I guess as long as you're not in Major Lin's hair he and General Tran will keep you as my side kick. Come on Tonto, Let's go over to the hooch and have ourselves a drink. I'll buy you an American beer and I'll have my usual ginger ale. I have some questions to ask about what to expect at a Vietnamese Thanksgiving Dinner. I've been invited to join Cindi Le and her mother," Angus said.

"Man! You two are getting too close! Next thing they'll invite you to stay overnight with them," Khoy quipped.

"Can't do that, Khoy. My military career comes first," countered Angus.

They toasted and continued to gab until Angus had to get back to his room to change into civvies. He and Cindi Le were to meet at the high school steps after she stopped at home. She had wanted to change from work clothes to her dating clothes.

The red Dauphine was waiting for Angus as he approached the high school steps. "Get in," Cindi Le stated as she leaned over to give Angus a kiss. He smelled the hint of citrus and sweet jasmine that filled the air surrounding her. By now Angus had learned an easier way to get in and out of the small Dauphine. "We're going to have a light dinner on the King Dragon boat in Sinh village," she informed Angus.

"OK, where's Sinh village?" he asked.

"Just a few miles up the Perfume River. You'll like this place. I picture it like a Texas tavern," Cindi Le explained as she drove along the river past Hen Island. Angus commented on what she was wearing, "Those cowgirl jeans look really good on you. Now that's you!" he gleefully said pointing to her belt buckle. It had a girl doing a barrel race. "That plaid shirt has Texas written all over it," he declared. Then looking down at her feet, asked, "Where did you get those fancy cowgirl boots?"

"I've got connections. Tell me what you think of your new commander Colonel Colt Cunningham? Did he tell you to call him Colonel Colt?" she quizzed Angus as she drove up the road to Sinh village.

Angus thought a while before commenting, "Well, I think he is more military minded than Colonel Lathon was. He'll want things done his way, that's for sure. What's your impression of him?" he countered back to her.

"He's more organized. He's already told me some of the changes he wants done. Maybe the paperwork will flow more smoothly from Hue to Saigon," she replied. Then she questioned, "How did he know about us?"

"I thought you'd told him." answered Angus.

"No way! Maybe the whole compound knows. Who cares? Right?" replied Cindi Le.

Angus pointed out, "He told me he had no problem with our relationship as long as it did not interfere with my work."

"I don't see that as a problem. Do you?" Cindi Le dispelled his concerns.

"No. Guess not. Is this Sinh?" Angus shifted his weight to be more comfortable.

"We're here. I've been told they have real pork bar b que here. Let's try it," she said opening her door. Angus had to shift his weight and twist to get out of the car.

"Come on, let's enjoy being together and some good pork bar b que sandwiches," Cindi Le invited Angus as she waited for him at the gangplank to the boat.

They spent the evening watching the setting sun reflect various colors off the calm waters of the Perfume River. They had their share of the house special: pork bar b que, sweet potato fries and drinks. They sat on a bench at the bow of the boat holding hands and discussing their future years together.

On Thanksgiving Day morning Cindi Le picked Angus up in front of the compound. "Happy Thanksgiving," she greeted him with a warm kiss on the cheek. The perfume she was wearing had a faint scent of Pine that reminded him of the pines on the ranch. It had a very enticing aroma!

When they got to Cindi Le's home, her mother was finishing setting the table, "Good morning, Angus." she greeted him as he handed her a box of chocolates with a "Thank you for sharing today with me." Kim Ly had a white traditional flowery silk tunic (Ao Dai) over her light blue trousers. Cindi Le had a bright yellow long-sleeved blouse tucked into a brown skirt topped with a wide, dark brown belt. Her skirt flared out just below her knees. She wore soft brown leather flats.

"You really don't have to keep bringing me sweets all the time. You're always welcome here," Kim Ly smiled as she accepted the box of chocolates." I enjoy having you come here. We'll begin Thanksgiving dinner in about ten minutes. Would you care for a glass of white wine now or wait for the meal?" she asked.

He replied, "I'll wait."

Cindi Le filled the empty glasses with water and poured the wine from a decanter. The table was ready. There were a couple of bowls placed around each plate. No turkey.

"I believe we're ready," Kim Ly announced. After Angus assisted in seating them and was seated himself, Kim Ly held one hand out for Angus and the other for her daughter and said, "Let's pray."

"Now Angus, this may be a little different than you're used to. We start with fried wantons," she said as she handed him a bowl, "This is baked shrimp on a toasted baguette."

Next a bowl of salad was served. Again, Kim Ly felt it necessary to explain to Angus what was in the salad," Angus, the salad consists of cucumbers, papaya, bananas, red cabbage and a touch of shrimp and pork. There's salad dressing if you would like."

"No ma'am, I'll pass on the dressing," replied Angus.

"This salad is tasty," he said in between bites. When most of the salad was consumed, Cindi Le went into the kitchen to get the twelve-pound roasted turkey and the stuffing, with sweet potatoes and dumplings. The stuffing was made of sticky rice, pork, shiitake mushrooms, chestnuts, pine nuts and seasoned with cognac.

When Angus tasted the dumplings he commented, "This taste really good, what's in it?"

Cindi Le spoke up, "It has shrimp, pork, ginger, garlic, sesame oil, soy sauce, sugar and jicama."

Angus inquired, "What is jicama?"

Cindi Le explained, "It's a sweet, crunchy vegetable root that looks like a large light brown turnip. We use it in a lot of different ways, for example we make chips out of it. Like in the states you have potato chips. Glad you like it."

"Angus, more wine?" asked Kim Ly.

"No ma'am. Thank you anyway. I could stand some more water though," he replied.

Cindi Le filled his glass with more water from the pitcher that was sitting on the dining room cabinet.

Angus was trying to slow down his eating habits to match Kim Ly's. He enjoyed the various dishes, but his favorite was the sweet potatoes. He had eaten more than his share of everything, which pleased Kim Ly.

"Got room for dessert? Or, would you like to wait a while? We usually sit on the back porch for a while before having dessert," Kin Ly recommended.

"Waiting a bit sounds good to me," he smiled

The two women picked up the dishes and took everything to the kitchen. "Angus, why don't you have a cup of coffee and wait for us on the back porch?" suggested Cindi Le.

"OK, unless I can help out in the kitchen," he responded.

Her mother called from the kitchen, "Three would be too many."

Angus sat alone on the back porch watching a gentle breeze moving ripples down the river and boaters floating with the current. He felt stuffed and relaxed. The coffee had a sweet smooth taste to it. He remembered that Christmas was the next holiday and he needed to get something for Cindi Le and her mother. He had already thought of sending his parents and Rob a framed 5" by 7 "photo of Cindi Le and himself.

Cindi Le was the first to join him. She sat down in a chair next to him. She leaned over and gave him a peck on the cheek, "What do you think? Did you enjoy having Thanksgiving with us?" she softly asked.

"Yes, it was different, but in a nice way. It must've been good because I ate more than I should've," he admitted.

Kim Ly soon came out and sat on a couch on his other side. She commented, "Cindi Le says your family raise Black Angus. Well we have something in common. Andre's grandparents raised Charolais cattle in Royan which is in western France. Since World War II it's become a seashore resort. Andre tells me they started introducing the Charolais cattle in the United States back in early 1930's. After the Holstein dairy cows, the Charolais is the most common beef breed in France."

"I'm a little familiar with them. Some of the herds in south Texas are moving up from Mexico and South America. That breed is good for cross breeding because the cows have less trouble calving. The bulls are a little too heavy for some of the lighter weight breeds. At the ranch we cross our Black Angus with the White-Faced Herefords. They do pretty well with the heat in our area," Angus remarked.

"Is that how you got the name Angus.?" Kim Ly asked.

"No ma'am. I was lucky enough to take the blue ribbon at the state Cattle Show. It came with a lot of prize money. Enough to pay for my college at Texas A&M. After that my high school buddies started calling me Mr. Angus and Angus just stuck."

"It was probably more than luck," Cindi Le injected.

Kim Ly then said that she talked to Andre about visiting Texas. He liked the idea and was wondering if it would be all right that he came too.

"Yes ma'am. I am certain my parents would be happy to have him visit our ranch too. I know my friend, Rob, would like to talk to him about rubber trees," Angus added agreeing with her.

"Well, then I want to warn you, we will soon start updating our passports," Kim Ly chuckled, confirming the plans for the Bonnay's to travel to Texas.

"Cindi Le, I think your young man here is ready for dessert and tea. Aren't you Angus?" suggested Kim Ly.

"Yes ma'am, as ready as I'll ever be," agreed Angus.

When Cindi Le brought out three bowls, she explained to Angus, "This is Che Chuoi. It has a sweet, flavorful chunks of local bananas with tapioca pearls, dipped into a hot coconut milk and topped with peanuts and sesame seeds. This will make you fall in love with Vietnam. I'll get the tea. What do you want Jasmine or Lotus tea?"

He replied with a grin, "You choose."

"Well I know you like Jasmine. You need to try the Lotus tea," she urged him.

"Wow, this is a real dessert," Angus agreed as he took his third bite.

"This is probably the most favorite dessert in all of Vietnam," added Kim Ly.

As they finished the dessert, Kim Ly started asking questions about ranch life in Texas.

There was noise at the front door. Kim Ly got up and said, "Must be the kids from the neighborhood. Come join us Angus. They will perform the lion dance for us and offer their blessing and good fortune on our home. Cindy Le get some money for them."

The three stood on the porch and watched the children dance and perform their holiday dances. The kids cheered when they got their reward. They all politely said, "Cam on ban (thank you)."

Kim Ly and Angus returned to the back porch. Cindi Le disappeared into the kitchen. When she joined them, she had a baked square shape mooncake for everyone. "Here is our mooncake for the holidays. I baked it myself," she proudly declared as she handed them individual pieces.

Later that day as Cindi Le was driving Angus back to the MACV compound, she said, "Angus, my mother really likes you and she knows my feelings for you. She is excited about dad joining us in Texas."

Their shoulders touched in the small Dauphine. When she stopped at the gate, Angus turned and put her face in both his hands and gave her a long romantic kiss. She ran her hands through his hair. Grabbing tightly, she pulled him so that he couldn't let go of her lips. He got an extra strong scent of that enticing fragrance she had dabbed behind her ears before taking Angus back.

"Guess I'll have to wait 'til Monday to see you," she softly whispered in his ear letting go of his hair.

"Yep. You know I'll be thinking of you." was all he could say getting out of the car.

The night orderly stood as Angus walked in and told him that Chaplain Henderson was shot while delivering Thanksgiving meals to the troops at one of the fire bases. It was a sniper shot! Colonel Colt wants to see you the first thing in the morning. He said he'd be there at 0700. I suggest you be in his office at that time. Angus felt a shock throughout his body. He and Chaplain Henderson had formed a close relationship. He had helped guide Angus through a couple of emotional experiences. The chapel was empty except for Angus, who knelt before the cross on the wall and prayed for the chaplain and his family.

Early Monday morning, before Cindi Le came to work Angus was sitting in Colonel Colt's office. "McKay, I guess you heard about what happened yesterday. Chaplain Henderson was a good man. A man of God for many religions. He was doing his job to the fullest. I am submitting his name for the Chaplain's Medal of Honor," commented the colonel. He stopped talking for a moment, then continued, "You probably got to know him better than anyone in the unit. I hear you helped him with some of his services. I can use your help with two things: first, go to his room and gather his personal belongings that we need to send to his family. And, second, I'd like to be able to add some personal comments to the letter need to write. Can you do that?" Colonel Cunningham asked.

"Yes Sir. I know they have two daughters and they had been married fifteen years. They met in a Japanese hospital. She was a nurse from Korea. We discussed marriages of different cultures," admitted Angus. "What will we do without a chaplain?" he asked in a concerned tone.

"There's one on the way. An Irish chaplain by the name of Captain Kendric Walsh. He should be here within three days," the colonel replied.

Angus first went to Chaplain Henderson's office and then to his room to box up his personal belongings. He felt sorry for Mrs. Henderson and her two daughters.

Later that morning Cindi Le was at her desk processing papers when Angus walked in, "Sorry to hear about Chaplain Henderson," she said offering her condolences. She could tell he was down because he did not radiate his usual big smile.

"Ye'ah, can't believe it. War can be cruel," he replied, looking at her and added, "I enjoyed Thanksgiving Day, especially your square mooncake. Thank you and your mother for sharing the day with me. I wrote my parents about it and about you."

The next morning Colonel Colt came cussing through the door. "Damn, cold rainy weather! Cindi Le is this monsoon season?" he blurted out.

"No sir, this weather is coming from the South China Sea. The wind doesn't help. It may be the beginning of an early monsoon. But normally next month is the start of monsoon season. Then, it'll really get rainy. Vietnamese people have learned to adjust to it," she stated with a matter-of- fact motherly tone.

"Guess I'd better get used to it huh," he reluctantly conceded.

CHAPTER 13

December 1967, Part I

The first week of December a forward scout plane reported an antenna poking out of a roof of a grass hut along the river. "It's not too far from Con Thien. Headquarters thinks it may be a radio station in contact with a Russian ship north of the DMZ in the South China Sea. Saigon wants another Search and Destroy Mission. I've contacted Major Lin. He has ten men ready and wants ten of our men to join them at Con Thien. It must be a small village, down river from Con Thien. He's sending Khoy over here as we speak," explained the colonel. "You might be able to fly this afternoon. You should be back either Thursday or Friday. Plan accordingly." Colonel Colt informed Angus.

"Yes sir." replied Angus.

It was Wednesday morning before Angus could schedule a helicopter to pick up nine marines and Lieutenant Bowman the platoon leader at Con Thien. It was Lieutenant Bowman's first search and rescue mission. He had arrived in Vietnam only two days before.

"According to the map, the huts should be about ten klicks west, along the river. The pilot will drop us off around three klicks west of them. Oh, I'm sorry lieutenant, a klick is short for kilometer and is 1.6 times a mile. Don't worry about it. You'll soon get the terms over here," Angus explained.

"Hopefully the scouts can locate the village," Major Lin said as he pointed to the map.

Khoy asked Angus how he liked his first Vietnamese Thanksgiving meal.

"It was really good. They had a turkey and everything. Dessert was really tasty and the square mooncake, baked by Cindi Le beat the downtown mooncakes by a mile," Angus chuckled.

"Turkey? Wow! Oh, so now she is showing you she can cook too! Too serious man," Khoy jokily countered.

"How many of these missions have you been on?" the lieutenant sheepishly inquired, interrupting their conversation.

"Khoy and I have been on a dozen or more since July," replied Angus. He looked over toward Major Lin and nodded, "he's been on more than all of us combined. He's Major Lin."

"I sure didn't expect to be involved in combat so soon," Lieutenant Bowman nervously responded.

"Hey, I recognized your sergeant back there. We were on a mission together a few weeks ago. Stay close to him. He'll help you," Khoy assured the young lieutenant.

"Good advice," Angus added trying to instill some confidence in Lieutenant Bowman as they boarded the helicopter.

The chopper flew toward the river. The pilot picked out a landing area of knee-high Elephant Grass and other wet weeds bending with the wind and rain about a half a mile south of the river. The rolling hills hugged the river all the way to the South China Sea. Major Lin sent out two sets of scouts. One pair was to follow the river banks and the other two men were to stay in the wooded area of the hills. They were told to head back within four hours unless they located the huts before then.

At 1400 both teams returned. They had located three huts that were less than four klicks away. One hut had a radio antenna. It looked like there were ten to twelve soldiers but no civilians. Tall bamboo trees along the river bed blocked the view from the river. A boat could be seen pulled up among the bamboo trees. The team from the rolling hills reported they saw two or three rice paddies to the south of the huts.

Major Lin met with the two American lieutenants about the best way to approach the huts. Major Lin would take the river route. The two lieutenants would take the wooded area. There was no jungle trail to contend with. Both teams should be in position to attack by 1630. They split up and headed out.

At 1630 the men were in position surrounding the huts; the winds kept blowing the misty rains sideways. All the NVA soldiers were huddled in the huts. Major Lin assigned two men to hit each of the two huts without an antenna with grenades. Lieutenant Bowman at the suggestion of his sergeant had his team line up to avoid any cross-firing casualties. Major Lin assigned two men to throw concussion grenades into the hut with the antenna.

The grenade teams timed their attack. Loud explosions blasted the silence. Men began running and screaming out of the huts as flames erupted. Black smoke engulfed both grass huts. The stench of burning bodies blended into the wind. The rains slowed the flames and left smoldering embers where the two huts had been.

Two men in black Northern Vietnamese Army uniforms came running out the door of the radio shack holding their hands over their ears to see what was happening. Neither one heard the shots and both fell dead at the steps. The raid had happened so swiftly that the NVA men did not have a chance to grab their weapons. Major Lin and Lieutenant Bowman combed the radio shack for files, codes, and military orders. The dead were searched for identification papers. There were two transmitters and two receivers inside the hut. Open frequencies could be heard blaring orders. Two men were sent to the river to destroy the boat that had been hidden in the bamboo trees.

The men could see the fog rolling in from the South China Sea. It was not a good sign for them. It meant no helicopters could be expected to arrive tonight. The radio shack had a leaky roof. Major Lin told the men they could stay in there, but two guards would each take a four-hour watch. Two of Major Lin's men made a makeshift palm leaf cover to protect the guards from some of the rain and wind. The shack was crammed with soldiers sitting shoulder to shoulder. The leaky roof was repaired with ponchos funneling the rain to flow through the holes the men had punched in the walls. Major Lin told the men not to complain because it was better than being outside.

It was 1000 before the whop-whop sound of a lone helicopter meant the men had been spotted at the edge of a wooded area. As was his custom, after they landed in Hue Angus shook hands with everyone that was involved with the mission. "Now you are an experienced soldier," he congratulated the young lieutenant.

The following morning, he was happy to see Cindi Le's smiling face. "Glad you made it back," she greeted Angus, "You look tired. I'll pick you up after work. Just you and me, OK?"

Angus finished his report and gave it to Cindi Le to type for Colonel Colt. "I'm fix'n to take a nap. Let's go for a quiet dinner. OK? Just you and me," he repeated back to her.

Angus headed back to his room to catch up on some lost sleep. At 1330 he woke up, showered, and shaved. He wrote his parents a quick note about the mission and one to Rob. He walked back to the office to mail the letters and check with Cindi Le. She had covered her typewriter and was writing down things to do tomorrow.

As they were walking to the car, he asked, "Where do you want to go for dinner?"

"Tonight, I'll treat you to my cooking. Mother's got a class 'til 9 o'clock. That's 2100 hours your time," she teased.

"Anything's gotta be better than the C rations I had last night," he ribbed her.

"You haven't tasted my cooking yet. You may prefer Uncle Sam's C Rations," she countered. "I'm testing to see how brave you are."

"Honey, you fix it and I'll eat it," he assured her with a Texan drawl.

At home she stirred up a shrimp salad with various Vietnamese fruits. Then she served bananas rolled in sticky rice and then roasted in banana leaves. The bananas were then sliced into pieces and served in a coconut sweet soup.

"Wow, don't know what you call it, but I call it GREAT!" he declared after the first few tastes.

The two washed and dried the dishes and bowls. They then headed for the living room. She sat down on the sofa and patted her lap. "Stretch out and I'll give you a Vietnamese back rub," she suggested.

"How can I refuse such an offer?" he replied as he laid across her lap.

She began to gently massage his back. She could feel his muscles under his shirt relaxing as she moved her hands to some key points around his shoulders.

"Right there," he responded. He turned on his back and reached up, grabbed her hair, and drew her face towards his. Kissing her on her forehead, then her nose then on her moist lips. She responded wrapping her arms around his neck. She encouraged him to continue. He sat up and began kissing her neck. She unbuttoned the top of her satin tunic; his kissing followed her fingers down her cleavage.

"Angus, I truly love you," she said, whispering in his ear with a soft kiss.

"I love you too," he confessed for the first time as he pulled her closer to his body, hugging her tighter. Her intoxicating perfume penetrated his nostril's.

He kissed her gently as he slowly let her go. Suddenly, he began to snap the buttons on his shirt, grasping to breathe, he weakly stated, "I need some fresh air. I need to sit on the back porch for a while." They were sitting on the back porch cooling off their heated emotions when the front door opened and Kim Ly came in.

"You kids still here?" she called out.

"Yes, mother, we're on the back porch," replied her daughter.

"Mrs. Bonnay, I was just fix'n to tell her it was time to send me home," Angus spoke up.

"I smell Che chuoi. So, Cindi Le cooked for you. That's nice. How was it? Would you two like a dessert?" offered Kim Ly.

"No thank you. It was a great dinner. Guess I'd better take a rain check on the dessert," Angus countered. "I really need to get back to the compound. Thank ya' anyway."

"Cindi Le, be careful driving home. I saw some strange looking men standing on the corners. I was a little scared myself. No one tried to approach me, but it didn't feel right," her mother remarked.

On the way to the compound, the two did see a few men standing on the street corners, but none bothered to look at the Dauphin as it passed them.

Angus asked, "Honey, did you recognize any of them?"

She replied, "No."

"Don't stop for any reason driving back?" he warned her.

"Don't worry it might just be some kids coming from a local village for the first time," she nonchalantly commented. They kissed and he watched her turn around and head back down Le Loi Street

CHAPTER 14

December 1967, Part II

The following morning Colonel Colt had a surprise for all units connected with the MACV compound:

HAND TO HAND COMBAT DRILLS WILL BE HELD EVERY WED. AND THURS. EVERYONE INCLUDED- THIS INCLUDES ALL CHOW HALL STAFF, ALL MEDICAL STAFF, ALL COMMUNICATIONS STAFF, CIA STAFF.

NO EXCEPTIONS,

EVERYONE NEEDS SIX (6) HOURS OF TRAINING. SEE THE CHART AT THE FIELD. SIGN UP FOR THREE (3) – TWO (2) HOUR SESSIONS. CHECK WITH SERGEANTS RAMOS AND COOK FOR SCHEDULED HOURS. MUST BE COMPLETED NO LATER THEN 14/12/67

A COMPLETED CERTIFICATE IS WORTH ONE DAY OFF!

SIGNED: COLONEL COLT CUNNINGHAM

"Did you know about this?" Angus asked Cindi Le as he walked into the office the next morning.

"Not allowed to say anything," she put her index finger to her lips.

Angus protested, "I thought we didn't have secrets."

"It's not mine. It's Colonel Cunningham's," she declared.

"OK! OK! OK! You win," he laughed.

"He wants to see you about another matter," she said to Angus.

Walking into the colonel's office Angus asked, "You wanted to see me sir?"

"Yes, Angus, this envelope came special delivery from Saigon. It was addressed to me, but has your name on the letter. "What's this all about?" he asked handing the letter to Angus.

Angus read over the chemical analysis of the two grenades he had taken from the tunnels and sent in for an analysis.

"Sir, this is from our lab in Saigon, before you had arrived in Hue, I had submitted two grenades from the tunnels. This is their analysis," Angus replied.

The lab report stated: *The explosive powder in the concussion grenade was diluted to about 30% low grade gun powder and 70% mixture of wood ash, fine sand, and salt. Effectiveness of this grenade will produce "poor" results.*

The homemade claymore analysis showed about 40% low grade gun powder, 60% mixture of wood ash, fine sand, and salt. Effectiveness of this claymore will cause "less than desired results."

"Sir in addition to tons of rice there were hundreds of weapons stored in those tunnels. I mean old French made Mas Rifles, Thompson submachine guns, World War II radios, and medical equipment in what must have been hospital rooms with cots, some with dried blood were there. Plus, we found rooms for eating. I was curious because there were so many kinds of weapons," continued Angus.

"Good thinking, Lieutenant. Now, what do you deduce from this analysis?" Colonel Colt quizzed.

"My first thought is that the enemy's manufacturers are low on quality explosive powder. Why else would they dilute it? Sir how would you, interpret the analysis?" Angus questioned the colonel.

"Let's not jump to conclusions, but I suspect you are pretty close to the truth. Saigon is still anticipating a build up for a major ambush following the New Year TET Peace Agreement," Colonel Cunningham pointed out.

"Sir it may not be anything, but last night Cindi Le's mother noted that there seemed to be more men than usual hanging around the streets. Cindi Le and I also saw some men standing on the street corners. She thought it was probably just some rural Vietnamese from the local villages. I do not know what to make of it. Probably nothing." Angus surmised.

"Angus, what does your friend Khoy say? See if he can pick up some unusual movement or comments from his friends," suggested the colonel.

"Roger that, sir! Will get right on it. Is that all?" he asked.

"Yes, McKay. Keep me informed. I believe we are on the same page," Angus recognized the 'dismissed' signal from the colonel and left his office.

Cindi Le asked, "What was that all about?"

He touched her shoulder on his way to his office and responded, "Not allowed to say anything," he put his finger to his closed lips getting even with her. "We can talk about it tonight."

"Your place or mine?" she teased back at him with a smile.

"You mentioned one time that you'd take me to Hen Island. What about tonight?" he suggested.

"Not tonight. Weekends are better for Hen Island," she commented and then added, "Pizza sounds OK with me."

"Fine. You want some Quoc Lui(Vietnamese beer) with your pizza?" he asked.

"Yes. Angus I've got some work to do. Let's meet here at 1700." she said over her shoulder as she returned to her typing.

"I'm gonna invite Khoy," he suddenly blurred out, "So make it 1730 instead at Coco's."

Cindi Le stopped typing, "Should be interesting. I'll try to find a date for him." she responded.

"OK, Khoy and I will meet you two at 1730 at Coco's," Angus reminded her as he dashed out the door.

"Hey, Khoy. What about a Quol Lui at Coco's tonight? I'm buying pizza. Cindi Le may have a friend for you," Angus shouted to Khoy who was talking to a guard at the gate.

"I'm in," Khoy shouted back trotting over to Angus. "Let's go to the hooch for some good ole American beer. It sounds interesting!" he said grabbing Angus by the shoulder. He gleefully added, " So Cindi Le came through for me. How do you say it in Texas? Bless her pea picking heart."

At the hooch over a beer and ginger ale, Angus asked Khoy if he had noticed more people standing around on the streets. He went over what Cindi Le's mother had said and what they had noticed driving back to the MACV compound.

"Do me a favor and ask some of your friends over in the Citadel if they've seen or heard anything around that may be suspicious. Maybe you could ask some of the vendors. What about the mama san? You remember, the one with the generator problem? She may be helpful," Angus explained expounding on his questioning.

At 1720 Angus and Khoy walked into Coco's. They found a table for four and waited for the girls to arrive.

Fifteen minutes later Cindi Le walked in with another young lady. Her friend had on traditional Vietnamese clothing (Ao dai). Her cute friend appeared to be a little nervous.

"Angus, Khoy, this is my friend Hanh Be. She is a junior at the university. We have a class together," explained Cindi Le, introducing everyone. Khoy stood up and jestered toward the chair next to his. "I'm Khoy," he announced with a broad smile. Hanh Be smiled and nodded her head, not saying a word. Cindi Le sat next to her.

Khoy spoke to her in Vietnamese, "Your name fits you., (Hanh Be means beautiful doll).

"Cam un ban (thank you), but I do speak a little English," she noted with a smile. Angus and Cindi Le glanced at each other and grinned.

"What would you ladies like to drink?" Angus asked, then added, "The pizza should be here shortly."

Both girls ordered the local beer from the Hue Brewery. The pizzas came with the two beers.

They talked about the Christmas break at the university. Angus asked about Hen Island. But no one commented on Hen Island. Hanh Be said she planned to go down toward Saigon where it would be warmer. Cindi Le said she needed a break from studying and was hopeful her father would be home for Christmas. Banh Dau Xanh (a dessert of mung beans, sugar, oil, and fat-resembling a yellow candy bar) followed the pizza, which had been consumed and the second round of mugs were empty. Angus covered the expenses.

Khoy walked Hanh Be back to her dorm while Angus and Cindi Le walked to the compound where she had parked her car. She reminded Angus he needed two more hours of hand-to-hand combat training. She knew that because she kept the records for everyone in the compound who reported for the drills.

"You may need it to protect yourself from me," she teased as she shut the car door leaving Angus speechless.

Friday morning Angus finished his two hours of the required drill. He handed the completed form to Cindi Le. "Here, I thought I'd better heed your warning of last night." he said needling her.

She looked up at him, grinned and then said, "Take me to lunch I have something to tell you. Oh! First, Colonel Colt wants to see you in his office."

Entering the colonel's office, Angus asked, "You needed to see me sir?"

"Yes, McKay, if the VietCong were to attack, which direction would they come from?" he asked pointing to a map of the compound that he had been studying.

"Well, sir occasionally snipers have been doing minor damage down at the end of the runway. A couple of the trucks and jeeps have had windshields shot out, the helicopter has taken some dings and the communications center had some windows shattered. I can't recall any damage at the front gate maybe some jeers and gestures," Angus answered.

"What about our guard tower? Doesn't it cover the back of the compound?" asked Colonel Colt.

"The back gate should be protected. After all, there are two guards on the ground to check for vehicles entering the compound, just the same as the front gate. The fire power we have in the tower should be enough to ward off any one coming through that gate," Angus assured the colonel.

"Well, I plan to separate our four tanks by putting the trucks and jeeps between them. We need to run some drills so the men will be familiar with the changes. I'll be calling another meeting with all of our officers," concluded the colonel.

CHAPTER 15

December 1967, Part III

The morning rains had ceased and the young couple scurried down Dong Ba for a quick bite for lunch. They found a vendor and ordered his shrimp and rice luncheon special.

"Well, what's the great news?" Angus was curious to know.

"My father is coming home for Christmas! I'm so happy! He told mother that he wanted to take us to D'ang T'ang a few days before the holiday. YOU, TOO!" she gleefully burst out, grabbing his hand.

"That sounds great, but, but," he stuttered, "Cindi Le, I don't know if I can afford that. I've heard it is an expensive resort area."

"No! You don't understand! It's a Christmas gift for all of us. My parents have been there several times when he was overseer for the Michelin Rubber Tree Planation. Besides you can get an extra day off for your certificate and a three-day pass. Angus, I have your three-day pass form completed and ready for you to sign. Father is reserving two rooms: one for mother and me, and one for you and him. He says we can take a train there. We'll leave the afternoon of December 12th, that's the day we celebrate Cake of Kings day, we will return to Hue the following Sunday. You don't want to upset my father, do you?" Cindi Le pouted.

"Wow! I can't quite grasp all of this. I never expected to meet your father this way," Angus admitted with raised eye brows.

"Trust me. You'll like my father. He's eager to meet you. I'm eager to show you off," she looked at her watch. "We'd better get back to the compound. What about going to Hen Island tomorrow? I'll pick you up at 11 hundred hours. We can talk more about D'ang T'ang tomorrow," she concluded taking charge. They sloshed their way back through the puddles because the rains and wind had picked up.

Chaplain Walsh had arrived and Angus was thinking, "maybe he could use some help moving in," as he climbed the stairs to the chapel.

"Chaplain, I'm Lieutenant Angus McKay with MACV," Angus introduced himself.

"Ah yes, McKay, I'm Chaplain Walsh. Glad to finally meet you. I see from the files you've been very helpful in this office. Chaplain Henderson had you down for being an assistant. Hope I can benefit from your assistance as well," the chaplain made his request known. Walsh had the rank of captain. He was Irish. His ruddy, wrinkled face showed years of military life. The graying of his bushy eye brows and his close-cut military haircut aged him.

"Yes Sir, what can I do to help you?" asked Angus.

"So, tell me McKay, what denomination are you?" Walsh wanted to know.

"I'm Episcopalian. But I'm getting serious about a young lady who is Catholic. We are talking about getting married in Texas when my time is up here in Vietnam," he stated.

"I see. You probably don't know this, but the church made some significant changes about five years ago. I'll be glad to discuss them with you sometime," the chaplain offered. Then added, "If you'll compare their Creeds, you'll see that they are the same."

"I'm anticipating she will be asking me to attend Mass with her. Sir, I've never been to a Mass before other than a funeral and a wedding," admitted Angus.

"Mass is pretty much like your church service. In fact, some of the Episcopalian priests are now allowed to become Catholic priests, including married men. That, my lad, was a big step forward for Rome! We can discuss all that later in more detail if you would like." Then changing the subject, "Will you take these candles to the chapel? I am starting a 1700 Mass for Friday and Saturday. It's Advent."

Angus began helping Chaplin Walsh set up. When he was finished helping and about to leave. Walsh said to him, "You're always welcome to assist me with Mass anytime you want. I will also be doing the protestant services on Sundays. I could use your help at any of the services anytime you're available." He looked at Angus and smiled, "Anytime! Any service."

Angus left the chaplain feeling good about him. He seemed like an understanding man. That night he wrote a quick note to his mom. He asked her to airmail his light tan western suit, the light blue shirt and the FFA bolo tie. He wanted to impress Cindi Le's father!

At 1100 Saturday morning Cindi Le drove up in her red car. "Ready for Com Hen at Hen Island?" she greeted as he wiggled himself in the front seat. She leaned over toward him and tried mimicking a Texas accent, said, "I need my good mor'n' kiss."

The sun was out and the top was pulled back to let the sun add a little warmth to the 68 degrees temperature. Cindi Le had her 'playful pony tail' under a wide brim western style hat with her rectangular sunglasses resting on it. The blue and silver tunic had flowers of various pastel hues. She was in a cheerful mood.

The drive to Hen Island took less than fifteen minutes. They crossed the only bridge connecting the main land to the island. They walked to the north side of the island until they found Hoa Dong which was a restaurant where they could sit and watch boats float up and down the Huong River.

Angus could smell the fish-like odor as they passed several restaurants and street vendors. He quickly understood Hen Island was not referring to chickens.

Cindi Le explained that the Com Hen is a baby clam. The muddy banks of the island at the river's edge is an ideal habitat for shell fish to breed. She reviewed the various dishes: Hen Chao-hen porridge, Hen Xao-hen salad with crackers, Banh Beo Chen- rice cake topped with prawns and pork rind, Cha- fish and pork cakes, Nem- cured meat, Banh Loc-shrimp and pork dumpling and Trung Cut–quail eggs. She recommended they order Huda beer for their drink.

Angus decided he would try the shrimp and pork dumpling. Cindi Le chose the hen salad with crackers. The Huda beer had more of a malt taste, Angus drank half and then ordered water.

A long-time resident, an octogenarian, spoke to them. He had been born and raised on the island and was always eager tell the history of Hen Island. He told how the emperor had wanted the land around the Citadel. Most of the poor villagers were forced to move. Many moved to Hen Island. He kept looking at Angus to make sure that he understood what Cindi Le was translating for him. When the history lesson ended Angus asked the senior from the island what he would like to drink. The old man smiled and said, "a Sua Dau Phong."

"What's that?" asked Angus looking at Cindi Le.

She chuckled, "it's peanut milk."

"Cam on ban, (thank you.) said the octogenarian nodding with appreciation.

"Khong co gi (You're welcome)," Angus proudly replied.

The old man, looked at him, again nodding, smiled showing his toothless mouth, and began drinking his peanut milk. The young couple sat and discussed the upcoming trip to the French Resort at D'ang T'ang. Then Cindi Le said, "We can go to my place. Mom has a night patient she occasionally helps. We can watch TV. I'll fix you an egg coffee," urged Cindi Le.

About a half hour later the two were sitting on the couch watching a blurry TV. "Ready for your egg coffee?" Cindi Le asked.

Angus had his arm around Cindi Le. When she stood up to get the egg coffee, his hand accidently touched her breast.

He quickly moved his hand. It was an embarrassing moment for him.

"Angus, it's alright." She assured him as she quickly sat on his lap kissing him. She took his hand and encouraged him to begin unbuttoning her tunic. Her sweet perfume captured his attention. When there were no more buttons, he pushed her tunic over her shoulders exposing a laced bra with the clasp in the middle of her chest. He fumbled trying to undo the clasp. First with one hand then with both hands. Finally, Cindi Le reached down with one hand and unfasten the clasp.

Angus began softly exploring her firm breasts. She leaned backwards and gently pushed his face downward. He began kissing between her breasts. The fragrance of her flowery perfume got stronger. He cupped her one of her breasts so he could reach it with a kiss. Then. Cindi Le raised his face to hers, her kisses forced him to unclench his teeth. He felt her tongue touch his. It was a new, explosive emotion for him that he had never experienced before. He reciprocated her aggressiveness. Then, suddenly, he backed off.

"Cindi Le, I've got to catch my breath. I can't breathe." He gasped sucking in as much oxygen as he could. "I need to go to the back porch," he said as he held his chest heading for the back porch.

"It's OK, Angus. I just want you so much," she implored.

The next day she talked to her mother about Angus being unable to catch his breath at times. Her mother explained to her that maybe he was hyperventilating. Medically it is an imbalance of oxygen and carbon dioxide. Could be the stress of the war or maybe he's anxious about being away from his home. She went on to explain that when he begins gasping for air Cindi Le should help him to relax and tell him to take deep breaths.

On Sunday Angus helped Chaplain Walsh with the 10 hundred hour protestant service. Angus was heading for the mess hall when he noticed a red car drive past the guard.

He walked over to the car. "What are you doing here on Sunday?" he greeted her.

"I came to see you and invite you to join me for a picnic. I know you like fried chicken and mashed potatoes with white gravy. It's all in the picnic basket. Get in. I'll take you to a beautiful waterfall outside of town. I cooked everything myself." Cindi Le urged, jestering him to join her by patting the passenger seat.

Angus replied holding up his hands to catch a few drops, "it's raining."

"There are covered picnic tables. It'll probably stop by the time we get there. Come on, I won't bite," she countered.

She was correct. The rain had stopped and a bright rainbow appeared over the waterfalls.

"See, I told you," she bragged. She put a plastic sheet on the picnic table and laid out the lunch.

"Angus, I hope the chicken is crisp enough for you," she said looking for his approval.

"If it tastes as good as it smells, I'll love it!" he grabbed her from behind and gave her a hug.

"What's to drink?" he asked snooping in the picnic basket.

"I brought some white wine for me and a ginger ale for you."

Angus enjoyed the southern style home cooking. He sipped a little of her white wine.

As they talked Cindi Le mentioned some of the things they can see and do at the resort. Then he let her know that Colonel Colt wanted each officer on guard tower duty one night.

"Yes, I know. You're to take the tower guard tonight from 2200 'til 0700 hours. Remember I typed up the guard duty schedule," she reminded him. "That's why we are here now. I probably won't see you tomorrow."

"Thank you for the lunch and the thought," he said as he gave her a gentle kiss on the cheek.

Rain drops began falling while driving back to the city. She pulled into the compound. They kissed and he sprinted to BOQ.

Angus stood his watch in the guard tower until his relief came at exactly 0700. He was happy to get out of the cramped area. The mounted machine gun and the cases of ammo took up over half of the square footage. Fortunately, someone had thought to take a chair and a cushion. Angus spent most of the night sitting down with his feet resting on a cannister of machine gun shells. The steady mist was followed by heavy fog. He pulled his poncho over his head tighter. He found it difficult to see the university a block down the street.

Monday morning Angus had a hearty breakfast of eggs, grits, and bacon, he took a shower and slept until 1400 hours. Angus headed for the office. "You survived the long night," Cindi Le greeted him with her flirty eyes and warm smile. "The colonel wants to see you," she informed him.

"Colonel Colt, you wanted to see me?" Angus inquired as he entered the door.

"Yes, Angus, Saigon sent a message early this morning. They want a search and assessment mission near Khe Sanh. Headquarters is anticipating a build up for a major attack after the TET holidays. Take Khoy. There's a helicopter scheduled to pick you, Khoy and Major Lin's men up at 1530. There is a platoon of marines waiting for you at Khe Sanh. See if you can uncover any type of buildup. Do not engage if you and Major Lin run into a hornet's nest where you are outnumbered. The boys at DaNang are on ready alert. Be smart out there! You would hate to mess up your three-day pass with Cindi Le," Colonel Colt chided in a more serious tone of voice and with a "That's all," comment.

The rains never ceased from Tuesday 'til Friday. Creeks and canals overflowed. Slippery mud paths slowed the search and assessment mission progress. Wet leaves in the jungle drenched everyone on the mission. Mosquitoes swarmed the men day and night wherever they were. Men ran out of mosquito spray on the second day.

Villagers along the rivers and creeks claimed they had not seen any troop movement for several days. There were empty boats floating in the swift running waters.

On Friday afternoon, the helicopters picked up the soaked soldiers. The men were grumbling about the failure of the mission and the terrible rainy weather. Angus was eager to wash off the red clay mud and get some sleep. He spent all day Saturday washing his muddy clothes and cleaning his weapon.

On Sunday he helped Chaplain Walsh with his 1000 service. He prayed his mother had airmailed his best western suit so it would arrive soon. As he was heading to the Mess hall, he noticed there was a red Dauphine in the parking lot.

Angus jogged over to the car. "I thought I'd come over to see how you're doing. I missed you," Cindi Le said taking off her sunglasses.

"There was a lot of rain, mud and mosquitos. That's about all," he replied.

"Hop in. I'll buy lunch. I just wanted to be with you," she admitted.

"OK, where to?" Angus said as he got in her car.

"This chilly weather calls for some good, hot pho. There's a popular place in Que Chu. Are you game?" she asked.

"What is pho?" Angus wanted to know.

"Pho is delicate, tasty Vietnamese soup. It includes rice noodles, broth, some local herbs, and beef bones. To add flavor, vendors add their own mixture of ginger, star anise, cinnamon, and cardamom. It's not Texas chili, but I think you'll like it. Maybe you can convince them to add chili powder," she stated describing what pho soup contained.

"Que Chu is a village just off Highway 1. It's just a few minutes outside Hue. There's a small restaurant on a side street called "Chao Mung (welcome)," Cindi Le explained as she turned onto Highway 1 and drove past the Citadel wall.

The owners were happy to see the two enter their quaint place. All the tables were round with only two chairs per table. A sheet of clear plastic kept the rain and wind from blowing into the restaurant.

"We both want to order your Pho and hot tea," she ordered.

The old woman nodded and scurried to the back of the restaurant.

"Guard duty was pretty tough on you last night, huh? Cindi Le remarked.

"Amazing how slowly time goes. I thought a lot about you, and us," he admitted

"Angus, remember what Colonel Cunningham said about not letting our relationship interfere with your military career," she reminded him.

They finished the pho and sat holding hands, watching it rain and enjoying the hot lotus tea. When they got back to the compound, he gave her a peck on her cheek. "See you tomorrow." He said.

He got out of the car and dashed through the rain toward the BOQ. Khoy was waiting inside.

"What brings you here at this hour?" Angus asked.

"Well, you suggested that I talk to 'generator mama san'. She agrees with you and Cindi Le. She did have some unfamiliar young men and women come to her restaurant and one of the questions a few of them asked was will she accept Hanoi money. Makes you wonder, doesn't it?" he questioned.

"It does, doesn't it? Khoy what do you make of it?" Angus wanted his opinion.

"We should keep a close watch on this. We need to know what they are up to," responded Khoy.

During the next few days Angus went shopping for new clothes to wear when he was with the Bonnays and a Christmas gift for Cindi Le. He was anxious about getting his good western suit from his mother on time.

He found a nice set of emerald ear rings and necklace. The green stone was circled with diamonds. The sale sign in front of the set of jewelry read: *Gift of True Affection*. He had the back of the necklace engraved with 'anh yeu em, Angus' (I love you, Angus). He paid half and told the saleslady he would be back the next day to pay the balance and pick it up. "Can you gift wrap it for me?" he asked, then added, "I'll be happy to pay you for gift wrapping it."

At the PX he picked out a couple of shirts and pair of khaki slacks. He stopped at the Post Office and was happy to find a package from his mom. He dashed to his room to open it to make sure she had packed everything. She had even included his matching socks.

The next day he paid for Cindi Le's Christmas gift. The saleslady had done a nice job of gift wrapping it.

Cindi Le had been busy studying for tests before the holidays. On December 15th Cindi Le finished all her tests. That afternoon she informed Angus she wanted to take him to Ruby's Bistro on Saturday night. It was only a few miles outside of the Imperial City. It was known for its French and German recipes and wine.

"I'll pick you up tomorrow at 1630. You should like Ruby's. Wear your dancing shoes," she warned Angus.

Ruby's had been a former warehouse that had been remodeled to offer a large dance floor. There were tables all around the wooden dance area. The menu consisted of French, German, and Vietnamese specialties. A record player provided the dancing music. The choices were waltz, polka, jitterbug, and slow dancing.

Angus and Cindi Le tried them all. They danced 'til 2130 hours. Angus's western shirt had perspiration under his arms and down the middle of his back.

"Can't remember dancing this much," he remarked as they strolled to her car.

It was late when she dropped him off at the compound. "Are you nervous about meeting my father? Don't be," she assured Angus as they kissed goodnight.

"I'm a little nervous. Hope I meet his expectations," Angus admitted.

"Don't worry. He already likes you. Last night, I told him all about you," she smiled in reply.

CHAPTER 16

December 1967, Part IV

The plan was for Cindi Le to introduce Angus to her father the next evening before the four took the train to the LeLieu de Sejour in D'ang T'ang south of DaNang the following morning.

The next evening Cindi Le said, "Angus, this is my father, Dad, this is Angus," as she grabbed each one by the hand, smiling with pride.

Colonel Bonnay had a solid build with square shoulders. He had a high forehead with an oval shaped face. His slightly bushy moustache rested on top of his mouth. His light blue piercing eyes and long dark eye lashes complimented his appearance. He had streaks of gray along his temples. He was wearing a dark leather sport jacket with a tan turtle neck sweater. His brown military shoes were well polished.

Kim Ly came in the room wearing an expensive looking, azure blue with a silver lotus pattern Ao Dai. She looked relaxed and fresh. Kim Ly had a wine glass in her hand. She interlocked her arm with Colonel Bonnay's left arm as he reached out to shake Angus's hand. "Glad to finally get to meet you. Both of my girls speak highly of you. Is it all right to call you Angus? Please call me Andre," the colonel spoke with a slight French accent.

"Sir it is my honor to meet you," replied Angus. "I appreciate your invitation to join your family at the resort. Thank you," he said.

The family sat in the living room. Cindi Le squeezed in the yellow chair alongside Angus. Mrs. Bonnay sat next to her husband with her legs tucked under her. She twirled her wine glass smiling at Angus and Cindi Le.

Andre asked, "Angus, how long have you been in Vietnam?"

"Sir I arrived in Saigon on July 1st. I graduated from Texas A&M University last May," he replied.

"And, you're already a first lieutenant? I'm impressed," commented Andre.

"Happened to be at the right place at the right time," Angus replied grinning at Cindi Le.

"We need to drink to our trip to D'ang T'ang. And, to Cindi Le's A's in school," Kim Ly spoke up. "Andre brought some French wine from our very own vineyard. Cindi Le get the wine glasses. I'll get the wine."

Angus thought the wine tasted exceptionally smooth with no bitterness. He continued to limit his drinks to one glass a day.

The wine stimulated the conversation which covered several topics during the next two hours, which included ranching, vineyards, cattle, Royan and Texas. It was agreed to continue the discussions over the next few days in D'ang T'ang as the two men got to know one another better.

Cindi Le broke into the conversation saying that it was time to take Angus back to the compound. Driving Angus back she told him how happy she was that he and her father got along so well.

"See you in the morning. We're going to have fun at the resort." Cindi Le assured Angus with a soft lingering kiss.

Andre had called a taxi to the railroad station for the next morning. The Bonnay family and Angus arrived at the train station in time to load their luggage and find their reserved private room. Kim Ly cuddled up next to Andre with her legs tucked under her and Cindi Le sat next to Angus. The train rumbled past Bach Me, the highest peak between Hue and Da Nang.

"This is beautiful countryside," Andre commented pointing at the towering peaks.

As the train stopped in DaNang, some passengers disembarked while others boarded. Andre commented to Angus, "This is a pretty port city. Has Cindi Le brought you here yet?"

"No sir, but she's been a good tour guide for Hue," he replied. Cindi Le smiled and grasped his hand.

It was late morning when the train pulled into the D'ang Tran rail station. There was a shuttle bus waiting to take them to LeLieu de Sejour Resort.

"Ah, Colonel Bonnay! Sir it's great to see you. We have your suite ready for you and your family just as you ordered," the driver greeted Andre.

"Good to be back, Frantz. Everyone still here from the old days?" the colonel asked.

"Oui! Where would we go? We just have more American officers and less French officers," Frantz chuckled with his reply.

At the resort, the head captain met them at the entrance. Angus was amazed at the beautiful, well-kept grounds with pine and flowering trees. He could see the influence of the French design in the large, white building. In the middle of the lobby stood a large Christmas tree with glistering tinsel and a star on top. Bright colored Christmas balls with French designs were carefully placed around the tree. Underneath was a nativity scene. The French crib included sentons, which are figurines such as a baker, a blind man, a woman selling fish.

"Welcome, Colonel Bonnay! We have missed you and your wife. Now you bring us your family. We are honored. I'll have your luggage taken to your suite. You are on time for a lunch. Should I have it delivered to your room?" Captain Marcel politely asked.

"Nice to see you again, Captain Marcel. I think we'll have lunch in the restaurant. How's your family?" Andre inquired.

"They have outgrown me! Two are back in Paris and my youngest is learning to be a chef here at the resort. Don't worry though, Regis continues to be our head chef," the captain assured Andre.

The foursome took the wide, carpeted stairways to the second floor rather than take the elevator. The premium suite was at the far end of the hallway decorated with French art. The double doors were open and the bell boy was waiting to be told in which rooms to put the luggage.

There were bedrooms on the opposite sides of a large living room. Cindy Le noticed the dining table decked out with a bouquet of fresh cut flowers. There were four dining room chairs at the table. A large leather sofa with three plush chairs surrounded an elegant glass table. A small kitchenette was tucked away in a corner of the living room. Palm shaped fans slowly and quietly rotated above.

French doors opened to a balcony that brought the outdoors in along with incredible natural light. The view of the lake at the bottom of the wooded hills reflected peace and tranquility. Palm trees in large pots were at the corners.

The individual bedrooms also opened to a long balcony. Twin beds were in each bedroom.

"Angus, you and I will share one bedroom and our girls will share the other one," he gave a smile as he pointed to one of the bedrooms for the bellhop. "She's still my daughter!" he added. Angus was surprised at his blunt statement.

"Let's freshen up a bit. Then we'll go downstairs and have lunch," Andre directed.

The lunch room had several tables open, and the maître d' led them to a table overlooking the flower garden that displayed various colors of roses, hibiscus, spider lilies, all mixed in with coconut, apple, and banana trees.

For lunch the men had a slice of roast beef, mashed potatoes, and dark gravy. Their glass of red wine was a perfect choice. The women chose the fruit salad with sweet tasting apples, grapes, watermelon, and a tangerine on top of a lotus leaf. Their white wine was equally satisfying.

Regis the head chef, came out to greet Colonel Bonnay.

"Colonel, greetings from the kitchen. When they told me you were coming, I got out some of your favorite recipes. How was the roast beef? I marinated it in red wine for four hours. You like?" Regis wanted to know.

"Oui! But ask my American friend here. He's from Texas. They eat a lot of beef there. Regis this is Angus," Andre introduced the two.

Regis looked at Angus, nodded and then at Cindi Le. "Colonel, is this little Cindi Le? She was this high when she was here last," he said, holding his hand at knee level. Regis turned back to Angus, he continued, "You are Mr. Angus, yes? You have good taste for beef, yes? And, French women, yes? What's your favorite recipe for beef?"

"Sir, guess the most popular is bar b que beef. Of course, a good T-bone steak is always a good choice," Angus replied.

Regis chuckled and said, "spoken like a Texan! I must return to prepare for dinner. Enjoy!"

Andre liked pointing out and explaining the various trees and flowers as they ate lunch. He said, "That bright yellow leafed tree is a 'cay keo bac, Americans call it a Yellow Mimosa."

"After dinner we can take a horse and buggy ride to the market area. Christmas decorations will be on display. We can try some local desserts," suggested Andre.

"Only if I get to pay for the buggy ride and the desserts," replied Angus.

Angus and Cindi Le spent the rest of the afternoon walking through the flower garden. She wore a lime green Ao Dai over white pants. They stopped and smelled the various flowers. Some of the flowers bloomed year around due to the tropical local climate. Cindi Le explained how the Vietnamese used the different plants in their recipes.

That evening the four sat in a horse drawn buggy heading for the market place. The cobble stone street slowed the horse's pace. The driver had the trip timed to take fifteen minutes. He spoke in Vietnamese, French and English about the history of D'ang T'ang and the French resort. He joked about no one stays at the resort very long indicating the absence of the French.

The street vendors were south of the village. Christmas lighting and colorful lanterns were dangling from the wires above the street. Christmas music in different languages filled the brisk air of the night. The Bonnays and Angus walked past the various vendors, judging where to buy the desserts. The decision was narrowed down to three kinds of desserts: a sweet potato and tapioca pearls cooked in a sweet coconut milk, or bananas rolled in sticky rice and then roasted in banana leaves, which are sliced into small mouth size bites served in a sweet coconut milk or the che troi nuroc, a sweet soup made with mung bean paste wrapped in gelatinous rose flour and then dipped in a warm ginger sauce.

"I know which one Angus will prefer," Cindi Le interrupted. "He will like che troi nuroc dessert. It's a sweet dessert for tonight's chilly air."

"I've got this," Angus said as he handed a five- dollar bill to the vendor. "Keep the change," he told the vendor. The dessert warmed them.

It was time to return to the resort. The twenty-minute walk back was well lit by the nearly full moon. Andre and Kim Ly were arm in arm; Angus and Cindi Le were holding hands all the way.

At the resort they agreed on playing cards. Choice of card games were Hearts, Whist or Bridge. Angus did not know how to play Whist or Bridge, so they started playing Hearts. At first the men played against the women. Later they played couple against couple. Andre and Kim Ly were drinking French wine, Angus and Cindi Le had ginger ale.

"Angus, we're going to have to teach you to play Whist," remarked the colonel.

"Yes sir. Thank you for an enjoyable day," replied Angus.

"Friday morning our plans are to go to church. It is Advent. We would like for you to come and pray with us. I understand you're not Catholic, but you can pray with us, can't you?" inquired the colonel.

"Yes sir. I would like that. Thank you for the invitation," Angus agreed.

Angus and Cindi Le told her parents they were going to walk down near the lake. The moon was almost full and cool winds had changed into a warm, calm breeze for the December night. The walk took ten minutes to get to the benches along the shoreline. They sat and shared their thoughts about the future. When they had returned to the resort, the staff had set out some nighttime snacks and drinks for them. The two took some desserts and sat on the balcony continuing their discussion about their dreams.

At 6:30 breakfast was delivered to the suite. Angus found a suite house robe and slippers on his side of the closet. Andre was sitting up in bed. Angus noticed a pair of Kim Ly's blue shoes were shoved half way under Andre's bed. Angus couldn't help but grin.

"Let's eat first," Andree said, "Just put on the robe. We can shave and shower after breakfast. Church is at 9:30." Angus was a little surprised at having breakfast in his pj's and robe with the Bonnay family. He felt a little timid when greeting Kim Ly and Cindi Le who were already at the table.

"Good mor'n," he said trying to look calm. He looked at Cindi Le, she was dressed in her night gown and robe, she smiled back at him. He winked, but said nothing. "Lovely as ever," he thought to himself.

The smorgasbord breakfast had a variety of choices and included Colonel Bonnay's standard order: oatmeal with raisins, a hardboiled egg, toast, and coffee. Angus had scrambled eggs, bacon, toast, and coffee.

When everyone was ready, they walked to a French chapel ten minutes away. The sun was beginning to warm the air. The chapel was larger than the one at the compound. French architecture was interwoven with the religious layout of the altar. Cindi Le and Kim Ly had a thin lacy scarf covering their heads. Both had on the traditional Vietnamese attire. Andre wore his French uniform. Angus had on his best western suit. Cindi Le sat next to him. Whispering in his ear, she explained parts of the Mass. Although he had been to a few Catholic marriages and funerals, this was his first time to attend a Catholic Mass. Even though the services were in French, he recognized parts of it. From previous experiences he knew to approach the priest with crossed arms to accept the blessing.

After Mass, Andre said, "Thank you for praying with us. You're welcome to join us for the Christmas Eve services on Sunday. Kim Ly and I are going back to the resort. I just happen to know that my daughter wants to take a 'Swan Boat' ride with you through the 'Valley for Lovers'. We used to call it 'Jardin Pour Les Amoureux'. You two are on your own."

"Cindi Le, let's change into leisure clothes before we take a boat ride," suggested Angus.

She agreed and the two hustled back to the Resort to get into something more comfortable for the swan boat trip. Angus changed into his western clothing with a fleece lined vest. She wore her cowgirl outfit with a blue jean jacket. She did her hair in a pony tail.

"Where are you two cowpokes going?" Marcel asked as they passed him.

"We're on our way to the Jardin Pour Les Amoureux for a swan boat ride," Cindi Le replied grabbing Angus' hand.

"Hold your horses! Where's your picnic basket?" Marcel tried to sound like a cowboy that he had seen in the cowboy movies. "Wait here, I'll be right back."

When he returned, he had a picnic basket compliments of the Resort. "Here, now you're ready for the Swan Ride at the Jardin Pour Les Amoureux." He explained.

They thanked him and headed to the twenty-acre park that included horseback riding. It was only a ten-minute walk to the dock. The water on the lake was calm. They swan boat scudded the two to a beach lined with pine trees. The piney smell reminded Angus of the ranch.

The picnic basket was packed with various kinds of sandwiches, pickles, chips and two bottles of white wine from Royan, France. A table cloth and a blanket were on the bottom of the basket. Angus spread the table cloth on a picnic table that was nearly invisible from the lake. It was farther back from the shore line. Cindi Le set the table while Angus spread out the blanket with the initials 'LSR'. The blanket was too tempting for the young couple and they sat on the blanket enjoying the lunch. Angus doubled his daily wine intake to two glasses. The white wine tasted perfect with the cake that the two had to share-one bite at a time.

She snuggled up to Angus and asked, "Are you having a good time?"

"Yes! I feel very comfortable with your dad. He's a straight shooter in my book," Angus replied. He grabbed Cindy Le and rolled her on her back. "Yes!" he said stretching her arms over her head and he began kissing her.

"Oh, Angus, if only you knew how much I truly love you," she whispered in his ear and then kissing it.

A stronger breeze came across the lake. "Guess we'd better clear the picnic table before everything blows off," she pouted.

As they paddled back across the lake, Angus threw crumbs to the fish. They would surface and nibble on the bits of food. "Look at that big fish," Cindy Le said. Sea gulls began swooping down competing with the fish. Three ducks quacking away swam over to see if there was any left for them.

Back at the dock they returned the swan boat. Angus had few more crumbs that he threw over the railing. Smaller fish swarmed toward the bits of crumbs. The couple had been told they could leave the picnic basket at the dock and the resort staff would return it to the resort.

The two decided to walk through the gardens. They chose a stone pebble pathway that led them on a clover leaf route. At the entrance was an intersection with gardenias at each corner. The fragrance of the sweet scent of the flowers had butterflies feasting on the nectar.

In the first circle there were many colorful flowers. Yellow, white, and red roses, chrysanthemums, ivies, hibiscus, honey suckles and small colorful trees with purple, red and green leaves of various hues. Taller narrow evergreens closed the entire circle.

The circle to the right led them to an area of several statues. One statue was a muscular man with a woman kneeling at his knees, another statue was of a woman holding a basket of flowers and another statute of a man and a woman with a torn blouse in a passionate kiss. There were other statues mostly of half nude women with water jars and some with flower baskets at the foot of a water garden. A willow tree on each side of the of the water garden dipped its branches into the water. Coi fish were swimming among the Lotus plants which were displaying white, red, and yellow blossoms. Two white swans glided over the water. Dragonflies were darting from flower to flower.

Angus asked, "Do you know how to tell the difference between the dragonflies and the damselflies?"

"No but I bet you're about to tell me," she replied with a grin.

"The dragonflies hold their transparent wings flat perpendicular to their bodies when they are resting. The damselflies fold their wings along the side of their bodies. They have a fluttery flight pattern. I learned that in biology class," Angus explained.

The path led them to the third portion of the garden. There were yellow and red flowering shrubs bordering the white pebble stone trail that attracted the small bees buzzing around the blossoms. It led to a waterfall. The rhythmical sound of the water splashing on the rocks below was soothing. They sat on a bench to take in the quiet of the moment. Sitting close together deepened their relationship with each other.

"There you are!" Another voice broke the silence, "We didn't know you were in the garden. This is our favorite place." Kim Ly avowed. "Mind if we join you?" she asked as she and Andree walked over to the young couple.

The four sat for several minutes listening to the relaxing music of nature. It was broken by dark black clouds and bolts of lightning lashing the sky followed by loud crackling sound of thunder. Angus put his jacket over Cindi Le's head as everyone began dashing back to the resort. The sprinkles were ahead of the downpour crossing the lake. They reached the resort just as the larger rain drops began to drench the garden.

The night smorgasbord had a variety of fruits: jackfruit, banana, mango, and coconut slices. The fish entrees were fried, baked, or grilled. Other meats included roast beef and lamb. The vegetables included carrots and potatoes.

By the time the Bonnay's and Angus finished their glass of Royan wine, the rain had stopped. The full moon's reflection on the lake brightened the night. Cindi Le and Kim Ly went upstairs and wiped the balcony lounge chairs dry. Cindi Ly noticed the fresh cut flowers on the table.

Andre and Angus lingered at the table while Andre finished off the bottle, "Do you and Cindi Le plan to go horseback riding tomorrow?" he asked.

"Yes, I know she likes horseback riding We have a scheduled a ride after lunch. I understand she did well in an Arabian Horse competition," Angus replied.

"Cindi Le loves horses and did well in competition," Andre proudly said as the two men went up to the suite. The balcony doors were closed since there was a chill in the night air.

After a few hands of whisk, Angus and Cindi Le talked about sitting on the balcony before going to bed.

Kim Ly offered her motherly advice, "Put on your house robes if you go out there."

Each got their house robes and headed for the balcony.

They overheard Kim Ly ask Andre, "Have you seen my blue shoes? I looked under my bed. Check your bed, see if they're under there." Angus looked at Cindi Le and they both smiled.

Sunday morning, the breakfast was catered to their suite. The routine was the same, breakfast in the suite robes, church, and a smorgasbord luncheon.

After church services Angus and Cindi Le changed into their riding clothes before lunch, then they headed for the equine arena. Cindi Le had her hair in a long pony tail with a bright orange cord intertwined. Two horses were saddled and ready for a two-hour ride zigging in and out of the resort's twenty acres.

She selected a black Arabian filly with a black mane and tail. He chose the chocolate Palomino stallion with white mane and tail. He'd never seen a chocolate Palomino before. They were given a map of the trail. Cindi Le proved her riding skills as she stayed with Angus. They stopped at the half way marker on the map to water and rest their horses. The horses enjoyed the carrots that the riders offered them.

Back at the equine arena, they helped the workers to take the saddles and bridles back to the tack room. The workers began washing the horses and walking them to their stalls.

"Boy! That brought back good memories. Cindi Le, I can tell you have good riding skills," Angus declared as they walked from the arena.

"It felt good to ride again," she admitted as she stepped in front of him for a quick kiss.

Back at the resort, the desk clerk called out, "Lieutenant McKay, sir you have a message."

The message read, *Return to the compound ASAP!* Colonel Cunningham.

"That's not fair, I wanted you all to myself." Cindi Le pouted.

Andre understood. Kim Ly felt sorry for her daughter. Cindi Le and Angus kissed good bye as the taxi drove up to take him to the railroad station.

CHAPTER 17

December 1967 Part V

A jeep was waiting for him in Hue. "You from the MACV?" Angus asked the young corporal sitting behind the steering wheel.

"You Lieutenant McKay?" was the response.

The calendar hanging in Colonel Colt's office showed December 17th, 1967. At 0700, Colonel "Colt" was at his desk.

When Angus walked in, the colonel offered him a cup of coffee and a breakfast roll. "Coffee sounds good. I'll skip the roll. What is the emergency?" asked Angus.

"Intelligence boys in Saigon say that there's a difference in your reports compared to the final report from General Tran. You indicate a buildup of traffic on Ho Chi Minh Trail. The General thinks the VietCong is withdrawing for the season. Now, Saigon reports PAVN divisions 320th, 324th and 325th have established strategic positions around Khe Sanh. Headquarters wants to know how you've arrived at an increase on Ho Chi Minh Trail." the colonel stated looking sternly at Angus his concern of the difference in the reports.

Angus studied the message. "Sir, I based my report on supplies not manpower. Khoy pointed out that bicycle and cart tracks heading south were deeper because they were probably loaded with heavier weapons and supplies. The south bound tracks were more to the outside of the trail, meaning foot tracks of men pushing or pulling the supplies were in the middle of the paths. The tracks heading north were not as deep, so we deduced there was less weight heading back north. The middle of the trail had both north and south foot tracks that made it impossible to determine whether the middle tracks could accurately predict troop movement either way. We both agreed that more supplies were being moved south. Plus, the tunnels we discovered had huge amounts of weapons and other supplies. Maybe there are more supplies stored farther south and west of Laos. We have been successful in disrupting the Ho Chi Minh Trail around Khe Sanh. They could have made new trails that we do not know about."

Angus continued, "There have been small skirmishes over the past few months. We probably caught them in their movement south. Sometimes our bombers have missed their targets by ten to fifteen miles because of the clouds. There may be some trails we have missed by not going farther west into the jungles of Laos. Plus, a local villager informed me to check boats going south on the rivers and canals, especially the boats hauling chicken eggs. Our Vietnamese inspectors are afraid of breaking the eggs and therefore do not check what's hidden under them. Weapons!" Angus concluded.

"Well, headquarters thought of adding forces in that area, but a final decision noted that it was not necessary to include Khe Sanh with the ongoing operations. Angus, I believe we have men in the surrounding area that are in imminent danger of a major attack," Colonel Colt sadly admitted. "Are you saying we need to be ready to send them immediate support? Khe Sanh does not have adequate cannon power nor the manpower should a major assault happen!"

"Yes sir, I am," Angus responded with a positive tone.

"OK, McKay. I will back you on the weapon supply traffic on the Ho Chi Minh Trail. My question is how did three PAVN divisions suddenly show up near that old French outpost of Khe Sanh?" the colonel needed answers. "You will meet with the captain in command at Khe Sanh tomorrow. Explain my concerns. They need to stock pile ammo for their weapons, especially ammo for their light cannons. Several men have been wounded by sniper fire. We will have marines on alert just in case," stated Colonel Colt.

On December 18th, Angus was in a chopper heading for Khe Sanh. The captain and Angus agreed on steps to take as outlined by Colonel Colt. They took inventory of men, weapons, and cannons. Both thought larger cannons were needed, but were not available at this time. There were only a few larger cannons at another firebase. Angus agreed to take back four seriously wounded men. It was dark by the time Angus got back to Hue. The wounded were flown on to DaNang.

Colonel Colt was waiting to see Angus at that late hour. He needed to talk to Angus about the report that the MACV reviewed on the security clearances of all nonmilitary personnel working in the compound. MACV had serious concerns about Angus' report.

"Angus, why are you recommending we do back ground checks on the Vietnamese working for us?" asked Colonel Colt in a stern voice.

"Sir, ever since we discovered the tunnels with all the abandoned weapons, ammo and food I have been concerned about someone passing information on to the enemy. Why would the North Vietnam Army leave all of those supplies without any protection?" That thought had been bothering Angus and Khoy for some time.

The colonel stood up, put his hands on his desk and asked, "Lieutenant McKay are you saying we may have been infiltrated by spies at this compound? That is a serious claim!"

"Yes, I am. Remember the operation called for B-52s to bomb the hills where we were told the tunnels existed. But the forecast for continuous rains cancelled the B-52s. I am suggesting that somehow the enemy was informed about the original message, but not the one cancelling the bombing missions. Look at the reports, the second message was on a weekend. The Vietnamese staff does not work on Sunday," he pointed out.

"I gather you have reviewed the entire report on that mission. Do you have any particular person in mind?" Colonel Colt continued his questioning.

"Yes sir. I do! I believe Quan has had the opportunity to steal our messages. He cleans our office and dumps the trash. The trash contains copies of those reports," Angus commented looking up into the colonel's eyes. "Sir, I'm suggesting a background check on Quan immediately," Angus strongly recommended.

"Lieutenant, I will take your report under consideration. You'd better get some sleep. I know it's been a long day for you," the colonel suggested as he turned off his office light.

Cindi Le was happy to see Angus come in the office that Tuesday morning. She smiled and said, "Welcome, good to see you again. Dad was impressed with you. He hopes you'll be able to spend Christmas Eve with us. You want to take in the Christmas decorations downtown tonight?"

That night the two walked the busy sidewalks filled with jubilant people taking in all the Christmas spirit. There were red, green, and white lanterns crisscrossing the narrow streets. Trees sparkled with colorful, lighted decorations. Food vendors were offering soups, candy, chestnuts, warm soupy desserts, and drinks. Churches had life-sized nativity scenes on display, their windows adorned by candles. Up and down the streets, Christmas music could be heard, even "Hello Good Bye", by The Beatles.

Christmas music around the compound was different. Songs like, *"I'll be Home for Christmas"* and *"White Christmas"* blared from the barracks and the hooch.

Angus decided to wear his western suit on Christmas Eve. Cindi Le had on a red and white traditional Ao Dai. It featured silver, sparkling snowflakes falling from her shoulders. She had a small white Lotus flower in her hair.

Kim Ly wore a Green French design dress. It had a lace neckline and cuffs. She also had a small white Lotus in her hair. A diamond necklace rested at the center of her cleavage. She wore a light shade of green eye shadow. Andre had a light green turtleneck sweater under his dark leather sports jacket.

Angus was surprised to see outside decorations on Bonnay's home. Lights were strung across the porch, the post on the porch was wrapped like a candy cane. Inside there was a five-foot tree with lights and Christmas decorations, Many wrapped presents were displayed under the tree. A nativity crib was on the China cabinet. Besides Baby Jesus, Mary and Joseph, Kim Ly had followed the French tradition of adding sentons, such as bakers, a woman selling flowers, a man selling fish, etc.

The Bonnay's welcomed Angus with a hearty *"Chuc mung Giang Sinh,* ("Happy Christmas")

"Merry Christmas to ya'll too." Angus returned their greeting, "Your decorations remind me of home. You have been busy decorating during the last few days," Angus noted.

Flickering flames from the three candles in the center of the dining room table added a warm homey atmosphere. Dinner began with tasty eggrolls. Beef Au Jus with potatoes and carrots were served to Andre and Angus. The women chose a small goose stuffed with chestnuts. Salad consisted of mandarin orange, apple, coconut, and jicama. Red wine was served for the men and white wine for the two ladies.

They laughed and talked about their trip to D'ang T'ang. Andre and Kim Ly told of some of their adventures in the earlier years at the resort. The Bonnay's had questions about Christmas in Texas. Andre talked about Christmas in France and leaving his shoes for 'Pere de Noel to leave little presents and candy in them. Kim Ly knew the Bonnay's would always have a *'buche de noel'*. It is a chocolate cake in the shape of a log.

After the '*buche de noel*' Andre suggested the four should get to the Cathedral around 2300 hours before there would be standing room only. The women began cleaning up the dining table and washing the dishes, they then handed the dishes to the men standing in the door way to put the plates and silverware in the china cabinet.

The women donned their lace veils as they headed for the Phu Cam Cathedral. The midnight Mass included the story of the birth of Jesus, dances honoring the baby, Christmas carols and hymns that put everyone in a festive mood.

"Now we open the gifts", Andre said as they opened the door of their home. It was just before 0200. Angus had put Cindi Le's and the Bonnay's gifts under the tree. He was surprised to see a gift from Texas with his name on it. Kim Ly set out some eggrolls and Christmas pudding. Andre opened a bottle of Royan wine.

Cindi Le loved her necklace and earrings. The engraving on the back of the necklace brought a tear to her eye. Angus helped her put on her necklace. She turned around, threw her arms around his neck and said, "I love your message on the back. I love you, too," she said.

Her parents gave her some new fashionable clothing from Paris. The Bonnays liked the photos of their daughter and Angus standing in front of the Cathedral.

Cindi Le gave Angus a brown leather sport jacket. His parents had sent gifts from Texas to the Bonnay address. The tan pullover sweater and a light western spring jacket from his parents fit perfectly. The McKay's sent some photographs of the ranch and of a black angus bull to the Bonnays. It was a relaxing and festive morning.

Andre announced that they would be spending New Year's Eve at LaParfum. The restaurant had a special dinner with music and dancing.

The question at the office for the rest of the week was whether the PAVN were retreating into Laos and Cambodia. Colonel Colt was concerned about the outposts and firebases around Khe Sanh. He had Angus and the rest of his staff working on various defensive plans to defend that area.

Wednesday night Angus returned to the Bonnays for dinner and a game or two of whist. Kim Ly prepared a glazed ham with sweet potatoes and a salad. After the meal Andre and Angus retired to the back porch to discuss some of the PAVN tactics used against the French. The two bonded when they were together. Cindi Le and Angus won two of three hands of whist. Andre claimed, "It was beginner's luck."

For New Year's Eve La Parfum served a smorgasbord with roast beef, turkey, and goose. A variety of Vietnamese and western appetizers, vegetables, soups, and desserts were enjoyed by the festive group. A bottle of champagne and appropriate glasses was the center piece of each table. Those attending the New Year's celebration were from western countries since the Vietnamese New Year was January 30, 1968. TET would be the Chinese Zodiac Year of the Monkey.

Cindi Le broke from the traditional Vietnamese dress style with an oversized Ao Dai with a daring 'V' neckline. It had a blend of black to green to white. The green was the same shade as the necklace. She wore a white skirt under the Ao Dai. Angus felt she looked stunning and held her tightly as they danced.

Kim Ly had on a traditional blue and white Ao Dai. Andre and Angus wore leather sports jackets over their turtleneck sweaters.

At 2200 the combo band took a break. The food was removed to make more room on the dance floor. Party hats and horns were distributed to help bring in the New Year. Couples danced to slow music and waltzes. The band included the *Hokey Pokey, Mashed Potato, Monkey,* and the *Loco Motion* for the younger generation.

Right before midnight the champagne bottles were uncorked, resolutions were made and everyone sang *'Auld Lange Syne'* followed by hugs and kisses which were shared around the table.

Andre had an early flight so the Bonnay's party left soon after midnight. For all four to fit in the Dauphine, Cindy Le and her mother had to sit in the back seat. Andre and Angus squeezed into the front seat their shoulders touching the doors. At the compound Angus twisted and turned to get out of the car. He turned to say good bye to Andre and Kim Ly. Cindi Le pushed the seat in front of her down and jumped out of the car into the waiting arms of Angus. The two hugged and kissed. When they finally parted, she looked into his eyes and cheerfully said, "This is our year!"

CHAPTER 18

January 1968, Part I

After the holidays Angus and Khoy spent more time observing Vietnamese people in the streets. Some looked like they were counting paces from one building to another or from a tree to an entrance of a building or bridge. People weren't just standing around! They were doing something, but what? There seemed to be more vendors throughout the city.

Khoy asked the owner of the ESSO station across the bridge from the compound if he thought there was an increase in the demand for gasoline. He replied, "Yes, so far gasoline sales this year have been much higher compared to last year." Khoy had grown up in Hue and he dismissed what most vendors were saying that the TET holidays were attracting the villagers. His experience told him that those from rural Vietnam did not come to Hue until five to ten days before they celebrated the Vietnamese New Year, never three or more weeks!

The colonel sent a memo to all MACV staff:

For your information. Recent background checks on our Vietnamese employees revealed there were two who were affiliated with the Communist Party. They are no longer with us. If you suspect any espionage activity, report it to me immediately. Colonel Colt Cunningham

Cindi Le planned to take Angus to the Azura restaurant in Cu Du village which was close to Hue for his birthday. It was known for its Italian menu and it attracted many of the college students not only for the food, but also because there was a small dance floor. On January

10th she picked Angus up at the compound. Angus had on his leather sport coat with a tan turtleneck sweater. Cindi Le was wearing a low cut, blaze orange blouse under a white sweater.

"Where are you taking me?" asked Angus.

"I know you like lasagna. The Azura is known for the best Italian recipes in Vietnam, just ask any college student. It's your birthday and I want to treat you," she explained pulling her light purple skirt past her knees. "We can dance at the Azura. I want to be in your arms tonight all night long," she flirted with him.

Scooters and a few cars were parked at the restaurant despite the rainy weather. The scent of Italian cooking met them at the door. The walls had posters of the Leaning Tower of Pisa, Saint Mark's Square, and the Canals of Venice. There were a couple of posters of Rome's famous fountains. The two found an open table.

A Vietnamese waiter wearing Italian style clothes brought a plate of focaccia bread to their table. Angus ordered lasagna, Cindi Le asked for a small cheese pizza. Both ordered red wine. The waiter brought another plate of focaccia bread with the wine. The record player had four or five Italian songs on the spindle to be played.

Angus and Cindi Le talked about the fun they had had at D'ang T'ang and the Christmas holidays. They danced to "Volare, *nel blu, dipinto di blu*" before their food was delivered. Angus held Cindi Le tight as she put her head on his shoulder.

The lasagna had real authentic Italian flavor. The waiters and servers came to their table and sang "Happy Birthday" in English, then in Vietnamese. The restaurant offered panettone for dessert. The sweet bread and egg-coffee was an added treat. Two more glasses of wine were ordered. Angus and Cindi Le requested they play *"Memories are Made of This"* for their last dance of the evening.

"Here is your birthday gift from me," Cindi Le said handing Angus a small box. It was a dark red garnet ring. "I muon duoc voi ban luon" was engraved on the inside. She translated it for him in English: *I want to be with you always.*

"Cindi Le, this is beautiful. Thank you," commented Angus as he slipped it on his ring finger.

The owner of Azura walked over to their table and asked them to dance one more dance. He pulled out another record and began to play it. Cindi Le smiled, stood up and took Angus' hand. She led him to the dance floor as the *Vietnamese Love Song* began. Angus could feel the meaning of the song as her body clung to him. Her sensuous perfume grasped every one of his senses. He could feel the firmness of her breast as she pulled him still closer. They were the only two on the floor because the others recognized that this was their moment. When the song ended Cindi Le threw her arms around Angus's neck and they embraced in a long slow kiss. A great cheer by everyone in the room erupted for them as the two headed for the door.

"This was a great 23rd birthday! Thank you," he said as they got to her car. The rain had turned to a misty fog. "Can you see to drive back to Hue?" he asked.

"Guess we'll have to try. We both need to be at the office in the morning," she acknowledged.

The weather conditions caused them to take twice as long to get back to the compound. The South Vietnamese gate guard recognized the car and waved them through. She turned the red dauphine around. Angus leaned over, grabbed her hair, and pulled her towards him. Their lips met and they hugged.

Finally, Angus sat back in his seat removing his roving hands from under her tunic. He quietly said, "We'd better stop before I won't be able to. I've got to go in."

"See you in the morning my love. Tell Colonel Colt the fog may cause me to be late," she joked buttoning up her tunic. Angus got out of the car and headed for the BOQ.

Friday afternoon Cindi Le informed Angus that her mother would be attending a medical conference in Saigon Monday and Tuesday. Kim Ly will be leaving for the seminar Sunday night. "I want to cook for you Monday night. We can leave the office together." She asked, "What would you like for dinner?"

"What about beef tips with mushrooms and gravy over rice?" he answered, " We can shop together after work. I can buy what we need at the commissary. Surprise me with one of your famous desserts."

"One other thing, Angus, will you attend Mass with me on Sunday?" she appealed longing for him to agree.

"Why certainly. What time do you plan to pick me up on Sunday?" he asked. After work the two went to the commissary to buy the groceries they would need for Monday night. She took the groceries home with her and Angus stayed at the compound.

Colonel Colt had called for another practice on that night. At 2200 flares were lit. The men knew the positions they were to be. Angus' assignment was to make sure each bunker had enough ammunition. There was some grumbling about the alert being conducted on a Friday night.

Sunday morning Cindi Le picked Angus up to go to Mass at Phu Cam Cathedral. After Mass and the couple were back in the car Cindi Le commented, "It seemed like there were more people than usual today. The priest seemed to be a little nervous." Angus did not respond but did make a mental note of it.

Monday morning Colonel Colt asked Angus if his friend, Khoy knew Russian.

"Can't say, sir. Do you want me to ask him?" Angus asked.

Later that day Khoy entered the colonel's office, "Did you want to see me, sir?"

"Yes, Khoy do you speak Russian?" Colonel Cunningham wanted to know.

"I'm a bit rusty. I've had two years of Russian in my military training. Why do you ask?" Khoy responded.

"We have a serious problem at the radio shack. There were six airmen who intercepted messages from the Russian's ship frequencies. Half of them are in the hospital with malaria. I would like to hire you as a CIA consultant. General Tran is OK with it. You would be paid a consultant's fee. Can you help me?" Colonel Cunningham appealed to Khoy.

"Yes Sir, I would be honored," Khoy committed.

"Good! Thank you. Here's your security badge that will allow you into the radio shack. Report to Captain Bates. He's expecting you. It may take a few weeks before the airmen get cleared to return to work," the colonel said as he stood and handed Khoy the pass.

"Thank you for the opportunity to serve you sir," stated Khoy. He turned and left the commander's office.

Khoy met Angus coming into the office. "You're on your own! I now work for MACV," he told Angus with a big smile.

Then he went on and explained to Angus about the meeting. Cindi Le looked up from her desk. "Good luck over there," she wished Khoy.

Late that afternoon, Cindi Le and Angus headed for her home and a home cooked dinner. There was a break in the dark clouds that had been releasing rain drops most of the day. The monsoon season continued with a windy, cold mist.

It was an easy dinner for Cindi Le. Angus turned on the TV and sat down on the couch. Cindi Le mixed up a fruit salad, stirred the beef tips and mushrooms while preparing the rice. She had added some herbs to enhance the taste. Angus helped set the table. He poured a glass of ginger ale for himself and a glass of red wine for Cindi Le. They held hands and said a prayer.

"Khoy seemed happy to help the colonel at the radio shack. I will miss having him around," Angus said. Khoy's assignment was the main topic of their dinner discussion.

For dessert, she served a mini mooncake that they had purchased at the commissary.

"Doesn't taste as good as the one you made," Angus mentioned as he took the last bite. He helped with the after-dinner chores by drying the dishes that she handed to him.

Cindi Le walked outside to check if the full moon was visible. She hurried back inside, grabbed a blanket and guided Angus to the back porch to look at the moon in all its glory. They sat under the blanket for several minutes before the cold misty night ground fog penetrated the blanket. They returned to the inside and sat on the couch.

She began gently kissing Angus on his neck and cheeks. She unbuttoned his shirt and started to rub his chest with her fingernails. He responded by kissing her forehead, the tip of her nose and then each ear where he got the hint of the seductive scent of her perfume before moving to her cheeks. She guided his hand to the inside of her blouse. He began slowly unbuttoning. At the bottom button Angus pulled her blouse open revealing a laced bra. He undid the snap and pulled her tighter to him. She locked his lips with hers in a passionate kiss. He could feel the rapid rhythm of his heart beat, his breathing became more difficult. He pulled away from her, gasping for air.

"Cindi Le! I need air!" Angus managed to say between wheezes.

"Are you alright?" she asked with a worried look. She wiped the sweat from his forehead.

"Just need some air," he said still breathing heavily holding his chest.

Cindi Le began getting her clothes back together. She hurried to the kitchen to get Angus some water. "Here, drink this, maybe it will help," she said handing him the glass of water.

After a few minutes, Angus could breathe more easily. He felt better.

"I'm sorry Cindi Le. I seem to get this way every time we get passionate with each other," he commented walking out to the back porch for fresh air. "Maybe I should see a doctor."

"That's a good idea. I'll try to control myself. Angus, it's just I love you so much!" she replied.

"Cindi Le, where did you learn to kiss like you do? Your touches excite me. Where did you learn all that?" Angus finally asked.

"I listened to the upper classmates at the French school. They would brag about their adventures with the French soldiers. Until I met you, I didn't even think of doing those things. You bring out the woman in me. Angus, I love you," she explained squeezing his hand.

The two went on to discuss the things they had in common and how they plan to address their cultural and religious differences until it was time to take Angus back to the compound.

CHAPTER 19

January 1968, Part II

The office atmosphere was tense the rest of the week. Colonel Colt had received reports from Khe Sanh about periodic enemy movements south of highway 9 intersection, also in the Annamite hills north of the special forces camp at Lang Vei, and up along the Rao Quan River. Khe Sanh area included four hilltop outposts, a mountaintop observation, the village of Khe Sanh and Lang Vei.

The colonel ordered the Khe Sanh Combat Base and all outposts throughout the area to be on high alert. The marines stationed at Hue were put on ready, yellow alert meaning no one was to leave the compound.

On January 21st Colonel Colt received a message from Khe Sanh Combat Base:

Heavy firefight launched by NVA at all firebases and outposts. Khe Sanh under siege. Combat Base under continuous bombardment. Est. over 2 divisions. Over 1,200 tons of ammo destroyed by direct mortar hit. Helicopters damaged by the blast.

"Angus, *l*ooks like your reports were accurate," the colonel remarked to the young first lieutenant. "Hanoi has introduced tanks. We'll need to get more ammo to the Combat Base."

"Sir, Highway 9 was destroyed last fall, before your time. NVA ambushed our convoy. All supplies in that area are now done by air," explained Angus.

Angus' orders were to coordinate Saigon and DaNang reinforcements and supplies to Khe Sanh Combat Base. Saigon approved two additional battalions, which required massive air support of helicopters, naval air craft and C-130's. A new technology that signaled advanced warnings of approaching enemy by sophisticated electronic sensing systems proved beneficial. It was being monitored from the Nakhon Phanom Air Base, Thailand.

On the following day the PAVN captured the village of Khe Sanh. Some villagers headed to Lang Vei, which was three klicks west, other villagers escaped to the Khe Sanh Combat Base. Then, typical of previous enemy attacks, the assaults ceased. But, not the enemy sightings and annoying shelling of 122 mm, 152 mm, and 130 mm cannons for the first time in the war. The rain and slimy red clay made it difficult for the men handling the cannon shells, to walk around stepping in mud holes. Red clay caked boots, clothing, and bare skin covered with clay made all movements difficult.

The day after the fall of the Khe Sanh village, the PAVN turned their tank Battalion and the 24th regiment forces to Ben Houei Sane. It was a small Laotian outpost of 700 Laotian soldiers. The Laotians surrendered to the North Vietnam army. After three continuous hours of pounding by the enemy tanks the Americans and the South Vietnamese made the decision to join the Ben Houei Sane villagers retreating to the safety of Lang Vei and the Khe Sanh Combat Base.

Angus and the MACV team worked through the week end. Angus and Cindi Le did not see each other.

Colonel Colt kept in contact with the captains throughout Corps I. Over their radios, he could hear the mortars and cannons hitting around the bunkers. The number of dead and wounded marines kept mounting. "Angus, see how quickly we can get some of the helicopters from Camp Evans to KSCB. We need to get the wounded and KIA to DaNang," the colonel ordered Angus.

On January 25th, C-130's with protection of the marine's jet fighters from the Midway Air Craft Carrier and from DaNang Air Base dropped food, medical supplies and a six-man Special Forces team at Khe Sanh Combat Base.

Colonel Colt kept telling his staff and other officers to stay alert. Everyone was on a twelve-hour shift to allow for rest and sleep. He wanted to be certain everyone knew their stations. He told Cindi Le and the other Vietnamese staff to take Monday and Tuesday off to celebrate the TET. The Khe Sanh offensive was not going well and the MACV office continued to communicate with each outpost around Khe Sanh.

On a dense foggy morning January 31st at 0340, six North Vietnamese dressed in South Vietnamese uniforms over took the two South Vietnamese guards at the back gate. The noise caught the immediate attention of the guard stationed in the tower. He turned his machine gun toward the back gate and began firing at the silhouettes who were running past the back gate. He could barely make out the figures in the dense fog, but he was successful in preventing a truck from entering the compound.

The enemy released over forty mortars and a shock wave of rockets into the compound area. The MACV compound came alive with men carrying weapons and ammunition scurrying to their positions. They could hear the high whining of the mortars falling from the sky. Flares barely lit the foggy morning. The tower guard continued relentless firing even after the tin roof of the tower was blown off and he was wounded.

Light from the explosions up and down the rows of trucks and tanks caught some of the North Vietnamese sappers moving out of that area. Sappers were the elite units of the North Vietnamese Army. They were lead units, trained to break through barbed wire barriers and other obstacles. The scout helicopter that had been locked in the repair shop for maintenance went unnoticed. Sharp shooters stationed in the second floor targeted the sappers and many were killed trying to escape the area.

Khoy and the airmen, with their backup sharp shooters held off the attack on the radio shack. A VietCong tied to a palm tree about ten feet up had good position to fire whenever the men in the bunkers stood above the sandbags. He was nearly invisible to the men on the ground. A sharp shooter on the second floor of the MACV Headquarters focused on the origination of the green tracers. He kept firing into that spot until there were no more green tracers.

The men in the bunkers that were six sand bags high at each corner of the MACV building stopped the PAVN from penetrating farther into the compound. There were bunkers at the base of the Truong Tien bridge and down at the Perfume River at the Navy's Landing Craft Utility.

Immense smoke from the mortars and from small arms blended with the fog that lingered all throughout Hue preventing air support.

On the north side of the Perfume River, forty PAVN soldiers had penetrated the great walls of the Citadel. General Tran's South Vietnamese army held off the PAVN as well as they could although only half of his troops had returned from their homes after celebrating the TET. But in the early hours of dawn, they eventually had to give up their position at the Hue Citadel Airfield and retreat to Fort Mang Ca yielding the Citadel to the enemy. All the airplanes at the airfield were destroyed, including two new Cessna's that had been delivered only the day before to replace the older models. The PAVN raised their gold-starred blue and red flag inside the Citadel for all to see.

The southside of Hue was being overtaken by two VietCong battalions. They had seized the Province Headquarters, the police station, the prison, hospital, the Post Office, and other government buildings along Le Loi Street. When they captured the local radio station the PAVN began broadcasting to the faithful supporters of the PAVN to join their cause and take part in the revolution.

By early morning all the PAVN military targets were secured except for the Navy's Landing Craft area, the MACV compound and the Mang Ca in the Citadel.

Since MACV had sent some of its marines to support Khe Sanh Combat Base, Colonel Cunningham requested reinforcements from DaNang. The TET attack on DaNang had been crushed within hours. Saigon approved the request and two units of marines were sent to Hue. It took almost two hours for the reinforcements to arrive. They crossed the Phu Cam Canal bridge south of the MACV and turned on to Phan Dinh Phung, a street that ran parallel to the canal. They immediately ran into enemy fire. The VietCong knew they were outnumbered and disappeared in the fog.

The DaNang marines included four M48 Patton tanks. The South Vietnamese soldiers had four Zippers(M67). This smaller version had a flame thrower that could belch out hot flames over the length of a football field. Each one carried a 250-gallon drum filled with a mixture of gasoline, napalm, oil, and other chemicals that created a flame reaching 1,800 degrees. The DaNang commander ordered the tanks to cross the bridge, but a North Vietnamese antitank shelling stopped the first tank.

The marines made it across the bridge but when they turned south, they were met with heavy machine gun fire up and down the street, from second story windows and from sharp shooters tied to palm trees. One marine ran toward the machine gun fire. He heaved a grenade in the direction of the machine gunner and knocked out the gun. Marines charged across the bridge and came under fire by automatic weapons and recoilless rifle fire from the enemy hiding in the shrubbery along the Citadel wall.

The marines began retreating across the bridge but they were caught in a cross fire. Wounded marines who had been caught in the cross fire were lying in the open. Other marines hotwired some of the Vietnamese trucks that had been abandoned. The vehicles were used to recover the wounded and the dead from the chaos. It was 1000 before the MACV Compound and a helicopter landing zone in the soccer field west of the Navy Landing Craft Utility ramp along the Perfume River were cleared of the enemy. Despite the foggy conditions (locals called it *crachin)* helicopters were called in to evacuate the more severely wounded even though the ceiling was below 500 feet.

Hue residents were rudely awakened in the early morning attack. Trucks with loud speakers were blaring at the residents to come out. Sympathizers to the PAVN and VietCong were pointing at homes that were considered to have helped the South Vietnamese and Americans. "There, nguy (a dirty term) Vietnamese," the collaborators yelled as they pointed to various houses along the street.

"Come out and let us re-educate you. Some of you will be sent to Hanoi." came from the loud speakers on trucks slowly moving up the streets on the southside of Hue. VietCong soldiers broke into homes dragging men, women, and children out into the wet streets. Some tried hiding, but search teams went into those homes. Any one arguing, hiding, or trying to escape was shot.

"Cindi Le hide your jewelry! Quickly!" Kim Ly shouted to her daughter down the hallway. Cindi Le quickly looked around. Then stuffed her jewelry, including the necklace that Angus had given her, between tampons in a half full box. She slipped on her ear rings as she ran to the door. 'Pray 'Our Father' and a 'Hail Mary' don't agitate them," her mother warned her. They were seized with fear, but peacefully left their home and joined hundreds of others, who were crying out loudly and hugging. All feared what was going to happen to them. They were loaded on trucks. Enroute to the Phu Cam Cathedral they passed, numerous dead and dying men, women, and children, many still in their rain-soaked sleeping clothes. The shock of hearing their cries for mercy and help struck at the hearts of those crammed into the trucks.

Four hundred, including Kim Ly and Cindi Le, were taken to the Catholic Cathedral, along with businessmen, teachers, and professors from the Hue University where they were encouraged to pledge their allegiance to the Hanoi government. A young priest and four young boys were hiding in a choir dressing room on the church balcony and peeking through the small holes which allowed fresh air into the tiny room to keep the choir clothing dry. They witnessed the kangaroo court proceedings conducted by the North Vietnamese officials. The priest and boys watched as over three hundred were marched outside to the church's cemetery. The screaming, the begging cries and shouting was horrific. Then, the ominous sound of gun shots filled the morning air. Cindi Le and Kim Ly fell silently into the mass grave.

The TET attack kept Angus busy supplying the bunkers with ammo. When needed, he helped the medics as they provided first aid to the wounded. He worked his way to the bunker near the bridge. Bullets flash by as he zigzagged toward that bunker. One dead marine was slumped over the top of the sand bags protecting the bunker. The dead marine had neck and head wounds. PAVN sharp shooters tied high up in palm trees kept taking pot shots at the dead man. The other marine had been seriously wounded and was wailing for his mother to stop the burning pain. Angus pulled him out of the sight of the sharp shooters closer to the front of the bunker, he called the chaplain on the radio. Chaplain Walsh was at the Naval Landing administering Last Rites. A marine saw the situation and fired a smoke bomb to provide protection for the chaplain as he worked his way running from cover to cover toward the bunker under the bridge. Walsh looked at Angus for a sign about the marine's condition. Angus shook his head, "no". The chaplain placed a crucifix in the marine's hand. The marine seemed to accept his condition and began his last confession, *"Forgive me, Father, for I have sinned. I stole jewelry from a dead Vietnamese, I gave some of it for payment at a whore house. I have killed the enemy with no remorse. Father, I'm*

sorry for all the sins I ever committed. Please don't tell my momma."
His empty eyes gazed at Father Walsh as he died in the chaplain's
arms. The chaplain gently shut the young marine's eyes. He turned to
Angus.

"McKay, you'll forget what you just heard! Never, I mean never
are you to repeat it to anyone! That's a violation of what is between
this marine and his God. Do you understand me?" he demanded
starring at Angus with piercing eyes. He stepped back and stood up.
A sharp shooter across the river saw the flash of the religious cross
on the chaplain's helmet, took aim and pulled the trigger. Angus
quickly reached out to pull him down out of harm's way, but it was
too late. The bullet smashed into the helmet and the top part of
Captain Kendric Walsh's head splattered against the back of the
bunker wall. Angus felt limp. Acids in his stomach burned his insides
and he could feel the sensation crawl up his throat. His mind clouded.
His knees caved in and he fell on his butt. His jaw locked up. It took
a few seconds for him to gather his thoughts.

He found the strength to radio for marines to join him in the
bunker. He pulled the three dead bodies to one side of the bunker and
covered the upper half of their bodies with his own poncho as best as
he could. He looked up and saw two marines running toward the
bunker. He pulled a smoke bomb from one of the dead men and
threw in the direction of the two marines, giving them some cover.
The marines jumped over the sandbags into the bunker. They looked
at the grim situation and one made the sign of the cross when he saw
the cross on Walsh's helmet.

"Keep close to the front of the bunker," warned Angus. "There's
a sharp shooter either in an upper window or up in one of the palm
trees somewhere across the river who is able to look down at an
angle so he can see the back of the bunker. We'll have to remove the
bodies later when we can. You guys OK? I've got more ammo to
deliver," Angus yelled over the constant noise of the mortars and gun
fire. He left the two marines hugging close to the front of the bunker

because they recognized the consequences as they stared at the pile of corpses.

Back in the MACV office, Colonel Colt saw Angus come through the door. The colonel caught the sign of bewilderment and fatigue in the eyes of Angus. He'd seen that look in Korea. Angus explained the experience in the bunker with the dying marines and Chaplain Walsh.

"I'm sorry about that, Angus, you need to rest. You've been running from bunker to bunker for hours keeping the marines supplied with ammo and food. I'm ordering you to hit the sack for a few hours and report back to me. I know it's a real chaos situation out there. However, we're beginning to get a handle on this attack," said the colonel whose clothes were wet with days of perspiration his eyes were blood shot and a three-day beard showed streaks of gray sounded exhausted himself. Angus agreed, but first headed to the chapel to find peace of mind. At the cross he fell on his knees praying for all those marines being killed and wounded, for all those civilians caught up in the war. He prayed for the safety of Cindi Le and her mother. Angus showered, shaved, and crawled in between the sheets. He could hear the continuous firing of small arms and of grenades exploding before falling to sleep.

Street fighting had killed many civilians trying to escape the chaos throughout the city. Dead and wounded men, women and children were scattered along the streets of Hue. The eerie night was filled with sounds people moaning, crying, and dying. Frightened animals wondered around searching for food. The slow flow of the Perfume River carried dead human and animal bodies farther downstream.

CHAPTER 20

FEBRUARY 1968

It was four heavy foggy days of continuous fighting before the marines could secured the University of Hue and the Joan of Arc School and church. Patton tanks rolled down Le Loi street providing protection and fire power for the marines. The enemy was well entrenched in each building along Le Loi Street.

The marines had to secure each room in the schools. They became easy targets for the enemy as the entered each room where the enemy was hiding. Angus heard the officers talking about marines walking into such dangerous areas but they were without any solutions.

"Maybe tear gas will get the enemy to try to escape," suggested Angus. "We have tear gas and gas masks on the third floor down the hall from the chapel."

A tear gas launcher held sixty-four canisters. It could fire 16 tear gas canisters in four volleys. The marines slipped on their gas masks and began clearing the treasury building. The eye burning gases chased the enemy out in the open gasping for air and rubbing their eyes. The tear gas program helped the marines to move more quickly from building to building. The next building to be retaken was the post office. In some situations, the flash grenades were effective in driving the enemy out in the open.

After the Hue hospital was secured the marines found the Mayor of Hue and his body guard hiding in the attic. They had been in the attic for four days. One wing of the hospital was designated as the psych wing. A few of the PVNA were mixed with psych patients, making it difficult for the marines to determine who to arrest. Military boots exposed the enemy dressed in gowns. At the city's prison, the marines captured a sharp shooter with a Russian rifle, M-16s and several grenades. The enemy began steadily pulling back. Later Colonel Colt received a message about Lang Vei being overrun and destroyed by PVNA. A few marines had made it to Khe Sanh Combat Base. There continued to be heavy fighting along the Laos border.

"We need to find out if the enemy is planning a counter attack," stated the commander.

"What about the CIA's helicopter? It has been in the maintenance shop but I understand it was ready to fly the day of the attack. The tower guard's quick reaction may have caused the snappers to skip the shop," suggested Angus.

"Does anyone know how to fly it?" questioned Colt Cunningham.

No one spoke up. "I know someone," Angus spoke up. "Khoy can!"

"Get him over here," ordered the colonel.

Twenty minutes later, Khoy was standing in front of the assembled officers.

"Khoy, Angus tells us you are a certified helicopter pilot. Is that true?" one of the other officers questioned.

"Yes sir, I am." Khoy replied with a prideful smile.

"You two get your butts out to the maintenance shop and see if you can crank up that 'Loach' (military nickname of the OH 6A Helicopter). It's been sitting there for weeks. Hopefully the maintenance crew has it ready to go." Colonel Cunningham directed his orders to Angus and Khoy.

The two found the helicopter had been repaired and was signed off to fly again. Angus grabbed a flak jacket and joined Khoy in the cockpit. "The colonel wants us to check out the territory along the river down to Khe Sanh Combat Base. Angus, do you have a camera and binoculars?" Khoy questioned Angus as he checked the gauges for fuel and oil pressure. The two were crammed inside the tiny cockpit.

The OH 6A, Cayuse, taxied clear of the shop. Khoy revved up the engines for a final engine check. The helicopter lifted upward and headed northwest to the river. "Man! This feels good," declared Khoy. He tested the various controls. "It's like riding a bicycle," he explained to Angus.

Khoy's scouting instincts started coming back to him. He dropped down 'til the skids of the OH 6A touched the tops of the Elephant grass. "Sometimes the VietCong would lay so low that the grass would cover them," he explained. Khoy had honed his skills so well he could detect a lit cigarette in the shadows of the trees. His keen senses allowed him to determine if tracks were new or old.

They zigzagged back-and-forth from the river to the south until they could see Khe Sanh Combat Base through the heavy fog. Then they turned around and headed back toward Hue.

"Wait!" Angus shouted above the air noise, "I thought I saw some Black Pajamas running from that tree line to our right."

Khoy dropped the helicopter below tree level. Green tracers flashed all around and pings pounded the helicopter. "Take this thing up and let's get out of here," implored Angus.

As they were climbing, a .51 caliber round penetrated the aluminum skin near the tail rotor. Angus and Khoy heard a loud whoomp sound as the ground-to-air missile exploded. The Loach began vibrating and bouncing through the air. The tail rotor was flapping in the wind. Khoy struggled to straighten the flight level. The pitch link, a rotor head component that's critical to maintaining level flight, had big holes punched through it. Khoy headed for the river to his left. He called, "MAY DAY, MAY DAY, this is FoxTrot One. Heading northeast along the Ben Hai River, five klicks northeast of Khe Sanh. Does anyone read me, over?"

"Roger FoxTrot One, read you five by five. This is Vulture One and Vulture Two. We're behind you at Lang Vei. Throw out some red smoke!"

"This is Hotel Two, the Jolly Green Giant. We read you five by five. We're over Hue and changing course to follow the river to you. Will let you know when we see the red smoke."

"Passing over Highway 9 east of the Rock Pile. Losing altitude," Khoy reported struggling with the controls to keep the Loach flying straight. Angus searched the back seat for a smoke bomb. Khoy flipped on the emergency frequency switch to start squawking his location.

"Enemy coming out of the woods! Firing at us!" Angus pointed down as the two flew over the tree line, "Ten or fifteen men."

Khoy yelled at Angus, "Throw the red smoke!"

The smoke grenade went flying out into space. As if fell from the sky it released a red smoke trail all the way to the ground.

"Foxtrot One, we got the red smoke!"

The two Vultures were A-7 Corsairs were off the Midway Aircraft Carrier. The jets had just been introduced in Vietnam. The swept back wings were less than thirty-nine feet. The subsonic jet was a new light attack aircraft that required only a pilot. It was designed to carry more weapons with better accuracy. It carried nine bombs and two side winders.

The two pilots began talking to each other, "Let me drop down and unload my two napalms. You follow with your cannon's a blazing."

"Roger that. Let's burn some ass!" Vulture Two waited until the smoke from the two bombs had cleared enough to spot any movement. He picked off three who were running toward a rice paddy. The flames from the grassland turned the green plants black. White smoke rose upward. Black smoke followed the white smoke.

"That should discourage them from chasing FoxTrot One. I'll hang around to see if any more want to show up. Saw some red bubbling up from the rice paddy."

"Roger, I'll jump ahead of FoxTrot One. Looks like he's struggling to pull up. Hope he makes it over those hills of trees!"

"FoxTrot One, this is Jolly Green Giant. We got you in our sights. Pull up! Pull up! You're not going to make it over the trees!"

"We're losing power," Khoy said to Angus in a calm voice. The tail rotor was twirling in the wind. Khoy tried to increase power by dipping the Loach downward as the trees rapidly came closer. The tail rotor tore into the branches. Leaves and limbs jammed the tail gearbox. The tail section had begun to twist. Blades of the main rotor began shearing the limbs. The two-man crew heard metal bending and the main frame screeching as it was being torn apart. Motors were whining and warning lights were flashing and a horn began to beep. The cockpit flipped on its side and slipped below the tail rotor. Angus was looking straight down fifty feet or more to a rocky ground. The OH 6A abruptly came to a standstill. Flames flared up as fuel began to drip on the leaves and broken limbs.

"Hey, what are you doing?" Angus cried out in a frightened voice.

"Saving your life!" Khoy pulled his identification tag from his uniform and stuffed it in Angus's shirt pocket. Then, he put both feet on Angus's chest and began pushing him backward out of the scout helicopter. Angus lost his grip on the seat and began falling head first down through the branches. Each branch scratched and ripped his exposed skin. A pain in his shoulder caused him to cry out. He tried to grab a limb only to be twisted another way falling sideways. Above him he heard the explosion as two grenades exploded. The OH 6A disintegrated into tiny pieces of hot metal piercing his clothing that was not protected by the flak jacket. He felt burning sensations on his legs and arms as he was twisted into a tumbling position and tossed around the branches like a pinball machine. He could hear himself groaning: "ouch!" "oof!" and "Ow!" There was a loud snap, sounding like a bat cracking at home plate, and he felt extreme pain below his left knee. He hit the rocky ground solidly on his left heel causing an electrical shock throughout his whole body. He felt a pain shoot up his leg as bones and muscles in his feet stopped abruptly. His body crumbled and he continued to roll ten to fifteen more feet down an incline bouncing off rocks.

The Jolly Green Giant crew of four witnessed the entire scene. The explosion had blown the cockpit into small pieces of molten plastic and metal. Flames charred the tail section of the scout chopper. It was all that was left of the OH6A. The pararescue team was already in a hover position trying to locate the victim at the base of the hill.

"I got him! He has rolled beyond the tree line to your right. Hold it there," the pararescuer instructed the pilot. The Sikorsky HH-3E moved to the right and held steady. The power hoist began unwinding the cable as the pararescuer began rappelling himself down toward Angus' crumbled body.

"Man, this guy is beat up. But, he's alive! Low Pulse. Signs of multi fractures. Dislocated left shoulder for sure. Knee badly damaged. I see bone! It's a compound! His feet are pointing in opposite directions," the pararescurer reported back to the pilot.

"Do what you can. Get him on the body board and let's get the hell out of here," the pilot commanded as he looked around for signs of the enemy. Angus was lashed onto a body board. The power hoist began winding and soon Angus and the pararescuer were inside the

Sikorsky HH-3E. The chopper rose above the burning trees and the black smoke.

The medic and the gunner began first aid procedures stopping the bleeding, applying oxygen, disinfecting his scratches, and wrapping the fractures. They were able to slip his dislocated shoulder back in place. Angus was given morphine. They kept questioning Angus to keep him from passing out. They pulled his trousers down and tattooed his buttock. It was a temporary ink-stamped "tattoo" of two green boots on his buttocks verifying the para jumpers had "saved his ass."

As the Jolly Green Giant approached Hue, the pilot called DaNang about the rescue. He was told the DaNang hospital could not take any more wounded. Their medical supplies and operating rooms were destroyed by mortars and they no longer had the necessary equipment to handle any wounded.

The pilot decided to land behind the MACV's compound. The city of Hue was secured, but fighting continued in the Citadel on the other side of the Perfume River. He noticed people gathered near the soccer field. TV cameras and reporters focused on six congressmen. As the helicopter set down a whirlwind of dirt and debris caused the crowd to turn their backs and cover their faces. The crew began transferring Angus on to a litter to carry him into the MACV building. Bloody bandages wrapped around his arms and legs where hot shrapnel from the explosion of the helicopter had burned his skin. Blood stains on the gauze that had been wrapped around his head down under his chin. The crowd gasped as they moved closer to the helicopter to see what was happening.

The congressmen were in Hue to assess the damage by the enemy. The senators were on the committee of the Secretary of Defense to report back to the president. Senator Vaughn was chairman of the committee. He represented Florida and Senator Morgan represented Ohio. The assistant to the Defense Secretary Randall Rockford was included in the factfinding mission. Captain

Carl Thompson was a medical doctor, who had joined the inspection team in Saigon. He was the doctor assigned to travel with dignitaries on their stops in Vietnam. Others in the audience included Colonel Colt Cunningham and other MACV officers from Saigon. Walter Cronkite, anchor news reporter for CBS and his staff had left the area earlier that day to fly back to the states.

General Tran and Major Lin with some of his men, and local Vietnamese dignitaries were in attendance. The Stars and Stripes reporters were on hand to take photos of the senators. The two corsairs dropped down to a thousand feet above the ground, waved their wings and headed toward the Midway Aircraft Carrier, twenty miles out on the South China Sea. Their fuel gauges had begun flashing "low fuel"

The crowd was looking up as Vulture 1 and Vulture 2 passed over head. The effects of the morphine began wearing off and Angus being mentally foggy, tried to figure out where he was and why are all those people were there looking up at the sky. He noticed a young Vietnamese boy running toward the congressmen. The boy tossed a grenade in front of them. Angus' military instinct took control over his mind and body. He rolled off the body board and just as he rolled on top of the grenade, it misfired with a flash of smoke and a loud fizzling sound. The force was enough to throw him up in the air. He landed on his back. The flak jacket had absorbed most of the blast. He felt the heat burning his chest. Sparks from the grenade ignited parts of his loose clothing. Two of the paramedic team saw what was happening and rushed to him and began extinguishing the flames that blackened his fatigues.

The crowd had turned to run away from the scene. The military police assigned to protect the congressmen pushed each man to the ground and partially covered them as they knelt over them. A Stars and Stripes photographer captured the moment Angus was blown backwards.

Angus blacked out. The rescuers immediately began trying to revive Angus.

The pilot told Colonel Colt that the local hospitals, including the Midway were either damaged or over loaded with wounded. Senator Vaughn ran up and asked in an irate tone, "Are you saying this officer, who just saved our lives, is considered collateral damage? I am not accepting that!"

Major Lin stepped forward, holding pieces of the grenade, "Sir, it looks like it was a North Vietnamese homemade concussion grenade. You can see from some of remains that the powder was diluted with ash and dirt," he stated as he showed his hands. "It was a defective grenade that saved his life and those of the senators from the United States."

Senator Vaughn was livid. "Fine! What are you going to do with this soldier?" he demanded.

The crowd was silent, no one answered.

"I tell you what I'm going to do. He's going back to Washington with us," he blurted out. He turned to the Assistant Defense Secretary Randall Rockford, "Tell some of the traveling reporters they will have to find another way home. There are C-7's landing in Washington every day." Then he turned to the Jolly Green Giant crew, "There's a Pan Am sitting in DaNang. Take this man there. Transfer him and as much medical equipment and medication that you'll need. He's going home with us!"

Angus was put back on the helicopter and immediately air lifted to DaNang. The pilot called up base operations and explained the situation. He told them that Senator Vaughn had taken charge. "There is a doctor from Saigon who is touring with the inspection team from Saigon. I think the senator is assuming the doctor will be going with them," he reported.

The medical staff at DaNang began collecting whatever they could afford to send on the plane. Two nurses headed for the commercial 707 to see what could be done to make a suitable bed. They had four rows of seats taken out to make space for a makeshift bed. No one questioned the decision.

The fifty-mile air trip to DaNang took less than a half hour. The air rescue team had already started administering oxygen and blood. They were also considering what medical supplies they could provide.

At DaNang the unconscious Angus was transferred to the jet liner. The crew had been alerted to the changes. The plane was topped out with fuel and a new flight plan to Washington had been filed. The senator and the traveling party flew back to DaNang with the Jolly Green Giant crew. The flight plan called for a stopover at Yokota AFB, Japan, there to McChord AFB, Washington and the last leg of the flight to Andrews AFB, Washington, D.C.

Captain Thompson began examining Angus's wounds. He noted a probable neck injury, and signs of a dislocated shoulder that had been slipped back in place. He saw a possible cracked shoulder blade, a fractured humerus, possible sprained wrist, a severed shattered tibia, fibula damage around the ankle, and moderate abrasions on face, nose, and arms. A cut across his forehead had dried blood covering that location of the cut. One black eye was closed. Angus' bridge of his nose had several deep scratches that would require stitches. A lip cut had bled down his chin. Branche cuts marked up and down both arms.

The medical team began carefully cutting through his charred bloody clothes. After cleaning and sanitizing his bare skin they covered him with a sheet and an army blanket.

The doctor started with a sling on his fractured left arm, resting it tightly to his chest to minimize movement while being cognizant of the dislocated shoulder. He wrapped the wrist with an Ace bandage that the nurses from DaNang had brought aboard as part of the medical supplies that the hospital could provide. They cleansed the blood from the scratches on his face and arms. Captain Thompson put a neck brace on him to reduce any head movement that could further worsen a neck injury. He then turned to Angus' compound leg fracture. He tied the upper part of the leg to the make shift cot to keep movement at a minimum. The same for below the area where the bone had broken through the skin. He carefully covered the exposed leg bone with some gauze that had been doused with Dakin's disinfectant solution. Last on his list was to wrap Angus's ankle tightly.

"What about wrapping his jaw?" asked one of the nurses.

"Yes, in case he has a broken jaw, we should take precaution with that too," concurred Doctor Thompson. "Which one of you volunteered to be with him to Yokota AFB? Understand you're getting five-day temporary duty status. Enjoy your visit to Japan," he added.

"I am going stay with him as far as Yokota to monitor his vital signs. Someone is to replace me there." the short, brunet nurse replied. "The TDY includes trading our surplus medical supplies for some we are short on. The TET attack emptied our supply of X-ray films and a few other items," she stressed.

"Good luck," Captain Thompson said as he left Angus and the nurse.

The 707 roared down the runway and lifted off to the Yokota AFB, 2,400 miles away. The two senators and the Assistant Defense Secretary were in the business section with three reporters. The pilot knew he had to find smooth air so there would not be too much jostling on Angus' wounded body.

The nurse sat on a seat across from Angus. His breathing was helped with the, oxygen being administered, via, a nasal cannula. The nurse's responsibility was to monitor his blood pressure and heart rate to make sure nothing dropped to a critical level, including his respiratory rate. The only bag hanging on the IVPB pole was to control the flow rate of antibacterial drugs. Blood plasma was handy if a transfusion became necessary.

Halfway through the flight the pilot and Senator Vaugh walked back to check on Angus. The nurse put down the book she was reading and told them, "He's doing fine so far. I tried to talk to him several minutes ago, but did not get a response. Vitals are holding. You must have found some smooth air. What is our altitude?" she asked.

"We've picked up some tail winds at 38,000 feet. We'll be a little ahead of schedule. I've notified Yokota of our revised time and ordered fuel, dinner, drinks, and snacks. We should be on the ground under two hours. The next leg to McChord is the long one. Oh, they have your replacement packed and ready to take off with us," the pilot informed the nurse. "Good luck on getting some of your needed medical supplies. Enjoy a little rest time, I understand it got pretty intense at DaNang," the pilot commented.

Senator Vaughn said nothing, but kept staring at Angus' puffed up, black and bruised face and the quietness of his expression.

The bright stars above and the runway lights below shined in the windless night. The pilot lined the Pan Am up on runway 18 and the huge plane began a smooth glide to touchdown. The wheels screeched and bounced as they touched the pavement. The plane vibrated and jerked as the crew applied brakes.

The nurse noticed a grimace on Angus' face. His one good eye opened wide and he nervously looked up and down, then his pupil moved from side to side for the first time since they'd left Vietnam.

"Lieutenant McKay, can you hear me?" she asked.

His blue eye focused on her in a blank stare.

"Sir, if you hear me, blink once," the nurse calmly stated as she stood up, walked over to him, and looked directly down at him.

His open eye blinked once.

"Lieutenant, you're in a 707-jet heading to Walter Reed Hospital. You have several broken bones that need immediate medical attention. If you are in severe pain now, blink once. If no pain blink twice," she instructed.

He blinked with a grimace on his battered face.

"OK, I've been authorized to increase your pain medication," the nurse stated and injected him with another low dose of morphine. "You'll feel a little better in a few minutes," she assured him. She soaked a small hand towel in cold water and laid it across his dry lips. She penciled in her report that Angus woke up during landing grimacing in pain. Communicates with one blink for 'yes' and two blinks for 'no'.

The lead vehicle led the plane to a parking space. A fuel truck was waiting to begin transferring over 22,000 gallons of fuel into the 707. Another truck pulled up with food and drinks. The crew, along with the two senators and reporters stepped outside on the runway to stretch their legs. The navigator walked over to the weather room to get the current weather report for the next leg of their flight to McChord AFB, 4,800 miles away. There were 40,000-foot thunderclouds building up near the Pacific shoreline of Washington and Oregon. The forecast was to expect tail winds on their descent at McChord AFB.

A tall, thin nurse with a short hair cut was walking from the terminal toward the plane. She stopped at the foot of the stairway to introduce herself. She was told where to find the patient and to go to the rear of the plane and relieve the nurse on duty. The two nurses discussed Angus' medical chart. The orders from the Yokota's medical team was to maintain his status if his vital signs allowed. Both nurses took his vital signs and recorded the results in their individual medical chart. Angus was no longer awake but breathing with slow deep breaths.

The flight plan from McChord AFB to Washington was filed and everyone was buckled in as the Pan Am 707 left runway 36 and began to climb into the night sky heading 90 degrees. As the plane leveled out at 36,000 feet, the pilot said to the co-pilot, "I'm going to grab a few winks."

"I'll wake you when we're half way there." responded the co-pilot," You got any coffee in that jug?" he asked, turning to the navigator. "We set up on the right frequencies? Keep me informed on the weather reports."

"Yes sir," was the reply as the navigator looked up from the book he was reading. The reporters had begun their card games. The smoke from their cigarettes and cigars was contained in the cabin where they were sitting and not getting back of the airplane where Angus and the nurse were.

"How we doing?" the pilot asked rubbing his eyes as he entered the cockpit after his nap. He picked up the latest weather report from the navigator. "Looks like we're about to catch up with the thunder storm," he commented. "I'll take it from here. You try to get some sleep, he said to the co-pilot. " Did 'ya save any coffee for me?"

The senators and reporters were stretched in all different positions the co-pilot noted as he made it toward the back of the airplane. "How's our patient doing?" he asked the nurse who had just finished checking Angus' vital signs.

"He seems to be doing fine. Not much change in his blood pressure or his heart rate. Both are high but that is to be expected for what he's been through. I just hope he can hang on until we get him to Walter Reed," she reported.

The 707 began to buffer as it entered the backend of the thunderstorm. The pilot could see the bolts of lightning flashing at the tops of the clouds. The plane began to descend.

The storm intensified as they dipped through the clouds. The instrument panel indicated that runway 33 was three miles straight ahead. The nurse smiled as she anxiously looked out the window. She could see the town of Buckley. Buckley was where she lived when she was not on the 90-day tour of duty at Yokota AFB. She would be home for the next seven days with her family.

The plane crabbed against the gusty winds until it was 200 feet above the runway. The pilot pushed the rudder pedal to align the plane with runway 33 as the wheels touched the rain-soaked pavement.

The jostling of the plane flying through the storm caused Angus to feel his pains. He opened his good eye. He moaned and beads of sweat dotted his forehead. He tried to move his legs, but they were strapped down. His arm was pinned to him. His first thought was "Am I a prisoner of war?" His head was in a brace and he could not move it. His eye went back and forth, then up and down. He saw someone sitting across the aisle from him. His moaning caught the attention of the nurse who immediately stood up and looked down at Angus and said, "McKay, I am Donna Bush, U.S. Air Force nurse. We have just landed at McChord Air Force Base in Washington. You are no longer in Vietnam. You're being transported to Walter Reed Hospital. You were in a helicopter accident and you saved the lives of several people by falling on a grenade. Can you hear me?"

Angus was unable to speak or move his head.

"Sir, if you can hear me, blink one time," the nurse repeated to Angus.

He blinked one time.

"That's good! You've put your body through a lot of stress. It's important that you do not move your legs and feet. We do not know about any neck injury but we're not taking any chances until you get to the hospital. Blink once if you understand. Blink twice if you're feeling intense pain," explained Lieutenant Bush.

Angus blinked one time, then closed his eye, and, then he blinked two times.

"Sir, I am going to add some morphine now. This will help with some of the pain you're experiencing," she assured him.

The plane followed the vehicle to the parking area. A refueling truck was waiting. The pilot walked back to see about the patient. He looked at Angus and then at Lieutenant Bush. "He awake?" he asked.

"Yes, I think everything is OK. No significant change in his vital signs. His heart rate continues to be up, but it has been steady. Isn't there supposed to be a nurse from here to Walter Reed?" she nervously inquired.

"There's a Lieutenant Blunt joining us. She'll relieve you and be with us all the way to Andrews AFB. I understand you have a few days of TDY here," commented the pilot.

About that time Lieutenant Blunt walked down the aisle. She was a lanky blond with her hair tied in a bun. She and Lieutenant Bush discussed the medical report. Both nurses inspected the compound break. "Do you think we need to put some more antiseptic gel on that exposed leg? How much morphine did you recently administer to him?" inquired Lieutenant Blunt.

"He indicated that he had some pain, so I gave him a low-level dosage," replied Lieutenant Bush. "He communicates by one blink meaning "yes", two blinks meaning "no".

"McKay, do you hear me?" asked Lieutenant Blunt.

He blinked once.

"Are you cold?"

Angus blinked once.

"OK, we can add another blanket and maybe the pilot can increase the temperature back here. We want you to rest as much as possible. Your vital signs are holding steady for your condition. There's no indication of fluids in your lungs. McKay, I'm going to be right here. Do you understand me?" she spoke in a soft, commanding voice.

He blinked once.

The refueling crew topped off the tank. Breakfast and lunch had been loaded for the final leg to Andrews Air Force Base. The plane lined up on runway 15, the pilot revved up the engines, released the brakes and 707 headed south, then banked left and was once again on an easterly flight. The pilot chose to fly south of the thunderstorm across the midwestern states.

The minor buffering on the 707 flying on the southern side of storm did not disturb Angus. He was resting with a grin on his face. Nurse Blunt noted his changing facial expressions in her report. Four and half hours later the pilot contacted Andrews for landing instructions. "We have you over the river VOR. You're cleared to Runway 19. There is an ambulance waiting to transport your patient to Walter Reed. Make a right-hand bank north of the airport. Line up with I-495. There's a Pan Am crew here to return the plane to Miami. Senator Vaughn will join them. Your mission is complete! Close out your flight plan upon landing."

The plane was parked near the truck with flashing red lights. Angus was gently transferred from the plane to the ambulance. The morning sun was coming up over Metropolitan Washington D.C.

The ambulance driver took route I-495N around Arlington. Then it was Interstate I-495W to Bethesda. The flashing red lights on the ambulance opened lanes as early morning commuters got out of the way and five minutes was shaved off the normal 45-minute trip. The next stop was Walter Reed Hospital.

Dr. Tanner thumbed through Lt. McKay's reports that the nurses had submitted after each of their legs of the flight. He noted that his vital signs seemed to change when the plane was landing and taking off. His facial changes included grimacing and grinning. Two of the nurses reported that Angus' body would twitch while grimacing. His blood pressure increased during those moments sometimes with beads of sweat. Nurse Blunt did not report any grimacing on the takeoff or landing.

There were short periods of time on each leg of the flight, especially the landings, maybe a minute or two, where he would open his good eye and be able to communicate with the nurse if he was thirsty, cold or in pain. Then he'd drift back into the unknown recesses of his mind.

Dr. Tanner surmised that Angus was reliving important events of his life. Some pleasant and some stressful!

CHAPTER 21

Walter Reed

Dr. Tanner called the surgery team together to discuss Lieutenant McKay's medical history and recommendations for his recovery.

He started the meeting, "Everything checked out with the patient's airway, breathing and circulation. The rescue medic did an excellent job in controlling the bleeding issues. I believe, the shattered leg needs immediate attention," he continued with his recommendation. He wanted to begin with an x-ray of that bone fracture to determine the damage of the break because it appeared the fibula and tibia were splintered. That would require at least two separate operations, and, possibly three, with a 3-week recovery time for each operation.

"There is a nasty rotator cuff tear on the same shoulder that has been dislocated. We do not know what damage the flight from Vietnam did to the wound. Afterward, we can start x-raying the rest of his body starting at the skull. According to his medical report, the rescue paramedic repositioned his dislocated shoulder," reported the doctor.

Most of the others at the meeting concurred with that decision. Another surgeon offered his opinion, "That's fine however, the skull and jaw were of concern according to the medics that rescued him. McKay was unconscious when they rescued him. He did not regain consciousness until the helicopter landed in Hue. During the flight to Washington D.C. he did not show any signs of being in a coma, only heavily sedated. I think we should not put off that x-ray until after the leg surgery but get all the X-rays initially."

Dr. Morgan, the doctor who would be doing the leg surgery spoke up, "I would prefer not moving that leg any more than necessary," he stated and then continued, "Besides, according to the nurses who flew with him, there were no signs of a blown pupil which should reassure us that we are not dealing with severe brain damage."

The decision to x-ray and do surgery on the leg only was the consensus of the medical team of the hospital. "Faith, I will need an x-ray of McKay's damaged leg as soon as possible," ordered Dr. Morgan.

"Sir how soon can you schedule a surgery?" asked Dr. Tanner's head nurse.

Looking at his schedule, Dr. Morgan made his decision, "I will re-arrange my day off. Let's look at the day after tomorrow."

A few days later, at 9:30 a.m. the telephone rang at the Bar MK ranch in Crockett, Texas.

"Hello" someone answered on the third ring.

"Is this Mrs. McKay?"

"Yes, I'm Grace McKay."

"Mrs. McKay, my name is Faith Henderson. I am a nurse at Walter Reed Hospital. I am calling you to let you know your son Daniel Andrew McKay is here at Walter Reed Hospital and he is in the care of Dr. Tanner. He survived a sixty-foot fall from a wrecked helicopter a few days ago. Also, you need to know your son is a hero. He saved the lives of some visiting senators and other government dignitaries by falling on a grenade that had been thrown into the crowd. Fortunately, it malfunctioned. However, he did receive severe burns from that. He has been in ICU for a couple of days. He is stable and improving. Do you have any questions for me?"

"Oh, my goodness! We received a telegram yesterday saying he was missing in action! We've been worried sick. Can I talk to him?" Mrs. McKay wanted to know.

"We do not recommend it quite yet. He's still under heavy sedation because he has several broken bones. His jaw may be cracked and it is difficult for him to talk. However, Mrs. McKay, we do not have any indication of a concussion. In situations like this it takes a while for the memory to reorganize itself. He keeps saying "Coee" or something like that. Does that ring a bell with you?" Faith asked.

"Khoy is his Vietnamese friend. They went on missions together. We have photos of them together. He wrote the date and K-h-o-y on the back. Has he mentioned the name Cindi Le? We also have photos of her," replied Mrs. McKay.

"Oh, maybe that's what he's saying. We didn't know for sure what he was trying to say. We thought it was Sandy or something like 'Coy'. Will you mail those photos to me? It may help him," Faith pointed out. She added, "Do you have a pen and paper handy? I'll give you an address and a telephone number where you can contact me. I will keep you informed of his progress."

"Just a minute," Mrs. McKay said as she laid down the yellow receiver.

Nurse Henderson gave Mrs. McKay her address and phone number. Just write 'Attention Lieutenant D.A. McKay"

"Miss, what did you say your name was? Oh, yes, Henderson. When do you think we will be able to visit him?" asked his mother.

"Mrs. McKay, I checked on the availability of the apartments we have available here at the hospital. I need to warn you he will be confined to a wheel chair for many weeks. Let's see, March is full. I would say, you may want to consider around Easter. It's on April 14th this year. But you need to make reservations very soon since that week will be filling up quickly. I'll mail you some information on that. One other thing, Dr. Tanner, his doctor would normally have called you, but he has laryngitis. I am sure he will call you as soon as he gets over that. He's one of the best," Nurse Henderson assured her.

Grace McKay sat down on a kitchen chair. She burst into tears! Her son was alive! She pulled a handkerchief from her apron pocket and wiped her eyes. The worn print dress with the apron tied around her waist was her on-the-ranch clothing.

Grace ran to the shed where her husband Connor was working on the green tractor. Tears were running down her cheeks, "Connor! Connor! Angus is alive!" she babbled.

He bumped his head getting out from under the tractor, "What are you jabbering about?" he uttered as he wiped his greasy hands on his bib overalls. Connor's graying hair and stubbled whiskers were signs of age creeping up on him. He rubbed his head as he grabbed his Deere cap from the tractor seat. "How do you know that?" he questioned her.

"He's in a hospital. They called to let us know." Grace ran up to Connor and tightly squeezed him, sobbing on his shoulders, "He's alive! Thank God!" Her tears flowed freely.

Connor swallowed, his heart beat increased, he cleared his throat, "What hospital? Where? How is he?"

"A nurse, her name is Henderson, called and told me, "Angus is not in Vietnam. He's at Walter Reed Hospital, some place in Maryland. He's has some broken bones, but should be all right. Isn't that great? Praise the Lord!" she sniffled wiping her eyes.

"Come in the kitchen. I'll tell you everything she told me." Grace said, grabbing her husband's hand.

After Grace went over everything Faith had shared with her and Connor had finished two cups of coffee and a few of Grace's cookies, she said to her husband, "We need to call Rob and let him know." As she picked up the empty cup and plate of cookie crumbs, she pleaded, "Connor, can we visit Angus around Easter time? Nurse Henderson said they have apartments available near the hospital."

"That's a good idea. They say you get better airfare rates when you book early. See what you can come up with. Ask Rob if he can help bale some hay in a couple weeks. My brother Rory is helping a church up in East Texas with a tent evangelizing mission. I doubt if he can get away from that." Connor replied as he closed the screen door and headed back toward the shed. "Thank you, Lord," he murmured under his breath.

Back at the hospital Dr. Tanner discussed the schedule with Angus, "Lieutenant McKay, the surgery team has decided it best that leg be operated on first. You will be in bed for a number of weeks depending on your progress. Your leg will have to be elevated in a cast for a few weeks. We'll get you into a wheel chair as quickly as we can. Then you'll be on crutches and later you'll have to use a cane. A physical therapy program will be included. We'll run a series of X-rays periodically to determine how well those bones are mending."

"We will operate on your leg the day after tomorrow. You have a simple fracture in your left arm. We can take care of that today. You will have to wear a cast and a sling for a few days. That will be uncomfortable and itchy. Your clavicle has a slight fracture at the sternoclavicular joint including a rotator cuff tear. That probably occurred when you dislocated your shoulder. That is the reason your shoulder is wrapped in a figure eight to give it support."

"Lieutenant you are lucky you did not rip your arm off. We do not want any movement from it for sometime. he nurses did a good job of wrapping your sprained wrist and ankle. However, we do think you have a lateral malleolus fracture in your ankle that will probably require surgery."

"The nurses were unsure about any neck injury, so they applied a neck brace just in case. We could not find any neck injury. The good news is that the flak jacket must have protected your rib cage. There are no broken ribs but you may be a little sore for a few days. You can expect some pain with normal breathing. Try not to twist too much. You have some black and blue bruises all up and down your back where the flak jacket must have been compressed hard against your back as you fell from the helicopter. McKay, you must have taken a hard tumble! We, however, believe you are over the hump and will recover in time," he tried to assure Angus.

"We want to keep you in ICU for one more day because we want to protect you from pneumonia. I know you are very sore and, ache all over. You'll be able to self-administer the pain medication as you feel you need it. Faith, my head nurse, will be with you through this whole process. Our goal is to get you healed and back to your old self." Dr. Tanner assured Angus then added, "Nurse Faith has talked to your parents. They are aware that you are now back in the states. They want to visit with you as soon as they can. I doubt you want them to see you covered with all the cuts and bruises over your face and body."

"We will be monitoring you to make sure you did not suffer a possible concussion. Sometimes these things take days to surface." Dr. Tanner concluded the review of his medical report to Angus. "By the way, you must have visited the doctor in Hue about some problem with wheezing when you were with your girlfriend. There was no follow up. You must have been wounded before you got to revisit him. His report says it was the perfumes that were causing you to have the breathing problems. He wrote in his report that stress and allergies don't mix well. He was going to prescribe some allergy shots to help you. I'll order some pills for you. Take them as needed, otherwise you'll feel the pain of wheezing all over your body."

Before the sun came up the next day, a nurse came into ICU. "Good morning, McKay, I am Nurse Henderson, we're going to the surgery floor and take care of that leg for you. I'm going to call you Humpty Dumpty and I am your fairy godmother who is going to put you back together again." Nurse Henderson joked with Angus as she helped the orderly roll him out of ICU.

Weeks passed and the doctors and nurses, especially Nurse Henderson, monitored his vital signs daily. His blood pressure fell to an acceptable range. Finally, Angus had graduated to a wheel chair. After a few weeks of pushing the wheelchair he noticed he was gaining more strength in his biceps. The soft cast had been removed from his arm. His clavicle had healed enough that a supporting bandage was no longer needed.

There were tiny bones that had been misaligned during his landing solidly on his heel when falling out of the helicopter. Surgery on his heel was scheduled for next week. He can expect to be in a wheelchair an additional three or four weeks.

Angus read in the Washington Post about the chaos and deaths happening in Hue. The Washington D.C. TV stations covered Walter Cronkite's assessment of the Vietnam War. He thought it was time for the USA to get out of Vietnam.

Angus had written a letter to Colonel Colt asking about Cindi Le. Weeks later the colonel notified him that Cindi Le and her mother were reported missing and presumed killed by the VietCong. The colonel expressed his sorrow and wished Angus a swift recovery.

McKay knew what the letter meant and he mourned for them and for all the American GI's and Vietnamese people who were killed or wounded in that chaotic country. Angus' thoughts and prayers were for Cindi Le and her mother. He was mentally and physically drained and sought comfort in the hospital's chapel. Images of dazed men, women and children wandering around crying out for help and the dead lying in the streets were surfacing from the depths of his mind. He had to accept life with all its harshness and continue with his life the best he could. After breakfast Angus would spend a couple of hours in the chapel.

"You know, Faith, I truly cared for that girl in Vietnam, but now I can't say it was a mature love. I believe we both were looking for affection. You know what I mean?" Angus would openly discuss his feelings about a youthful romance and Faith was the one who was there whenever he needed to talk.

"Any other girls in your life?" asked nurse Henderson.

"Nah, Mary Beth. We met mostly at FFA meetings. We dated off and on for five or six years but it was more of a brother and sister relationship. Her mother died before she was in high school. She was young and her father was too busy with his boat and guiding business to spend time with her during those tender years. She felt comfortable with me because I helped her with the FFA projects." Angus remarked, then added, "Guess the girl in Vietnam was the only one I was truly attracted to. We had talked marriage, but there was no engagement ring. So, maybe I was not fully committed."

"Possibly you're right," Faith replied with relief because over the past months she was beginning to have sentimental feelings for him.

A few weeks later, Angus was still in the wheelchair when two military officers visited him. They explained that because of his Vietnam injuries he would not be physically able to continue his military career. They handed him his Honorable Medical Discharge certificate. He was to receive a token monthly $275 check for the rest of his life for his services.

Angus was visibly shocked. His lips quivered. His muscles tightened. He stared stone-faced at the two officers during the entire duration of the abrupt, unexpected visit. His mind could not believe what the officers were telling him and the disastrous news rattled him to his very core. His lifelong dream of a military career was over. There was no warning. No hearing. No recourse. He had experienced disappointments before, but never one that left him as hopelessly empty as this one. It was like a death sentence for Angus.

Over the next few weeks, Faith began noticing that his behavior was changing. His smile was missing. Angus was no longer friendly with her nor the other patients. He did not like being around loud noises or bright lights. He closed the blinds to his room and shut the door to keep noise and people out.

"Angus, are you sleeping OK at night?" she inquired one morning, "Your sheets and pillow are damp with perspiration."

"I'm fine," he snapped back at her.

"Lieutenant McKay be honest with me, are you having vivid nightmares?" Faith pressed for answers.

"So, what if I am! Just leave me the hell alone, I'll be fine," Angus countered angerly.

Faith talked to Dr. Tanner about McKay showing symptoms of slipping into depression. "It may be a combination of receiving notice of his medical discharge and battle fatigue," the doctor remarked. Faith knew about another possible issue, Cindi Le. Maybe it was more than infatuation!

Later, she again reported to Dr. Tanner that Lieutenant McKay's nightmares were becoming more serious and his attitude toward the staff was uncooperative. He was even contrary toward Senator Vaughn who had not missed one month of bringing him flowers or books.

"He has fallen into self-destructive behavior like smoking cigarettes. That is not the way he was bought up. He has had positive support from his family and church, but he has stopped going to services on Sundays and he no longer helps the chaplains with their

Sunday and Wednesday services. And, I caught him ripping up his Vietnam photos. He seems to want to destroy his past," Faith discussed these recent changes with Dr. Tanner. Then she added, "Sir, he's reluctant to talk to me about his nightmares. All he tells me is that he's falling from the sky with flame like demons chasing him. Sir, I recommend we put a night nurse with him to see if that will help us determine the root of his problems."

"He's been with us for nearly a year," commented Dr. Tanner. "The kid evidently experienced a lot of internal stress over there. The medical discharge might have been the straw that broke the camel's back. That was a psychological blow for him. Let's enroll him in the group hypnotherapy program. It has proven to be effective in most cases. The surgery on his heel will have to follow the therapy program since he will be confined to bed for at least six weeks. Let's start him out on a low dosage of tricyclic antidepressant and monitor him closely for four weeks. If he doesn't gain excessive weight or show other side effects, we may increase the level."

The therapy program required Angus to discuss his feelings and nightmares with some of his hospital buddies. During the first few weeks he refused to share his thoughts with those who were also attending the sessions. His buddies understood because they had been where he presently was. They did not give up on their encouragements.

He trusted Faith. She was the one person who was there with him whenever he felt the need to talk. Many times, she pushed his wheelchair out on the patio so they could enjoy the spring like air. She helped him write down what his nightmares were doing to him. The months of therapy began to make sense to him. Seeing the written words of what was causing the nightmares had an impact on his attitude. Angus began to readjust his life. His attitude toward the medical staff, especially Faith, and his hospital buddies began improving. The medication program helped rewire his brain from the war memories to experiencing everyday thoughts, and thinking more about his future.

His parents also noticed an improvement in the way he shared more of his thoughts without becoming irritable. Grace visited him once a month and Connor did, whenever he could get away from the ranch. His mother would bring his favorite cookies and photographs of "Apple", his horse. They noticed that he was becoming more like he was during the days before he went to Vietnam. His smile, his interest in talking to other people, and encouraging his fellow soldiers to be positive had returned.

Over time, Grace McKay and Faith developed a certain warm relationship, both were concerned about Angus. Faith began to better understand him through discussions with his mother and photographs of the ranch and of Vietnam. She began to recognize his true personality. She felt his determination to overcome his war wounds and nightmares. She felt his grief when the Army gave him the honorable medical discharge. The two would take walks outside the hospital, and sit on the benches. With Faith's encouragements Angus began to overcome his depression. He looked forward to their walks and their talks. He felt her energy when she touched his shoulder or grabbed his hand when they prayed together. A bond was drawing them closer to a relationship that neither recognized. Their eye contact with each other was warmer and longer. His jokes and carefree attitude blended well with her life style. He liked her direct responses to his questions. He liked the fact she felt comfortable enough to disagree with him. Their feelings toward each other were growing deeper than a nurse and patient relationship. Both felt a longing to be with the other.

When Senator Cary Vaughn heard about his medical discharge, he called a college buddy who was one of the chief supervisors at the Internal Revenue Service. The Senator was told that there was an opening in the Gas and Oil Division of the IRS, and since this young man was military, he would have priority over nonmilitary applications. Of course, he would have to pass an IRS Gas and Oil exam.

"He's your man! I'd like for you to send one of your top agents over to Walter Reed and start preparing him for the test," Senator Vaughn was adamant about his request.

"Cary, I don't know if I can do that or not," protested the IRS Director.

"Don't let me down on this. Remember, I gave you help on that multi-million-dollar computer system," the senator reminded him.

"OK! You're right. I owe you one. Now, we're even. I'll have to get back with you about who will tutor him," retorted the IRS Director.

Senator Vaughn had brought books and flowers to Angus every time he had visited him. He had not missed one month in over a year. He sent Angus special cards every holiday. He is the one who attached an amendment to a bill that authorized the field promotion for his bravery in time of war. Angus was given the rank of captain by the act of congress. Many congressmen did not see it buried with a bill approving additional funds for the experimental F-105X.

Nurse Faith thought that Angus would respond better if he got away from the hospital atmosphere. The operations on his foot required him to wear a boot and use crutches for several more weeks. Angus could feel the strength in his arm muscles becoming more visible. He had physical and hypnotherapy Tuesdays and Thursdays. The IRS trainer was there Mondays and Wednesdays. On Sundays Angus returned to assisting the chaplains in their Sunday worships.

In June, Faith recommended that because of his progress, Angus should be allowed to leave the confines of the hospital and live in one of the government's apartments while he continued his physical and hypnotherapies. He still had at least two more weeks to wear the boot and another six weeks of therapies.

The hospital staff agreed with Faith's recommendation about his move. She helped him find a one-bedroom apartment near the hospital. She and Angus walked to the apartment complex to inspect the small, one bedroom fully furnished. The rent was acceptable. It would be available any time after July 10th.

Angus found the tax laws challenging. He would question Monroe Hartman, his trainer when a regulation or phrase was ambiguous. Sometimes he would call his father to get clarification on the wording in their gas and oil agreement. He learned where most of the errors were showing up on the gas and oil tax returns. Angus looked for reasons 'why' those questions were generating more errors than other parts of the forms.

The weeks passed, Angus' mental and physical health continued to improve. Dr. Tanner had recommended he consider an insert for his left foot because the bones in his heel had not aligned as nature intended. Angus' left side was a quarter of an inch shorter than his right side. According to the podiatrist this could cause serious joint problems later in life.

His depression and nightmares were no longer controlling his life. Flashbacks of Vietnam were very rare as he gained more control of his life. His broken bones and wounds had mended as well as could be expected.

He passed the Gas and Oil Tax exam and was offered a position with the IRS Department at a Grade Level 7, which paid $1,200 per month. With his medical government check he was earning $1,475 per month. "Angus, our combined income is nearly $3,750," Faith said hinting at a possible marriage. Angus replied, "That's not a bad salary for 1968."

Angus and Faith went out for a nice dinner to celebrate his job at the IRS. When she drove to pick him up at his apartment, Faith got out of the car to let him drive. She was wearing a scoop neck, blue lace jacket dress. The thin silver necklace that he had given her had a bright blue topaz stone that matched her eyes. Her ash blond hair was shoulder length and had a swishy, gorgeous twist. Angus had not seen her so dressed up. As a nurse her hair was always in a bun. She seemed more businesslike wearing her nursing uniform. Other times when they were together, she had her hair in either pig tails or a pony tail.

Angus held the door for her as she gave him a peck on the cheek. He helped her into the car, "You look absolutely dazzling," he complimented her.

Angus wore a gray western cut suit with his black lizard skin boots. He felt good about himself wearing a light gray shirt and black western tie.

He had made reservations across the state line in Virginia. The restaurant was at the corner of Old Dominion and highway 309. It featured wood fired steaks and sea foods. Faith ordered the smoked salmon, Yukon mashed potatoes and green beans with pecans. Angus had read on the menu that they served Black Angus beef. He decided on the 10 oz. steak with Yukon mashed potatoes and grilled asparagus. They both had sweet tea. For dessert they shared a chocolate velvet cake.

They were comfortable with each other as they discussed where they were in life. Both were their mid-twenties. She was a year younger than Angus. He let her know he hoped to find an apartment closer to where she lived.

She and another nurse shared an apartment on Dorset Road, which was between Chevy Chase Village and Kenwood. It looked as if Angus would have to find a place northeast of Washington, D.C.

He knew, too, that it would take time to learn the routine at his new career. The new job allowed him to think of the future and less on the past. Yet, his thoughts were about Faith. She gave him signals that she felt that way about him too.

They were holding hands after the waiter had picked up the empty plates. He casually mentioned to Faith, "How would you like to go to the ranch? I know you've met mom and dad. You've even met my buddy Rob and I've met your roommate Sarah. I have until December 1st to begin work at the IRS," suddenly he couldn't contain his thoughts and he blurred out, "Faith, I've fallen in love with you!"

Faith whispered back to him with a warm smile, "Angus, you know I was engaged when they first brought you into the hospital. I broke off that engagement a few months after I met you. It was always you. You don't pretend to be anyone else. I have waited months to hear you say that you love me."

"I'd like for you to meet my parents. We can fly to Wilmington so you can meet them. They want to meet you. I have written and talked to them about you…about us," she proposed.

"I like that idea. But I've got to find an apartment first," he replied. He had time to find an apartment closer to the address where he would be working 1111 Constitution Avenue NW, Washington, D.C. He and Faith spent three weekends looking for an apartment in the areas of Riverdale and Silver Spring, Maryland. They could find nothing to match what Angus' wallet would allow. Over the Labor Day Weekend, they finally found something suitable south of D.C. The Hickory Hill apartment complex in Suitland, Maryland would have an opening in the middle of September. The 1,200 square foot apartment had one bedroom, a den, kitchen, and a sunken living room. It was twice the size of the apartment he had been in the past three months. The lease was within his budget. A bus could take him along highway 5 straight to Pennsylvania Avenue and then to Constitution Avenue NW in 40 minutes during rush hour, but it was a farther distance from Faith. She worked and lived on the northwest side and Angus would be on the opposite side of D.C.

Faith helped him pick out furniture for his living room, den, kitchen, and bedroom. The question on the bed was it to be a king size or queen size. Faith kept hinting to him, "Think about the future." Angus argued that some of the furniture was too girlish. Faith would counter with, "Maybe someday I'll be moving in!"

The furniture was to be delivered on Saturday, September 20th. Faith was there with Angus. She pointed out to the delivery men where to place each piece. By the end of the day all the plastic was removed from the furniture. They sat at the kitchen table and ate take out Chinese for dinner. Angus looked around his apartment and declared, "I think I can live here."

With the cost of the furniture and a deposit on the apartment, Angus had to call home to take out extra money from the trust fund his parents set up from the sale of EZ Boy. His parents were excited about seeing his new apartment later in the fall.

He asked Faith to join him on a week end to try out the jacuzzi in the apartment building. Angus suggested they both needed a relaxing week end. She was eager to join him. When she came out of his bedroom, she had on a single piece blue and light green bathing suit that was tied behind her neck. He wore plain black swimming trunks. It was a crisp but warm day. They bundled up in beach towels and headed for the jacuzzi. They sat in the tub for twenty minutes before Faith suggested that was enough time.

They wrapped themselves with big beach towels and hurried back to his apartment. They stood in the middle of the sunken living room looking at each other. He reached out for her and she took her towel and wrapped it around both of them. Their kisses became more passionate. His hands worked up and down her back, finding the bow, he untied the strand that had been holding up the top of her bathing suit and tugged. The top of suit felt to her waist. She dropped the towel and pulled him closer to her. He could feel the firmness of her breasts touching his chest. They didn't want to let go as they stared into each other's wanting eyes. Angus ran his hand down her sides and found the top of her bathing suit and pulled it up covering her breasts.

"I love you," she said as she dashed into his bedroom to get out of her wet swimming suit. He could hear the hair dryer humming in the bathroom.

When she came out, she was wearing a navy blue knit sweater over a pair of light tan pedal pushers. Her hair was in a pony tail. She looked at Angus wrapped in one of the towels. "Your turn to change into dry clothes. Need some help?" she grinned at him, "I'll fix something to eat. What's in the refrig?" she asked opening the refrigerator door.

CHAPTER 22

Before he was on the payroll, Angus would take the bus to and from the hospital apartment to the IRS office. His supervisor, Bill Wallace, was helpful in introducing him to the staff. They, in turn, would mentor him for an hour before he would go to another station. He always had questions for them.

Bill Wallace was hosting a Halloween party and had invited Angus and his lady friend to the party at his home in Arlington. Faith talked Angus out of going as a Vietnam soldier. She dressed as a nurse and dressed Angus as a doctor. He wore green scrubs, a surgical cap, and a head mirror. A stethoscope hung from his neck. She had painted his face to look like Groucho Marx, who was a popular comedian with a big bushy mustache on television. The party goers took turns answering the door for the 'trick or treat' kids. The children laughed when Angus and the others opened the door wearing their silly Halloween costumes.

On the way back to Suitland, the two discussed the best way to raise children. Angus' farm background was stricter than Faith's. Her parents mostly sent her to her room when circumstances called for punishment. She agreed that a stern method would be necessary in certain cases but preferred the way she was raised.

It was nearly 11 o'clock. when he pulled up and stopped at the apartment, he lingered in her car as they embraced and kissed. The center console was a deterrent for such occasions. Her 1966 Ford Mustang Coupe was a two-door silver model with a black top. Angus often washed it and filled the gas tank for her. On Sunday after church, as usual, they had brunch and discussed the coming week. This time Faith asked Angus if he would like to fly to Wilmington and spend the Thanksgiving Holiday with her family. It would be first time her family would meet him. She had found a United Airways flight for $160 each round trip if they book early. The flight is only one and half hours. "There's a Sunday afternoon return flight that gets us back by 3:30. I know you had said December's busy with end of the year reports," she said, to let him know she knew what was on his mind.

"Why not! It would be nice to meet your mother and father," he agreed. Angus had been secretly looking at engagement rings. Now, he had to make a choice. He, also, had to think about how he was going to approach her father about asking his permission to marry his only daughter.

The following week Angus invited Faith to his apartment for a pasta dinner with a salad. She arrived at 6:30. She had put in a ten-hour shift at the hospital. He offered a glass of wine since the pasta was not quite ready. She had kicked off her hospital shoes and taken off her white hosiery. Bare footed she helped him in the kitchenette. The pasta bowl, plates, salads bowls and glasses filled the small round kitchen table.

"Acute strep throat is taking its toll, especially with the soldiers at Fort Meyers. We have whole wings of patients suffering from an outbreak at the camp. We're also watching for symptoms of rheumatic fever, which can affect the heart, scarlet fever and even meningitis. All of them can be easily spread," she grumbled. After the evening meal prayer ended. "Nice to be with you and your pleasant smile," Faith commented as she softly touched his cheek. "Thank you for making dinner for me. Sarah had the late shift, so she's not there and I would have had to eat alone."

"Ye'ah, I know they keep you hopping over at the hospital. I remember when I was in there and you were going from patient to patient. I know you did spend time with me giving me sponge baths, changing my bandages and emptying my bed pan," he grinned at her. "I must have been a real pain in the butt."

"No, I wished some of the other Vietnam vets had the attitude you had. Some of them just gave up on life. It makes it tough for everyone around them," she said. Then abruptly changing the subject, she added, "I ordered the airline tickets today. We leave on Saturday the 22nd at 2 o'clock. We'll come back on Sunday, the 30th at 2:30. That gives us time to go to church with my parents and have brunch. You owe me $160."

They washed and dried the dishes together. Then she said, "I'm bushed. I'm going to my place and get some sleep."

Angus suggested, "you can sleep here. I'll take the couch."

"Not on your life. I don't trust myself. Tired and alone in your apartment after all of that pasta and wine I would not have my defenses up," she said smiling at him, but meaning every word. "But I do appreciate the thought," she responded putting on her white working shoes and grabbing her white nylons. "I love you too," were her last words as she closed the door.

Angus' request for a few days off at work was granted since he did not officially go on the payroll until December 1st. He called Faith to let her know.

On November 22nd at 11:30 am, Faith picked Angus up to go the airport. "I know I'm early, but this gives us time to have lunch and park the car for nine days," she remarked.

Everything went smoothly as Faith had planned. Her mom and dad were at the gate to greet them. They walked with them to the baggage area.

"Mom, Dad this is Angus McKay. He's the one I've talked to you about so much. Angus blushed when he heard her introduction. "Sweetheart, this is my mom, Alice and my dad, Henry, we call him Hank."

"Glad to meet y'all. Faith has told me a lot about you. Sorry it has taken so long to come to Wilmington," Angus apologized as he shook hands with Mr. Henderson. Mrs. Henderson reached out and gave him a hug, "You can call me Alice," she whispered to him.

Hank and Angus put the luggage into the Chrysler 300's trunk. They drove to the Bayshore Landing. Big Oak trees lined both sides of the street. They lived on Lantana Court in a beautifully landscaped, two story home.

"Here we are," Hank said as he pulled into the driveway.

"Nice home." Angus remarked. He liked the southern columns on the front porch. The house faced eastward toward the ocean which was a couple of miles away.

They unloaded the car and Alice showed Angus the upstairs bedroom where he could make himself feel at home. She pointed out that Faith's bedroom was at the far end of the hallway.

"I know Faith wants to show you our downtown and the beaches. Would you be interested seeing the naval ship we have? It has become a real attraction for the city, " Alice explained. "Dinner will be at 6 o'clock."

"Thank you, Ma'am. Let me freshen up a bit and I'll be right down," Angus replied.

"Faith told me you like southern fried chicken. So tonight, we're having chicken with mashed potatoes with gravy and okra. Is that all right with you?" Alice proudly announced as Angus walked into the kitchen, "And, I baked a peach cobbler for dessert."

Faith came into the kitchen wearing white capris and a V-neck wildfire knit tunic. Her hair flowed down on her shoulders. "Thought I better come down and help mom with dinner," she said while blowing Angus a kiss.

After the blessing was said. The Henderson family wanted to hear all about the McKay Ranch in Texas. What did they grow? Do they have oil wells on the ranch? Angus answered their many questions. He had not been there since he left for Vietnam in 1967.

"Would you like some more sweet tea, or would you prefer milk with your peach cobbler?" Alice offered him a choice.

"Sweet tea will be fine," he answered. Hank, feeling left out, spoke up, "I'll have a cup of coffee."

"We understand you and Faith have been going to her church up in Bethesda. We thought all Texans were Baptist," Hank joked with Angus.

"Not all, Sir.! We have a pretty good mix in Texas. There are even some Missouri Lutherans," Angus countered back because he knew that was the church of the Henderson's.

There was a chuckle at the dinner table. "Touché,'" grinned Hank.

"We normally go to the 10 O'clock services on Sunday. You're welcome to join us, if you'd like," Hank offered, then he continued, "Tomorrow, we'll go for brunch after services. We generally go to the Pin Cushion restaurant downtown. They serve a great brunch that's deeply rooted with southern tradition."

"Yes sir. That's fine with me. Faith has mentioned they serve good food," agreed Angus.

After dinner, Faith sat next to Angus and talked about him having moved into a new apartment, and how she had helped him pick out furniture. She told them that he had passed the IRS exam, and about his job at the Gas and Oil Division of the Internal Revenue Service.

The next day after the Sunday services they headed for the Pin Cushion restaurant. Mr. Henderson and Angus ordered the Sunday special of eggs with grits and hash-brown potatoes, biscuits, and

Carolina ham. The women chose the French Toast with North Carolina persimmons, candied pecans, and orange sabayon over berries.

On Monday, there were clouds and a chill in the breeze so Faith wore a denim jacket. She borrowed her mother's Dodge to drive around the area showing Angus where she went to school. She introduced Angus to her friends. They crisscrossed the Cape Fear River several times. The famous Airlie Gardens Park was not open to the public, but he could see through the gate the beautiful old trees with limbs loaded with Spanish moss. He enjoyed visiting a historical home of the colonial era. The Bellamy Mansion was built on the eve of the Civil War.

That night the two took a romantic horse-drawn carriage ride around the town. The two cuddled and kissed sitting in the back of the carriage. They were enjoying the time being with each other.

On Tuesday, they toured the World War II U.S.S. North Carolina battle ship. The tour included photos of all the ships named North Carolina and memorialized all North Carolinians who had served in the Second World War.

Fort Fisher was twenty-one miles south of Wilmington. It was a point of entry for the confederate supplies to get past the U.S. government's blockade during the civil war. Angus was interested in the museum's many artifacts.

The day before Thanksgiving, Faith wanted to help her mother with preparing the main meal for the next day. Angus helped Mr. Henderson with trimming front yard hedges. Hank had some questions about the Vietnam War. He knew that Angus had been at Walter Reed for over a year and a half in recovery. He asked Angus about his future with the government. Angus recognized that Mr. Henderson's concerns were for his daughter. Her parents had been surprised when she broke up with her fiancée over a year ago. Faith and he had met when she was in nursing school and he was in premed classes. They had dated for a couple of years. After the trimmings from the bushes were bagged the two men sat down on the lawn furniture. Alice brought out some sweet tea and cookies hot from the oven.

"Mr. Henderson, Faith and I have known each other ever since I entered Walter Reed. We agree that we enjoy each other's company. I start with the IRS December 1st. With your permission, I intend to propose to Faith over the Christmas holidays," Angus stated.

After some moments Hank asked, "Does she know?"

"I think she senses it," Angus responded.

"Well, Angus, as you know, she has her own life to live. Alice and I discussed that's probably one reason you came to Wilmington. If Faith says, 'yes', we will support her decision. We would welcome you to our family," Mr. Henderson assured Angus.

"Thank you, sir. I'll do what I can to make her happy. You can count on that," Angus happily replied with a sigh of relief.

On Thanksgiving morning Angus woke up to the aroma of turkey baking in the oven. It had been several years since he experienced a true home cooked Thanksgiving meal. He thought he had better telephone his mom and dad and wish them a Happy Thanksgiving. Alice told him it was all right to make a long-distance call to his folks. His uncle Rory answered the phone, he was always there for Thanksgiving. Grace told Angus to wish the Henderson family a Happy Thanksgiving and special wishes to Faith who she thought was such a sweet and thoughtful young lady.

Finally, the announcement was made that the turkey was done. Time to eat. The dining table was decorated with little chocolate candy turkeys on each plate. The turkey was in the center surrounded by cheddar cheese-green bean casserole, fluffy mashed potatoes, sweet potato casserole, corn bread dressing. There was choice of either soft dinner rolls or buttermilk biscuits. Each setting had a smaller plate for the cranberry gelatin salad.

Mr. Henderson said the blessing and thanked God for the opportunity to meet Angus. Table discussion was about warm weather over the Thanksgiving holidays. The food was delicious and everyone had their fair share of helpings. It was decided to have the pecan pie later. Mr. Henderson wanted to watch the San Francisco 49'ers and the Cowboys football at the Cotton Bowl in Dallas. The game ended in a tie 24 to 24.

On Sunday Angus and Faith put their luggage in her dad's car. Right after church they had to rush to the airport to catch the flight back to D.C. As they unloaded their luggage, Hank shook Angus's hand and with a sincere grin said, "Good luck."

Later, on in the airplane Faith asked, "What did dad mean by 'good luck'?"

"He was wishing me good luck with the IRS," he answered.

On December 1st, he was eager to begin work with Gas and Oil Division. The first part of the morning, he had to complete the employee paper work. Faith called him to see how he was doing. Within a few days he was at a level that he did not need supervision when he reviewed the tax forms but he knew he had support whenever he needed it. Angus was well accepted by all his peers.

During the following weeks, Faith would pick Angus up at his office after work and the two would go Christmas shopping. Both had to shop for their parents and friends. She helped him pick out gifts for his mom, dad, and uncle. On the nights that Faith had to be at the hospital, Angus would take a bus to the mall. He looked at many engagement rings before he chose the one that he wanted Faith to have.

He had fixed his famous pasta dinner on Saturday and invited Faith over to help him decorate the Christmas tree that he had purchased for his apartment. After some discussion about where the tree should go, Angus conceded that her recommendation was the best.

Angus was making plans for their special night. He made reservations at Rose's Luxury. It was on 8th street in Washington, D.C. Rose's Luxury offered specials for engagements, weddings, or office parties. They arranged for a cozy corner table with fresh flowers and a bottle of wine for Angus and Faith. He agreed to pay $10 extra for a small cake with sparklers.

When Faith picked him up at his apartment, she had on a white pleated georgette skirt and a turquoise V-neck, long sleeve top. A topaz necklace encircled her neck. A white shawl collar shrug that matched her skirt, covered her shoulders. Angus wore a blue blazer with gray slacks and red and blue striped tie. He had practiced saying, "Will you marry me?" several times. He thought he'd propose to her when the sparklers were lit. He knew that Faith was the one for him. He had told her that he had something to ask her when he called for the date.

The scene at Rose's was romantic. A large window allowed the two to view the Washington Monument at a distance and a decorated Christmas tree partially blocked the corner area from other diners.

They started with a shrimp cocktail followed by an Italian salad. Both had the Rigatoni ala Vodka. The Pinot Noir wine added an elegant balance of spice and fruit for the special occasion. The entre' was delicious. Their dinner discussion was mostly about their work. Angus was eager to let her know that he felt comfortable working for the government. He asked her what she wanted for Christmas. Did she plan to fly to Wilmington for the holidays? "Maybe we can fly to Texas then to North Carolina," he suggested.

The waiter cleared the table and abruptly left without saying a word. Angus looked uneasy. "Are you still available to go to the office Christmas party with me?" he asked.

It was not the question she had been expecting. Faith tried not to look hurt. Taking his hand and calmly, trying not to show her disappointment she replied, "Angus, I've had that on my calendar for several weeks. I am looking forward to meeting your co-workers."

The waiter brought the cake and lit the sparklers. He turned and hurriedly left the area. Angus took Faith's right hand, pulled the tiny box from his coat pocket, opened it so she could see the diamonds flashing with the sparkles flitting in the air, "Faith will you marry me?" he proposed.

She teared up because she had just gone from a low emotional disappointment to one of sheer joy and happiness. "Sweetheart! Yes! Yes! to both of your questions," she eagerly responded. "Angus, you know I love only you," she sobbed as she wiped away her tears of joy.

He got up and walked to her side of the table. As he took her hand, he put the ring on her finger. They grabbed each other and he kissed her warm, quivering lips. She didn't want to let go of him. Cheers and clapping rose from the other diners on the other side of the tree. Rose, the owner, came to their table with a polaroid camera.

"Would you like a photo by the Christmas tree?" she offered. She took three snap shots. "Here, send one to your parents and keep one for yourself," she said as they waited for the pictures to slowly develop.

They finished the cake and the wine, and as they walked past the tables on their way-out people congratulated them and wished them well.

"Let's go call our folks," suggested Angus.

First, they called Faith's. "Hi mom, your future son-in-law wants to say 'Hi' to you."

"Hello, Alice. Your daughter just made me a very happy man."

Alice replied, "We're happy for both of you. Congratulations! Have you set a date?"

"No date yet. When we do, I'll let you know," Faith replied while all the time gazing into Angus's eyes.

On the second call to Crockett, TX, "Hi mom, your future daughter-in-law wants to say 'Hello' to you."

"Oh, my goodness. Faith, we are so happy to hear this news. I've told Connor many times how nice it would be to have you as a daughter-in-law. Thank you for all you've done for Angus. I feel like we know you. You were always so kind to Connor and me when we visited Angus all those times while he was in the hospital. I am so excited for you two."

After the parents were notified of the engagement. Angus opened a bottle of chilled wine. Both were beaming with happiness. "To us," he toasted.

"Now and forever," Faith warmly responded. They set the empty glasses on the kitchen cabinet and began hugging and kissing. His hands moved up and down her back as he pulled her tighter to him. Her body responded as she wrapped both arms around his neck.

It was 2 o'clock when she drove back north to her apartment. Sarah was up waiting for her. "I want to hear all about it," Sarah blurted out as she looked at Faith's left hand. "It's gorgeous! You are one lucky girl!" The two sat up another hour as Faith relived in detail how the evening had unfolded.

It was noon when Faith woke up. She immediately called Angus, "Just wanted you to know last night was the best night of my life. I love the ring and I love you. What about you and me going to the mall this afternoon? You know we've got to take a silly gift that is less than $10 to your office party for the Chinese gift exchange and I need to get a few extra gifts for my parents. I'll pick you up at 3 o'clock," she told him.

The mall was crowded with Christmas shoppers. Angus and Faith walked the mall holding hands. They found a sign with, 'My job is taxing!'. She looked for something she could wear to the office party. They took a break and had a bite to eat before continuing their quest to find gifts for her parents. Angus wanted to find something for Rob and his wife, Tina. They had gotten married when Angus was bedridden in the hospital.

"Let's see 'Butch Cassidy and the Sun Dance Kid'. I just love Robert Redford," Faith mentioned casually. Angus jestered, "Is this my supper?" as he purchased a box of popcorn and shared a large soft drink with her.

After the movie they were walking out of the mall Faith asked, "Do you have wrapping paper and ribbons in your apartment?"

"Nope. Good thing you thought of it," he admitted.

"One more stop and then I'll drop you off at your place," Faith stated. She told Angus that they could wrap the gifts on Sunday after church. They kissed good night and she drove toward her apartment.

The next day the two went to church and then for brunch. "I'm sorry about last night, but Sarah and I stayed up way too late Friday night. I'll make it up to you tonight," she promised Angus.

After they finished the gift wrapping, they sat at the kitchen table to talk about their wedding plans. Angus opened a bottle of ginger ale and Faith finished the last of the wine from their Friday night engagement date. The first decision was to determine a date. Faith wanted a June wedding. Many other questions followed, where to go on a honeymoon, where to live, etc. Faith wanted the wedding in her church in Wilmington. Saturday, June 6th, 1970 was selected for their wedding date. They started their 'to do' list in preparation of their day of marriage.

Emotions took over them and they retreated to the couch. She removed her shoes and began slowly undoing her nylons one garter at a time. She could see that Angus was puzzled as to what he should be doing. "Sweetheart you want to help me?" she invited him. The garters dangled just below her lacey panties. Angus undid the rest of the garters and gently slid her nylons down her smooth legs. She wiggled her toes to help him take the nylons off. They embraced each other. He held her head in his hands and began kissing her forehead then her cheeks working his way to her waiting lips. Then, he kissed her ear and down toward her cleavage. She responded by unbuttoning her top two buttons and throwing her head back to expose more of her breast.

The telephone rang. On the fourth ring Angus picked up the receiver, "Hello," he answered.

"Hey Angus it's Rob. Your mom just told me the good news. Congratulations! Hope I didn't wake you, I forgot you're an hour ahead of us," Rob rambled on. "I think she's a sweet lady. Of course, I've only met her when she was taking care of you at the hospital. You must have impressed her since she's agreed to take care of you the rest of your life."

Angus replied, "I was lucky she said yes when I proposed to her." The two talked for several minutes. Faith was straightening out her blouse and skirt. She brushed her hair while Angus and his buddy continued talking. After they hung up, she remarked, "Boy! Talk about good timing!"

She walked over to Angus and gave him a kiss on his cheek, "Call me tomorrow after work and remind me that you love me," she said running her fingers through his messed-up hair, "I love hearing that from you."

The department Christmas party the following week end was at the home of Mr. and Mrs. Bill Wallace in Arlington. There were a variety of snacks. It was a BYOB. Angus took a 32 oz. bottle of ginger ale to mix with a little bourbon. Faith said she would share with him. She mixed her drinks stronger than Angus did. In fact, after the first two mixed drinks, Angus did not add anything to his ginger ale.

The gift swap was fun. Faith's gift was a pair of plastic garden gloves, which she traded for a cactus plant. The gift that Angus chose was a pair of patriotic socks which he elected to keep. The topic among the women was the engagement of Angus and Faith. The married men fired gags and jokes at Angus.

Faith flew home to spend the Christmas holidays with her folks. Angus joined them on the 23rd. Their home was neatly decorated for the holidays. This time Angus was welcomed to their home as Faith's fiancé. Faith and her mother began planning for the wedding. They called the church to reserve it for June 6th.

The Henderson's gave Angus gifts for his apartment that Faith had recommended to them. She gave him a stylish shirt and tie and professional photograph of herself. He gave her parents a $50 certificate to the Pin Cushion. To Faith he gave a pink cashmere sweater with a white pleated skirt. He had kept the receipts so she could exchange his gifts for something else if she preferred. Angus called his parents and mentioned that he and Faith were trying to find a date when they could visit them and to wish them a Merry Christmas. Faith talked to Grace and assured her they would be coming to the ranch as soon as their schedules allowed.

Both flew back to Washington, D.C. after church services the last Sunday of the year.

Faith had RSVP'd for a new year's party at her Nurse's Association. They would dine and dance to bring in the new year at a ballroom in Fairfax, VA. Angus and Faith shared a table with Sarah and her boyfriend, J. Roy Madison. They danced to live band music until the New Year. At midnight, they kissed and hugged, Faith whispered in his ear, "I love you, Angus. I wish tonight was June 6th."

It was 3 o'clock when Angus drove up to his apartment. He was concerned about Faith. "Tonight, I sleep on the couch and you sleep here. I will not allow you to drive through D.C. with alcohol on your breath," he stated in no uncertain terms.

She knew she was a bit tipsy and he had had only two weak mixed drinks. He was right.

"Maybe you're right," she reluctantly conceded.

He gave her one of his Texas A&M sweatshirts and slowly closed the bedroom door. It was not what he wanted, but it was the right thing to do tonight.

Faith slept until 11 o'clock. She could smell eggs and bacon cooking. Angus looked up from the stove at Faith standing in the doorway wearing his sweatshirt over her panties. Her hair needed combing.

"It's 1970! Now I know what you are like in the mornings. You're as lovely as ever! Yes, I can get used to this. How do you like your eggs my dear?" he asked with a big smile.

"Honey, why did you let me sleep so long? Thanks for not letting me drive home last night. Guess that's a sign of true love," she commented and walked over and gave him a lingering good morning kiss. "Does this mean I can expect breakfast every morning?" she quizzed in a light manner.

"Now you're an Aggie by association! Better eat your breakfast before it gets cold," he encouraged her as he put her plate on the table and pulled out a chair for her.

After Faith ate, she went back into his room, showered, and got dressed. When she came into the living room, her hair was in a pony tail. "I'm keeping the Aggie sweatshirt," she declared as she plopped down next to him on the couch. Angus was only half listening because his Cowboys were in a playoff game with the Detroit Lions.

His team won 5 to 0. She had stretched out and laid her head in his lap and dozed off.

Their jobs kept them busy and they were not able to see each other as much as they would have liked. They did talk a lot on the telephone. Angus' birthday and Valentine's Day were the only weekends they were able to be together. He gave her a 'Build a Pearl Necklace' for a Valentine gift. On several Sunday's Angus would wash her car after church. Faith and Sarah spent the weekends looking at wedding gowns. She flew to Wilmington a couple of times to coordinate wedding plans with her mother. They also looked at wedding dresses at Camille's Wedding Dress Shop and Coastal Knot Bridal.

During Faith's short trips to Wilmington she and her mother discussed the invitation list, the floral arrangements, videographers, or photographers or both. They visited the bakery to look at various cakes. The question and the cost of a disc jockey or live band got Hank involved with the discussions.

Alice helped Faith schedule appointments at BeBeautiful Salon, WakeUp MakeUp, and Aunt Anne's hair salon.

Faith enlisted her dad's thoughts on the reception following the ceremony either at Southern Beach House or the Beal Rivage Golf Course. Her thoughts were whichever he chose, she would recommend the other place to Angus to host the rehearsal dinner.

CHAPTER 23

Angus was surprised at the huge number of tax returns that began flooding the Gas and Oil Department starting in March. His group was the first to review the tax forms, then they were double checked by another group of inspectors. By May, it was obvious that the tax forms that Angus had reviewed had far fewer errors than the others in his group. Mr. Wallace rewarded Angus with a grade level promotion. He was now at a grade level 8 which meant a 10% increase in income.

March 22nd was Palm Sunday. Angus had accepted the pastor's invitation of being an usher. He could now look at the statue at the front of the church of Jesus lying in Mary's lap without being reminded of the image of Father Walsh holding the soldier in his lap as he heard the man's last confession. During the week Faith attended the daily services at the chapel in the hospital. That Saturday, the two headed for Walter Reed Hospital. They handed out Easter lilies and chocolate Easter bunnies to each military man in the wing that Angus had been in for over a year.

Easter Sunday was a warm sunny day. Angus remembered his dad buying an orchid for Grace every Easter. So, he gave Faith an orchid when she picked him up at his apartment. She gave him a kiss on the cheek as he pinned it on her, "It's so sweet of you. I've never had an orchid for Easter," she commented. Later, they walked the mall of Washington D.C. enjoying the sights and fragrances of the flowering cherry blossom trees. They paused at the Lincoln Memorial to take in all the beauty and meaning of living in a free country.

Angus discovered that April was an extremely busy time for his department. He could not believe the costly penalty fees caused by simple errors that kept showing up on the tax forms. He had been working twelve-hour days and began showing up at the office on Saturday. He had been used to working like that on the ranch.

On Monday morning, his supervisor called him into his office. Angus had been there since seven o'clock. Mr. Wallace pointed out that he had noticed the extra time Angus was logging in and, although he appreciated the effort, it hurt the morale of the other agents. Mr. Wallace instructed Angus either stop coming in on Saturday or knock off at five p.m. Angus told Mr. Wallace, "I'll leave work when the others do." He apologized because he did not want to upset anyone in the office.

Then Mr. Wallace told Angus that in reviewing tax returns by state, Texas had far more rejects than the other two states he had been reviewing. "I want you to prepare and conduct a series of training classes in Dallas-Fort Worth, Houston, Lubbock and Tyler. From now on you will be reviewing only returns from Texas. I know you're getting married in June, so, let's get the meetings scheduled for August or September," he said assigning the project to Angus

That evening during his telephone conversation with Faith, he mentioned he was called into the office and told to cut back on his overtime hours. "Honey, city people are more concerned about the hours they work, not when they finish the work. On the ranch we worked 'til the chores were complete," he lamented. "From now on I will be reviewing only Texas tax forms. Mr. Wallace wants me to develop training sessions for Texas. Looks like I'll be traveling to Texas this fall conducting training classes," Angus added.

That night Faith was telling Sarah what Angus had said. Sarah replied, "Guess it's true what they say about farmers, you can take the boy away from the farm, but you can't take the farm away from the boy!"

Faith responded, 'Sarah, I wouldn't have him any other way!"

By mid-April the wedding plans were scheduled. Angus still had not chosen where to take his bride on their honeymoon. One choice was Halifax, Canada. But Faith had grown up on the shores of the Atlantic Ocean. So, he decided on the honeymoon capital of the world, the Niagara Falls. It would be a romantic place in early June. He reserved the honeymoon suite at the Water Falls Inn on the Canadian side of the falls. The suite included a bottle of wine, a wine country tour, a massage for two as well as a boat tour around the falls. There were other milestones marking the significant events of a new chapter in the lives of Mr. and Mrs. Angus McKay.

In May the McKay's were surprised to receive a letter from France. They didn't know anyone in France:

Dear Mr. and Mrs. McKay,

It is with heartfelt emotion that I write this letter. I found your address in Kim Ly's belongings in Hue. I continue to mourn the loss of my wife and my precious daughter, Cindi Le. Both were executed by the North Vietnamese Army during the battle of Hue. I am now retired from the French army and have returned to my home in Royan, France. I did have an opportunity to meet your wonderful son. He talked about his family and how proud he was that you so readily accepted Cindi Le. Angus and I quickly bonded. He was the kind of man I would want for a son. I had looked forward to having him as my son-in-law.

Enclosed is the necklace (sorry I never found the ear rings) Angus gave to Cindi Le on Christmas. The engraving on the back is "I Love You, Angus" in Vietnamese.

The USA army will not give me any information about Angus, other than he is missing in action. I pray for my two girls and for Angus. War can be cruel. You are always welcome to visit me in Royan.

With Regards, Colonel Andre Bonnay

Grace couldn't believe it. She and Connor discussed what to do with the letter and the necklace. "Definitely not the right time to bring this up with Angus and Faith," stated Connor. "Put them away someplace and let me think about it," he instructed his wife.

On June 6th Faith and Angus exchanged their wedding vows and the pastor announced they were now married in the eyes of the church. Sarah was the maid of honor. She and the three other bride's maids wore light blue satin dresses that matched the blue-ribbon which Faith had braided in her hair and flowed down the back of her wedding dress.

Rob was the best man. He and the three men were in grey tuxedos with matching blue bow ties and cummerbunds.

No one noticed if any small problems occurred during the wedding. Nothing affected the romantic atmosphere of Angus and Faith. Everything went as they had expected except Rob had secretly taken the blades from Angus' electric shaver. Angus wouldn't know about that until he tried to shave the next morning in Canada.

The country club was elegantly decorated and the luncheon was as superior as they had expected. Mr. and Mrs. McKay were happy for Angus and their daughter-in-law. Faith's parents expressed how proud they were of her and their son-in-law to everyone attending the wedding.

After the photographs and the reception had ended, the families of McKays, Harrisons, and close friends watched as the airplane as it left Wilmington with Mr. and Mrs. Angus McKay onboard headed for New York. Passengers on the plane applauded them and wished them well when the pilot announced there were newlyweds on the plane. The airline crew offered them a glass of wine.

The two enjoyed their honeymoon at Niagara Falls. At last they could fulfill their pent-up desires for one another. Faith was impressed that Angus had reserved the plush honeymoon suite. They ate at the Watercolors Mark, rode the Hop on-Hop off double decker bus, went to the top of the Skyland tower, and took the five-hour journey behind the falls, where they learned that rain coats were not enough protection.

The McKay's had decided to move into the apartment in Suitland until they could find something closer to the Walter Reed hospital. Their search ended right after the 4th of July when they found a three-bedroom home in Falls Church. A widow was moving to Florida and she was not ready to sell her home. It was a three-story home with two bedrooms down stairs, a living room with a fireplace and a kitchen with modern appliances on the ground floor, and upstairs one bedroom, bath, and large sitting room. She had agreed to leave the furniture in the upstairs. She favored Angus because he had been wounded in Vietnam and her husband had been wounded in World War II. They moved into their new residence the last week of July.

CHAPTER 24

In August Angus left for Texas to conduct two-a-day Gas and Oil Tax classes in Dallas and Tyler. He met Mr. Jerry Johnson and the Fischer family which consisted of a father and two sons at the Dallas classes. Mr. Johnson invited him to dinner at his place on Lake Ray Hubbard. Mr. Johnson had taken a sincere interest in Angus. He recognized that Angus had full knowledge of the tax regulations and offered good suggestions on how to reduce the errors that Mr. Johnson's accounting department was making.

The next day the class members began asking questions about how to improve their tax reporting procedures. Angus set his notes aside, wrote down the questions and began answering the individual questions.

That evening he drove to Crockett, TX to spend the night with his folks. The McKay ranch was only 80 miles south of Tyler. He knew if he left there by 6 o'clock he could be on time for the 7:30 a.m. meeting. It was first time he had been able to be with his folks since the wedding. He called Faith that night to let her know where he was and that he was thinking of her.

The Tyler meeting went much the same as the Dallas meeting had. Those attending began asking questions like those he had heard in Dallas. It became a question and answer session. Angus deviated from the script, again, and began discussing what the accountants could do to reduce the errors and penalties. Angus was beginning to better understand the concerns of those who were filling out the tax forms.

It was Mr. Johnson who approached him again at the Tyler meeting, "Mr. McKay, there are some special friends who would like to discuss a proposition with you the next time you are in the Dallas area. Here is my direct phone number. I can't share anything with you now, but I can tell you, it will be worth your while to listen to it."

Following the Lubbock and Amarillo training meetings, Angus called Mr. Johnson early one morning to let him know he had a three- hour layover at Dallas Love Field on Friday afternoon. "I'll pick you up at 11 a.m. at the airport," Mr. Johnson told Angus.

He was waiting at the gate for Angus as he got off the Braniff plane from Lubbock.

"Mr. Johnson. it is important that I catch the flight to D.C.," Angus pointed out before he climbed into Mr. Johnson's 1971 brand new Oldsmobile.

"We're meeting the others at the Cantina Laredo. It's only two minutes away. I'll be sure to get you back in time to catch your flight," Mr. Johnson assured him.

The Tex-Mex restaurant had a small private room. Three men from the Fischer family and two other men were waiting. The senior Fischer welcomed Angus to the meeting and introduced him to the others. "Mr. McKay you have impressed us with your knowledge and the ability to explain everything to us so we can better understand the regulations. You talk our language. We are offering you a monthly retainer of $3,600 to open an office in Dallas. This offer is guaranteed until the end of 1976. We have a legal contract drawn up for you to study. Any outside business you get is yours. Naturally we expect to be your key accounts. We think we can help you generate other clients. To be honest we are tired of hiring consultants who do not give us correct answers. In fact, in several of our cases, we end up paying more in penalties because of their advice."

Angus was stunned since he had not expected such a lucrative offer. He looked at each oil man sitting around him, trying to gather his thoughts. His mind was whirling with all sorts of questions and concerns. Leaving the IRS had never entered his mind for the future.

"Gentlemen, I appreciate your offer, thank you. I'll need some time to consider it. It appears to be a great opportunity, but I need to discuss this with my wife," Angus said responding slowly with a grin. Then he deliberately added, "Can't say I would not welcome the opportunity to get back to Texas."

"You discuss this with your wife. Think of your future in the gas and oil business! Let us know your decision and how soon you can move back to Texas!" the senior Fischer said with confidence because he knew it was a great opportunity for the young man.

Mr. Johnson pulled up to the curb at Love Field and looked at his watch, then at Angus. He had another offer for Angus. "You can help me with an investment issue," he said to Angus. "There is a section of land north of Dallas with a large rock quarry on the northwest side of it that's for sale. I would like to purchase that land. I believe that Dallas will be growing northward. It will include the township of Preston Prairie. There are 120 acres on the southeast side. It has a nice farm house that was built in 1968. It also has a small barn," he handed Angus an envelope and added, "Read this when you get an opportunity. I am willing to sub-lease the 120 acres to you for 10 years at $400 per month. You will be responsible to pay the property tax. At the end of ten years you can purchase the land for $800 per acre. The land is deeded as agriculture, so the taxes will be based on an agriculture tax rate. Angus, I am not doing this for you. I am doing this for myself. The only way I can swing this deal is to generate some income from the 120 acres. I don't have time to be a farmer. You can grow crops or run livestock on the of 120 acres to help pay for the lease and taxes. Read the sub-lease agreement and let me know."

Angus shook his hand, and said, "Thank you. Mr. Johnson let me study this and I'll let you know within a few days. Of course, I'd like to see the property before I commit."

Faith was waiting at the gate for him when he walked toward the baggage claim. He had so much to say to her about the trip. He did not want to talk about it until they got to Falls Church. His mind was still juggling figures when they sat down. He tried to explain the job offer first. Faith had never been to Texas. She had a lot of questions. She was not saying, "No", but was concerned about their future. He pointed out how much it was costing them to pay the Virginia taxes, plus, what D.C. taxed him on the money he earned there. He pointed out how much they would save monthly. He would be earning more than twice his current income. There were too many questions to make a decision. They agreed to fly to Dallas and see the property.

Angus called his father to discuss the situation with him. Connor told him that he understood that area had good producing soil. When his father heard the names of the Fischer family, he recognized them as being highly respected throughout the oil fields of Texas.

They booked a flight to Dallas for the weekend. Faith was interested in knowing if there was a hospital where she could apply for a nursing position. Mr. Johnson met them at Love Field and gave them a map to find the property. He gave them a key to the farmhouse.

The McKays rented a car and struck out for Preston Prairie, Texas. Just north of Frisco was the small town with a railroad track running down the main street. There was a bank, a feed store, and a few other retail stores.

The two-story brick and rock farmhouse were set about 100 yards off Highway 287. It was a three bedroom and two bath home with a living room that had a fire place. It had a large kitchen with an island on the ground floor. The upstairs consisted of two large bedrooms sharing one bathroom. Faith was impressed with all the cabinets and closet space. A small office or sewing room was also upstairs. The home had been well cared for. A large two car garage was attached. A barn and shed was twenty yards behind the house.

Faith wanted to know how far it was to the nearest shopping area, especially a grocery store. Denton was west and McKinney was closer to the east. The unincorporated township of Preston Prairie had future growth potential. The Collin County property tax was reduced substantially because of Angus' being a wounded Vietnam vet.

The gravel pit was out of sight behind a patch of pecan trees on the back side of the section.

This was a difficult decision. Part of Angus wanted to return to Texas. Faith agreed to be with her wherever his job took him although she loved her job at Walter Reed.

They decided to do a 'Not Accept' and a 'Accept' list. On Sunday, they stayed after church after everyone had left and prayed for the right decision. That evening back in Virginia, each wrote their answer on a sheet of paper. Both agreed to accept both offers. They were moving to Preston Prairie, Texas. They had agreed they were young enough to take the risk.

They both agreed to give their current employers a thirty-day notice. They called their landlord in Florida to let her know of their decision. She graciously let them know she understood that the move to Texas may be an opportunity of a life time and offered to return their down payment.

September passed quickly for the young couple. Grace was available to help Faith prepare the home for their furniture. She was thrilled that the kids would be closer to Crockett. Angus was busy looking for office space in Dallas. He found a suitable office near the SMU campus and law library. Brenda, a young receptionist served six companies who leased executive office space on the 5th floor.

The seasons passed by quickly and in July Angus received a telephone call from Mr. Johnson, one of his key accounts.

He and the Fischer family had been discussing the future of the oil industry with indications that the Vietnam War was showing signs of winding down and what the effect that be on oil prices.

"Angus, we have come to a conclusion that the oil prices will drop off significantly after USA brings all of our troops back home. We thought you would be able to put together a five-or ten-year projection of what you think the oil market will look like," suggested Mr. Johnson.

Angus replied, "Mr. Johnson, that's going to take some time to put together. How soon do you want this projection? I've got some good sources to call on. Let me see what I can come up with. Give me a week to think about it and I'll get back to you."

Angus hung up the phone and began thinking how lower oil prices would affect his business. He needed some input from others. He dialed his buddy, Rob Palmer, who had an office in Midland, TX.

"Palmer Petroleum Field Services." Rob speaking.

"Hey, Rob. it's Angus. How are things out in your neck of the woods?"

The discussion about how they both ended up in the oil business was always the beginning of their conversations. Then, it turned to families. He had met Tina Gomez, a young lady finishing her doctoral degree in veterinary medicine. Rob was in his final year of earning his master's degree in Petroleum Engineering. The two decided to set marriage aside until they knew where Rob would be working after graduation . Tina figured she could find a job anywhere Rob worked. During the summer months and semester breaks Rob worked in the oil fields around Midland-Odessa. He was a hard worker and his roustabout jobs included working under ground to climbing to the top of a rig. He had worked as a field hand and a floor hand. He learned about repairing equipment and he " fished" for broken pipes and bits 800 feet below ground. He found that each rig was different. Rob found the Permian oil field was ideal for gaining field experience and he had some contacts from his Aggie days who helped him with the many jobs available that would give him experience in getting oil out of the ground.

"Rob, let's get together. Bring your bride Tina to the ranch. I'll bring Faith. The girls can get to know one another better," suggested Angus.

"Sounds good to me. I do need a mini vacation," admitted Rob.

"Well, let's call it a part vacation and part business," Angus responded. "I have been asked to put together a projection for the next five to ten years for the oil industry in Texas. Some clients had experienced the drop in oil prices right after the end of World War II. They think we may experience a decrease in oil prices again in the next several years. What do you think?"

"I should've figured you had something up your sleeve. Set a date and Tina and I will be there. I have not been able to help your dad since we moved to Midland. What about dove season? How does that sound?" Rob asked looking at his work schedule.

"Sounds good. You start making some notes and let's see what we can come up with." Angus replied. He had already written down some prospective well-known names in the industry who would be willing to sit on a discussion panel. The list included the Railroad Commissioner and university professors to discuss how low oil prices would impact Texas. He was hopeful that maybe a couple of executives from major oil companies would agree to join the panel.

The Fischer family had sponsored Angus's first year of membership to the Petroleum Club in Fort Worth. The dues squeezed his budget but he was becoming more well-known with established people in the oil business. Another advantage was the membership allowed him access to Petroleum Clubs in Houston, Dallas, Midland and San Antonio.

The two friends talked back and forth on the telephone several times over the following weeks. Rob told Angus about an individual in San Angelo, TX who was beginning to buy used oil equipment, and cleaning it with an explosion proof water pressure system. He has a lot of money tied up in cleaning equipment and storage.

A few days before dove season opened the two couples got together at the McKay Ranch. The McKays were thrilled to have Faith visiting as well as Rob and Tina Palmer. Angus and Rob practiced shooting clay pigeons to hone their timing for dove hunting. Uncle Rory told them he saw doves on the ponds flying in and out of the Davy Crockett National Park.

They discussed what world events could adversely affect oil prices, and who would be invited to be guest speakers. Some had been contacted and agreed to attend and make comments. The Railroad Commissioner thought a meeting would be important and agreed to attend. Shell Oil, Exxon, Mobil Oil and Conoco Oil agreed to send representatives. The governor would not commit but did say he would send someone from his office. A decision was made to see if the San Antonio Petroleum Oil Club would host the meeting.

Rob suggested, "Let's see if our wives would like to tour San Antonio while we're at the meeting. We can get together for dinner."

After a few weeks, the meeting was fully scheduled. San Antonio Petroleum Oil Club agreed to host the meeting with a smorgasbord luncheon. A panel of guest speakers consisted of the Rail Road Commissioner, two state representatives, division vice presidents from Shell, Exxon and Conoco oil companies, and Jimmie Jenkins, of San Angelo. Mr. Jenkins was the gentleman who was buying and cleaning used oil equipment.

The Shah of Iran and the Ayatollah Ruhollah Khomeini were the main topics of most of the national news and conversations of those active in the oil business. Oil prices had dipped to under $15 per barrel. Street fighting had broken out in Tehran and Beirut. There was talk of possibility of Iran invading Kuwait's oil fields. Some experts were forecasting that the world would run out of oil by year 1985.

Attendees came from Pampa, Wichita Falls, Kilgore, as well as Dallas-Fort Worth and Houston. Some were oil producers, some from banks and saving and loan firms. There were two sessions. The morning session had the Railroad Commissioner, two professors of economics, and the president of the Texas Oil & Gas Association on the panel.

There were nine round tables each with seven chairs. The tables were covered with white linen tablecloths. A pitcher of water surrounded by glasses and glass ash trays for each table. Waiters wore white gloves with their white jackets and black bow ties.

There were concerns about how the world production would be affected by what was happening in the middle eastern countries. The Organization of the Petroleum Exporting Countries (OPEC) banned oil shipments to the United States and other countries that supported Israel in the Yom Kippur War when Syrian and Egyptian forces attacked Israel on their holiest day.

The Railroad Commissioner thanked Angus McKay and Rob Palmer for putting the meeting together. Then, he showed charts pointing out the importance of oil and gas production for Texas. Billions of dollars from taxes and royalties goes to schools, roads, and rescue organizations. His charts, also showed that plastics, medicines, computers, and life saving devices were industries benefiting from the by-products of oil and gas. He projected the embargo will cause pump prices at gas stations would double to $1.30 a gallon of gasoline and there would be gasoline shortages over the next ten years. The two economists thought the price would be $3 a gallon. His final chart showed that Texas had over 400,000 miles of pipe lines from oil fields to oil refiners. "We need to stabilize the price of oil to a manageable level that will keep employment levels up and generate profits for our companies and our state. It is the opinion of the Railroad Commission that prorationing production will not benefit those who are not considered large oil producers. We will continue to monitor the gas and oil markets," concluded the Railroad Commissioner.

The federal and state governments were considering prorating oil production. The two major oil producers in Texas as well as major oil companies were in favor of limiting oil production, but smaller independent oil firms thought it would cause a high rate of layoffs throughout the industry.

The morning session ended with a better understanding of the overall potential of the oil and gas industry in Texas. During lunch Mr. Johnson and the Fischer family told Angus that he had done a good job, but they were looking for solutions to staying profitable during the turbulent future.

"You will hear some more during the afternoon session," Angus assured them. Then he added,

"Time to think outside the box!"

The panel for the afternoon session consisted of two professors of oil engineering one from the University of Texas and the other one from Texas A&M University. Jimmie Jenkins of Jenkins Used Oil Field Equipment was included. The fourth member was the divisional manager of Field Operations of Conoco Oil company. The fifth member of the panel was from the governor's office. He welcomed everyone for attending the meeting and thanked Angus and Rob for getting the oil and gas experts to share some ideas that have been on the drawing board for some years. And, the sixth speaker was Mr. Dawson from the Federal Department of the Gas and Oil Division. Texas governor Dolph Briscoe was a surprise speaker. He was running for his second term and elections were a few weeks away. He talked about the importance of the gas and oil business to Texas and how he had worked hard with the Texas Oil & Gas Association as well as other organizations to make sure there were fair regulations for companies to grow and profit. He briefly mentioned how fracking had progressed in the past few years and that he fully understood the potential for it in the future. He thanked Mr. McKay and Mr. Palmer for spear heading such an informative meeting. His busy schedule prevented him from staying for the entire session. His parting words were, "Hope to see you at the polls in November."

The two professors reported on their findings of Hydraulic Fracturing (Fracking). They were followed by the Haliburton Company and Jenkins Cleaning Systems.

The two professors discussed innovations that showed promise in meeting the regulations of hydraulic fracturing. One professor showed graphs of using above ground water tanks for managing well fluids to limit the danger of well fluids getting into groundwater. He reviewed how this method was meeting the Safe Drinking Water Act, The Clean Water Act, The Clean Air Act, and the National Environmental Policy Act. He noted that some of these acts are still pending in Congress, but the industry is already ahead of the government.

The other professor's research project showed how sound control and surface management allowed safe drilling near city buildings and homes. He stated that though hydraulic fracturing had been around since the 1940s, it hadn't been until recent years that modern horizontal drilling technology had opened opportunities for millions of jobs and economic growth for the industry. He predicted that, in the future, fracking would account for nearly fifty percent of the total U.S. oil production and up to two-thirds of natural gas production. The gas and oil industry should celebrate this new era.

Jimmie Jenkins, although not a public speaker, held the attention of the audience by explaining that his two-year-old company of cleaning field equipment in San Angelo now had the capability of cleaning on-site. He showed a photograph of his operation in San Angelo and one of his latest investment for on-site cleaning. His cleaning service helps equipment last longer, flow smoother and reduces contamination problems. He added that as a new service, his company was purchasing old, used field equipment, from oil wells to rigs to trucks.

The next speaker was Mr. Dawson from Washington D.C. He was the head of the department that reviews income tax returns for errors in the gas and oil industry. He drew laughter by starting with, "I do not write the regulations, I just enforce them." He continued with explaining the changes for the following year's tax forms. Mr. Dawson closed by stating that the person he goes to for interpreting the tax regulations is with us today. "Mr. Angus McKay will you please stand up and let people know you better?"

The Halliburton Western Division Vice President was the final speaker. His charts showed that 70% of the world's oil production from mature fields. And, that 80% of mature fields were controlled by the middle eastern countries, Russia, and the United States. Half of the world production came from 30% of giant fields. Halliburton Oil performed the first two commercial hydraulic fracturing operations near Archer. City officials thought we were going to empty Lake Kickapoo and Lake Arrowhead. We have grown with the process. Despite the higher operating costs in those early years we kept improving and today we are seeing the fruits of our labor. The savings can be attributed to the fact that fewer vertical wells are needed to access the same volume of rock area.

Then the vice president announced that the company had three patents pending for Safety Valve for Use in Wells, Well Safety Valve System, and a Method and Apparatus for Gravel Packing. "If anyone wants more information on these, see me after the meeting," he concluded.

Angus thanked everyone for attending and hoped it was worth their time. Several men approached him. Many offered their business cards and commented about getting together to discuss penalty fees.

One gentleman edged close to Angus and announced in a loud voice, "this man saved me $300 on each of my three wells."

Rob Palmer had several men approach him about inspecting their operations to see how they might save money. One rancher asked if Rob would come to his ranch near Gruver, TX to see if fracking could reactivate some old wells that were no longer producing enough oil to continue.

Mr. Dawson , from the IRS Gas & Oil Department, waited until the crowd had left. "Angus, got a minute or are you exhausted?" he asked.

"Always have time for you. Thanks for the endorsement. Glad Mr. Wallace allowed you to come to Texas to participate." Angus took a deep breath and loosened his tie.

"Angus, I need to share something with you. Thank you for your support in helping me get promoted. I've gotta go, have a plane to catch. Call me when you're in D.C." Mr. Dawson said as he hurriedly left the banquet room.

Mr. Johnson walked over with a drink in his hand, "Angus, that was a swell presentation." He congratulated Angus with his big, friendly smile. "The Fischer's were really impressed. We did not expect such a meeting. You and Rob did great. In fact, we want to learn more about this Jimmie Jenkins. You know, I think there's a lot of money to be made in buying used equipment and selling cleaned equipment. It's a matter of timing, and I think the time is ripe. Do you think he would be interested in having some investors in his business? We think he may need some capital to be able to pay cash."

Rob Palmer joined a few others to meet with the Halliburton vice president about the Well Safety Valve System and the Safety Valve for Use in Wells. He was invited to visit the company in Carrollton to inspect the two safety systems.

That evening the McKay's and Palmer's got together for dinner at The Iron Cactus Mexican Restaurant on the River Walk. They were pleased to have a table outside on the patio.

The men ordered Beef Fajita's with guacamole. They each ordered a bowl of queso with the chips. The women ordered chicken quesadilla's with guacamole. Rob ordered a Prickly Pear Margarita. Tina ordered a Virgin Cola Das and Angus and Faith asked for sweet tea. The women discussed their sightseeing experiences, especially their visit to the Alamo. They insisted the husbands take them on a Riverboat cruise. The men agreed to have an early breakfast to discuss their meeting in more detail.

Rob reported that the bank in Amarillo had invited him to come to Amarillo and then they would introduce him to some small and medium size oil companies. Also, a bank in Wichita Falls had asked that he call them to set up an appointment.

Angus talked about his two key clients being interested in talking to Jimmie Jenkins about investing in his company, maybe even forming a partnership. Their thinking was that maybe with more capital to work with, his bank would be willing to increase his line of credit. Angus said that he would be interested in making a small investment.

Rob said, "I get to meet a lot of drillers in the field and could recommend Jimmie to them about cleaning their oil well equipment or buying it. I don't have enough to invest, but maybe the company could pay me a "finder's fee" or something like a finder's fee in company shares. Bounce that off them."

"Let's plan a meeting in Dallas with everyone and see what they are thinking." suggested Angus. Then he added, "I don't see how this future company could be profitable for at least three years, maybe five. Depends when the oil prices get over $25 per barrel."

The next day the McKay's drove back to Preston Prairie.

CHAPTER 25

Monday morning, Brenda greeted Angus at the office with a warm smile, handed him his telephone messages and pointed out one message in particular, "A newspaper man, Johnnie Porter, was here. He says he really needs to talk to you. He wouldn't tell me what it was about, but said you'd know."

"Thanks Brenda. I have a few more important calls to make, then I'll call him." Angus looked through the telephone messages walking down the hall. He had two calls to prospective clients in Electra, TX, just west of Wichita Falls. Then he needed to call a banker in Wichita Falls who had given him a business card at the San Antonio meeting.

The first phone call was to Mr. Johnson about a meeting with Jimmie Jenkins. Angus had to coordinate the meeting with Jimmie Jenkins, Mr. Johnson, the Fischer group, and Rob. He had to leave a message with Rob. The others had open dates the first two weeks in October. He decided that the Petroleum Club in Fort Worth would be a good place for everyone to meet.

Angus' schedule allowed him to drive to visit the banker and the two prospective clients in Wichita Falls the first half of September. During the second half of September he needed time to train his two key accounts on the bookkeeping system for the new taxes next year.

On his way to lunch Angus stopped at the SMU library to get a book on setting up a corporation in Texas. He wondered what Jimmie Jenkins would want to do.

Returning from lunch, Brenda handed him a telephone note from Rob. It read 'call me ASAP'.

"Guess I'd better handle this. It sounds urgent." He said to her as he headed back to his office.

"Hello Rob, what's happening in Midland that's so urgent?" he asked.

"Jenkins, his attorney and his banker would like to schedule a corporation meeting proposal in Fort Worth a week from tomorrow. Can you arrange it at your end?" Rob asked.

"I'll try. The Fort Worth Petroleum Club should work with us. Are you bringing your attorney and banker?" Angus joked with his friend. "Let me get back with you as soon as I can."

Mr. Johnson and one of the younger Fischer sons had plans to leave a week from Tuesday morning. They requested an early Monday breakfast meeting. The other members of the Fischer family were all right with any day that week. This meant that Rob and the three business men from Midland would have to be in Fort Worth Sunday night. The Petroleum Club had a meeting room that would available Monday morning and it could serve up to twelve people.

Angus called Rob to let him know they can have the meeting at the Petroleum Club on Monday morning. Then the two discussed that Midland was 300 miles from Fort Worth. It would take over four hours for them to drive up for the meeting. A flight to Dallas Love Field would take only one hour, but may be too costly for them. If they decide to drive up, we could take them to Joe T Garcia's or, if you want to go top shelf maybe The Keg. They could stay at the Worthington Renaissance. It's near the Petroleum Club. They could walk to the Petroleum Club from the hotel.

Rob agreed to call them to see what they wanted to do. Mr. Wright informed Rob that they would fly into Fort Worth Meacham Airport in the bank's corporate jet. They would make their own arrangements for a rental car and hotel.

That following Monday Angus left earlier than usual to beat the morning rush hour in order to be at the Petroleum Club to make sure everything was set up properly. The club provided a buffet breakfast in the private room where the meeting was to be held. The buffet consisted of scramble eggs, biscuits and gravy, bacon, or sausage and some soft tortillas. Hot coffee and assorted juices were available.

Angus thanked everyone for making the early morning meeting and turned it over to Mr. Jimmie Jenkins. He talked about his business of buying, cleaning, and storing old, used oil field equipment until the oil prices return to normal levels. He stressed the opportunity to sell the clean equipment at a higher price to those returning to the oil business when it recovers. He turned the meeting over to his banker, Mr. James Wright and his attorney, Mr. Preston Peterson. Angus and Rob handed out the prospective packets.

Mr. Wright's position was that Jimmie is undercapitalized and too cash poor to take advantage of today's oil situation. The banker knew from experience that there was a lot of old, used equipment lying in the fields now in bankruptcy. Everyone nodded in agreement with his statement.

The attorney then spoke up, "Jimmie is an honest, hard worker. He probably could stand another cleaning truck and another flatbed truck to haul the old pipe and equipment back to his warehouses for cleaning and storage. He explained that Jimmie would be a lot more profitable as a corporation. "He could personally scrape up about $50,000 by mortgaging his home, a few acres of farm land and some equipment he already owned. The problem is local bankers are afraid to invest in Jimmie's low cash flow business based on where the oil industry is at this low point."

The Midland banker agreed and added, "Major banks are not ready to get back into oil yet. Mr. Peterson and I have studied Jimmie's Profit and Loss Statement and his Cash Flow. He is unable to buy in volume from some of the oil well diggers. This is causing him to have to pay higher prices for the used and old field equipment.

Mr. Peterson and I have projected that with proper financing he can buy low and sell at 20-25 times when the market improves. To do that we think some of the larger banks, such as the Midland National, some in the Dallas-Fort Worth area, and maybe one or two up in the Panhandle would be able to increase his line of credit that would improve his financial position."

Mr. Peterson said, "We would like to reach our goal with only Texas investors. Our figures show a minimum of a $500,000 line of credit. The board of directors of the Midland National is only currently allowing him a $25,000 line of credit. We believe with substantial investors that the $500,000 goal is reachable, despite today's market prices. One major Texas oil company has agreed to match up to $250,000. That's half of our goal! We need to raise the other half. It's all in the prospectus. You can read how the investor's will be compensated. We believe the market is on the verge of bouncing back. We know this industry tends to hit peaks and valleys. A price of $2.50 per share means we need to sell 200,000 shares. The oil company that's matching what we raise up to $250,000 would require a place on the board. Maybe you gentlemen would have some input on that. There is a former Texas Rail Road Commission board member who says he would invest $10,000. That's 4,000 shares. Gentlemen, this concludes our portion of why we're here this morning. What questions do you have?"

The room was silent until Mr. Johnson spoke up. "as I understand it, this will be a short time corporation. Once the market begins peaking, the corporation will dissolve. The investors will split the proceeds. Is that correct? What does Jimmie get out of this?"

Mr. Peterson replied, 'Jimmie would not sell his cleaning business. He will be paid for the cleaning of the oil field equipment. He is mortgaging that business as part of his investment. Mr. Johnson you are correct about liquidating the investment company. We project somewhere in five to ten years; the shares of the corporation will be in the range of $15 to $25 a share."

Then Mr. Wright commented, "Yes, your next question is what happens if the corporation goes into bankruptcy. The answer is the board has the right to bring in another manager. Knowing Jimmie like I do, that's not a likely situation. We know that none of us is making any acceptable oil money right now." Then he added, "If our current Rail Road Commissioner decides to cave in to the larger oil companies on the prorationing oil, the market will be in a worse economical oil drought.'

Senior Fisher speaking in a soft slow tone, said, "That sounds like the dumbest recommendation I've heard this year! I agree with you both. You can expect my company to invest $75,000, and I am fairly sure, Mr. Johnson and some of his oil buddies can do the same."

Everyone in the room was shocked. Senior Fischer was known as a conservative business man. What he had just heard was that there was a light at the end of the tunnel. His sons all nodded in agreement with their dad.

"Well, Jimmy what are you going to do?" he looked directly at Mr. Johnson adding, "I remember when you were starting up, you did several things that were out of the box. Look at you now, a wealthy oil man. I know you're a man who is not afraid to stick your neck out and not be like a turtle that draws its head back in its shell like some are doing in this industry."

Then he continued, "Mr. Jenkins, We've got used and old oil equipment we've written off. Hell, it's not doing us any good lying out in the fields. In fact, the government is yelling at us to clean up our mess. Mr. Jenkins, let's discuss what the value of our old equipment is to you."

It came out of the blue! It was like a famous Putnam Investment ad: 'When Putnam speaks, people listen.' Mr. Fischer had spoken and his words would spread around the Texas oil industry.

Jimmy Johnson shook his head. "Can't say I can invest that much right now, but I know some people who would be willing to invest with me. There are some pioneers in east Texas who believe in the Texas spirit. I am honored to join up with Senior Fischer."

Mr. Wright and Mr. Preston began clapping. They knew the meeting was a success. "Gentlemen, there are more copies of the corporation proposal on the table by the door. Take one with you. To be honest it is a cookie cutter proposal. You are welcome to add bells and whistles. Send the changes as you feel necessary to Mr. Peterson's address in Midland. He will try to incorporate your thoughts in the proposal. Is a three week notice too soon? Another year is right around the corner. Let's start making money again." concluded Mr. Preston who began standing up and walking to the door to shake hands with each person.

Mr. Johnson put his hand on Senior Fischer's shoulder saying, " Those are the most words, I've heard you speak since we've known each other. I think we both saw ourselves in the kid's determination to make it in the oil business. Sir, you just gained yourself more of my respect.

They shook hands and smiled for they have been known to be fierce competitors in the oil fields.

Angus and Rob were elated with the success of the meeting and happy that they were working with two of the top oil experts in Texas. Mr. Jenkins came over to shake hands and thank them for their support. All three young men were looking at a brighter future.

Mr. Wright and Mr. Preston thanked the two for organizing the meeting. Mr. Wright looked at Rob and suggested he stop in the Midland National Bank and meet some of their oil clients. He hesitated and commented to Angus, "You must be good at what you do if those two giants use your services. It was a good meeting. I've got to get back to Midland. I have a golf game with the financial officer of Halliburton at 3 P.M. My sons will be handling the corporation proposal."

Within four weeks a corporation was approved by all the parties. Investors across the state had invested $300,000 to match the $250,000 that a major oil firm had offered. Major banks called to offer higher lines of credit. The shares were valued at $2.50 each. The Fischer firm owned 30,000. Mr. Johnson owned 20,000 shares and the other investors in his investment firm owned the other 10,000 shares. The former Rail Road Commissioner purchased 4,000 shares. Angus and Rob each had 2,000 shares.

The oil and gas magazines and newsletters printed articles about the J.J. Oil Service company. Jimmie Jenkins had to hire and train field men to be able to determine the value of the old, used oil equipment. As his cleaning business grew so did the value of the stock. The cleaned oil equipment was tagged by usage and footage. The warehouses began filling up, waiting for the next oil boom.

It was almost six o'clock and when the phone rang, Angus was finishing up writing his instructions for the bookkeepers of his key clients on the changes for the gas and oil tax form. His first thought was it's probably Faith.

"McKay," answered Angus

"Angus, it's Rob. You got a minute?"

Angus replied, "Sure, if it's good news."

"You won't believe this. I just got off the phone with an experienced field manager from the Santa Fe International Corporation, in Arizona. He says the company is shutting down their drilling department. His wife wants to move back to Texas to be closer to the grandchildren. He offered to work for me part time. He was at the San Antonio meeting. He has contacts with several gas and oil companies in Texas. He thinks he can get some of them to call me," Rob said in an excited voice.

"Sounds like your business will be expanding. That's great! What do you know about this guy?" Angus asked. "What's his name?"

"His name is Lee Martin. I've talked to a couple of the companies that know him. Everyone has nothing but positive comments. They say he is a professional in the field with years of experience working mostly in South America. I did learn that there are more oil companies down there who are closing their drilling departments," commented Rob.

"Have him send you a resume and I can run it past my two key accounts to see if they know anything about him. That is, if that's what you want," suggested Angus.

"That's why I called you. Thanks for offering to help. He's sending me one this week and I'll mail a copy to you. Are we still going to hook up in the Wichita Falls area?" Rob asked.

"I thought that was the plan. I've got to run over to Electra to talk to two men who may be interested in fracking some old, unproductive wells. You should plan to go with me," Angus said.

Then he added, "Have you talked to Mr. Jenkins about the companies dropping their drilling departments? If not, you should. Maybe it is an opportunity for him to buy some used oil equipment, especially if a lot of companies are doing that. It could mean an excess of used equipment at lower prices just to get rid of it."

"Good thinking. I'll call him tomorrow morning," responded Rob.

As Angus walked through the door of office 500 the next morning, Brenda was talking on the phone, "Wait! Mr. Palmer, Mr. McKay just walked in." It's your friend from Midland," she whispered to Angus.

"Tell Rob I'm on my way to the office." Angus told her.

"Hey Rob, how come you're working so early?" asked Angus.

"Mr. Martin, he's the guy from Santa Fe International, and I talked on the phone again last night. He is willing to send me $15,000 to put into the company's bank account. He wants a guarantee of $2,000 per month for the first six months, less 15% of the total quote on any account he brings to the company. He thinks he can generate an income of $30,000 or more a year just on commissions. And, any balance in his account at the end of six months is to go as an investment in Jenkin's used equipment company," Rob excitedly explained.

"Rob, that really sounds great! It won't hurt to have an experienced sidekick working with you," stated Angus. The two long time buddies continued to encourage and support each other. Both had faith in the future of the oil business. Both men were enjoying a good reputation in the oil fields.

CHAPTER 26

Faith double checked her "to do" list for the upcoming month. She had written, Bi-annual *Medical checkup with Dr. Tanner*. Faith knew getting Angus to break away from his business was going to be difficult.

"I feel fine. Really don't understand why Dr. Tanner needs to see me. Everything is fine," Angus argued explaining why he did not have time for a medical exam. In the end, he relented and told Faith to schedule a short trip to Washington D.C. "Maybe I can take 3 days off, if you insist," he finally agreed with her.

Faith contacted Dr. Tanner's office to make an appointment.

The flight to Washington D.C. arrived at 8 pm. The McKays took a taxi to the American Inn on Wisconsin Avenue in Bethesda. The hotel was within walking distance to Walter Reed Hospital.

"Boy, this brings back memories," Faith said as they stopped at Jerry's their favorite restaurant for a dish of ice cream. "Honey, remember our little chats here about what we thought our future would be?"

"Ye'ah, we thought we had it all planned out. Never thought we'd be on our own in Dallas," Angus uttered sitting down. "Jerry's hasn't changed much."

Back at the American Inn, Angus grinned as he looked up to see Faith coming from the bathroom wearing a sheer, enticing night gown. It was tied with a big bow in the front. "Wow! What's on your mind tonight?"

"Oh, you noticed? Angus, it's the same night gown I wore on our honeymoon. You do remember our honeymoon, don't you?" she appealed.

"Come over here and refresh my memory," Angus gestured holding out his arms for her. She waltzed into his open arms, he pulled the dangling ends of the bow and she moved closer. He gently removed the gown from her shoulders. He pulled her hands to the pit of her back causing her to lean back, her body pressing heavily against his. He fell backward and her body followed to the king-size bed.

"Angus, let's plan an Easter trip to Padre Island. Sort of a mini-honeymoon," Faith suggested.

"Remind me in the morning," he replied as he rolled over.

At 4 o'clock she snuggled up to him and began running her fingers nails across his back and up his neck. She knew that would get to him. Angus slowly rolled over and began kissing her between her breasts. She grabbed him by his ruffled hair and pressed his face tightly into her cleavage. Working his way up to her neck, the fragrance of her perfume became more intoxicating as his kisses reached her waiting lips.

"Padre sounds pretty good," he later admitted.

"Today we see Dr. Tanner this morning at 9:30. Senator Vaughn agreed to meet us at the Union Pub for an early lunch and dinner is with Randall Dawson, your replacement at the Gas and Oil Department, at the Hill Country BBQ at 6:30. He said he has a bunch of questions for you," she remarked as she reviewed their schedule with her coffee and roll at Jerry's.

After breakfast they walked to Dr. Tanner's office and signed in. There were two other patients waiting to see the doctor.

"The doctor will see you now," the nurse said to the McKays. She held the door and pointed down the hallway. "It's room 102. He'll visit with you shortly."

"Well, well, Captain McKay and my nurse. Hello Faith good to see you again. What's this I hear about you moving to Texas?" asked Dr. Tanner said reviewing Angus' medical file.

"We're still in the process of settling in. So far, Angus has been busy with his consulting company. I'm getting used to it. Things are a bit slower there compared to here. Another change for me is that there are no strangers in Texas. People are really friendly," she stated.

Dr. Tanner thumbed through the thick medical report. Then he sat back in the chair and crossed his legs. "Angus, since I've not heard from you since last spring, I assume the demons are no longer bothering you. Are the nightmares still in the envelope locked up in your safety deposit box? Do you have any of the medication left in the cabinet?" he questioned Angus.

"Yes, and yes"

"Great! You can toss out any of your outdated pills," Dr. Tanner suggested. He, then, directed his attention to the present, "Bring me up to date. How has it been going?"

"Well, doc to be truthful with you, Faith is the best medicine for me," Angus admitted.

"She steers me away from those negative thoughts. Getting my consulting business established has kept me busy. I'm enjoying my marriage, my life, and my work. What else could a man ask for?" he commented.

Doing his routine medical checkup, "I want to run some blood tests this morning. Your heart and lungs sound good," he said. "Angus have you been to the VA hospital in Dallas?"

"No sir, I have not had any need to go there. Why do you ask?" Angus responded looking at Faith. She shrugged her shoulders because she too wondered what Dr. Tanner was leading up to.

"Angus," Dr. Tanner continued, "I would like to send your medical records to them. There is a Doctor Kirk Scott, who is on staff there. He's a top-notch doctor. We wanted him here, but he preferred Dallas. He has handled several Vietnam cases. His brother was killed over there so you can understand his interest in trying to find long term solutions. Faith, maybe you remember him, he was an intern of mine while Angus was going through recovering. Dr. Scott knows you. He was instrumental in several surgery recommendations that he learned at the naval hospital before transferring here. I am certain you'll like him. I strongly encourage you to schedule an appointment to see him in the next six months."

"I have no qualms about that." Angus interrupted, "Why schedule an appointment there in six months if my medical file is here?"

"Good question. I want to follow your progress. I have an invested interest in your case, besides you stole my head nurse. Who knows , someday I might write a case study about you. Seriously, he is much closer in case you would need immediate medical treatment down the road," Dr. Tanner said, looking over at Faith for support.

Faith got the message and supported the recommendation, "That's a good idea, we will contact Dr. Scott. How long do you think it will take to get his files there?" she asked.

"Give me a week or ten days," he responded to Faith. "Also, Angus, I recommend you learn to take some quiet time. The American Psychiatric Association is doing in depth studies on supplemental transcendental meditation along with standard physical therapy. Trials show that by taking only twenty minutes twice a day to close out the outside world helps our brain to rewire or rebalance itself. You indicated you're putting in a lot of hours at your consulting business. That constant stress can become too much for your lower brain to continually absorb it all. You don't want to grind down your brain."

"How's the shoe insert working out for you?" he asked Angus. Then before he could reply Dr. Tanner added, "You know x-rays showed you did a real bang up job on that foot. Your talus looked like a 1,000-piece puzzle. Dr. Rogers, our head foot surgeon, got as many of the bone fragments back in proper alignment as he could."

Angus replied, "The shoe insert seems to be doing its job. It took a while to get used to."

"That's about all I can do for you. You'll like Dr. Scott as you Texans say, he's a good ole boy. But, anytime you're in the area, stop by and bring me up to date on your lives. Faith, a hospital in Plano, Texas inquired about your qualifications. If that's the position you want and they don't hire you. Let me know."

The taxi pulled into the no parking zone in front of The Union Pub at 11:30. Senator Vaugh was standing at the bar near the door and saw them enter. He had a dark blue suit with an American flag on his lapel. Under the flag was a pin of Florida with a diamond showing the location of the state capitol. His Florida suntan reflected an active person in good health.

"By golly, Angus good to see you. Hi Faith," the Florida senator greeted them . He always wanted to give Angus a hug and this time he included Faith in his hugs.

"Been waiting long?" asked Angus.

"Nope just ordered a drink which hasn't come yet. What would you two like?"

"I'll have a glass of wine, blush, please," Faith responded first.

"Angus, what about you?" he asked. Angus looked at Faith for an approval sign. She nodded her approval. "I will have a glass of red wine," he answered.

Senator Vaugh touched a waitress' shoulder, "Ginger, add a glass of blush wine for the lady and red wine for my friend. We will be at my usual table."

She gave him a big smile and said, "Yes, Mr. Vaughn."

Sitting at the senator's usual table, he remarked, "Tell me how your new venture as a gas and oil tax consultant is working out for you? Bet you like being closer to your ranch."

Angus grabbed Faith's hand and replied, "Thanks to you, we've been blessed." With a big smile he replied, "The consulting business is growing more than I ever expected. It was a leap of faith for me to leave the gas and oil division of the IRS and to venture out on my own. We felt that we were at the age where we could take the risk. It was the right decision. We're enjoying living north of Dallas."

The three sipped their drinks and discussed the future of the oil business in Texas and in Florida. "Well, Angus I am glad I was able to help. I owe you my life and you know you can always count on me to do whatever I can do to help you and Faith." He looked at Faith and said, "Faith make sure I have your Texas address."

The Union Pub was known for good tasty luncheons. Ginger delivered their food soon after she had taken their orders. She served the senator's usual tilapia and diced red potatoes. Angus and Faith had ordered the luncheon special. The food was well prepared and had a savory flavor.

The senator asked Angus if he would be interested in being a guest speaker at next year's gas and oil conference in Florida. They discussed dates and locations. "We are interested in extracting oil from the ocean floor around Florida." Senator Vaughn stated. He also let them know he was planning to run again in the next election and that he had a strong committee supporting him. He felt good about his position in the Florida polls and his re-election. Faith noticed the senator was nearly finished with his plate even though she and Angus were only half done.

"Listen, good seeing you kids again. Call me any time you're in the area or if you get to visit my great state of Florida. Faith, I can help you find a nice place on the beach," he claimed looking directly at her as he grabbed the bill for the meals and drinks. "You can get the next one. Who knows, maybe I will come to Texas for a good Angus steak. Any bets on the Dolphins and Cowboys game? Be sure to tell your Senator Shay there in Texas, I could his his support on my oil bill that allows Florida to increase our deep-sea oil extraction," he appealed for support as he stood up from the table.

"You got it. You can count on it," Angus assured the senator.

"Oh, if you want another drink, put it on my tab. Ginger knows me here. I just told her it was OK," he explained to the McKays.

"Appreciate you, senator. We have another meeting with the IRS. Still have friends there," Angus stated. They finished their luncheon and decided to visit the mall and St. John's church, the church of the presidents. The four mile-distance was too far for Faith to walk in high heels. So, they hailed a taxi.

"St. John's church at 1525 H street NW," Angus gave address to the driver. The ten-minute drive was $12.50 plus a tip. At the church Angus and Faith sat in the front pew thanking their Maker for all the blessings they are enjoying. Faith asked for guidance in making the right choice on which hospital to accept a job offer.

From the church they took a bus to the Pentagon City Mall. Faith looked at the dress styles for the coming year. Angus couldn't believe the price tags on some of the dresses. She did find some Thanksgiving napkin holders and napkins she thought were unique. The napkin holders were designed to hold individual napkins, folded in such a way that the napkin was the tail feathers of a turkey. She took ten sets.

Later they were taking a bus to the Hill Country BBQ to meet Randall Dawson, who had replaced Angus when he accepted the offer to move to Texas and start his own business in gas and oil tax service.

The bus stop was two blocks from the restaurant. Randall was sitting at the bar having a draft beer when the McKays walked in. He greeted them with a big smile and a warm handshake. He led them to the back corner where a table had been reserved for them. There they did not have to compete with the country western music that was blaring outside to attract the people walking near the restaurant.

Randall's wrinkled shirt showed he'd had a hard day at the office. The loosened yellow tie was standard for him. His black framed glasses gave him the 'Clark Kent Look' of Superman days. "It sure is good to see you two again," he said. "I didn't expect to see you so soon after you moved to Texas."

About that time the waitress appeared with the drinks and asked if they wanted to order anything. She was wearing tight fitting cut-off jeans with a big belt buckle. Her western blouse and red boots matched the red and white checkered table cloth. The top three buttons of her blouse were unbuttoned exposing cleavage. The western décor included a roll of paper towels for napkins.

Faith looked at the waitress and with a thick southern accent said, "Honey, bring me a cold mug of beer."

"And you, sir?" she asked Angus who was still looking at Faith with a 'where'd-that-come-from' look on his face.

"If you have ginger ale, I'll take that. If not, a glass of sweet tea,' replied Angus. He glanced over at Faith who was nodding in approval. The waitress shrugged her shoulders, turned, and sashayed back to the kitchen.

Angus asked, "Randall, how do you like your new position at the office?"

The waitress returned with the drinks, a beer, and a glass of sweet tea. "Ma'am, would you care to order anything else?" she directed her request at Faith.

Faith ordered a chopped pork sandwich with potatoes and gravy, and a small bowl of succotash. Randall and Angus each ordered the sliced beef special with sauce, French fries, and okra.

"Well, since you asked, the constant changing of laws and regulations causes us to be attending more meetings than I anticipated. They try to explain why the changes were implemented and how to work them into our teaching manuals. They have meetings to schedule meetings! I swear, congress generates more paperwork every year. The only people who really benefit are the document shredders. Congress keeps trying to squeeze more money out of those gambling on finding gas and oil holes. Angus still can't thank you enough for recommending me to be the head of the department," Randall stated as he held up his mug of beer, "Cheers to your consulting business."

"I knew you were the best person for that position. Yes, it's a demanding job, but you have the personality that will not let the executive manager get under your skin," Angus replied.

Faith wanted to know how his family was doing, "Randall, how are Kay and Johnnie? The last I heard you had moved to Alexandria, is that right?"

"Thanks for asking. Yes, we did make a move to Alexandria. Kay started working in the procurement office for the Defense Department. She likes it, except next year little Johnnie starts school. She has been considering being a fulltime mother. Who knows we may have another baby." Randall looked sheepishly at Faith.

Randall Dawson are you trying to tell me something?" she pressed for an answer.

He leaned over toward her and whispered, "Well, Faith, we are not certain right now. I'm not supposed to say anything about it yet."

Trying to change the subject, Randall asked, "Angus how is it on the front lines working with the oil and gas people?" Faith took a sip of her drink, gave him a big wink with a knowing smile.

"To be honest, there is so much misinformation floating around by some who don't have the foggiest idea on how to fill out a tax form. Then there are those who think they know all the loop holes. For example, the change coming next year about reducing the percent for inventory carry over which will cause a lot of red flags. I've already started directing my key clients to make the necessary changes. They already know to expect higher taxes, but they won't be hammered with penalties," Angus explained taking a drink from his glass of sweet tea.

The cowgirl waitress with the ponytail delivered their order. She deliberately gave Faith her pork chops and potatoes last. During their meal, Randall ordered another mug since he had more information to share with Angus, "Congress finalized an approved a bill authorizing our department to purchase a computer system from IBM. Big Bucks! IBM claims they can develop a software program that will cut our workload in half. I'll believe it when I see it. I am not completely comfortable yet about using computers to handle our processing. You've heard 'garbage in, garbage out'. As you know the tax laws can be very complex and they change year to year."

Angus responded, "I agree with you. People are still uncertain about putting their trust in computers. Good luck on that."

Randall took another sip of his beer and added, "Also, for your ears only, I have reasons to believe congress is about to announce an Environmental Protection Tax within the next few years. Upper management keeps asking for reports on how the oil rigs are damaging the environment after the oil crews pull out. I may be calling you to get some photos supporting their claims. Keep your eye on that. "Last week, I got yet another special assignment. You probably heard about a county commissioner getting murdered near Houston," Randall started telling Angus and Faith how he is now involved with the FBI's investigation.

Angus quickly looked at Faith and slowly shook his head because Faith knew of his involvement with the case.

Randall continued, "The FBI wants me to run a background check on the assistant commissioner, the mayor, and the entire board of the Houston ISD. Angus, that's an old case from a few years ago and they still haven't been able to arrest anyone for the murder. Didn't you have to conduct some background checks when you were here?" Randall looked at Angus wanting a response.

"Randall, those background checks may take several months to complete. Do not get in a hurry with them. Be certain that your facts can be verified. There were three Jamaican banks that were known for working with United States citizens who did not want to pay taxes." Then Angus added, "I do remember I had to get some political backup to get the banks to comply. The weirdest one was when two brothers, who were presidents at different banks kept transferring this guy's bank balance back and forth. That one took some time to solve."

"The FBI wants a full report as soon as possible. Executive management says I am to drop everything and assist the FBI. Of course, I do the leg work and they'll get the credit, Right?" Randall lamented with a grin.

"Gee, man I'll be glad to go do Jamaica for you. That is, if Faith can go with me," Angus chuckled glancing at Faith who gave him a weak smile.

Randall wanted to know, "When you had an assignment like that, how did you go about it? I mean where did you start?"

"You start by comparing the deposits made by the citizen or company to what the bank is showing," he advised. "I got lucky when the bookkeeper saw the difference in what the bank was showing compared to what the company's books were showing. I let them think that maybe they could be arrested for being part of the bogus transactions. I tried to put the fear of God in them. Usually they didn't want to go to prison for something their boss did."

Angus continued, trying to put Randall on the right track, "I don't know much about your situation but generally there is a shell company that is used. Maybe someone on your list is involved in a small business that is showing more dollars than his competitors in that market area."

The dinner crowd was thinning out at the Hill Country BBQ. The McKays had had a full day and needed to get back to their hotel. Angus and Randall shook hands as they departed. Faith whispered in Randall's ear when he hugged her, "Tell Kay to keep me informed about your family."

The McKays took a taxi back to the American Inn after a full day in Washington D.C. The next day they boarded a plane and headed back to Dallas, Texas. Angus discussed the idea of getting a minicomputer to handle the gas and oil tax forms with Faith. "The more I think about what Randall said about IBM installing a computer system I wonder why a mini computer wouldn't work for me?"

CHAPTER 27

Angus took the elevator to the 5th floor and walked through the Executive Offices door to his office. Brenda the young neatly dressed receptionist greeted him with a smile and said, "Welcome back, Mr. McKay". She handed him a fist full of telephone messages. She added, "That Johnnie Porter from the Houston Daily News is a real flirter! He called me twice asking for a date after he dropped in unannounced. I told him you would be back in the office this week."

"Well, he has good taste." Angus chuckled as he walked down the hall. He had a small office on the fifth floor. There were ten offices: six different firms, one receptionist, one conference room, one break room with a refrigerator, microwave, and a modern coffeemaker. His small, ten by ten office consisted of desk and chair, two chairs for clients and a file cabinet, which had half of one of its drawers filled with file folders. There was one small five-foot book shelf with a few issues of the Gas and Oil Journal. The office was northeast of downtown Dallas. Angus liked the location because it was close to Southern Methodist University. He frequented the Underwood Law Library at SMU where there were study rooms for privacy, helpful library services and three floors of law reference books.

Angus looked through his messages and recognized the names on most the messages except for two. One message was from Johnnie Porter. There were two from the Dallas FBI agency that had begun assisting the Houston FBI when Angus had moved to Dallas. One was from Mr. Johnson and another from the Fischer family. Each family was asking how he was doing. One other message was from a Mr. Allen Watson, a prospective client, who was asking Angus to look at his taxes. He had just paid nearly a thousand dollars in gas and oil tax penalty fees. Angus replied to his key clients first. He told them everything was fine, that he was just dealing with an old battle wound. Next, he contacted his latest prospective client Allen Watson to schedule an appointment to review his taxes. Then he called FBI Agent Guy Hopkins.

"Agent Hopkins," the FBI agent answered the phone.

"Agent Hopkins, this is Angus McKay returning your call," Angus replied.

"Yes sir, our department is assisting the Houston FBI office and we could not find your fingerprints in the files. Could you come to the Dallas office? We're at One Justice Way, off I-35E. We need to take your fingerprints. You do not need to make an appointment," stated the FBI agent.

"Why do you need my fingerprints?" Angus curiously asked.

"It pertains to a County Commissioner's murder. Our report shows you stopped and administered aid around three years ago. You're not a suspect, Mr. McKay, but we're gathering missing information," Hopkins assured Angus.

"You mean they have not made an arrest in that case? What do I need to do?" Angus asked.

"Sir, they do have a few leads but no arrest has been made. As you probably read in the papers, the commissioner and his wife were babysitting for their son and his wife, who were on a cruise. The district attorney believed that the judge would not allow the children to be introduced in the court because neither child could legally appear in a grand jury. The oldest is a four-year-old boy who has Down Syndrome. He just says, 'gun, bang' when asked what he saw. No appointment is required, simply stop in our office. It'll take less than 15 minutes," Agent Hopkins responded.

"All right. I should be in that area within next two weeks," agreed Angus.

"That's fine. Look forward to meeting you, sir," the agent said hanging up the phone.

Next Angus called Johnnie Porter. "Maybe he wants to apologize for the way he darted out of the White Bear restaurant several years ago," he thought to himself.

"Porter here," Johnnie said answering the phone.

"Mr. Porter, this is McKay. I dialed a Dallas number. I thought you were in Houston. Did you move?" Angus asked.

"No. I am doing a follow up story on a report that a Dallas county commissioner is scheming money from home builders, I'm temporarily using an office at the Dallas Morning News. I heard you had a tough time in Vietnam and have made it back to Texas. Glad you made it back. I would like to buy you a lunch again as a way of saying 'thank you' for putting me on the right track. When and where would you like to meet?" asked Johnnie.

Angus looked at his calendar. "I can meet you tomorrow at the El Fenix at 11 o'clock, if you promise not to run out on me," Angus reminded Johnnie of their past meeting.

"No problem. See you there tomorrow for lunch," Johnnie replied with a chuckle.

The El Fenix opened at 11 o'clock. Angus parked his car at 11:10 and went in to wait. Mr. Porter walked through the door at 11:40. He had a camera that belonged to the Dallas Morning News hanging around his neck.

"Mr. McKay welcome back to Texas," Johnnie greeted his guest.

"Mr. Porter, thank you. Glad to be back," replied Angus.

As they sat down at a table in the back, a chubby waiter brought them water and warm chips. Both ordered tacos. Porter ordered a beer and Agnus had sweet tea.

"I have reasons to believe that the Mafia bugged your phones in Crockett. They may have already bugged your home in Parker's Prairie," Johnnie informed Angus.

"What? Are you sure?" Angus asked with a surprised expression.

"I said maybe. But if it is, you wouldn't want the Mafia to know what I've learned about the shooting 3 years ago. McKay, thanks to your suggestion of finding out 'why' the commissioner was killed, I began a two-year investigation immediately after our meeting. Even the Houston FBI was impressed when I shared with them what I was finding. McKay this could be a best seller mystery for me. Thank you," reported Porter.

"What exactly did you learn in your investigation?" Angus asked when the food was delivered to their table. Both men took a sip of their drinks.

"Well, some of this is subjective, but it makes sense. The commissioner had discovered a man everyone called Mr. C, who owns a service station within three blocks of the Independent School District bus maintenance lot. His cousin Bobbi Ray owns a medium size fuel delivery truck. The shop manager had been instructed by the superintendent to order either the diesel or gasoline from Bobbi Ray because he had the lowest delivery price. Mr. C just happened to also be on the ISD board and the one in charge of reviewing the expenses of the ISD maintenance shop. What if the gasoline meters on Mr. Ray's truck had been altered to show more fuel being delivered than what was actually delivered?" Porter stopped and took a couple bites of his tacos.

He continued, "The balance of the load would be taken three blocks to Mr. C's service station. I've checked his gas station net profits compared to the other service station in his market area. He's gotta be running two sets of books. I suspect he's getting some free gas and it's not showing up on his profit and loss report." Johnnie confided to Angus. "Somehow the commissioner must have figured it out and probably confronted Mr. C with this. That is why I believe the commissioner and his wife were murdered. He knew too much," the reporter concluded.

"So, you're saying that Mr. C is somehow connected to or may be involved with the Mafia?" Angus asked after considering about what was just pointed out.

"I have not been able to confirm everything yet, but Mr. C must have been related to the Mafia. I am certain that the Houston ISD has been short changed on what they have been paying for fuel not only for their school buses, but for all their automobiles and pickups over the years. Also, in my investigation, I learned that Mr. C owns a rundown tavern south of New Orleans. I have a detective down there gathering more information," Johnnie finished his report and ate the last of his tacos.

"Johnnie, sounds like you've been busy since our last meeting. What you say makes sense," Angus said agreeing with the information from his investigative." Angus continued, "As I told you earlier, the only thing I could understand from Joey King was that I should tell his wife he loved her. You say you discussed this with the FBI in Houston. What did they say?" McKay wanted to know.

Johnnie responded, "They thanked me for the information. I know from some close sources they are still looking at very few leads. I asked them to let me have first right to release this information when it gets to a grand jury. Yes, you're right, I do have some 'iffy' information, but I truly believe it will explain not only 'who' but 'why' the commissioner was shot to death," the investigating reporter stopped to take a few bites of his cold tacos.

Looking at his watch Angus said, "Well Johnnie I'd be interested in having a signed copy of your book."

"I'll keep you informed on my investigation. I still believe there's more to your story," Johnnie looked directly into Angus' eyes waiting for a reply.

"Don't you think that if there was more, I'd told the police?" Angus questioned Johnnie.

"Not if your family was be in danger," countered Johnnie as he stood up and reached to shake Angus' hand. "Thanks for your time and for teaching me a valuable lesson. You put me on the right track on this story for a reason. That, I believe. We will meet again," he picked up the tab and turned toward the door.

Angus followed Johnnie to the parking lot and drove to the FBI office to be fingerprinted.

The gray granite walls held the American flag and a portrait of the president. He passed the big 3-D letters on the wall as he walked up to the counter. "Agent Hopkins wanted me to come in for fingerprinting," Angus said to the professionally dressed receptionist who looked like she could be an agent herself.

"And you are?" she inquired looking up from her paperwork.

"My name is Angus McKay I am here to be fingerprinted," he said as he introduced himself.

"Yes, Mr. McKay. Agent Hopkins said to expect you. He's at a meeting. My name is Mary Ann, I will take your fingerprints," she politely said, "He did mention that I was to let you know that you're definitely not a suspect. This is strictly routine for our files pertaining to the case."

"How long will this take?" Angus needed to know. "I have a 3:30 appointment at my office near the SMU campus.

"Allow me ten to fifteen minutes and you can be on your way," she answered as she led Angus to another room. Her hands were silky smooth. Her freshly polished finger nails were a bright red. Her perfume released a sweet flowery aroma as she stood beside Angus. Mary Ann gently guided his fingers one at a time on the ink pad and then rolled each one on a form that had Daniel McKay written across the top. When the fingerprinting was completed, she handed Angus a paper towel to wipe the ink off. About that time Agent Guy Hopkins walked into the office. Mary Ann introduced the two men.

"Thank you for coming in so quickly," Agent Hopkins said.

"Sir, I am concerned for the safety of my family in Crockett and my wife. I have been informed that the Mafia may have bugged my phones. Is there any way I can tell if my phones have been bugged?" Angus asked.

"Mr. McKay let me have the phone numbers and your address and I can check to see if your phones have been bugged. If so, we can de-bug them for you. Do we have your permission to do that? Either way I will let you know what we find?" replied Agent Hopkins.

"Yes, you have my permission," agreed Angus.

Less than an hour later Angus entered the elevator, pushed number five, and headed up to his office to wait for Mr. Allen Watson.

Mr. Watson's coarse voice had a Texas twang that could be heard as he introduced himself to Brenda.

"Mr. Watson I'm Angus McKay. Angus to my friends," he greeted his latest client as they walked toward his office.

"Pleased to me meet you, I'm Allen Watson," he stated removing his tattered cowboy hat.

Angus picked up a yellow paper pad and pen from his desk, pulled up a chair and sat beside Mr. Watson and said, "Let's start at the beginning. Tell me where you're from and how old your wells are."

"Well sir I'm from Garden City. It's northeast of Midland-Odessa. The five wells began pumping in 1970. My first oil check was in 1971. The IRS went back last year and say I owe about half of my annual oil income," complained Mr. Watson.

"How did you learn about me and did you bring your tax returns with you?" Angus continued questioning.

"Your name came up a week or so ago when I was having my daily coffee at our local Dairy Queen. I was bitching about the IRS to my friends. That's when they told me about you. Yes sir, got 'em, rat here," he replied handing Angus a banker's box half full of paper.

"Mr. Watson, let me go through your receipts and tax returns to lean if I can be of any help to you. It will take me a couple of weeks. I have your phone number in case I have questions. Do you come to Dallas often ?" Angus asked.

"My daughter goes to Texas Christian University over in Fort Worth. I try to see her as often as I can." He smiled at the thought of his daughter. "She's the first in our family to go to college," he proudly announced.

"I know you must be mighty proud of her. If you have no more questions, that's all I need to know at this time," Angus said concluding the meeting.

"Thank you, Mr. McKay fer your time. I look forward to hear'n from you," he replied as he left Angus' office. He tipped his Stetson hat to Brenda and politely said, "Thank yah ma'am." As he passed her desk.

McKay reviewed his to-do list. Next on the list was to get names of computer companies.

CHAPTER 28

"World Wide Rugs. This is Rooster, how may I help you?"

"Rooster, this is Deggs."

"Oh hi. Whatta you got fer me?" he asked.

"Nothing to help you, except there had been a Houston Oilers Ice Chest cooler in the trunk of Joey's car. There had been a couple of bags of ice, but the ice had melted. There weren't nothin' inside but water and two empty plastic bags. Joey's finger prints weren't the only prints found. Forensic guys are trying to find out whose finger prints are on the ice chest besides Joey's. They've run different tests, but the tests do not agree. The lab report is inconclusive. So, the FBI and the Houston police still have nothing solid to go on. Who would put only ice in an ice chest? huh? The guys at the station think Joey was planning on heading for a grocery store for food and disappearing for a few days," Police Officer Deggs stopped talking briefly to crush his cigarette beneath his shoe.

Rooster anxiously wanted to know, "Was there any money found?"

"Not according to any police reports that I read. Was there supposed to be?" asked Deggs.

"Just asking," Rooster quickly stated, dodging any further discussion.

"Look, Rooster I gotta go, I'm on duty pretty soon. If I learn anything else, I'll give you a call. Deggs hung up without waiting for a response. Rooster walked into Frankie's office and reported what

Deggs had just told to him about the ice chest and there was no money found.

Mr. C was getting nervous about his 25 G's. He dialed Trigger in Gretna.

"Last Resort." A deep bass voice bellowed.

"Trigger?"

"Nuh, I'm a customer, Just a minute I'll get him for you."

"Trigger here."

"Trigger, why are customers answering the phone? Where is Twyla?" Mr. C asked in a frustrated tone.

"Oh, it's you, Mr. C. Twyla's up in 'New Or'leens. She says she needed some new clothes. I think she needs to get away from this place occasionally. You're on my list to call. Our Houston police contact says the only thing they've found in the truck of Joey's care have is an Oilers ice chest. The outside was scarred and burned but did not melt, the inside had water and two empty ice bags. The Feds think Joey was stocking up to disappear somewhere. They did find Joey's finger prints on the ice chest, and there also were some prints that they have not been able to trace because they were too smudgy. They have no license plate numbers and nothing about an airplane. Actually, Mr. C, I don't believe the guy who gave Joey first aid, had an opportunity to even look in the trunk. He spent all his time doing the Good Samaritan Deed," Trigger concluded his report.

"Well, someone has my twenty-five thousand! Maybe Maria has it! By God, someone has it!" Mr. C 's frustrated voice kept getting louder.

"Frankie talked to our newspaper guy in Houston. His contacts had no information of any value, only what's in the newspapers. Mr. C, I'll keep working on it and let you know as soon as I learn anything." Then, deflecting the conversation to a more positive topic.

"We have a new source for two kilos twice a month. It comes in from Haiti via Mexican Airways on a regular weekly flight in a medical package for one of our doctors. I checked it out. Good stuff. We can divide it up among our top producers. They have been threatening to go somewhere else. This should keep 'em happy for a while."

"OK Trigger. Keep me informed. Maybe I should raise your rent! Ha Ha," he chuckled slamming down the phone.

In New Orleans, Twyla put down her packages and dialed a local number. The phone rang a couple of times before being answered, "Good afternoon, this is U.S. Pest Control. May I help you?"

"Sara, this is Twyla. Put me through to Walt."

"Twyla, how are you? How's my top DEA agent? What do you have for me?" asked Walt.

"Walt, I understand there may be some heavy medical shipments on Mexican Airways twice a month. Don't know when it will start. Shipments are supposed to originate in Haiti, but that may be a cover stop over. It may be worth investigating. Listen, I've got to get back to Gretna. I'll call you if I find out anything else. I suggest we activate our file on Haiti-Gretna," she advised ending the phone call.

She gathered up her bags from the various stores where she had made purchases and went out the door of the Canal Plaza. Twyla did not look the same as The Last Resort customers knew her. Her hair was down around her shoulders, her make up highlighted her dark brown eyes, she was a shapely size eight. At work she had either worn a ponytail or pigtails, no make-up, and fake glasses that made her look twenty years older. It was something she learned at the beauty school when she was in the CIA.

One bag was from BCBGMAXAZRTA, a very high-end department store, where she had purchased a lace trimmed, black sheathe. At SOLSTICE SUNGLASSES she picked out a pair of Ray Ban Wayfarers. The frames were large enough to adequately cover her face. At Saks Fifth Avenue she purchased a Kender 148 New York blouse to match the Abris Pung Scuba Velvet Pencil Skirt. Then she headed back to The Last Resort.

A yellow cab pulled over as soon as the driver saw her waving her hand. He figured since she was just leaving Canal Plaza, the nice-looking lady had to be a good tipper. He did something he rarely did, he got out and opened the door for her.

He asked in a pleasant manner, "Where to, lady?"

"Gretna! I'll give you the address when we get closer," she replied.

"You musta won the lottery or sumthin'. Nobody comes out of Canal Plaza with an arm full of bags and heads for Gretna! That's a warehouse district for unloading ships," the driver asserted as he got into the mainstream of traffic. "Nothing like that. I've been saving for a special occasion and want to look extra nice for my boyfriend." she replied.

"Lady, you look nice enough. He must be a pretty lucky guy!" The driver drove south to Gretna. It took less than fifteen minutes.

The fare was fifteen dollars. She gave him twenty-five dollars.

"Thank you, ma'am, call me if you need a ride anytime, anywhere. Here is my card." He flashed a friendly smile and drove away. Twyla entered her modest one-bedroom apartment and put the sun glasses in her top dresser drawer and her newest clothes in the closet. She activated her new cell phone and put it away for future use. Then, she redid her hair and put on her barmaid clothes before heading to The Last Resort.

Trigger asked, "Hi Twyla! How was the big city trip?"

"Oh, I was just looking and dreaming." she replied.

There was a couple at the bar. The ash tray in front of them was overflowing with ashes and butts. Smoke from a partially smoked cigar looked ghostly reflecting in the bar mirror. The customer was fading and the woman next to him knew she had a meal and a place to sleep that night. Twyla had witnessed this scene many times. Her heart felt for the woman who looked like she was on her last leg.

"Here, have one on the house." Twyla said as she shoved another glass of cheap bourbon his way. She smiled, looking at the woman, "Here's one for you too." The woman's glass had ginger ale. She recognized the difference by the fizz. She looked at Twyla and mouthed 'thank you'.

Twyla began cleaning up a couple of the tables and swept the floor. Trigger was on the phone with one of his street workers who he hadn't heard from lately. She claimed she was short of cash but would contact him when she had enough to buy. "Trigger, you know me I'm a true customer," begged the desperate woman. Trigger hung up on her and came out to talk to Twyla.

Trigger mentioned to Twyla in a quiet voice, "Mr. C called."

"Ye'ah, what did he want?" Twyla asked with an uninterested voice. She opened an exit door, turned the overhead fan on high to clean the stagnant air of the smoky smell. The squeaky fan noise drowned out the tick tock of the clock on the wall.

"Joey's money is missin'. Mr. C wants it back," he whispered so the couple couldn't hear.

"What money?" Twyla blurted out.

"Oh," he hesitated, "I think Mr. C paid Joey twenty-five grand to take care of the job with that commissioner in Houston. Now Joey's dead and Mr. C wants his money back. You didn't hear that from me?"

Twyla knew why Trigger hesitated. He wasn't supposed to share that information. She now had more pieces to the puzzle: Mr. C, Joey King, and a missing twenty-five thousand dollars. She made a mental note, 'Walt needs to hear about this' and kept on cleaning.

The following week Trigger was overly happy about something. He got that way when he knew there were some drugs being moved and he always took his share. Twyla asked Trigger if she could take off for a couple of days. He told her he needed her around for a few nights, but maybe Saturday night when the tavern traffic drops off because the warehouses will be on reduced shifts. The ploy worked! Based on his answer she figured there would be a drop off within the next few days. She had to find out when and where.

From the telephone booth down at the filling station, she called Mexican Airways to get their arrival schedules into New Orleans. There was one on Thursday night at midnight. Flight #2833. It was worth a call to U.S. Pest Control.

"Hello, U.S. Pest Control. How may I help you?" was announced.

"Sara, it's Twyla. Can you put me through to Walt?" she asked.

"Walt speaking."

"Walt, there may be a two or four kilo shipment of cocaine on Mexican Airways on a midnight night flight #2833. She explained what she had learned. It's a guess, but worth checking out. This is a bi-weekly flight on Thursdays. Probably addressed to some doctor or medical clinic. Think you should check this out!" stated Twyla.

"Doubt it on such a short notice. If not, didn't you say they are expecting a shipment every two weeks?" asked Walt, then he added, "Can you confirm a future shipment date? I'll get some men in place at the airport to check out the baggage for flight #2833."

"Also, I may have some information worth checking on the Houston commissioner killing. Joey King was killed in a mafia hit. I understand Joey was paid twenty-five thousand dollars to kill the commissioner. Mr. C is upset because he wants to know who has the money or where it is." reported Twyla.

"Good job. I'll pass the information to the FBI in Houston. Try to keep me informed on the dates of the shipments. Twyla be careful, don't be asking nosey questions." he warned.

Several days later Twyla learned that Mexican Airways flight continued to Houston. She wondered if maybe the drugs would be going to Houston and not New Orleans.

Walt studied the New Orleans-Gretna file and began reviewing the major players in the drug ring in the area. He recognized Tony, alias Trigger as being a minor player and wanted to nail someone farther up the ladder. Tony was a gofer man for Mr. C. His twin brother, Frankie, handled Louisiana for the mafia. Both were young men with records. Walt wanted to get Mr. C behind bars. It may be time to get Twyla out of Gretna. He began planning Operation Pelican. His plan was to follow the drug route from the airport, to the packaging and all the way to the streets.

Six days later Trigger was in his office with his office door closed. Twyla knocked twice.

"Just a minute," Trigger cleared his throat and yelled.

Twyla waited and knocked again. This time Trigger told her to come in. Upon entering his office, she noticed white powder under his nose. Trigger's clothes were all winkled and he looked like he had not slept. She knew immediately the shipment had arrived the night before. She motioned that he needed to wipe his nose.

"Oh, that. That is some powdered sugar from the beignet's. I was at the Café du Monde in New Or'leens last night. Just had my last beignet." Trigger casually commented.

"If you say so," Twyla remarked with sarcasm. "I've been thinking of a vacation and was wondering if you can handle everything here for a week," she asked.

"Does Mr. C know about this? Have you talked to him?" Trigger asked as he wiped his nose with the handkerchief from his suit pocket.

Twyla responded, "I thought I'd clear it with you first."

"Ye'ah, I can do it. I can handle my business by phone. Talk to Mr. C and if says it's OK, it's OK with me," Trigger agreed to her request.

"I'll let you know his answer," she replied retreating to the bar.

Walt's Pelican Operation required that Twyla not be in The Last Resort when the Drug Division raided it.

Twyla talked to Mr. C about taking a vacation. At first, he begged her to just take a long weekend, but she insisted a full week off.

"Well if Trigger agrees to it. Guess you deserve some time off. Where do you plan to go on your vacation?" he asked.

"Not sure yet, maybe one of the Caribbean Islands," she replied.

"Call me when you get back. Send me a photo of you in your bikini," he said teasing her.

Before Twyla had some work to do before she could leave. She needed to bug Trigger's phone but she had not been given the signal from Walt to leave Gretna. Walt had three men stationed in an office of an abandon warehouse. He had two men at the New Orleans Airport working on the flight line.

CHAPTER 29

Thursday night at 9:30 Trigger's office phone rang. He answered after the fourth ring, "The Last Resort."

"This is Henry Garcia. I have a package," said the pilot. "I'll be at the LaGalerie Hotel."

"After you check in, call the hotel clerk and ask for Trigger Ramos. I'll be in the lobby waiting for your call," Trigger spoke softly.

The Drug Enforcement team at the warehouse immediately called Walt at his office in Washington D.C., "The drugs are not with anyone on the passenger manifest. It's the pilot, Henry Garcia! He's heading to the LaGalerie Hotel to meet Trigger Ramos. We can be there in fifteen minutes. What are your orders?" asked the DEA supervisor.

"Get to the hotel. If you have an opportunity to follow Trigger after they meet and make the trade, maybe we can catch a bigger fish. Otherwise, take the pilot to your New Orleans office and see what information you can get from him. I'll be here no matter how long it takes," directed Walt.

The three DEA officers locked up the warehouse and headed north on the West Bank Expressway to I-90 and Decatur street. One agent walked into the LaGalerie. The hotel clerk asked, "May I help you?"

"I'm waiting for someone," replied the agent as he picked up a magazine.

Forty-five minutes later, Henry Garcia, entered the hotel. His flight crew of a co-pilot and three airline flight attendants accompanied him. All were wearing the Mexican Airways uniforms. He carried his pilot's black nylon flight case and a traveling flight bag up to the reservation desk. "I'm Captain Henry Garcia." he stated handing the desk clerk his company credit card. The co-pilot had a separate room and the flight attendants had a double bed with a pullout couch.

"Yes, Captain Garcia, we've been expecting you and your flight crew. Here is your room key. Do you need a wake-up call?" the hotel clerk asked.

It was 10:45 pm when Trigger walked through the door carrying a brief case. He walked over to the reception desk and picked up the USA newspaper. "I'm waiting for a phone call." he told the hotel clerk. Ten minutes later the hotel telephone rang. "Mr. Ramos, a call for you sir," the young clerk announced pointing to the phone.

"This is Trigger Ramos," Trigger answered.

"Suite 412."

Trigger handed the receiver back to the clerk and headed for the elevator. The agent waited until elevator door closed. He watched as the floor level flashed as the elevator passed each floor. The DEA agent took the steps to the fourth floor.

Trigger softly rapped on room 412. The door slowly opened and Garcia was smiling as he opened the door all the way for Trigger. "Come in, my friend," he welcomed his guest with the brief case.

The pilot wanted to know, "Do you have the money?"

"Yes! Didn't expect you 'til after midnight. Where is the merchandise?" responded Trigger.

"Yes, the company changed the flight schedules to New Orleans," Garcia replied as he set his flight case on a coffee table in front of the couch. He took out two Jeppesen Airport Chart Maps, IFR maps, an Airport Reference handbook, and a New Orleans Sectional Aeronautical Chart map. The flight case had a false bottom. He reached down and pulled out one kilogram of cocaine wrapped in a plastic bag.

Trigger cut the plastic with a knife and gave the white powder a taste test. He smiled and said, "Good stuff!" He handed Garcia the brief case with $10,000 in bills of hundreds and fifties.

Garcia looked Trigger in the eye, "There's more where this came from! I fly to New Orleans every other Thursday night. The airline books us at this hotel. Do we have a deal?"

"Yes. Can you handle two kilos a trip?" asked Trigger.

Garcia replied, "I'd rather not. One kilo works better for me."

The two agreed on one kilogram every other Thursday. Trigger headed back to his car with his merchandise in his briefcase. The DEA agents had put a tracer under a rear fender of the black Lincoln. They waited for the third agent to come out of the hotel.

Trigger headed west on Highway 90 toward Thibodaux. At the Des Allemandes exit he turned where an old dilapidated 'Catfish Capital' road sign beckoned visitors. The road led to a boat landing at Bayou Gauche, where his 16-foot motor boat with a 150-horse powered Mercury motor was parked. He then headed south. He passed several old shanties some with inhabitants, some empty. Trigger tied up the boat at a boat dock that had four other boats tied to it. He climbed up a ladder to get to the front porch of a cabin that had been empty for decades and entered to be greeted by four men and two women.

On an old kitchen table there were two big gallon pots and a pound of powdered sugar. Trigger carefully unwrapped the kilo of cocaine and poured half in one pot and the other half in the other pot. Then he measured 15 teaspoons of powdered sugar into each pot.

"That should do it," he said. The two women put on their face masks and industrial safety glasses. They began rapidly stirring the mixture.

After three minutes, Trigger said, "That should be enough. Let's bag it."

The mixture in each pot was carefully poured into six smaller bins with a chute at the bottom. It was an archaic and labor-intensive method of filling small plastic bags with one gram of the '12.5% stepped up' mixture of cocaine and powdered sugar. The powdered sugar allowed Trigger to increase the total number of bags from 2,000 bags to 2,250 bags. It was four o'clock in the morning when all 2,250 bags were filled. Each person received 40 bags for their pay.

Trigger headed back to Gretna with 2,010 bags of 'stepped up' cocaine plus the bag of pure cocaine he took for himself.

It was 2:15 the next afternoon when he tried to sneak in the squeaky back door of The Last Resort. Twyla heard that sound. "She must have been a tiger!" she needled him.

The DEA team had called Walt to let him know Trigger had taken a boat down the bayou. Walt blew up! He wanted the bust to go down as he had planned. More discussions from the field agents indicated that there was no way they could get back into the bayou without revealing their presence.

"How do we get agents there without anyone knowing," he asked the Pelican Project team who were gathered in the conference room.

One agent spoke up, "We had a similar situation in Vietnam. We helicoptered six men and one motorized rubber raft into the area. We were dropped at a low level. The chopper was skimming the water. In fact, we climbed down a ladder into the raft. We hit a village that night and caught the Vietcong off guard. They never saw us coming."

Walt looked at the agent, nodded and asked, "Anyone have a better suggestion?" No one offered to say anything. "Let's do it. We know they meet every other Thursday. We can get an overhead photo of the bayou. My bet is it is the last cabin along the canal. We will make an early morning drop. Locate the cabin. Disappear into the swamp and wait. We know they'll have to take boats to the cabin. They'll lead us to it. I want the man who brings the 'cake' to the party. This time he won't get away," stressed Walt.

He then called his New Orleans office. "We need the Keesler Air Force Base to do a flyover to take photos of our bayou as soon as possible. Then, we need a chopper to ferry six men and three motorized rafts on an early Thursday low level delivery. Let's see if the agents can train for this exercise in Mississippi, any place but Louisiana."

The Secretary of Homeland Security over the DEA approved the Pelican Project and the week of special training and supplies needed for the operation. The plan was for a helicopter from Keesler Air Base to drop three motorized rubber rafts, and six especially trained men. The DEA team was ready at sunrise on the third Thursday of the month. They were equipped with special CAR-15's, smoke and flash bombs. Each agent was carrying two cans of mosquito spray that the Vietnam vet had highly recommended. Each raft would hold twelve people including six DEA agents. Each team had trained to rappel down a rope from the helicopter to one of the two rafts. The drop off area was a mile from the targeted cabin. The men had to sit under camouflaged netting from sunrise until darkness. Each man knew where he was to be once inside the cabin. They could expect to find three or four flat bottom boats tied to the cabin dock. The dock was attached to the ladder leading up to the cabin. The trailing agents were to radio the agents sitting in rafts when Trigger got into his boat. It, too, had a tracer that the lead raft could monitor.

Ten days later a couple of grungy looking dock workers walked into The Last Resort. They found a clean table. Twyla walked over and asked what they wanted. One answered in a gruff voice, "Two po'boys and two bottles of beer, Sweetie."

Sweetie was Twyla's code name. She figured something was about to happen. She delivered the order with several extra napkins. The two customers took their time to eat the sandwiches and drink the beers. There were no other customers in the tavern. When the two finally left, one of the napkins had a note, 'get out of town'.

On the third Thursday of the month. The same two dock workers came in an hour before noon. She recognized them and asked, "Two po'boys and two beers, right?"

"You got it, Sweetie," the gruff voice replied.

This time the note was written on a ten-dollar bill, 'get out of town'. The two grabbed their sandwiches and beer bottles and departed. Twyla knocked on Trigger's office door. She yelled through the closed door, "Trigger, I don't feel good. I think I'm coming down with something. I need to go lie down."

Trigger pulled open the door and objected in an angry tone, "You can't take off today. I've got an important meeting to attend in New Orleans."

"So, Trigger, close early! I can't make it!" she coldly smirked.

Trigger slammed the door shut so hard that a beer sign fell off the wall. Twyla closed the door and headed for her apartment. She packed what clothes she wanted to keep and called the taxi driver that had left his card with her. She had told Mr. C that she was taking a vacation.

By 10:30 The Last Resort was empty of customers. Trigger locked the door and turned the sign on the door to read "CLOSED"! He went back into his office and turned off the bar lights. He grabbed the briefcase with the $10,000 and headed for his black Lincoln. He was running a little late for his meeting with Henry Garcia. He had a couple of half ounce cocaine packets in his pocket. He could get $15,000 of 'street money' for them. But these were his private packets. They had not been cut. He arrived at the hotel just as his contact and the rest of the flight crew were checking in at the reception desk.

They nodded at each other as the pilot picked up his flight bag and his small suit case. Ten minutes later Trigger heard the desk telephone ring. Trigger was the only person sitting in the lobby. The night clerk waved the receiver at him, "Sir it's for you."

Trigger took the telephone and heard, "Room 422." He grinned as he handed it back to the clerk. He grabbed his briefcase and walked toward the elevator. He saw himself in the elevator's mirror and straightened his stylish haircut.

He quietly knocked twice on 422 so as not to bother other hotel guests. The pilot opened the door and let Trigger into his suite. His flight case was on the coffee table with the aviation materials scattered around it. He pointed to the opened flight case and said, "Check it out."

Trigger took out his knife and punched a tiny hole in the bag. He poked the thin knife blade to withdraw a small sample from the bag. Neither man saw a tiny amount of cocaine fall to the bottom of the case.

"Has this been cut?" Trigger asked while checking for foreign sized materials.

"No. I've been told a bag that has been cut will have a warning notice, 'Do not use this with an IV injection!'" Mr. Garcia informed Trigger.

Trigger opened his brief case showing the $10,000. "Same agreement in two weeks?" he asked the pilot, who closed the false bottom flight case and was returning the aviation books, maps, and other flight tools. He looked up at Trigger and nodded his head in agreement. Trigger wrapped the bag in a hotel towel and put it in the brief case.

The DEA agents were in a van with government approved eavesdropping devices. They had it all on tape. Two of the agents were chosen to follow Trigger all the way to the boat landing. They were to radio the lead raft that he had gotten into his boat and was heading down the canal to the cabin. The New Orleans Police Department agreed to provide a NOPD van to transport the drug people to the jail.

Each team took down the camouflage netting and tested the two spot lights on each raft as well as their night goggles.

It was 11 o'clock when Trigger tied his Chris-craft to the dock. The DEA agents would start their assault the next hour. A Sikorsky HH-3E helicopter was scheduled to be over the shanty at midnight to provide additional light and a M-60 machine gun for additional fire power if needed.

Trigger's helpers already had their masks on as well as their industrial, protective eye goggles. They were busy setting up the table with five additional bowls and a bag of powdered sugar for cutting the cocaine. Each worker took one box of 200 milliliters size plastic bags from the shelf.

According to Trigger's calculation a ½ ounce measuring teaspoon was equivalent to one gram of cut cocaine. This time he experimented with 10 tablespoons of powdered sugar to cut the cocaine 12.5%. and began blending the two. He stirred for five minutes and looked at the results under a microscope. After testing several areas, he said, "That's good enough. Let's bag it." He carefully poured the drug mixture into the other five bowls. The helpers slipped on their Old Navy face masks and goggles to wear before they started filling the bags.

The blaring music drowned out the noise of the DEA teams as they tied up the rafts. They flashed signals to the helicopter. They quietly climbed up the ladder two at time. One stayed on the dock and two remained on the porch When the last man was on the small porch, one agent opened the metal door of the utility box and flipped the main switch turning off all the lights to the cabin.

The night goggles were flipped on and they charged through the door. Screams and cursing filled the air. Trigger and the men were trying to locate their guns and the women crawled under the table. Trigger ran for the open door, but tripped over a DEA agent's boot and fell at the feet of the agent, who immediately grabbed him and tied his hands. The helicopter's spot light lit up the porch and the ladder to the dock. Trigger was the first to be put into a raft. In twenty minutes, the four men and two women were cuffed. There was not one gun shot fired during the take down. The signal was given to the helicopter to return to the air base.

The lights were turned back on and photographs were taken of the drugs in bowls. All the equipment that was being used to cut and bag the cocaine was tagged and bagged. Trigger had his usual two bags of pure cocaine in his pockets. During the chaos of the assault, cocaine was spilled on the clothing of the workers. A call had been made to the NOPD for a van to pick up the seven drug traffickers. The last agent turned off the lights and headed down the ladder to the remaining agents.

Each raft was driven by an agent and carried two men and one-woman prisoner. One agent drove the Chris-Craft with Trigger tied to its anchor. Each of the three remaining DEA agents picked a boat. The six-boats with one empty flat bottom boat tied to one of motorized rafts looked like a parade motoring its way to the boating ramp and a waiting police bus.

At the New Orleans headquarters Trigger was allowed one telephone call. He called his attorney to let him know his current situation and told him to call Mr. C in Dallas to let him know there was no one available to open The Last Resort. Twyla was on a vacation.

Captain Henry Garcia was arrested at the airport later that morning when a police dog sniffed the drug in the false bottom of his flight case. He was booked on drug trafficking when the Norco Test showed positive cocaine. He was also booked for not declaring the $10,000 he was carrying out of the country. His piloting days were over!

Mr. C was livid. How could all of this be happening? He broke one of their agreements and called Frankie in Houston to ask him to fly to New Orleans and open The Last Resort in Gretna. Mr. C planned to hire a manager and a bar maid because he intended to fire Twyla when she came back. Frankie negotiated a deal to go to Gretna for a month's salary and expenses. He needed to visit his brother while he was there. Trigger was looking at a $50,000 bail. His sentence could be twice that with jail time of ten to twenty years depending on the attitude of the judge. Frankie knew that neither Mr. C nor the Kansas City Mafia would support Trigger. Frankie was beginning to think about his future with the mafia. He discussed hiring someone from the mafia to manage The Last Resort, but Mr. C wanted to be the in between contact to the Mafia. He had to answer to them about the drug bust which meant he had to fly to Kansas City to accuse Trigger of doing some side deals and blaming Trigger for the missing $25,000 that was paid to Joey King.

Frankie flew first class and rented a sporty Buick convertible. From the New Orleans Airport, he called a couple of employment companies and told them what he needed in Gretna and what his budget would allow for a manager and a bar maid. Both positions offered minimum pay and long hours. He gave The Last Resort's phone number. He stopped to visit Trigger, but was told his visitation rights were only on Wednesdays and Fridays. Frankie then drove to Gretna to re-open the tavern and to interview any prospective employee looking to take on a job for Mr. C.

The Last Resort was dusty, there were dishes and beer mugs in the sink. He checked out the inventory to report to Mr. C. He left out two cases each of Jack Daniels and Wild Turkey. The refrigerator shelves had a couple piles of hamburgers to be grilled, lettuce, cheese, and pickles. Trigger had purchased a number of Po'boys from a local truck driver who was also a drug dealer. He'd have to check for the beer delivery schedules. Then he started dusting and sweeping. The push sweeper was so old and ineffective that he threw it away. He then mopped the floor with soapy water. He had to throw out three buckets of muddy water. Cleaning the two toilets wore him out. Besides being unsanitary there were no paper towels nor toilet paper in either of the restrooms. Frankie's hard work made the tavern more presentable. Some day he would have to go to the hardware store to get light bulbs to replace those that had burned out. He tore down the calendars from last year.

He then went into the office. It had a private toilet and a closet. The back door led to the parking lot. There was a New Orleans Saints Football on top of the metal file cabinet. Frankie checked out the four drawers of the cabinet. He found some photos of people in incriminating positions. He looked through the desk drawers to see what he could learn about the bills and the vendors who delivered to The Last Resort. Frankie was more organized and business minded than his brother. He knew if he found any incriminating information that could be used against his brother as evidence, he would destroy it. He found a wall safe behind the file cabinet. The combination was taped to the top of it. Frankie had to try three times before it clicked open. There was over $100,000 in 100's, 50's and 20's. Under the cash there were more photos and a 35-mm video tape. He looked for anything that would play the video, but found nothing. He'd have to check Trigger's apartment in New Orleans. Frankie gathered the photos from the file cabinet and from the safe and stuffed them in a box. He pocketed the tape.

The first inquiry call came in at 8:00 pm. A man was asking about the position that had been posted on the Employment office board. "I can be there within twenty minutes," he said in a raspy voice after asking a few questions.

The prospective employee knocked on the window because he could see Frankie sitting at the bar drinking a beer. Frankie waved for him to come on in and then yelled, "The door is not locked."

The man slowly opened the door and entered The Last Resort. The two shook hands and introduced themselves. The man was pushing sixty, his ruddy face had not been shaved for days. Black and white whiskers blended with dust from some warehouse nearby.

They discussed the responsibilities of the open position. When Frankie gave him a tour of the old tavern, it was at the office that the man had the most questions. He noticed a bag laying on the desk. The shaggy man pointed to the door of the closet, "What's in there?" he asked.

"Oh, that's a..." were the last words Frankie ever uttered. Two quick pistol shots rang out one to the chest and one to the back of the head, and Frankie's body slumped to the closet floor. The gunman saw the safe. He pulled the string on the single light bulb and saw the combination taped to the top of the safe. It took him one attempt to open the safe. It was empty! He wiped his finger prints from the handle, stepped over Frankie's crumpled up body. He checked each pocket of the corpse. He pulled the tape out of Frankie's pants pocket and stuffed it in the same pocket where he had put the safe combination. He opened the bag sitting on the desk. His eyes opened wide when he saw all the loose money. He flipped through the photos. Then he slowly pulled one from the others. "This is the one I want," he said to himself out loud.

He hurriedly walked to the door, wiped the handle, and got into the car. The lady sitting next to him asked, "Did you find it?"

"Yes, we're safe from now on." He said to her as he patted her leg. Then they drove off.

Several days later Frankie's body was found in the closet. A beer truck driver had stopped to unload an order and looked around for Trigger. When he walked into the office, he got a whiff of a strong putrid odor. Opening the closet door, he saw that the body had been found by spiders and cockroaches. The driver quickly shut the door and ran to his delivery truck where he radioed his company.

The Gretna police officer and the county morgue employees wore face masks as they loaded the body into a hearse. All the windows on the hearse were down as they took the body to the New Orleans morgue. The Gretna police station called the New Orleans Police Department since both were in Jefferson Parish. The NOPD already had a back log of investigations. The Gretna robbery/murder report went to the bottom of the pile.

The Times Picayune-New Orleans Advocate newspaper ran a story of a robbery at The Last Resort in Gretna. Frankie Bocavinii, the manager had been murdered. Trigger's heart sank when he read the article from his jail cell.

CHAPTER 30

Angus discussed with Brenda about his decision to investigate using the minicomputer for his business. He had decided to contact three different computer companies to schedule appointments. After reading 'Minicomputers for Dummies' he selected Wang, Data General and DEC. He made a list of questions he thought he should ask each one. He wanted to learn about the RAM (Random Access Memory), CPU (Central Processing Unit), Hard Drive (peripheral storage) with each minicomputer, and what other components would be needed to be able to process the various gas & oil tax forms that Federal and state governments required.

The Wang representative could meet with him Thursday afternoon at 2 o'clock. He had yet to hear from the other two companies.

On Thursday at 2 o'clock Glen Steen of Wang came through the door. He wore a light tan suit with a green tie. He carried a dark blue canvas briefcase with Wang imprinted on the side. He was a young man with a friendly smile and curly reddish hair.

"Mr. McKay, my name is Glen Steen. I see you are in the gas & oil tax business. Tell me why you are interested in Wang's Computing Calculators," the salesman began.

"I know nothing about computers. You said computing calculators. I don't need a calculator! I thought Wang 2200 was a minicomputer!

"You're correct! It is a computer. In fact, it *is* a minicomputer." Mr. Steen assured him.

"I am interested in seeing if I can incorporate a computer into my tax computations. My goal is to reduce penalty fees and hopefully, speed up the process of filling out gas and oil tax forms," replied Angus.

"Do you know anyone who can program your computer to do what you want it to do?" asked Mr. Steen.

"No, I thought you would do the programming," replied Angus.

"Mr. McKay, most of the Wang 2200s are sold to value added resellers, who customize your software program to fit your needs. This computer has some built-in features that makes it the first of its kind. It has its own CRT, cassette tape for storage and uses BASIC language. This means you do not have to purchase these separately," he pointed out. Mr. Steen added, "Two more features you need to know about are (1) the Intel microprocessor produces 60,000 instructions per second, and (2) the Intel model that the Wang company uses has 2,300 transistors."

Angus stated, "That is all impressive, but what other items will I have to purchase?"

"Your programmer will need to understand your tax forms and the formula required to fill them out. With the proper programming, I am certain this minicomputer has the capacity to do your tax computations. The hard drive with the code to store the language is included. We use the BASIC language for proper programming with our operating system. I recommend two programmers from Texas Tech. They can handle your specific program," explained Mr. Steen.

Angus wanted to know, "Is there anyone in this area who is using your system?"

"Yes, we have two hospitals and one laboratory. Would you like to visit one to see our minicomputer in operation? I can arrange a meeting for you," replied the Wang rep.

"I was thinking of a turn-key minicomputer," explained Angus.

"The two young guys at Texas Tech that I mentioned can design a software program that will handle the needs of your company. They'll know what additional peripherals your Wang 2200 System will need. I've recommended them several times. In fact, one of the hospitals used them. That one would be a good one for you to visit. You can see how it is working for the hospital and ask about the capabilities of the programmers. How does that sound to you?" the Wang rep questioned.

"Mr. Steen, I do not have the budget a hospital has. How much are we talking about here?" wondered Angus.

"The standard Wang 2200 minicomputer is being introduced at $6,700. The programmers charge for their services. Of course, any additional memory required will be added to the total fee. There's a gas and oil attorney in Odessa, that has a system. Although not a Wang 2200, but the word is he paid somewhere around $40,000. He says he has recouped his costs by cutting down his penalty fees. I would guess your cost would be less than that." Mr. Steen estimated.

"Wow!" blurted Angus shifting his position in the chair.

"Think of the savings, Mr. McKay, less in penalty fees, being able to submit tax forms in less time and allowing you to handle more clients. Isn't that your goal?" he reminded Angus.

"OK. See when you can arrange a visit with the hospital. I have a meeting out in the Panhandle in October. I would like to meet the programmers you're recommending then," concluded Angus as he stood up.

"I can do that." Mr. Steen said. "Which would you prefer a morning or an afternoon visit? Here are the programmers' business cards, and the Wang literature.

"Afternoon visits would be better," responded Angus.

Angus was concerned he had yet to hear from the DEC or the Data General reps. The next morning Brenda handed Angus a telephone message from Jim Stewart the Digital Equipment (DEC) representative requesting an appointment for that afternoon after lunch. Please call.

Angus looked at his daily calendar. He had planned to go to the SMU Library to read more about minicomputers. He could postpone that until after the DEC salesman was finished. He dialed the DEC rep and told Mr. Stewart that after 1 o'clock would be fine. That gave him a couple of hours to review the tax claims that were submitted by two of his newest clients who he had met at the San Antonio conference.

At 12:50 Brenda buzzed Angus that Jim Stewart of DEC was there. "Send him back," replied Angus. When Mr. Stewart entered his office, Angus saw a middle age gentleman wearing a western suede light tan jacket over dark brown slacks. He had on a lime green turtle neck sweater. His cowboy boots were polished.

After the two greeted each other. Mr. Stewart asked, "Why are you interested in purchasing a minicomputer?"

"Currently. I am a tax consultant for clients who are in the gas and oil business. It is a very complex tax program. Right now, I am doing the calculations on an $89 electric calculator. It is much quicker than the old mechanical Marchant adding machine, but maybe the minicomputer can help reduce my time and improve the accuracy in processing the tax forms," answered Angus.

Mr. Stewart started his presentation, "This is DEC's Program Data Processor, we call it PDP for short," the DEC rep said handing him a photograph. "We are the leaders in the minicomputer industry financially and technologically! As your business increases you will be adding employees. With DEC you will be able to run multi terminals from the DEC's minicomputer. That alone will be a considerable saving for you as your business grows," continued the

DEC salesman. He added, "You are looking for accuracy and less processing time, right? We offer an extended arithmetic function that adds financial symbols, such as dollar signs or per cent signs that you will probably be needing on the tax forms. The PDP uses a line printer and a monitor that lets you view as you type directly into the computer. No punch cards or punched paper tape! It uses the 64-bit memory and you benefit by the integrated circuit design that the DEC PDP offers."

Angus asked, "Does your price compete with other minicomputers?"

"When you include the add-ons that other minicomputers require to be functional, the answer is 'YES'. That is why DEC is a price leader. We purchase some pieces direct in bulk from the manufacturer, you will have to purchase other parts from a vendor at a much higher price. I know some competitors have a base price of $4,000. That minicomputer will not be able to handle the financial input/output you need. You need to add $4,000 for additional RAM and that may still will be too slow. Another savings with DEC is we're the first to offer 16-byte as opposed to the 8-byte that most competitors are offering. It costs to add bits! Our basic price is $10,000 with the memory included. There are other add-ons to consider. Programmers for one. Each system is different but programmers that I know tell me that the DEC/PDP is easier to program. I know that some companies are paying somewhere between $40,000 to $50,000 to get up and going. I will have to go back to my office to give you our quote. My experience is DEC will be 10% to 15% less than any other total quote."

"Do you have any local clients I can visit?" questioned Angus.

"We have a university lab over in Fort Worth. They have a multi-terminal program. There's a small medical clinic in Irving. Which would you like to visit?" then he quickly added, "I would say the clinic may be better because they are in a growth mode and looking to add on two more terminals yet this year."

"I agree. Can you schedule a visit with them sometime next week?" asked Angus.

"Should be no problem. I'll arrange a time and call you to confirm." answered Mr. Stewart.

"Mr. McKay, I have to ask. Are you the McKay the newspapers are saying tried to save the killer of the commissioner few years ago?"

"Yes, but I was unable to save him," replied Angus. "Why do you ask?"

"I'm a nephew of the commissioner who was shot," Mr. Stewart sat back down. "You know the month before he was killed, there was a family Valentine Day luncheon in his back yard. He loved to grill pork tenderloins. Anyway, the topic got on politics. He casually mentioned that he's finding some fuel charge discrepancies at the Houston Independent School District bus maintenance shop. He said that when he approached the commissioner about it, he just sluffed it off as an over sight of the manager. My uncle made note that the over sight had been going on for several years according to what he had uncovered. A few weeks later he was murdered in his own home along with Aunt B." Mr. Stewart finished and stood up to leave the office.

"Wait! Mr. Stewart. Did you ever tell this to the FBI? asked Angus.

"No. No one from my family was ever approached by the FBI or Houston Police. We figured they had found out who did it," the DEC rep stated. "My dad was the youngest of the family, so there is really not that much communication unless there is a family gathering. Wait! I do remember dad saying a Houston police officer stopped around 9 o'clock one night a few days after my uncle was killed. Dad said his name was Diggs, Dagart or something like that," recalled Stewart.

"What's your dad's name?" Angus wanted to know.

"Jack Stewart. He lives in the Woodland area," the young Stewart answered.

"Sorry to bring this up. I've got another appointment I need to make. I'll arrange an appointment for you to visit the medical clinic in Irving," he concluded as he left the office.

Angus sat down and dialed the Houston FBI.

"FBI! How may we help you?" a lady's voice answered after two rings.

"My name is Angus McKay. I would like to speak with either Agent Al Ramos or Agent Guy Hopkins"

A soft voice responded, "Yes, Mr. McKay. Al Ramos will be right with you."

"Mr. McKay. This is Al. How are you doing?" answered Agent Ramos. "We have not heard from you for a few years. My phone you're calling from Dallas. Did you move?" he asked

"Agent Ramos. Yes, spent some time in Vietnam and there was some recovery time. Are any new leads to the commissioner's murder?" questioned Angus, anxious to hear his response.

"We have a couple leads, but nothing to report as this time," stated Ramos. "Why do you ask?

Do you have the Houston police reports on this case?" Angus wanted to know.

"We should have. Why are you asking these questions?" Agent Ramos questioned him.

"You might want to check the Houston Police report about an officer calling on the commissioner's brother, Jack Stewart. I understand the Stewarts had a family gathering on Valentine's Day. See what officer Diggs or Dreger or something like that reported a few days following the murder. Mr. Jack Stewart may have some answers that may be of help in your investigations That's all I know for sure," replied Angus.

"McKay, have you discussed this with anyone else?" the FBI agent asked Angus. "How did you learn of this information?

"I met someone in the Stewart family a few minutes ago. He commented that his uncle was concerned about some over charging on fuel fees at the Houston ISD. A week after my uncle had discussed his allegations, he was murdered. I'll let you handle this as you see fit," Angus felt like he was not getting the response he expected

"Thanks for the information. I will personally check this out for sure. I suggest you not talk to anyone else about this," recommended Agent Ramos. Then he added, "Angus, we have enlisted the support of the Dallas FBI. Since you now live in the Dallas area, I'll have someone from the Dallas FBI contact you."

"There was an agent who called to let me know the Dallas FBI was joining the investigation. He told me that since no one has tried to make contact with me after all this time, my family should no longer be in danger. He let me know they had a complete copy of the file on the murder of the commissioner and will be following up on some old leads."

CHAPTER 31

"Brenda, if the Data General rep calls for an appointment, see if he can make it around 10 o'clock any morning next week. I plan to be in the office all next week reviewing the tax returns for our new clients, but I want to hear what he has to say about the minicomputer," directed Angus.

"Boy, Mr. McKay you're getting pretty sure of getting a minicomputer, aren't you?" Brenda remarked.

"We'll see, the price tags are more than I expected, but I believe it will help cut penalty fees for our growing list of clients. I may be needing a larger office space," he commented.

"I am not supposed to say anything, but the office at the end of the hall will be available within the next two months. That office space is one and half times larger than yours. Please do not tell anyone you know about it," pleaded Brenda.

"Don't worry. I won't." Angus responded, "See ya' in the morning."

It was 8:30 the next morning when Angus walked up to Brenda's desk. "Here's the message from Mr. Preston Hudson, the Data General rep," she said handing Angus the message, "Looking forward to meet with you in the morning at 10 to discuss the Nova minicomputer." Preston Hudson.

"Thanks Brenda. OK, let's work him in our morning schedule. Buzz me when he arrives, please," Angus said looking at the message.

Preston Hudson walked up to Brenda's desk at 9:50. He was wearing a blue blazer with gray slacks, a light blue shirt with a red and blue striped tie. He had youthful facial features. He handed Brenda his business card. "Ma'am, I am Preston Hudson from Data General. I have a 10 o'clock appointment with Mr. McKay."

"Yes sir. He will be out to meet you in a few moments," she informed him.

Angus shoved some papers in a file folder and put it in the desk drawer. He walked out to meet Mr. Hudson.

"Mr. Hudson, I am Angus McKay. My friends call me Angus. I look forward to learning what you have to say about the NOVA model minicomputer. Come on back to my office," Angus said as Brenda handed him the business card.

As usual Angus sat in the chair next to the one Mr. Hudson sat in. He did not like to sit behind his desk with initial discussions. His method seemed to relax the other person. He used his yellow pad to make notes.

"Tell me what you are looking for in a minicomputer, Mr. McKay," Hudson wanted to know.

"I am a gas and oil tax consultant. The forms can get very complex and they are changing just about every year. I am hoping a minicomputer will allow me to handle more clients with fewer errors. Errors cause penalty fees! I am not up on minicomputers. I am interested in a turn-key operation," explained Angus.

"It sounds like beside the cost issue, you are interested in a reliable minicomputer. The Super Nova is a favorite in industrial and lab situations. We use a mother board which reduces the cost of manufacturing while providing more reliability. Mr. McKay, we are offering a basic price of only $4,000. If you need additional RAM to handle the work load you are expecting from your minicomputer. The cost will be increased by $8,000. A lab department at a local university has one of our units up and running. We have sold over 500 Super Nova units in the past year and half," stated Mr. Hudson.

He continued, "Data General's Nova 2 is being introduced this year. Our engineers have reduced a three-board circuit system to a single board. Also, important to your situation is the fact the Nova 2 has a 16-byte compared to 8-byte operating system that our competitors are only able to offer. Today we ship the 840 in a large 14-slot case. 840/14 means more memory space to handle your needs faster and with fewer errors. With the Intel semiconductor base memory, we are getting 1,024 bytes on a single chip and running at much higher speeds. I will have to see a sample of the gas and oil tax forms to better advise you of the size memory you will need for your business. Your additional expenses will probably be somewhere between $25,000 and $35,000. Do you have any questions at this time? Do you have a timetable for starting to use a minicomputer? Would you like to visit some of my local customers who already using the Data General Minicomputers?" Mr. Hudson asked the multi questions.

"Not at this time. Call me when you have your quote ready and you can schedule a visit to one of your customers," Angus replied as he stood up to escort Mr. Hudson to the reception area.

Days later at the medical clinic in Irving that was using the DEC minicomputer, Mr. Stewart kept pointing out the benefits.

Angus asked the office manager, "Who did you use as programmers?"

"We went with Mr. Stewart's recommendation of two programmers from Texas Tech. Once we went through the computations we needed, they drew up a schematic, and after a few changes, they understood exactly what we needed to produce the required results. We did a few runs to make sure the program did what we needed," she responded

"Did it save you time? Was the output accurate?" questioned Angus.

"Yes. We were spending over three hours a week putting together our weekly report for the owner of the company. With the minicomputer it's one third the time! We do a double check on all the medical codes, to make certain they match the codes of the prescriptions and medical services. We still catch one or two occasionally," she confessed.

Friday of that week, Angus called Mr. Hudson of General Data to say he had decided to go with a competitor. He told Mr. Hudson he was no longer interested in visiting the university lab that is using the General Data minicomputer. Mr. Hudson asked if price was an issue.

"No, if fact your quote was 5% under theirs, but I've made my decision based on some other factors. You had a good presentation and have a good product. It's nothing personal Mr. Hudson. Thank you for your time," Angus said as he hung up the receiver.

Angus began reviewing the gas and oil tax forms and the steps in completing the many questions, credits, and the tax on underperforming wells. The tax department in Washington D.C. had calculated it should take two hours to do the bookkeeping, forty-five minutes to know the laws required to fill out the forms and another hour to fill out the forms. That did not include the Daily Drilling Report required on each well. That could amount to over sixty blanks to fill out on each well every day. Angus was thankful that he needed only the year end cumulative rig information.

He lined up appointments to meet with the Lubbock banker and his gas and oil clients. He also included a meeting with the two programmers at Texas Tech. They suggested he bring tax forms to show them what he needed to have programmed. Since a banker in Wichita Falls wanted to discuss the tax regulations on marginal wells Angus decided he would drive. He called Rob to see if he would like to join him on these calls. Rob agreed to fly into Dallas and stay the night with Angus and Faith.

Late Sunday afternoon, Angus met Rob at Love Field. The two had not been together since the San Antonio conference. Both were eager to discuss how they benefited from that meeting. That evening Angus grilled some steaks and Faith served a baked potato and a salad.

Monday morning Angus and Rob took highway 82 to Wichita Falls. The bank was on Stone Lake Drive. Coffee and donuts were available for the meeting. The banker had eight of his gas and oil clients attend the meeting. Most of the discussion centered around marginal wells and if the cost of fracking would be profitable. Rob told them that he would have to inspect each well separately. He would like to see the daily drilling reports when the wells were first opened. Angus informed the group that marginal wells may have unused credit due them depending on how they reported their income tax. He would be happy to review their tax statements that were filed in the past five years. Five of the eight clients agreed to have Rob come back to the Wichita Falls area as soon as possible. All eight said they would submit their previous tax statements to be reviewed. Both men felt good about the stop in Wichita Falls.

In Seymour they picked up sandwiches and drinks at the Dairy Queen along highway 82. They were still over two hours away from Lubbock. The Lubbock National Bank was on Main Street. It originally opened as the Security State Bank and Trust in 1917 at that time Lubbock's population was 30,000. The president of the bank had invited over twenty-five of the bank's top gas and oil clients. The legal department of the bank was also at the meeting. The conference room was re-arranged to handle those attending. Tea, lemonade, and cookies were set out for the meeting. Again, the discussions centered on marginal wells, penalty fees and unused credit. Rob took the lead and discussed merits of fracking, especially for the current price of oil. Angus handled the questions pertaining to the penalty fees and how to benefit from the unused credit.

The bank had been closed for two hours when the meeting ended. Both men were anxious to get back and discuss the responses they got at Wichita Falls and Lubbock. Rob decided to fly back that night to Midland. Angus accepted the invitation of the bank's president to have dinner with him and his family. The president called the Overton Hotel downtown to make reservations for Angus. After dinner they discussed the prorationing of oil issue and Angus learned that the president of the Lubbock National Bank had played football for the Red Raiders in the 1950s. He thanked his host and drove to the hotel.

The desk clerk gave him the preferred king suite for the price of a standard room. It was a large luxurious suite. Angus had two important phone calls to make. The first one was to invite the two Texas Tech programmers to meet him for breakfast at 7:30 in the morning at the Pecan Grill in the hotel. The second call was to Faith. Although he was physically and mentally tired, he was always happy to talk to his wife. He asked her about her day. She let him know that everything was all right in Preston Prairie. He let her know that he and Rob had had a successful day.

The next morning the two programmers Tom Henderson and Cole Armstrong met him at the Pecan Grill. Tom had played basketball. He was tall at six-six tall and wore a tight fitted Red Raider t-shirt under his black jacket. Cole was a former 225-pound linebacker. He wore a western shirt, jeans, and cowboy boots.

Angus and the graduate students enjoyed a hearty breakfast before going up to Angus' suite where they could discuss what he wanted the DEC minicomputer to do. Tom and Cole studied the various tax forms to be programmed. As Angus talked, they drew a rough schematic. They asked questions to be certain they understood. Angus was anxious to get a ball park figure of what the programmers thought their total fee would be. They did some calculations to determine the number of hours it would take to complete the programming and a list of what was included in their quote. It included defining the program in detail, programming, and calculations, designing and reports, testing and debugging, revisions and follow up contact. Both agreed that the fee would be between $20,000 and $25,000 which included traveling to Dallas a minimum of three times. They would accept $10,000 earnest money and the balance when the project was complete to Angus' satisfaction.

It was after lunch when Angus left the programmers in Lubbock. He had about five hours of straight driving before he would be home. On his drive back to Preston Prairie he checked his list pertaining to the minicomputer. He had agreed on purchasing the DEC minicomputer and on hiring the Texas Tech programmers. The office at the end of the hallway had to be locked in.

CHAPTER 32

Angus walked into his office to begin a new week. Brenda had a message from Mr. Stewart, the DEC rep. He would like to meet with Angus on Tuesday morning at 9 o'clock. Also, there was message to call Mr. Dawson.

"That's tomorrow," Angus grumbled, then turned to Brenda, "I've got to get busy and review some tax forms. Brenda, who do I need to talk to about the office at the end of the hallway?"

Angus wrote out two thank you drafts to the presidents of the banks with whom he and Rob had met. Brenda would correct his errors and type them up before having him sign them. He had a stack of tax forms to review which required more filings for the growing number clients.

But first he thought he should return Randall's call.

"Angus, I want to share this with you. Remember our discussion when you and Faith were in D.C.? We met at the Hill Country BAR B QUE. Your advice about the FBI investigation was helpful. The FBI tells me the bookkeeper is willing to work with them on the Houston murder and drug operation in Louisiana.

"Thank you. I was told I'll get a grade promotion for my efforts. Just wanted you to know. Hope the family is doing well. I've got a staff meeting to run to. Let's stay in touch." Randall quickly hung up.

Mr. Stewart was at the office when Angus walked back to Brenda's desk. He and Brenda were talking about the pleasant fall weather. Angus greeted him and they walked back to his office.

"Mr. McKay the company would like to introduce a finance program to you. You are the first one to be offered a lease agreement," the DEC salesman anxiously announced his news before Angus pulled up a chair next to him. "You mentioned you would like a 'turnkey' program. DEC is offering you a four-year lease agreement. The monthly fee is only $300 per month with option to purchase the minicomputer for $6,000. The company will provide all the necessary peripherals except the programmers' fees. That's as turnkey as you can get!" declared the DEC rep.

"That sounds great, Mr. Stewart, but we may have a problem. I do not have the space and it will be two or three months before I can move into a larger area. Plus, I am already thinking I may need to hire someone," responded Angus.

"That's no problem. I've been authorized to add another terminal at no extra cost. The offer is good for 90 days. We just need your approval!" Mr. Stewart urged Angus for an approval.

There was a long pause while Angus was considering the offer. His concern was how much Tom and Cole were going to charge to program the DEC minicomputer and how much would a larger office space cost per month.

"I have to re-examine the company budget. Can I have three days to let you know? I really like your offer, but I need to figure out how all this will affect my cash flow. Can you call me Friday for a definite answer?" asked Angus.

"I understand. Mr. McKay, we projected your potential growth over the next four years. We believe in you and your business. I'll call you on Friday." Mr. Stewart replied as he got up to leave the office, "Can I tell the company you are 90% sure you will accept our offer?" Mr. Stewart pushed for a positive response.

"Call me Friday! No promises." Angus harshly responded because he didn't like being rushed to make such a major financial decision.

The rest of the week Angus was busy reviewing tax returns and scheduling appointments with new clients. He also had an appointment with his banker who assured Angus that, if needed, he would provide a line of credit that would help him with the purchase or lease of the minicomputer. The banker questioned if the minicomputer would be worth $6,000 in four years.

Friday morning Mr. Stewart entered the reception area. Brenda told him that Mr. McKay was waiting in his office. "Is it good news?" he asked Brenda as he headed past her and toward Angus's office. She replied, "It's his news, not mine."

"Come in Mr. Stewart. Angus was moving the coffee table between two chairs. "I suppose you're wanting an answer from me. What was your question?" he teased.

"Mr. McKay, my question is, do you accept our lease offer or not?" responded the DEC salesman missing Angus' teasing.

"Well, I took the DEC lease agreement to my banker. He thought the $6,000 was a bit steep because the minicomputer won't be worth that in four years. I tend to agree with him. Does DEC offer a 10% discount for vets?" Angus asked with a deadpan face.

"I'll have to contact my sales manager. That's above my pay scale. May I use your telephone? If he agrees, will you accept the offer?" Mr. Stewart asked, trying to get an agreement.

"You can tell him I'll accept the offer if DEC will wait until I find a larger office," replied Angus.

It was a short telephone conversation. DEC agreed to knock $600 off the purchase price at the end of the lease, and they would need a two-week notice of when they could deliver the minicomputer.

Jim Stewart had a big smile on his face, "McKay, you drive a hard bargain! Thank you for allowing DEC and me to serve you. I truly believe you will be satisfied with what it will do for your business. I understand you were able to meet with Tom and Cole in Lubbock. I know they do not look like business people, but they know their programming. It's the new generation. You will have to coordinate with them about when they can begin programming your minicomputer." Angus walked Jim Stewart to the reception area. Mr. Stewart thanked Brenda.

CHAPTER 33

Angus was able to move into his larger office earlier than expected. He called Mr. Stewart to order delivery of the minicomputer. It would be two weeks before they could deliver it. He then called Tom and Cole in Lubbock to schedule them to begin programming.

The Wichita Falls and Lubbock trips were proving to be successful. He was getting three to five packages a week from new clients. He was anxiously waiting for the programmers to finish their work. They informed him it would be mid-January before they would be ready to do a test run.

The new year was rapidly approaching. His mom and dad invited Faith and him to come to Crockett for Christmas. Faith encourage him to take a break because he had been putting in over fifty hours a week reviewing gas and oil tax forms and making recommendations that saved his clients on penalty fees.

The program that Dr. Tanner had recommended had eliminated the nightmares. Angus was no longer facing the demons that they had burned up on the shore of Lake Texoma.

Faith was busy getting ready for Christmas holidays and learning more about the Preston Prairie area and people. She helped Angus at his office sorting tax receipts to match expense claims, etc. The two were happy and busy with their new environment. She however, was not overjoyed that Angus lugged some boxes of tax receipts when they drove to Crockett for the holiday.

The time on the ranch was good for the couple. The slow pace gave them time to be together and relax. Angus rode his horse,

Apple, nearly every day. Faith began riding a horse that Connor picked out for her.

On Sunday, the 27th after church they said good bye to his parents and drove back to Preston Prairie. Faith mentioned to Angus that she was not feeling too well. "It must have been too much of Grace's home cooking," she shrugged it off.

The Lubbock programmers called January 4th. They had been in the Dallas area for the holidays and wanted to stop by to see if they could do a trial run. Angus was elated that he could fulfill his dream of being able to take advantage of using the minicomputer to process the gas and oil tax forms.

Angus had invited Mr. Stewart to be present when they did their test run. However, the test run showed that a couple of spaces where figures were to be, did not line up properly and the figures printed out above the space. This was an easy problem to resolve and soon all the figures were in the correct places. They entered two more tax returns that Angus had previously done by hand. The minicomputer was declared operational. He paid the programmers their final payment. They told him when they would be back in the area and at that time would check to be sure the programming had no errors.

The minicomputer allowed Angus to do ten more contracts each week over what he had been able to do by hand. He was finally getting caught up on his workload. He was anxious to see what the tax season would generate.

On Valentine's Day Angus took Faith to a nice restaurant in Dallas. He noticed she did not order wine and was picking at her food. "Honey are you alright?" he asked in a concerned tone.

"Angus, I think we are going to be parents!" she confessed to him. "I was waiting for a better time to tell you, but guess now is as good a time as any."

He was flabbergasted. He had a big smile. He got out of his chair and walked around to her. He bent over and kissed her. "It's wonderful news. Faith, you will make the best mother any child can ask for. Do we know when the baby is due?" he asked.

"August or September," replied Faith, half smiling, half feeling nauseous. Her feathered hair style was current for the times. She looked radiant in a sparkling blue scoop sweater. The heart shaped red ruby necklace that Angus had given her for Valentine's Day was displayed between her breasts.

"Honey, I love you,' he kept saying to her all the way back to Preston Prairie. "Wow, me a father! Wait 'til our parents hear this. They will be overjoyed," he gleefully declared.

Angus called Rob to tell him the good news. Rob congratulated him, "I knew it would just a matter of time. Faith will be a great mother. You, I am not so sure," he jokingly kidded, then said, "No, Angus you will be a great father. Guess that makes me sort of an uncle, huh?"

The soon-to-be grandparents in Crockett and Wilmington were excited for Angus and Faith. The future grandparents began planning. Grace tried to make a trip to Preston Prairie more often to help Faith. Grandpa Connor didn't say anything to anybody, but he began looking for a good Shetland pony.

Angus was free of the demons of Vietnam, the helicopter accident, the military career, and the Unsolicited Confession.

EPILOGUE

Angus and Faith had a that August and two years later they had a girl. His tax consultant business grew to a multimillion-dollar company, which he sold in 1981. He remained Chairman of the Board. For their 10th anniversary, Angus and Faith visited Andre Bonnay at his vineyard in France.

Rob Palmer and Angus remained best of friends.

The Used Equipment Cleaning company liquidated in 1980 at $30 a share.

Johnnie Porter made the bestselling mystery book list.

Mr. C, Trigger and the Houston ISD superintendent were locked up for 15 years.

The Last Resort mysteriously burned down.

Twyla and Walt married and retired from Department of Drug Enforcement Agency.

Frankie's murder remains at the bottom of the unsolved cases file.

Preston Prairie was absorbed by the growing city of Frisco.

Officer White had taken the $25,000. He retired and donated all but $5,000 to local charities.

Senator Vaughn was elected vice president of the United States.

ACKNOWLEDGEMENTS

A big thank you to all who have contributed so much of their time and talents to make UNSOLICITED CONFESSION a possibility. My loving wife, Marlene, for her love and patience, such as waiting at the dinner table while I finish one more sentence or two or three…

Cathy Carlsen	Editing
Anna Turner	Social Media Marketing Coordinator
Charlene Raddon	Cover Design (www.silversagebookcover.com)
Jeff Turner	Legal Advisor
Carolyn Williamson	Process Advisor
Dr. Bryan Turner	Medical Advisor (JordanHealth@gmail.com)
Brad & Susan Turner	Computer & Word Recovery
Tom Heinkkinen	Minicomputer History/Technical Advisor
Steve Brodie	Gas & Oil History Advisor

Unsolicited Confession would not have been possible without my family and friends who continued to provide love, prayers, and much needed encouragement especially Brad and Susan Turner, Dr. Bryan Turner, Jeff and Zoraida Turner, Chad Turner, Steve Brodie, Carolyn Williamson, Mike and Cathy Carlsen, Tom and Diane Heinkkinen, Anna Turner, and many others who supported me even after they read portions of the manuscript.

CPSIA information can be obtained
at www.ICGtesting.com
Printed in the USA
FSHW012347020221
77911FS